My Heart, My Fate

Timothy Lynn Singleton

Table of Contents

Prologue

As the Grimm's faery tale of Snow White said, she had hair as black as midnight, skin as white as snow, and lips as red as blood. She turned every head as she meandered through the crowd, as only the truly graceful can do. Both men and women were captured by her presence, some because she caught their eyes directly and others because, though she was dressed elegantly, her wardrobe was a bit archaic.

Everyone except Will, that is. Will, dumb as a creek rock when it came to women, just wanted to listen to a little music and go home. He was handsome enough, just distracted as a rule, and could sometimes be off-putting.

He had made his weekly Friday trip to the bookstore, dined alone as usual, and watched a movie. He decided long ago that a relationship was just too much trouble. He didn't see her in the mirror as she passed from behind him, though he smelt her perfume, and that piqued his curiosity. Not seeing anyone, he returned to his coke and plate of lemon wedges, looking forward to eating pizza and reading a good book later at his townhouse. He had been waiting for Stephen King's "The Shining" to be released on DVD, and he intended to watch the video and eat himself into a coma.

Sitting down at an empty table next to the dance floor of the pub, the raven-haired girl ordered a club soda and lime as well as an innocent daiquiri and proceeded to watch the folks in the club like Will. Shortly afterward, a blonde joined her and ordered a couple of drinks.

"Are you teetotalers?" The waitress asked when the blonde specified no alcohol like the others.

"Yes, we are," replied both in unison and broke into laughter.

"Good enough," Said the waitress and went away.

Will figured he would ask a few women to dance and then go on home. It was almost midnight, and he felt himself getting tired. *Used to be a solid rock. Why did I let myself go this bad?* He got up and went to a table to try his luck. Unfortunately, he got turned down by one of the girls. He then diverted his attention toward the raven-haired beauty and asked if she wanted to dance; only then was Will struck by that same dark beauty.

"No, thank you," she replied.

"OK," he said, strangely frustrated. Usually, a turn-down is no big deal; he just liked to dance and didn't care much with whom. Will walked back to his seat. Suddenly, he was not tired anymore but confused. Looking into the mirror, he tried just to observe this woman who caught his eye and couldn't locate her. He looked over and saw her seated at the table. *I'm just tired, I guess. Screw it. Time to go.* He got up and walked outside, enjoying the cool air of November as only those whose ancestors are native to cold climates can. The freezing air invigorated him, cleared his head, and made his blood flow hotter; he could feel it. Will was one of those polar bears who leaped into pools, creeks, and such during freezing weather. Most of his friends thought he was crazy; Will thought they were probably correct.

There was commotion at the pub across the street. Will sat in one of the outside chairs where people often ate lunch. It was wet from the earlier rain showers. Irritated for the second time tonight, Will decided that since he was already wet, he might as well sit and see what was happening across the street.

A policeman was escorting a guy out of the pub who was not happy to be leaving. A second, quieter man was also being escorted out. His expressions were one of distraction and rage. This fellow exchanged a few words with the officer, and it looked like he intended to get into his truck and leave. The first unhappy gentleman lunged away from his guard and popped the distracted fellow a good one on the left temple with a sound like a rubber mallet hitting a coconut, driving him to his knees in a puddle of water. The blood dripping from his nose was visible even from across the street. *Shee-it, that HAD to hurt!* Will thought.

The police officers struggled with the unhappy gentleman, and it wasn't clear who would come out on top, what with one of the guys radioing for backup.

Drugs, he's stoned and feels no pain.

Will stood as if to help when he remembered he was a civilian, so there was no need to get involved. He started across the street to help the victim still in the puddle. It quickly became clear that the quiet fellow was unconscious and possibly not breathing. Bending down, Will touched the kneeling man, who promptly fell over.

"He's dead, I think," Will said, with no particular emphasis. Then, "Looks like you officers need to take this man for killing as well as being an idiot."

This led to one of the officers releasing a hold and drawing back his fist, which gave the man an opening to slip away from the other officer as well and, as they say in the South, haul ass, which he did, quickly cutting down an alley.

They'll never catch him now, morons. Will thought as he turned back to offer what he could in the way of first aid.

He knew an ambulance was on the way because one of the cops was hindered in his running by requesting an ambulance on the radio. *Correction: he was hampered because he was too overweight to be a street cop.*

As Will hoped, the victim still had a pulse. *He was not breathing but still had a pulse.* As he worked on the man, he heard a gunshot, which was quickly followed by the police car's radio screaming, "Officer down, officer down." It took some effort, but he got the guy running again with a weak, unsteady breath.

"What happened?" he asked Will in an unsteady voice.

"You just got the shit knocked out of you. What was his beef with you?"

"He got pissed off because I cut in on him and my wife."

"That sucks, buddy. Look, I am putting my coat over you because I don't want you to be shocked. You need to keep talking to me because I want you aware and with me until the professionals get here with an ambulance, OK?"

"Sure, I guess."

As he covered the guy, Will continued, "Come on; talk to me. I don't care if it recites all the phone numbers you can remember. Just talk."

"Alright, I work a lot and am tired a lot. I wanted to go home. My wife said she was going dancing even if she had to dance with some other man. She waved at some guy walking by, and he led her out to dance. I had had enough and tried to stop it. He and I got into a pissing contest inside, and the law told us both to go. She stayed."

"My man, that sucks. Hard old world and love hurts, huh?"

"Yeah….love hurts. But only as long as you let it."

A brunette runs up and says, "Stanley…? Oh no!"

"Meet the wife. Her name is Cheryl."

"Good evening." No effort to look up was made as Will further tucked him in.

"What happened?" Terrified, near tears, as if she couldn't comprehend that she was responsible for his injury.

"Look," began Will, "I'll field this one. Your husband came out and was giving the cops no trouble. He was going to get in his truck and go when the other asshole broke loose from the cops and landed a haymaker in your hubby's left temple. He was knocked unconscious and…."

The ambulance's siren wailed.

Yanking the equipment boxes out, the paramedics ran to Will and the quiet man, "What happened?"

Will yelled over the other ambulance, pulling into the alley for the policeman, "He was struck in the left temple! He was knocked to his knees! I came to help, and when I touched him, he fell over. He wasn't breathing but had a pulse. I did CPR and got him breathing again! He is awake but REAL fuddled!" The siren continued blaring, and the wife's screaming could still be heard. *I scream, she screams, we all scream for ice cream!* His mind laughed out of character in a naturally screaming laugh. *What the hell is wrong with me today?*

"Do you know how much he drank?" The balding paramedic asked.

"I have no clue!" Realizing he was yelling to be heard over a siren that had subsided, Will quietly added, "But maybe you should ask the troublemaker here. She is his wife, after all, and as far as I can tell, why this shit started."

"One beer," she said numbly, voice breaking. Then she continued, "Thank you for saving Stannie's life. I…"

"Whatever," not bothering to look in Cheryl's direction, squatting down at Stanley's feet and raising his hand so the semi-conscious fellow could see him and be out of the paramedics' way at the same time, Will continued, "Stan, my man, take some advice from me. When your woman is to the point of talking directly to your face about enjoying the company of another man, it is maybe time to put '50 ways to leave your lover in the CD player and get the fuck out. Best of Luck, Dude."

Walking away, hearing Little Miss My Ass Is the Center of the Universe, finally get enough brain cells firing at the same time to figure out what he just told her "Stannie" to do and yell a heartfelt, "Fuck you!" at him, Will raised a bird without looking back and laughed out loud.

Will didn't realize it, but he had a couple of observers watching this little tableau of current American family values who were quite taken with his actions.

Walking to clear his head, rather than take a cab as he usually did, Will just wandered around, moving in the general direction, more or less, of his flat in one of the nicer sections of Southside. Mulling overseeing another man so graphically get his heart ripped out, and his head pounded in at the same time brought back a lot of memories. He stood there looking into the sundries and used items store, that was the actual sign above the front door, 'A Sundries and Used Items Store.' unseeingly for ten minutes when he finally became aware that he was treading old thoroughfares from his married life.

Memories he had no desire to tread through and, why,

yes! Yes, here they were, those oh-so-sweet memories of his heart deciding to just get up and leave! Also, just as punctual were the warning signs of a just super special, number 9, going to screw up his next two days, headache coming on to make his evening one that lasted about what seemed to be a week. He described them as kidney stones between the ears. His doctor quit trying to get him off the Fiorinal, settling for Will, just trying to control his intake and get checkups fairly often.

Oh, crud...this one is coming fast and hard. Gotta call a cab anyway, or I will be one hurting SOB...shiit! Battery is gone... These are Will's thoughts as running steps come down the old brick-paved ally next to the second-hand shop where he and his ex-wife used to come to spend time when they had no money.

Turning on a dime, Will saw two women round the corner of the building with terror in their eyes. With heaving breath and a wandering step of what Will imagined was exhaustion, they stopped as if to listen. It was easy to hear a group running up the alley and determine that it was a crowd of drunken men.

"Please, can you help us? Our car broke down, and when these guys offered to help..."

"Come inside." Pushing the glass around the doorknob with his elbow, Will reached into the shop and unlocked it. Then, he pulled one woman in while the other followed.

"Get down behind something," Will said and stepped outside.

Five men, three of whom looked like rejects from a biker flick and two who looked like Joe College, looked around the corner, trying to understand where the objects of their pursuit went.

Why it is some rich kids want to hang out with the scum of the earth is beyond me. I just don't get it. Not only did Will not get it when children of privilege chose to identify with what he considers scum, he also had no patience with them. Not that he blamed them per se. He saw it as a case of a daddy not doing his job when men are little boys.

"Evening, guys," Will spoke casually as if closing shop for the day. He looked as he tried to figure out what had happened to the door.

"You see two bitches run by here?" asked one of the biker dudes.

"Nope. Hadn't seen any dogs at all today. I guess Animal Control is doing a good job, huh?"

"Very funny. You must have seen them. A blonde and a black-headed one."

"Nope, didn't see anyone…."

This biker dude, apparently the older one and the leader, grabbed Will and spun him around. He was about to yell as to how he was in absolutely no mood for absolutely no shit, and if Mr. Ain't seen no dogs didn't believe it, he was going to have to have his head surgically removed from his ass.

Will reacted with an over-the-arm loop and trap that went a long way towards dislocating a shoulder and followed with a sharp sweep to the right knee, which in turn caused the biker to spin to his left. Will stepped to his left, sliding his left arm around the biker's face to the right side of his jaw. Whipping the fellow's face to the left, he pulled out his straight razor, a party favor he kept in his pocket for such festive occasions.

The biker found that his voice had entirely deserted him when he felt about 8 inches of razor lying neatly across his carotid artery, followed by:

"Don't move."

"Ok."

"We will all slow down and take a few deep breaths. You others get down on your knees, cross your ankles, and put your hands behind your heads. Now."

"Fuck you, let's get him," one of the college boys said, looking all seventeen years old.

"David, I swear, if you do and I live through this, I'll kill you myself," says the biker in Will's embrace, showing that wisdom is indeed a trait of leadership. So, everybody froze.

"Tell them now, or I will kill you and then them. Believe me, I have one bitching fucker of a headache coming on, and if I don't get my medication soon, I will be three days fighting it off with booze and drugs. I want to close up shop and go."

"Now, I am willing to let you go, and you guys move on, but hear me good on this. I know I can't take all of you. But I can kill one of you. Any ideas which one that will be?"

"Me?"

"GIVE this asshole a damn DOOR prize! Yes, you. They will kill me, and I will kill you. I will only hit you; I will only cut you. Yours will be the only one whose insides I want to see in the moonlight….well, streetlight, but I think we understand each other. Right, bossman?"

"Fucking A! Don't want anything but to leave you alone and be gone," the boss biker is shat his pants in an effort to not move against that oh-so-sharp edge that was the only thing separating him from the next life.

"Good enough. See ya."

This was a madman's bluff, but Will was mad enough not to be in his right mind; too many memories had come back to him, he was in pain, and his moral code would just as soon slaughter a group of rapists as not. Will would deny it, but part of his subconscious almost wished they would jump. He made it worse by simply sitting down on the step, remarking that a bad blow was sweeping in from the gulf and how the storm might help him sleep, looking at the sky all the while. The bikers moved down the street, but Joe College didn't have enough.

"Where you guys going? We got the drop on him now. Come on!" He was ignored, of course. Some men, like stray dogs, knew when the alpha male was pissed and when it was time to go. The bikers knew it was time to go. Joe College followed their lead. This pup, however, needed a more pointed lesson.

Casually, Will looked the young man up and down and asked, "You ever been in prison, son? Maybe St. Clair or West Jefferson?"

"Hell, no."

"Well, I only ask because you look like one of the best girlfriend boys I have ever had. I bet you're him! Man, I miss coring him. He would twist and scream like a banshee, and man, what a nut he could make you get! You guys go head-on. Junior and I here have some catching up to do." With that, Will stood and made a halfhearted grab in Joe College's direction. This sent him running in blind fear. The older biker, still backing up and away, couldn't help but grin just a wee bit while muttering to his cohorts, "Keep your pie holes shut and your asses moving."

They were out of sight quickly, and Will heard

movement in the shop and muttered quietly without looking inside, "Don't come out for 15 minutes. They'll wait 5, maybe ten, before they move on. They don't have the brains for patience."

Something like 15 minutes passed, and the two women stepped out. Will realizes it is the woman from the club and her companion.

"You ok?" He was fairly sure she was, but it was the right thing to ask.

"Never better, and thanks. Weren't you terrified?"

"Sometimes my mouth takes over." Remembering why he was walking home and the memories that had been dredged up, he added, "Besides, there are things worse than death."

"True, all too true." Both women remarked in unison, like some feminine stereo.

"Well, I need to go ahead and call a cab. I was very serious about my headaches. Once they get bad, it is like fighting a brush war and takes days to knock it down, mostly by staying fu...uh, messed up."

"This will help," the blonde said and stepped up behind him, embracing him with an unbelievable grip. Her small, slender arms felt as though they contained bundles of steel cables.

Will woke up the next day feeling well. He didn't remember getting home, so he called his doctor to say he needed an appointment. Since he wasn't a man who felt that current events were all that important to him, he completely missed the morning news covering the discovery of three bodies, four heads, and five bikes. Well, there were three bodies worth of parts anyway. They didn't match.

Chapter 1

Considering his circumstances, Will was a pretty happy man. He struggled with bouts of severe doubts and depression, mostly because he lost his wife and partly because he couldn't understand why things kept going wrong.

His wife left him because, in her words, "Things never get any better, Will. You keep screwing up over and over and making the same mistakes. You have ruined my credit by being irresponsible, and what good credit YOU have, you have because I sat down and paid the bills. YOU have good credit because it was ME that paid the bills!"

She is right, of course. Will knew and agreed that he was guilty of everything she accused him of. He forgot things. He forgot appointments and lost mail. He was genuinely an out-of-sight, out-of-mind kind of guy. His distraction drove his wife to distraction, and he couldn't seem to change. He tried for a while, then lost a bill, which was late. His losing the bill led to his forgetting to pay it, which led him to spend the money and the Friday night fights.

It got so bad that he dreaded her going to the mailbox for fear that she would find something. *Well, at least I don't have to worry about that anymore, so happy effing days. Right?*

Will didn't bother to answer himself. Though self-imposed, his current state of isolation was a clear indication that he was not exactly ready to face up to all the ramifications of what happened in the last 18 months or so. As he finishes getting ready, he is idly listening to the television. There is something about murder, something more common in Birmingham than you would think based on the local news organizations. Something about there being enough body parts for three people, but at least five individuals contributed to the pile.

Teeth marks. Effing freaks, Will thinks to himself. *Of course, they will get the bastards off. After all, the fact that they committed this act is ipso de facto proof that they are mentally ill. Right? Then again, maybe they were just hungry.*

This last thought was accompanied by the idea that perhaps he wasn't getting enough red meat in his own diet here lately. He called Robert, a pure-D fool but a good guy to play spades with, and asked if he and Payne wanted to come over and cook out and play spades till the wee hours of the morning. Robert said he would come this weekend. He would call later and confirm. He hoped Robert would not bring a girl. Robert tended to favor the loud redneck babes who always put a period at the end of the evening by puking after having too much to drink. *Well, maybe one day, he will figure it out and finally get a good one.*

With that, Will called a cab to work and didn't think much about his heroism for three months.

He went to work and got into fights – well, arguments-in traffic. He apologized half the time to the other party, not out of fear but because he realized he was beginning to act like a huge asshole. *So. Avoid traffic.* Then, wryly, *My social skills and options are beginning to come into play.*

Will also thought that maybe the doctor was right in telling him to take a vacation to the other end of the world to get some space between him and his divorce. At any rate, and his doctor had said that was correct, whatever it cost, it would be worthwhile for him to go away for a while to relax. Business and life were good, and the management contract he took out with one of his competitors turned out to be a goldmine for them through concentrated markets and efforts. He spent two days with his manager and CPA confirming it so he could afford to take off some time. Say, for 3 to 6 months! *Money in the bank, no problems, someone else to take care of the crap. Why not?* Will calls his mom in Pensacola to say he will be down to see them for a few days, maybe even a week.

He called Robert to see if he would care for his cat Solomon. Once again proving he was a limited friend and not a buddy, Robert refused. So, Solomon's fat butt goes into a pet motel anyway. *May not even remember me when I get back. Then again, he might remember me as the SOB who put him in there and left him. Well, at least they are getting paid to care for him. They won't let him out or put him to sleep when they tire of caring for him.*

Petting Solomon a bit more, he said, "Then again, Solomon, maybe I will just send for you from the Caribbean. Who knows?" Solomon, being held up under his front legs with his belly poking out, looked at his owner as cats almost always do, like the man had lost his mind and couldn't grasp how boring the feline race found human commentary. Ending the goodbye, Will left through the lobby, waving to everyone, and started his vacation. The next time Will saw Solomon was under very strange circumstances.

Pensacola was great. His parents' house was boring, not because he didn't enjoy them; it was just strange not to be able to talk to them about how it had ended, and this always led to unexpected quiet spaces in the conversation, so he split after five days. Still, his parents didn't feel slighted. He his longest stay before was three days, so... you know how the rest goes. It was just time to boogey.

And boogey, he did. His business was going VERY

well. He lets the money roll in. Will did what Will was good at, and taking his partner's advice, he hired a bunch of paranoid, truly dedicated money managers from New York. In addition to his business continuing to grow due to his management contract, his ability to sell, and his manager's caretaking, he could retire. Well, he did not retire, per se, but went to work when he felt like it. *Too bad she didn't stick around.* Then, Will laughed. *Oh yeah, isn't that just too damned bad. Then she could drag my ass into a bar like that poor SOB back in Birmingham.* Then it occurred to him: *Didn't she say something like that once?* It wouldn't come back to him.

Whatever, it doesn't matter anymore. Working his way down the Gulf Coast, Will finally chartered a plane to one of the Virgin Islands and spent a month walking up and down the beach until he knew every cove, inlet, and tree by heart. He became known as the quiet American who never tanned, though he eventually did. He suspected it was mostly due to all the freckles running together, a gift from his redheaded mother. He read his statements monthly from the banks, his profit and loss statements, and generally stayed out of the way of his partners and money managers. For the first time, Will was considering retiring.

"Hey, Will, how ARE you?" Patricia asked. She was one of his business partners.

"Fine...fine. You?"

"Everything is going along just fine. You had a visit from an interesting couple yesterday."

"Really? Who, what, and what did they want?" lazy days, lazy Sun, and he had an itch in his short hair telling him it may be time to go and leave it all. *Shit.*

"Yes, a couple of ladies from Germany want to meet

you."

"Huh. Isn't that interesting?" *What the hell is going on now?* In the past, Will tended to forget things, and he did not like surprises or things out of the blue. *What did I eff up now? He tries to think, but nothing comes.*

"They seemed to think you would remember them, small, one with black hair and one blonde. Ring any bells?"

Oh yeah...THOSE ladies. Well, yes. As a matter of fact, she did. "No, not really. What did they want?"

"Well, she is quite insistent on seeing you personally. They both are. Something about a heroic exploit of yours and a biker gang? Really, Will, when DID you become the caped crusader type?"

"You are enjoying yourself, aren't you?"

"Yes, I am. The last three months, you have been as relaxed as ever since I have known you, and yet, you never said a word."

"I didn't think it was that big a deal."

"Modesty as well. Been reading The Art of Virtue?"

" No, it just didn't seem to be the sort to bring up in polite company. The whole thing about maybe KILLING somebody didn't seem to go well with 'Hi, how are you? How are the kids?' Anyway, what did they want?"

"They want to see you, something about our managing certain of their American business interests. How was it, she put it? Oh yes, 'We need a man of old honor, courage, and chivalry to handle our interests in our absence, which is often extended for a long time.' I believe you have made a conquest of the heart."

"Does this need me there personally? Can't you handle

it?"

"They were quite insistent that you handle the preliminaries personally. She even agreed those subsequent things could be left to someone like me. You know, come to think of it…"

"What?"

"She seemed to know a good deal about our business arrangement. Your company is the only client we have taken on in this manner. Have you been talking out of school?"

"No!" Then he adds, "Crap."

"Did something occur to you?"

"Nothing but the fact that it looks as if I need to come back to the States to see whatever this is. Give me a week and make the appointment for ten days from now."

"Good enough. See you soon."

Chapter 2

There are desperate men, and there are decent men. Generally, you do have a few truly evil individuals, but mostly desperate men get there an inch at a time, little by little until they wake up one day to find that they are no longer considered an upstanding member of society. The sad thing is their motivations are almost always honorable.

Their reaction to finding themselves reviled by society is not what many expect. Surprise, anger, disappointment…they are all there, of course. The main feeling is one of betrayal. By the universe, by God, by the family who've deserted them just when they needed them the most and most searingly, like a hot branding iron constantly laid to their brain and heart, their own common sense.

"How could I have been so stupid?" is a constant metronome beating in their heads, as if they can rectify the situation by just figuring out what went wrong.

Will Johnston is such a man.

How could I have been so stupid? The thought goes on and on, as if providing a back beat to most of his thoughts as he moves through the day's routines. He is making progress with all his company's creditors since his partners screwed him, but it isn't easy. *Especially The Asshole of the West, that asshole. He'd like to stick me with a piece of driftwood and break it off at the nub.*

Unlike most of his creditors, Robespierre doesn't give a shit about the fact that Will is operating on the basis of someone else's word; he wants Will's head on a plate. *Well, he wants somebody's head, anybody's head, so he can not take his part of the blame. Thank God for one more miracle, Will thinks. Paranoia, thy name is mine.*

Will is pretty sure he understood Robespierre's actions, but he will deal with that issue later. Right now, the important thing is to pay off the money, put it behind him, and go about the business of rebuilding what he once had. Will also made the decision that it is better to build his business one small customer at a time and never put all his eggs in one basket again, no matter how big the customer is.

That is unless that customer wants to pay up front for the entire project, PLUS guarantee that cost overruns will be covered. Won't ever happen, but hey! I can always dream.

"Sylvia, would you call John for me? I need an appointment with him on Friday."

"Certainly."

John is their accountant. Will always pays by certified check since last year. He always enters the charges into the checkbook, the PAPER checkbook, I might add and also stays in touch with the bank as to when service charges are deducted in any individual month. I make this point because you need to understand that Will makes his CPA balance his checkbook at his full rate at least once a month and sometimes more when he gets to thinking about it. You could say, and John often does, that Will is overly paranoid. Today is no different.

"Mr. Johnston? John would like to speak to you. Want me to transfer it to your office?"

"Sure." After a second's delay, John's handset is ringing.

"Will, how are you?"

"Fine, fine. You?"

"Doing pretty well, things are really beginning to heat up, we're getting things off us, and customers are coming back. We are really very excited about all this."

"Well, that's good; glad to hear it. Will?

"Yes?"

"I balanced your checking account not even two weeks ago. Are you ok?"

"Yes, John, I just get freaked out sometimes. Last year was a heart-stopper for me, and I really haven't liked to write checks at all since then. You know that. I have explained to you that it is worth it to me to pay you too much, so I don't have to worry."

"I understand, as I said before. Love the billing hours, too. I just feel bad for you. You are okay with every business metric I use." There is a significant pause, and then John continues, "Will, might I suggest you see a therapist or something? Your anxiety levels are way out of line with your financial situation. You know that. Why are you torturing yourself? You were completely exonerated of all wrong doing."

Another pause, then, "I think maybe you should seek professional help."

Silence ensues. There is no comment for what is a hell of a long time on the phone. Then Will responds calmly and with certainty, "John, I want you to take this in the spirit in which I give it, OK?" He continues on without waiting for ok, or no, or taking a flying leap at a rolling doughnut, "I understand your concern. My behavior is not exactly normal right now. It is, however, how I choose to deal with the demons that chase me in my dreams. My wife is gone, and all my last damn therapist could ask me was, 'How does that make you feel?' as if I didn't feel like shit. Everyone offers advice, and no one offers any solutions."

"Therapists can't help me. Most of them are WAY more fucked up than I am. Keep me happy. Balance my checkbook when I ask and at least once a month. Enjoy the extra money I pay you. No worries, ok? Besides, I think just balancing my checkbook hardly covers the analysis I ask you to run every so often."

"Well...if you..."

"I DO. I do insist. This nightmare will be over in a few years, and I can figure out what to do then." *...and WHAT is that scent?*

"Will, are you still there?

"Yes, John."

"Okay, it seemed the phone got full of static for a second."

"Probably the gremlins in the building."

"The what?"

"Gremlins, spooks, haints. Who knows? I keep smelling lavender strong enough to go looking for it. I guess my nose is screwed up because I smell it all the time."

"Huh. Anyways..."

"Anyways, you keep doing what you are doing, and I will keep doing what I am doing. Enjoy the billing hours, John. This is on me; I know you are not gouging me on time," and Will laughs and continues, "because I have to argue with you to bill me for more. Like you tell me, relax."

The scent of lavender, a breeze. *Go home now.* The thought is that alien voice again, feminine to the extreme. *I really am going crazy*, Will thinks. *I really am losing my mind, and oh, God, Baby, I miss you so much.* If asked, Will could not have told you to whom he was speaking in his mind.

Will's resistance to tears is worn almost to nothing, which is why he spends a lot of time in his office with his phone put on do not disturb. He thinks he has everyone fooled, but not his secretary.

Sylvia heard his tears one early morning when she decided to come in early since she couldn't sleep. Will had slept at the office the night before on the couch and had been crying in his sleep. She thinks to wake him and check on him. More than once, she has also thought about just leaving, but her pay is better than elsewhere, and he has never mistreated her. Just as she is about to enter his inner office and wake him up, she is buffeted by a cold air current and paralyzed with fear.

She turns from her planned route and returns to her desk.

What is there in that room with him, making him cry and terrifying me? The idea that she can ALMOST see a form in the room, next to the sofa on which he sleeps, is quickly dismissed. She had left with that thought on her mind and had left the door open so she could watch him on the couch.

Should I call his ex-wife?

She had the number and knew that they were estranged, but not what the situation was now. *NO, you will not call her! It's an odd thought to have, but ok. Something…I can't remember…well. Okay. I won't call.*

Sylvia gets up as if to check on him as she had been dithering about doing for the last half hour or even perhaps to wake him when the door to his office slams shut. The door slamming shut is not what makes her get up to take a personal day. The lock snicking and the clock snickering do that. She is of South American heritage and had been brought up in a superstitious home.

It is time to go. 30th floor, no open windows, I am here, and no one else is, cold breeze, Will crying in his sleep, alien thoughts that aren't mine, doors that lock by themselves and clocks that laugh, yes, indeed, it is time to go. She lies to herself and tells herself that she doesn't hear the office's outer doors lock as she goes towards the elevator.

Later that afternoon, she is surprised by Will's call.

"Are you alright, Sylvia?" He pronounces it as he understands she likes, like back home. Sylv-ya.

"Fine. Just got a bug." Then cautiously, she adds, wrapping herself tighter in a blanket, "How are you? I noticed you didn't go home last night."

"Fit as a fiddle. Why?"

"Well, I just wondered if it might be something you already had." She has not been able to get warm all day and is becoming more and more fatigued as this conversation goes on.

"Look, I am beat." She is beat. She also wants no part of him until he is done with his trouble.

"Well, just let me know if it looks like you'll miss tomorrow, too. Why don't you go ahead and go see a doc?"

"I suppose I should, but I think I'll just see how it goes."

Will hangs up with Sylvia, feeling as if he has passed some unseen marker on whatever fucked up road he is on.

There is no one here but him; he is truly expecting no calls, and he is sleepy, oh so sleepy. His head feels as if it weighs a thousand pounds. *Rest, Dearest Knight. Your trials will begin soon enough.*

"Huh? Who's there?"

He really is tired. As he lay back on the sofa, it is as if he feels soft, cool hands-small and ladylike-pressing his shoulders back onto the couch. He passes out and into a dream.

She is ethereal. Her laughter tinkled through his office and out the high-rise windows, all of which were now open. *I didn't think you could open the windows.*

There is that sweet giggle again. "You can't, Sugar. I opened them myself. I'll put them back again if you like. I just love the way the wind feels across my skin at this height."

Will stares. This is not a conscious response. She is floating in the air above him, naked, her blonde hair, hip length swirling around her naked body, revealing the lush, tight curves of her pale cream skin. Behind her, he sees two indistinct images, one lightening bright white, the other a dull, rusty maroon that invokes images of blood-soaked instruments of death rusted with age and rot.

She sees it in his eyes, or perhaps she simply reads him. Whichever it is and whatever she sees or reads, it startles her, and some of the magic flees the room.

She whirls, startled. The male part of his mind noticed that her perfectness, her roundness everywhere that had excited him so darkly, did not go. *Whatever she is, she really is this beautiful.*

She appears to concentrate, and the magic returns.

"Why do you sing so? Do you not realize you are as beautiful as you are? You make my heart ache in my chest."

She had not opened her mouth, yet it seemed to Will he heard singing.

"I wishwhat you say were true. Yet you know not what I am or what you need to be about yet as it is not up to me to tell you. One day soon, you'll meet me under circumstances where your mind will not be able to say it was just a dream. I hope you feel the same way then. Now, however, you need to sleep and forget for a time.Looking at the exhausted man as he fell into a deep sleep she thinks, *You will never die, my Knight. I promise you you will never die, and you will never be alone again.*

Monday morning, Will calls Sylvia and lets her know he is feeling better. He hopes she is, and does she think she will be all right by Monday?

"I am sure I will be."

"Good, good." A pause in which he coughs slightly, saying shit under his breath as always. "Sylvia?"

"Yes?"

"What happened yesterday, exactly? I was very sick and didn't remember much about it." Actually, he remembers quite a bit, an angel floating naked above him, making his heart ache so badly in his chest he wondered if he were having a cardiac event.

Dreams aren't so bad. Hell, what is troubling Will is that he has awakened, naked, in his office, with his clothes strewn all to hell and gone, with lavender on his clothes and all over his skin and his face. Weak-kneed, Will staggers about for a few minutes, wondering why it is so quiet.

He laughed. *She put the windows back. How thoughtful. Now I don't have to explain to the building managers why my nighttime girlfriend took out the suicide-proof windows*

He is losing his mind. He has been cheated, deserted, almost jailed, analyzed, poked, and prodded, and now he is losing his mind. *Well, at least I feel better about it all.* He walks stiffly about, sore in the good muscles one is really never sore enough in, at least for single men and most married ones, picking up his clothes. As he gets dressed, it occurs to him that he ought to call Sylvia.

"I mean, I did not say anything out of the way, did I? I had some things on my mind, and I was not well," Will is suddenly worried about what point Sylvia may have gone home.

"Well, nothing out of the ordinary. You were upset when you…"

"Sylvia, I am sorry. I DO remember that part. Things just seem to get the better of me since my divorce. It is getting easier overall, I think. My mother seems to think I will get over it entirely in time. I am beginning to think she is right." Sensations in his memory threatened to bog down his thinking, so he moved on. "Anyway, I will see you Monday, OK? Be prepared to help me map out a new strategy for this quarter and the fall. I think it is time for me to quit feeling sorry for myself and take the fight to the bastards who tried to destroy me. What say you?"

"I say it is about damn time you felt this way." The shock on both ends of the phone, thunderstruck silence, then laughter, belly laughter, the kind that you know will come back again and again throughout the day, rolls out of Sylvia's headset. "Well", she continues, "it is the truth."

"Ah, Sylvia, come run away with me. We'll find some far away glen where the fairies still live. I understand all the stars in the sky are different colors and blaze like torches there, like gems on a jeweler's black felt." The chuckle is still in his voice, and it is good to hear him this way. It is as if she hears the turbines in his soul gearing up.

It is a massive, throaty sound that comes out as an undertone whenever he chuckles. "So, I will see you Monday?"

"Yup. Have a good weekend, dear heart." As she hangs up the phone, she wonders, not for the first or last time, what HAD happened last year.

Something few people realize is how hard the wind blows at high altitudes. Folks like Crystal know. She loves to get as high as possible, then simply fall towards the earth until she reaches terminal velocity. The object of the game is to see how closely she can get to the earth before pulling out of the dive. Vampires are immortal, but you can still seriously physically damage one to the point that it could take years to recover. One horror tale that circulates amongst the People is the one where a vampire is so damaged by irate townsfolk that he cannot defend himself. His carcass is then dumped into a coffin and buried. The vampire, immortal, it is true, is also so damaged that he cannot free himself from his coffin prison until he feeds. He cannot feed because he is in the coffin. The idea of being trapped in a coffin for millennia while your brain turns more and more to insanity, unable to die, gives even those not subject to death the willies.

Some say she is trying to find a novel way to commit suicide without it being a suicide. Crystal's retort is always something along these lines, "What, and miss all this fun? The truly excellent quality of life I have? I can't see the sun again, ever. I will never again have children that can see the sun, ever. My husband is dead. My children have been dead for some 2000 years, and none of my descendants know I exist. They not only don't know me, they don't even know they had an ancestor."

"I walked up on a child some weeks ago in a mall. It was my great to the twentieth granddaughter, I would guess. Her mother is SO proud of her. She laughed and remarked on how much I looked like her mother, the child's maternal grandmother. Little did she know who I was or that her baby was definitely going to be left-handed and run like the wind, out running most of the men in her life. Let me be clear on this. I don't know, nor could I care less if I die on impact. I am already dead as far as I am concerned. I did not ask to be a vampiress, living off the blood of scum. I do not fear hell; I didn't ask to be here in this awful state. If I die, I am free."

I wonder if Will will miss me. Crystal is going home. Her path across the Atlantic toward the land of the People describes a gigantic wave up and down as she moves toward the castles and hidden lands of home.

Once, just for fun, she had let herself simply dive into the water at slightly over 120 miles per hour. It hadn't hurt, but all her clothes were basically shredded off. When she had come blasting up out of the water next to a South African tanker, it had been quite amusing to see the slack-jawed crewmen on deck.

"Where the hell have you been?" Monica is into a fine fury this evening. Crystal had been out running wild while she had to stay here and deal with these fools amongst the people who can't count, the application being that their population is just over four million amongst a world population approaching seven billion. *Idiots. They have an almost unlimited lifespan and the ability to accumulate vast wealth. We never get sick, and yet, it isn't enough. What was it someone once said about the accumulation of wealth? Once you have enough to never worry about gold and silver*

"Well, if you must know, I have been looking after the good Sir Will. He has been having a horrible time, and I hate to see him suffer so."

Crystal isn't trying to hide her encounters with Will from Monica. She couldn't anyway. She didn't bring the subject up, though, either. For her own reasons, Monica decides not to pursue the matter. It is sad, but being a regent often leaves one with hard choices, such as now.

"Crystal, we have some hard, dangerous work ahead of us this next fortnight. We will be challenging some very powerful masters on their home turf. It bothers me that we three have become so sure of ourselves, our power, and our uniqueness that we really can't conceive of failure."

"Well," Crystal replies, "are we not the strongest of any three People? Who can stand against us with Melissa's glamours, your ferocity, and my speed?"

"I have spent the last several months pondering just that question, and I cannot answer it. So, why do they move to challenge us? It cannot be purely a foolish act on their part. We have a missing piece of information. Melissa!"

From far down the central ventilation shaft, Melissa's voice replies distantly, "Yes?"

"Come!"

She arises out of the shaft and settles near Crystal on the divan. "What's up?" Melissa had begun to absorb a lot of the speech patterns of modern TV. Monica did not think it was an improvement.

"We need information, and I think I have a thought on how we can get it. If you were able to get to Danco and assume his place, we would be able to learn about their plans and strategies. Do you think you can glamour strong enough to fool a crowd and individuals?"

"It would be child's play, but the appearance isn't the problem…"

"Well, what is?"

"…I am getting to it, just thinking a bit as I go. His closest allies and cronies would be able to see through my glamour not on physical attributes but on actions and mannerisms." Hanging her head over the edge of the divan so she is looking at the room from an upside-down angle, she continues. "I suppose we would need to keep him a few days before we kill him for interrogation. That is to be his final fate, correct?"

"Yes, he has harmed too many innocents amongst the cattle, I mean amongst the human, races to be allowed to continue. That fact alone may explain his actions. He knows I will kill him sooner or later for what he has done. So much blood and murder! Can they all have forgotten that they were human once?" It is a rhetorical question, so neither bothers to answer it. *Besides,* thinks Melissa, *in many cases, is not true.*

"…and I could probably take out a few of his cronies at the same time. Yeah, I could do that. I will need to find and interrogate him and a couple of his hangers-on. What do I do with the bodies?"

"Burn them." The People, many of whom accuse her of preying unrighteously on the People who tried to exercise their destiny, call her a predator.

Monica's response is always, "Really? You do not prey unrighteously on humans?" People quit responding after a while. It became clear, when she reserved true vampire feeding for use as a capital punishment for People who fed on humans, that she is serious about the People and humans being able to share the planet.

Melissa, like Crystal, likes to fly naked. She flies up the canyon ways, avoiding the human radar. It isn't that they could detect her, but they could and did detect her jewelry and weaponry when she flies. For some damn reason, she has a signature equal to a fighter craft, and it always makes her nervous. Humans can be quite disturbing when territorial issues come up.

Finally, she spots the mountain range called "dragon's hump," though no one living can tell you why.

The Lord Danco is holding a feast. Upon arriving, Melissa hides herself between two rocks. An army sniper searching for a heat signature in the night would have missed her. This is no surprise. Her body temperature is the same temperature as the surrounding rock. *Well, I knew it wasn't going to be an easy one.* This thought came on as she was assessing the crowd's numbers. *Better than 75, I think. At least I don't have to hold back.*

She is going into that place in her mind where she creates her glamour. If she explained it to you, she would say something very similar to what she said to Crystal when she was her tutor.

"It is very much like closing your eyes and visualizing what you are thinking about; only do it with your eyes open. Concentrating on making your eyes see what your mind wants is the trick."

Crystal had tried that and, to some degree, was successful, but not like Melissa. It's as if she actually warps what IS, rather than just creates visions.

Well, that should do it for a few days, anyway. Plenty of time for Monica to get the intelligence she needs.

Gnashing of teeth, wailing on the part of his buddies, nails gashing long scores into the rock walls of his prison, Danco is seriously pissed. Monica decides it is time to do an "interview."

"Lord Danco. Thank you so much for the visit, especially right in the middle of your party. Such devotion will not go without reward."

"You bitch. Save your sarcasm for someone who is impressed by it. Why am I here?"

"Why to answer doubts in my mind as to your loyalty, of course. Some say you are the leader of a group who is bound to the destruction of my reign. Answer me truthfully, for you know I will know a lie."

"My loyalty is to the destiny of the People as rightful rulers of this world."

"I see." *How sad. He believes he is telling the truth.* Monica continues sadly, "How unfortunate that you believe what you say and still must die."

"How can you say you are a just ruler? Why will you not lead us in our quest for what is rightfully ours?"

"Because what you seek is not yours; because you believe what you say, you will not suffer." Rather than make his punishment overly long, she simply takes his head off and feeds on the spouting stump of his neck. It is over for him and the others within seconds. Their efforts at resistance were hardly acknowledged by the powerful Monica.

Surveying the carnage around her, she wondered, not for the first time, why humans make life hard. *We are still human. Being a vampire only makes it easier to be murderous*. She and those close to her sat back in stunned horror as they watched World War I unfold across the continent of Europe and even more so as they watched Hitler take down millions of innocents in the name of a master race.

Heaven help us if someone like Hitler ever gets turned, Monica thinks.

Hitler had known of the People and had even sought them out. Thankfully, even the most hardened of the 'Divine Right' crowd wouldn't touch him. Most of the People had a bit of second sight and could see nothing but a long line of destruction and extinction leading away from the point of Hitler's turning. He was, according to some of the oldest among them, a true son of Cain.

Shuddering, Monica leaves the now silent chamber and returns to the upper chambers, where she finds Crystal and Melissa in a high state of confrontation. The bodies of Danco and his cronies will be burned before the day's beginning.

"What in the hell do you mean?" Crystal is angry and red-faced in the manner only enraged People can get. A red-faced vampire is where the red devil image began.

"I mean, he is bound and chosen to be Monica's King because she is the MBIC. What are you thinking?"

"He is better than that, and he doesn't want anything but to live in peace, have kids, and die an old man with his grandkids around him. Damn it, we can't take it from him. He is a Good Man."

"Really? Why is he so capable of screwing your brains out if he is so pure? He is still married, right? Doesn't sound too good to me." Melissa is honestly flamboozled by Crystal's rage and wonders, *Just what the hell is happening here?*

"Because he is lonely! That bitch left him, and it broke his heart. Besides," she is a bit quieter now, "he doesn't know I am real, and yes, he is legally and completely divorced from her."

"Excuse me?"

"A dream, a fantasy, a delusion. He thinks I am another symptom of his mental illness and that his mind is simply deteriorating."

At this point, Crystal's voice completes its migration from the roar of an enraged vampire to that of an upset young girl to this dead, affectless monotone. The monotone is more troubling than the rage.

"Crystal." Monica's voice cut through the hall. "Are you all right?"

"No."

"What is it?"

"I want to have babies that can walk in the sunlight again. I never will. I want to be human again. I never can."

The next morning, Crystal was gone. She often disappeared for months at a time, always listening for the call. Sometimes, she could be found in the polar wastes where nothing seemed to stir unless is was some kind of archaic bacteria, just hanging out in the truest solitude on the planet or sometimes wrestling with polar bears like they were just big old German Shepherds on the other end of the planet. Sometimes, she walked the Amazon ceiling, giving the indigenous people reason to tell their kids stories of a tree ghost that occasionally wreaked vengeance on evildoers.

No one was surprised. Will still needs protection.

Chapter 3

Will felt spoiled by his high-speed connection to the Internet at work. Remembering what it was like trying to work over a modem connection, even a 56K link, makes it even more enjoyable. *No, enjoyable does not cover it. PLEASURABLE. Now, there is a word with all kinds of undertones that just about explains the feeling.* During the closing days of his marriage, a 56K or an expensive ISDN line was the best a consumer could do.

Will's troubles with the phone company started as a result of his being able to exploit the tariff legislation for home based businesses. His was a home based business using a corporation's worth of pipeline from the phone company; he was tearing them a new one all day and all they could do was comply and it just KILLED somebody at the phone company.

A buddy from Outer Edge Electronics interrupted Will's anti-nostalgia, wanting to know if he wanted to cruise over to InterOp and maybe catch a gun show as well.

"Sounds like fun. What time we need to leave? Atlanta is about a two hour drive, isn't it?"

Will hung up the phone and realized that it was almost quitting time and he had not had a teary eye all day.

Thank the Good Lord. Maybe I am going to be okay after all. He was half expecting to get a whiff of some perfume, though he was not aware of his expectations. Will had begun to realize his ex was losing no sleep over him, nor were his past associates. *Quit being a little bitch and worrying about what else you could have done. You did all you could; fuck everybody else.*

Making his goodnights to Sylvia *Sylvya*, his mind corrected, as it always did, and the rest of the staff, all of whom were temps at this point, Will made his way down towards the elevators. *It was worth it to get a view like this for our clients to see. Makes them more comfortable with who we are. Come to think of it, who are we now? How did our company wind up where it is now?* Then, *Not the same, not the same by a long shot.*

It occurred to Will as he waited on the elevator that OEE might need his skill sets, in particular network security. As he rode the elevator down to the lobby floor, he was furiously making notes to nail down his thoughts for the ride to Atlanta.

One year later:

Success is ours again. "I just wanted to take a few minutes to thank everyone who helped us get here today." Will spoke from the podium in one of The Wynfrey Hotel's conference rooms in Hoover, a suburb of Birmingham. It had been built as a star attraction of the Birmingham Galleria. Will had no idea whether or not it met its backers' expectations.

Will continued, "I especially want to thank all those customers who stayed with me, us, as I went through a tremendously dark period in my personal life, a period which severely affected my business life as well." On the faces of his audience there were looks ranging from pain to interest to anxiety. A few were kaleidoscopes in emotional motion, not knowing what was coming next. Will took a breath then continued.

"I especially want to thank all the folks at Outer Edge Electronics. These folks had faith enough in what I was trying to do with Infosurge that they weathered all the bad periods long enough to enjoy the second-to-none service we offer today. Mr. Browning, would you stand and be recognized? You'll have to excuse me, folks. This wasn't planned but it seems to me the right thing to do."

An elderly gentleman of about 90 stood up. He wore one of the looks of interest. The other twelve guests at his table were looking on. This group would have stood out anywhere. He mouthed a question to Will, who laughed in response.

"Yes, Sir. This is what you get for beating me so handily at racquet ball." Then he continued, more sober and serious, "Mr. Browning, you are my friend and mentor. You stood by me when I had no one else. You said to me, 'Keep going. No matter what, keep going. Rest when you have to, do without when you have to, push ahead when you can, cut your losses when led to do so by God and good sense, but above all, Keep Going.' You also said that when you feel like you are going through hell, don't stop." This was followed by some laughter and applause.

"We have kept going, sir. Your pledge, backing and faith helped us get past the first sticking point and your continued encouragement helped me, and us, to find our way past the others. Late night conversations about all things didn't hurt, either." Will did not know it, but he had just identified himself as someone who had the Senator's ear to several interested parties. He cleared his throat, and finished up with, "Let's have a hand for Mr. Browning, Infosurge's spiritual savior!"

After the applause died down and Mr. Browning returned to his seat, his face serious and thoughtful, Will continued, "We can now say from day one, we have had a return on investment of over 11%. In the last year, that has risen from a horrendous minus 41%. This is called turning the tide." He grinned. Why not? He deserved to grin. Everyone was dead certain that he had bottomed out and was a financial ruin. But he proved them wrong by overcoming it all and bringing his company to soaring heights as one of Birmingham's star children.

There was more applause at this as he finished up, "My thanks to all whom decided to come share our celebration. Each of you, through your decision to continue on with Infosurge as we fought our demons, has contributed to our success. It is my hope that this evening of dining, dancing, and music can convey some small idea of my gratefulness to you, our customers and vendors."

"Now, let's enjoy the rest of the evening."

Coming down from the podium with the other guests, Will found himself surrounded by well wishers. It was a big night and Will had been looking forward to it with great anticipation. It had taken a toll on him but he was glad everything had ended well. He didn't drink as a rule, but had applied a pre-emptive strike against a headache. That strike together with the unexpected turnout of well-wishers for this party made him feel light headed.

Meeting Crystal didn't hurt either. *God, she is so beautiful...but be cool. Got to remember, be cool.*

Crystal was his girlfriend of 3 weeks. They met at a Hoover bookstore where Will almost bowled her over coming around a corner in the stacks. He had managed to catch her from falling. She had thanked him and laughed it off, proceeding to the magazine stands that lined the entire back wall of that particular Books-A-Million. She was redheaded, petite, blue eyed, and had a smile that lit up her face when she was animated, which she often was. She also had an off-putting manner of speech. As Will perused the books, he kept looking at her, wondering why the curve of her calves in open toe heels made him feel homesick. She then surprised him by saying when he walked up to her that she had started a running bet as to how long it would take him to finally come over, was he always this slow to take a hint?

Crystal was here tonight to support Will. He was nervous about this but she encouraged him to be bold and daring. She was dressed in a royal blue, sequined dress that fit her form perfectly. She was, as his dear old mom so aptly verbalized it, perfectly suited to separate Will from his IQ. She laughed when she said it, but her eyes didn't. Will was her first born after all, and she was a bear when it came to what was best for him.

"That went wonderfully, Will! See? Didn't I tell you? You were a smash! As for not being good in front of a crowd, that was masterful the way you singled out Mr. Browning. You'll be the talk of the town."

"Well, I don't know about being the talk of the town, but I do know that Mr. Browning deserved every word of it. He kept me going."

Will and Crystal were interrupted by a familiar face, asking them for a moment of their time.

"Are you kidding? Anytime the senior senator attends a local function it is written up. Surely, you know that," Crystal responded as she turned to their questioner.

"I suppose I did; I just had not thought about it," Will said, still looking at Crystal.

The face of their conversational interloper seemed to be desperately trying not to appear predatory and greedy, which meant that is exactly how it appeared. It was a familiar face not by personal acquaintance but by having it burned into your mind by the TV, day after day.

Recognition, but not the name, hit Will. *It is, golly-gee-whiz, a reporter from the local Fox affiliate. Great, what cluster fubar is coming down now?* Will thought to himself. Like any man or woman who has built something from the ground up, Will distrusted the press if for no other reason than they never report good news. If she was here, Will would feel inclined to think something has gone wrong and that he missed something.

DAMNIT! Will smiled as if he was politely interested.

"Mr. Dupont? Could we have a moment of your time?" The mike was placed in front of his face, the camera was on him, and the red light was winking at him as if to say, "Okay, guy, don't screw up. If you do, it will be seen in instant replay for all your old friends to laugh over. You didn't really think you could have an evening where you didn't have to deal with all those old friends, doubt, anxiety, and fear, did you? Did you?"

"I'm sorry, what?" Will looked as if he had been a bit pole-axed, like perhaps the petite reporter just used a rubber-covered mallet to the forehead to soften him up for the interview. Later that evening Will would tell Crystal she looked for the entire world like a match on two legs just itching for someone to rub her the wrong way and set her off.

"We were wondering if you'd care to enlighten us to the extent that Mr. Browning helped you save your company."

"What? I don't…"

"We would like to know to what extent Mr. Browning helped to save your company. Surely you can see that in light of the on-going Senate investigation into Mr. Browning's activities while chairing the telecommunications sub-committee it is important that…" The reporter droned on. It hardly mattered. Mr. Browning came over and asked what was going on. The legal team not yet a week old but led by a Bryan Ismael from Mobile quickly interceded.

"Mr. Dupont has no comment at this time. We will shortly address the issue."

"No position at all? Why not? Surely Mr. Dupont can see that this will reflect…" Will was spirited away quickly with Mr. Browning on one arm and Crystal on the other. This left the reporter on the defensive which almost always led to belligerence in that peculiar breed of humans.

"Mr. Dupont has no position at this point because he had no idea he would need one. We have no knowledge of the hearings you refer to nor will we have a response until we do. You can contact me at the office on Monday. Perhaps I will have more information then. Please, feel free to enjoy the food and entertainment…though if I had slipped in under the guise of goodwill as you have, I would have the good grace to leave." Bryan turned his back and walked away to check on his boss. Others who were watching this exchange looked away and began conversation or trips elsewhere. *I'm not finished yet!* The reporter growls internally.

"Excuse me, but are you telling me to leave? I have a right to be here, you know. I simply want to know his connection to Mr. Browning." Denise was a reporter and did have a backbone. You just don't give up this early in the game.

"Why, not at all!" Astonishment that looked real on his face again set her off guard. "Mr. Dupont has had a very trying year and a half. He managed to save his company, but not his family. I am sure I speak for Mr. Dupont when I say that you should stay and enjoy the party. You will understand that since his presence is upsetting to you, he will simply leave you to enjoy yourself."

Looks from lookers on gave her no confidence that staying would resolve anything. A few attempts to interview some folks nearby resulted in several "you have got to be kidding," a couple of just plain scary stare downs with no response to her questions, and being called a bitch.

"Cut tape. Let's go." She had never felt dirtier about her job. *And why not? This guy comes out to enjoy surviving, and we jump him. Somebody at the office screwed up with this one. DAMNit.*

Denise felt soiled and that wasn't easy to make her feel. *There IS a story here; it is not dirty dealings. But what?* In a room of 300 people or so, not one agreed to be interviewed, good or bad. There was more than just a sound byte story here. She kept these thoughts to herself as they returned to the studio, though, because she couldn't find a way to explain what had transpired.

The camera crew kept their mouths shut as well, especially Nathan, who could always be counted on to get something on the wild side of an on site broadcast, even if they didn't use it. It never occurred to Denise that the story she sought might be one with a happy ending; she was a reporter after all.

"Well, Nathan, anything interesting?"

"Not a thing. Nope, not a single, solitary thing. No story here. Nope. Not at all…let's just split. This one is a waste of time."

"You okay, man?" Asked Buddy the driver.

"Yes, I am ok, asshole. I just want to leave and go home.

I…I don't feel well! Yes! I feel like shit and need to go home. I won't be in tomorrow, most likely. Need to see a doc." He looked lookedback over his shoulder at odd times. In fact, he either looked like a rabbit that couldn't see where the eagle was or like an addict who was having tremors or something. In any case, Nathan was sincerely ready to go. When someone suggested they go ahead and stay for the party, Nathan nearly went apeshit.

"No, I got to go. Take me back to the studio and you can come back. If you're crazy enough to…" but then Nathan stopped, looking as if he had said too much and finished. "I am going back to the studio, now. I don't feel well and if you all want to stay here in this…this place where we are clearly not wanted, well then go to it. But I am going and I am going to take the van if no one else does. Phil or someone can come and get you all."

Why is everyone acting so weird? Denise looked at Nathan as if he had just grown a third eye. *Good grief, what a wasted evening*, she thought. In the end, they all decided tonot stay. Nathan was beside himself with joy. *Why does he keep turning and looking out the rear view window and the back?* Buddy asked himself, observing Nathan's strange behavior. *Goin' right off'n his gourd. Doctor sounds about right.*

The next day, Nathan called in his resignation, and left with no forwarding address. Everybody agreed he was severely stressed the night before. As usual in the face of bizarre behavior on the part of a co-worker, everyone scratched their heads, puzzled, and promptly offered a few theories and moved on to the next big thing. After awhile, no one thought about Nathan anymore and life carried on.

Chapter 4

Nightmare on Will's Street

"Hello, human," the thing on the ceiling croonedin a voice that made Will nearly weep, not out of outrage, fear or disgust but out of joy. This was a voice that drove men to kill each other and destroy themselves just to be near its owner. Hot prickles of fear sweat seeped out of the pores in his skin on his face. This caused Will to repeatedly wipe his face against the sheet, causing the sheets to stick to him, making him understand his mortality. He then asked a simple question, "Who are you?"

The thing giggled in response. It began to migrate away from the ceiling fan and towards the ceiling/wall joint right above the headboard. Migrate is really the only word that fits. It doesn't crawl, for it has no legs. It doesn't climb, it seems as if it is stuck to the ceiling and, yes, there it is, a slime trail. This *has GOT to be a dream,* Will thought. *Looks like I will find out up close. It is coming this way.*

This congealed his horror into a clear concept for Will as its image failed to do. The damned thing was trying to get into bed with him. "Fuck!" he exclaimedas he scrambled out of bed. The sheets seem to maliciously hold him back as if they were lovers who were playfully trying to keep him in bed. They seemed almost to be silently saying, "Just a little while longer, lover boy. Just one more round, me and you, okay?"

Again, the horror on the ceiling giggled as it reached close enough to touch the wall against which the bed was pushed. Amazingly, and here Will went slack jawed for a second, one eye seemed to swivel independently towards the wall and a tendril of flesh shot across the gap and anchored itself to the wall. More and more fleshy tendrils anchored themselves against the wall as the bulk of the visitor got closer. Then, with a dry sucking sound, it dropped against the wall and began to move downward towards the bed. "Oh Will, you are such an example of a fine, strapping young man! So strong, so full of heat and sweat and BLOOD!" With this, the thing sprang in air above the bed, somehow giving the impression of a spider, snail and leech, all at once. Below is an orifice: round, puckered downward and ringed with what appear to be fangs of different colors, all indicating deep decay and filth.

Will was now in that mental zone where when an attack is being made the seconds seem to tick by like temporal hang shots. Looking at those teeth, he realized each one had a minuscule hole in the end, large enough to take a serious amount of blood in but not large enough to blunt sharpness.

Rolling out from under the falling, squirming mass of tendrils onto the hardwood floor, banging the hell out of both elbows and knees, Will was excited about the idea of being somewhere else. Looking up, he heard the thing's voice muffled by the sheets and mattress it was entangled in. In its ardor to tear a ring shaped hole out of Will's flesh and certain of hitting its target, it instead managed to drive all teeth about four inches into the mattress and through the sheets, which responded much the same way they had with Will.

"Stay with me," the sheets seemed to cry as the thing tried to get traction against the mattress. The sheets were interfering again, and wound the thing up in a shroud that was as convoluted as the thing's limbs. *You sheets are such sluts; you'll sleep with anything.* This brought maniacal laughter to Will's lips, which couldn't contain his mirth.

"Bedbug!" he cried and began laughing in long, loud peals of deep-throated humor. This had an effect on the thing with the angelic voice. It became a blur as, like some small dogs would do, it began to furiously shake and try to disentangle itself from bed.

"Oh, how yuwa suhher!" Will did not need a translator to know what the thing was saying, "Oh, how you will suffer." Still laughing, he added, "You know, you little motherfucker, what I need is a big can of Raid to put on your ass." The thing fell silent. Will continued on, suddenly happy and determined. He walked out of the bedroom and stepped down to the spare one, retrievinghis shotgun. He muttered to himself, "Goddam, partners STEAL, my customers leave like a bunch of damn dickey birds running as their free lunch rolls over in the mud, my wife leaves. "I can't let you destroy me financially," she said. JEEsus Christ. I would have fucking died for her. Now," he hesitated before grabbing the buckshot box and the shotgun and stepped back into the room with the thing. Now, it was panicking and struggling. Somehow it was completely entangled in the sheets, like two ropes knotted up together, and just couldn'tget loose.

Click. Slick. Will chambered a round and walked up to the bed, leveled it at one disbelieving eye. BLAM!

The Thing, as Will had already named it in his mind, giving it a proper-noun status, stopped struggling and screamed in high falsetto, like you would imagine some crossover dresser scream; imagine Barry White trying to sound like Melissa Joan Hart. It suddenly began to dig down with all tendrils into the bed.

"Son of a bitch." He placed the barrel of the gun against the central sack of the Thing, and pulled the trigger, which blew a satisfying lump of gut and startling gout of blood up against the head of the bed.

"Fuck with me, fuck with ME!" Will was in a fine rage

now. "Come into my house and try to fuck with me. MY House!"

Will proceeded to empty the gun into the Thing, which was becoming even less well organized than it had been. It was a bit mesmerizing to look at. Bits and pieces of what had been Will's terror but was now his prey were spread across the upper half of his bed and all across the headboard. "I don't even like my FRIENDS to show up unannounced!"

Looks like I killed a pig in here. The Thing obliged this train of thought by beginning to squeal, a sound that horrified Will not by its sound but by how much he was enjoying it. He didn't trealize it, but he was experiencing what a rabbit experienced when it came up on a dog that had just been hit by a car: pure joy.

"Oh, yeah, you goan suffer. Well, you little FUCK, how do YOU like it? Huh? Love it? Love it? Want MORE of it?" Belatedly, he realized that he was cycling the gun and then clicking it dry for how many times he didn't know. He is out of shells. *Well, I fucked Thing up for sure.*

But had he? On the bed, pieces of meat that belonged to the creature began to crawl across the bed towards a single point. Those that made it began to twist into each other, knitting up the carnage caused by Will's 12 gauge.

"No." It was a whisper, a tired whisper. *Can I wake up now, God? Pretty please?* He stomped on flesh and brought it to a mince again, but to no avail. *Can I get off this horse now? This can't be anyway; I will just wake up in a minute.* Standing there, he looked at the Thing and saw it had begun to coalesce again. Willwas struck with fatigue and a warm feeling of lassitude came over him. *This is just a dream...relax, Will.* Then something in his eye began to burn.

Something burning in my eye? Then, *This isn't a dream.*

The thing lying on the bed's mouth pulled itself together again. Being overbalanced, it fell over with its mouth open towards Will. It began to snap open and shut, and Will noticed the second curious thing about the mouth. The teeth were in slots into which they slid incessantly. *In and out. Which is probably how it chews its victims.* Will knew instinctively that running away was useless. Tonight he will die. If he ran down Main Street right now and a thousand folks saw him, none will remember it tomorrow. *Because people forget. They forget dreams and child abuse. Because of the horror, the horror and the truth. The universe is a mad place and we all lie to each other about how shallow the rabbit hole is.*

I hurt it but I can't destroy it all at once. He stood there, the better part of ten minutes watching as his destruction assembled itself again. Will was not feeling fear right now but a cold, assessing determination to absolutely fuck up another being's existence. The two eyed each other, the Will and the Whatzit, with hate streaming between them like live wires of lightening. Noticing the fireplace in the bedroom, Will turned and ran to the basement, screaming, "Oh yeah, motherfucker, I got something f' ya' ass!" Down the stairs and doing a loop back around the hallway wall to the basement door, Will almost lost it, but managed to pull it out.

Almost busted my ass. Then he was through the basement door and down the stairs, taking 3 at a time, grabbing what he needed. Instant replay in reverse and he was back in his room, standing by the bedside, sweating and heaving.

"Welll, allllrightty then!" he said, mimicking Jim Carey. "I got something for you."

Will gleefully emptied half a five-gallon can of gasoline ontotheinsanely incensed occupant on the bed, his glee seeming to feed off the rage of his attacker. Sensing its peril, the thing began to writhe around on the bed, trying to avoid entanglement with the sheets again and trying to roll up all its missing parts like some baker picking up all the bits and pieces of leftover dough.

Will stepped towardsthe door of his bedroom, struck a match to a sock, and peered deep into the eyes of the Thing. One was on the central mass again, finally. The other eye was still twisted up with some of the bedclothes. Both looked at Will in amazement.

"Goodbye, Thing." He threw the sock at it. The bed instantly lit up in flames, as did the floor where the gas had spilled over. There wasthen a flurry of activity as the Thing tried to run in all directions at once. Ghostly things, looking like gray handkerchiefs blew out and began to circle the room in a wind that first, knocked things over, then picked them up, and finally slung them in all directions. *Time to tip my ass on out the front door.*

Then, Will ran down the steps for a second Heisman trophy performance he was sure, and out the front door.

Gasoline doesn't burn, it explodes. While Will was fast, he wasn'tfast enough to completely avoid the flames and suffered some significant burns all up the backsides of both calves. While these were cared for by paramedics, a firefighter asked Will how the fire started. He was curious and not just concerned. Then, the smell of gasoline hit Will in the face again..

Being quick in his mind as well as on his feet, he explained that he had gone into his house and changed clothes downstairs. He had gas on his hands because he had seen liquid lying on the floor near his closed bedroom door. Thinking it was water, he had gotten a towel to clean it up. When he stood up with the towel, he heard a roaring noise coming from his bedroom.

"I guess I didn't give it much thought where the water had come from. I have been working a lot of long hours lately. Anyways, when I touched the bedroom door handle, it burned me. That is when I decided it was time to get the hell out and call you guys." This was followed by a sheepish boy's grin, then sorrow at his loss. That part wasn'tfaked. He'd loved his house. It was his haven. It was a total loss.

There was the usual investigation, but all the facts fit the story, with the notable exception of how the gas got to the upper floor. "I was using it to thin some paint. Stupid, I know."

As I say, all the facts fit the story, if not the entire truth and the fire department is happy enough to let it go at that.

With no record and no motive for burning his own house down, the matter of Will's loss was closed in short order.

The sun coming through his office windows was insultingly bright, as if it had decided to aggravate Will with its brightness this morning.

Will was groggy, all right. His inability to focus made it terriblydifficult to move forward. His head swam in circles and his mouth was dry. He now begam to worry that the line that usually cracked running straight up the center of the inside of his upper lip might be turning into a permanent feature.

Can you get a cleft palate from sleeping with your mouth open? Will wondered.

Will had taken up the habit of a few Darvocet in the

evening because the burns on his legs prevented him from sleeping well. The pills helped without the inconvenience of affecting his judgment the next morning. At least, he was pretty sure it didn't affect his judgment. The fact that he could and often did choose to go without it at times seemed proof enough that he was not addicted. Will was concerned about his dreams, though. They were crystal clear in their experience and it seemed he wanted nothing more than to fall asleep in the evenings around 8PM. She almost always showed up soon after. He was pretty sure that mental health professionals would worry.

Well, the hell with 'em. They are STILL worse off than I am, a thought followed by swallowing two Darvocets.

He lay back on the couch. Lately, he had been simply keeping clothes at the office as some days it was just too much trouble to drive home. No one was there, so why bother?

Hope you show up tonight, Baby Girl. He hadn't dreamt for a few days now and it was beginning to bother him. He may not be getting addicted to Darvocet, but he sure as hell was addicted to Crystal, his dream girl.

Baby Girl was identical in some respects to the young woman Crystal he had been seeing on and off for some weeks, but this dream girl…well, she was the Dream Girl. There were oddities about her, though. For instance, Will was almost certain her ears were mobile like a cat's ears and occasionally when startled it seemed her muscles were attached further away from the joint for the briefest second.

What in the world would cause me to dream those things? She is nothing but candy and then when something creaks or the wind blows too hard against the house, she changes slightly? Then, Will knew and understood. *I am probably just halfway waking up and making mental mud-pies out of my ex, that thing I killed and my girl, Crystal.*

Like the story Will gave the firefighters in the aftermath of killing whatever the hell it was in his bedroom, mental mud-pies fit the available facts.

He slept in the office again, Sylvia thought. She is was for her boss, but was glad to see him awake to the fact that he wasn'tdead yet and that there were other things in life besides having and losing the wrong wife. Still, this constant sleeping in the office was surely taking a toll on him. At first it didn't seem to bother him; he seemed energized . Now, though, since the last few days, Will was developing a haunted look that bothered her.

What was that thing? Was it real? They found nothing, though, so who can say for sure? Will thought aboutthe fire and how it started again when Sylvia stuck her head in the door. The certainty of living in a rational universe is quick to dull the memories of things beyond the pale.

"You know, you are really spending too many nights sleeping on that couch. It is starting to look like it has been lived on." Sylvia was worried about him, not the couch, but didn't choose to put it that way.

"Yes, well, it looks as if I will be spending every night here for a while."

"Why?"

"Last night I…" he almost said 'I had to kill a 120 lbs. talking spider bent on strewing my guts all over my bedroom.' Instead, he paused, and then added , *Entrails was the word it used, not guts.*

"Last night my house burned down. Everything is gone." *Well, Mom, I am now rid of all my pictures of her.*

Happy now? This wasn'tfair to his mom and he knew it, which was why the thought would never see the light of day, certainly not in a conversation with his mom.

Sylvia laughed, not being able to help herself. "When you talked about locusts, plagues, and frogs yesterday, I thought you were kidding. Should I stand this close?"

"Ha ha. Go…be useful."

Chapter 5

Crystal did not show up that night. Will had explained the night before how he had burned down his home. *He is talking about an arachnid. It can't be anything else. How? He is just human, and humans are dead meat when confronted with an arachnid.*

Crystal was disturbed. She would have called for butterfly nets and white coats if she were a normal human being, but Crystal was not. *How did he live?*

As I say, arachnids aren't, strictly speaking, human anymore, if they ever were, which is a metaphysical question unless you are one of the people who sign onto the idea that those supposed humans who transform into Arachnids are more like mockingbird babies; perhaps only human in appearance and from a different genetic tree altogether.

They take many forms, but the most common are a lack of any organized skeletal structure, immense speed and strength (even vampires fear them), no memory whatsoever of their lives as humans, and a rage and ferocity that is terrible to behold. As far as Crystal's People knew, those who changed into arachnids were incapable of intelligence above a certain verbal cleverness; much like a predatory fish that uses light to lure other fish, which would seem to go towards the case for non-human origins.

Humans seem to have it hardwired to forget or revise their observed history when confronted with one taking out a victim. Many hit-and-run accidents have been victims of these genetic freaks. If no one in the neighborhood heard or saw ANYTHING? Most likely, it was an arachnid murder seen, fled from, and forgotten. As Monica explained to a young general who was being briefed on the People and their relationship to first-world countries' militaries, "You don't believe humans will just stand by while another is butchered and killed in broad daylight, do you?" Diplomatic silence followed.

For the last four or five centuries, those amongst the People who considered themselves academics have tried to figure out what to look for in someone who was being considered for the change that will indicate a higher than normal risk for becoming an arachnid. The only thing they could find was the troubling fact that some 80% of arachnids came from the same population that produced 80% of the world's male serial-killers of European descent. There is no record of a female converting to an arachnid, so they don't reproduce. Whether they are mules or not is unknown.

Monica needs to know about this. Then a horrible thought occurred to Crystal: *No...!* She head off for her castle home at a blurring speed. She needed to see Monica and Melissa now.

Crystal was terrified of her thoughts and failed to tell Will she was leaving. After three days, his unanswered phone calls were given up as a bad job.

Well, another one bites the dust. Good riddance. Besides, my house is quiet, and I have no one to deal with after working all day.

Will had gotten much better at lying to himself.

She isn't coming. The clock on the wall said 10:30 PM. *Man, you ARE losing it.* Will often considered whether or not he was still sane. The idea that he was a nutcase wrapped in a normal outer shell was a recurring thought. When Crystal had gone MIA, Will thought perhaps Baby Girl would show back up in his dreams.

Crap. What now? Will's phone rang.

"Yes?" Then, "What?" followed by an "I couldn't be LESS interested." Will hung up on the caller, probably more abruptly than he intended. *Telemarketers…glad I don't have to do that…anymore.* Grinning wryly, Will thought about some of the stupid jobs he had held over the years. The phone rang again.

"I said I wasn't interested!" Naturally, it isn't a telemarketer, but his Buddy Siggy from Outer Edge Electronics.

"Well, fine! I will take all the money, women, and fame for myself. Youooo ssoorrry INGRATE! I am SO hurt."

"Sorry, yes, ingrate, no." Will wiped his other hand across his forehead and realized he was looking forward to sleeping and dreaming. Thinking this was unhealthy, he continued, "I am glad it is you and not another telemarketer. What? Yeah, I guess. The hell of it is it doesn't do any good to change your number as they do a random calling of all possible numbers on an exchange." Will was sure this is true because he put his name on the national no-call list to no avail.

Pausing to lean back in his chair and swivel to look at the skyline, Will asked, "What's up?"

"I and some guys are taking off to the beach for a few days. Want to come?"

"Actually, I do…"

"Great!"

"…but I can't. I'm cooking right now and can't leave in the middle of it. How long did you say you would be there?"

"Don't rightly know. We can't move ahead on some

things here until we get the Power19 machine from IBM, and they have run into some manufacturing delays…Will, hang on a sec…"

Will heard Siggy telling someone in the background that he was skipping lunch and leaving early, then "Anyway, the old man said go get a tan, so we're going. Could be three days, could be a week."

"Well, call me on Monday. We'll see where we both are then."

"I would tell you I'd be thinking of you, Bud, but it would be a lie."

"Yeah, you're a giver that way. See ya, Dude."

Later that night, at the security offices of Outer Edge Electronics, a furious discussion took place. Will had friends, and it was clear that the fire that destroyed his house was not entirely kosher, even though Will himself was keeping mum.

"I knew he was in trouble again, and I could just feel it. He had that edge, which meant he was entirely somewhere else. None of which explains why you asked me here after hours." Browning was not used to his security chief being so clandestine with him. *What has him so wired that he wanted only to see ME?*

"Listen to this tape. It is from his house, bedroom specifically." They listened as the Orson Well's Martian edition of the story unfolded.

"Oh, how yuwa suhher!" The tape in Outer Edge Electronics security offices had been painstakingly analyzed.

"You bugged his house? Why? I just said watch out for him."

"What you said was do what is necessary to protect him. If nothing had ever happened…the tapes are erased daily. These seem different."

"Different, how?"

"Well, you know how some folks here are always screaming about how much on pure, undirected research we do here at OEE?"

"Yeah, but what's that…?"

"I am getting there soon enough. I want you to be sure you know that I checked this out and need more info from sources in OEE that I don't have access to or that I need to hand this off to someone else."

"Alright…what has your wind up so bad?"

"Well, we did voice stress analysis of this person Will was arguing with just prior to the fire…you know, routine since we are now hooked up with Interpol on a number of things. I had hoped the voice would turn up in a databank somewhere. Since Will was so emphatic in his denials of anyone being there with him, he might be hiding something. We also wanted to eliminate the possibility of Will talking to himself."

"I hadn't considered that."

"Right." *This is why you pay me to be paranoid.* "Well, Will wasn't talking to himself. Analysis shows that there are clearly two voices there, very different. When I got nothing from Interpol or other national resources, I turned on the global knowledge search parameter with no search priorities to cast as wide a net as possible. A reference to a project headed by Dr. Loki called VEL was brought up. I tried to get more info but was stonewalled. Now, there are no references to VEL in the system."

The old man's face didn't change, but stoniness still existed there. "Go on." *Damn. I must consider what to do about that,* thought the Senator. *Secrets always slip out, sooner or later.* Briefly deliberating on how hard it might be to deal with this unexpected turn of events, the Senator decided it could wait until another time and turned his attention back to his security chief. He had missed something critical.

"It briefly pulled up a file on predatory insect studies. Why would it do that?"

"THAT is an interesting question. I have no idea. You sure it wasn't just a bad entry on your part? What could all these things possibly have to do with each other?"

"Sir, I don't know. I could not pull up the file again a few minutes later. Do this for me…as a favor."

"Yes?"

"If you need me to stay out of the loop on certain things, just say so."

"You need to stay out of the loop for a bit. Is there anything else?"

"Yeah, the stress patterns are all wrong, like a mechanical voice is completely different under analysis, so is this one."

"This is a recording or synthesized speech?" Browning looked oddly relieved. *I will have to think about that later, too.*

"No, sir, it is not mechanical. It is as different from a speech synthesizer as a synthesizer is from human speech."

Chapter 6

"Will survived an arachnid shaper. By himself. Unaltered and unchanged." Monica's voice was flat and full of wonder simultaneously, a strange combination. Then, "How was he able to do that?" Sitting on her throne, one leg slung up over one armrest and leaning on the other, Monica toyed with her sleeves. This was not a lack of interest but an intense inward consideration of Crystal's revelations.

"All the details aren't known yet. He burned down his own home to do it, though. Fire kills even the arachnids, as you know." Crystal was astounded, too, but admiration was clearer in her face.

"What do we REALLY know about Will? What is his heritage? There is no record of an arachnid ever falling to a lone human."

"Quite a juicy mystery, isn't it?" Crystal clasped her hands to her chest like a ten-year-old on Christmas morning. She was relieved. It was her job to check on him from time to time, and she was upset inside from the fact that he could have been killed.

"Yes, but how did he get away or have enough time to set it…or get the thing to stay still long enough to burn?"

"He is quite clever." Then she added, "He even had enough presence of mind not to tell what really happened."

The two women didn't know Will and were filled with sudden hatred upon sighting the arachnid. He didn't know the name but knew something against nature when he saw it. He never hesitated in his reaction to the thing, not in the usual freeze-up humans fall into when confronted with such an extreme event.

Again, Arachnids weren't strictly speaking human anymore. A vampire can claim 99% of the human genetic code it started with (compare that with the Chimpanzee's 98%), but the arachnids could not. The arachnids were what humans feared in the dark. Whether from racial memory or just being faced with what was an unbelievable shock to the higher brain functions all at once, there was a reaction that drove the human organism into the extreme stages of fight or flight. A human is never stronger, faster, or more desperate than when faced with an arachnid, not that it does them much good. Their revulsion is pure. That is, until Will. His revulsion was still pure; his hesitation was non-existent.

Will knew how to hate. Boy, howdy, did Will know how to hate. Even at twelve, he didn't just sit by and allow events to run him over.

Like a bright, shiny ice pick driven through the meat of his memory, he remembered Johnny Baldwin from his sixth-grade class. If there were ever a scab of a human being, he guessed Johnny would qualify. There he was, a scrawny, diseased, tubercles-infected runt of a man. But at 16, he towered over them as sixth graders. The fact that he was allowed to stay in school after failing four grades was one of the odder situations public education sometimes faced.

Oh, he was bad, he was mean, and if anybody forgot who was boss dog in this man's sixth-grade class, a quick sucker punch to the gut, when the teacher wasn't looking quickly, brought the kid's attention back to speed. Will wondered whether Mrs. Verde's attention had wandered as often as he had previously thought when she and the boss asshole (as he began to think of Johnny Baldwin in the days leading up to Christmas vacation) got into it one day.

"This IS my classroom, Johnny, and I have had enough of your crap." She was angry, red-faced, and terrified. It was sickening to watch. Like most kids, Will had problems with authority and didn't want to be told what to do. Then again, in his stomach, he realized he depended on Mrs. Verde to protect him from guys like Johnny. *What if he hurt her?* This thought wasn't exactly clear, perhaps because of its thundery, cataclysmic implications. Maybe nobody was REALLY safe, and what exactly do you do with THAT? Will had not figured it out yet, but he was thinking hard.

"Well, I tell you what. Why don't you put five or six of your big ones in this class on me? I'll take them all on. Ain't nobody gonna tell me what to do." Grinning, like some hateful troll, Johnny defied her to make him behave and challenge her. Even Will saw with disgust that she could do nothing if he were sufficiently determined. Years later, after having grown into manhood and running into this piece of two-legged detritus at a gas station, he looked at a grinning little troll with no power. Still, he towered over the diminutive Mrs. Green just as he did over the sixth graders in her class.

Five or six of us. Five or six of us? Un-huh, that's what HE said. Five or six of us. This thought keeps occurring to him throughout the night and well into the next day. Will is growing up. He is beginning to grow into a man who believes in defending women. Will is beginning to be brave, and he is also beginning to develop the ability to assess risk versus rewards.

"Look, CC, I have been thinking..."

"Dangerous work for one so challenged," CC grins as he says it, but not meanly.

"Un-huh. You copied off my last three tests, so take a few breaths while I talk. This is serious."

CC looks at Will with his full attention. Will thinks to

himself, *CC is a cutup, maybe because he is about 2 feet tall and named Clarence, maybe just because his brain never seems to stop spinning in his head. I never know for sure. He is smart, but he can drive me batshit crazy by joking around until you cut him off.* CC asks, "What's up?"

"Boss asshole."

"Oh, Jeez. What now?" Clarence, like everyone else in his class, caught hell on an almost daily basis from this terror. Johnny had bloodied his nose when CC wouldn't let him copy on Friday's math test. Well, 'Couldn't' would have been a better word. The dumb ass was two rows away and would've had to have Clarence hold his paper up and have a set of binoculars to pull off this little bit of educational assistance. His insistent whispers led to his being booted by Coach Curley. Yes, friends and neighbors. By this point, Mrs. Verde had given up some of her authority to the next room's teacher, Coach Curley, because she feared Johnny. As some in the military might say, the situation was deteriorating rapidly. Def Con 3 was about where Will put it in his mind now or would have, had he known the term.

"Well, see, I figure we got to do something. Now."

"DO something. I don't getcha." CC was afraid that he did indeed get him and was losing his frock mind. If he was talking about him and his little butt, CC, going up against Johnny, he knew he had gone high, wide, and happy into the loony blue yonder.

"Well, I think you do. Now," and here he saw CC get ready to interject some objection, but he cut him off, "Hear me out, OK? You can say I am crazy later."

Which is exactly what I will say, hombre, CC thinks.

"OK." He settled back onto his haunches like only kids

and very small people do.

"We have to do something."

"You said that already."

"I know, just shut up and listen, OK? Jeez." Continuing, Will said, "You could have gotten hurt really bad after the math test. If Coach hadn't been around, you would have. As it was, I thought Coach was going to get hurt." The coach, as opposed to Coach Curley, was Coach Walker. A nice enough old fellow, but one who had no concept of how close Boss Asshole had come to firing one or two off at him. *He doesn't see*, is the thought that went through Will's mind as Coach frog-marched Johnny out of the classroom. The second thought was *Coach may get hurt* as he watched Johnny shrug the Coach off and walk toward the principal's office. "Anyway, Boss asshole is coming unraveled, and he may hurt someone or do something really bad."

The phrase "really bad" was the only way Will could express what he thought of as monstrous, horrific, or bizarre. He was about a year away from mastering these words, so "really bad" was about as clear as possible.

"Yeah, I know, like busting my nose again for talking to a lunatic who wants me to get in his way. Again. On purpose. Are you out of your mind? Just what do you think you and I can do against him?"

"Re-arranging your face maybe ain't such a bad thing, what with you being so frocking pug ugly..."

"Yo, mamma..."

"Speaking of which, I asked her the same thing, and she said you looked like your daddy, and I said, 'How can you be sure....'"

"Shut up, you fucker," it was good-natured ribbing, but

CC could see that Will intended to have his say, so he quieted down and let him roll on, on his own. A word like horrific may take mastering, but the good old F word grew into many kids' vocabulary like a fungus that will not die.

"...anyways, I think Johnny Baldwin, AKA Boss asshole, AKA the worst man in his mind, may have solved our problem for us. And...I am afraid he may hurt Kim." Will, a sixth-grade child, didn't have the vocabulary to say any more than that, only to feel a sick gut punch dread and an engine inside him trying to spin up for the first time when he saw Johnny giving her a hard time. "But, like I say, he may have solved the problem for us." The engine was idling now, determinedly and happily humming.

"Huh?" CC had been hurt, terrified, insulted, and now confused relating to one scab of a kid in the space of two days. "What ARE you talking about?"

"Well, Johnny told Mrs. Verde to put five or six of us big ones on him. She wouldn't ever do it, but I guarantee that if myself, Mac, Keith, Tracy, Cliff, and you...well, that would be five and a half, but close enough." Will was grinning in a friendly way to take the sting out. CC pulled his weight in a scrap, and everybody knew it. He would go on to do bantamweight in Golden Gloves in high school. "I think we ought to catch the bastard in the bathroom and try to put his ass in the hospital. Maybe we can get him to quit school. Fucker is 16. What I can't figure out is why he stays. Can somebody be so stupid they don't know how stupid they are?" This last question was a puzzle for Will, who was bright and knew it but somehow couldn't get his head around the mental problems of someone like Johnny Baldwin.

"I don't know. I wouldn't count on Keith, though. Mac is tough; Tracy will stand with you, Cliff, maybe. What about getting some of the black kids to help?"

Will hadn't thought of that. Some of the black kids were tough, too. Why, Will bet one kid, named Georgios, *course with a name like* Georgios *you had to be*, a thought flitting through his mind, *might even give old Johnny a run for his money. Yeah, well, they were always saying kids of all colors OUGHT to work together, right?*

"What's funny?"

"Let's talk to Georgios, maybe he and one other."

"Yeah!" CC and Georgios sometimes worked out at the Y together. Georgios would go on a growth spurt in another three months and wind up leaving CC in the dust weight-wise, but they knew each other, too.

It wound up being Will, Georgios, CC, Mac, and Tracy. They were careful. What finally tied them together was watching Johnny put his hands on Kim, which drove Will nuts. Kim was the girl who made him understand that girls' legs can be pretty. She wore a green, pleated skirt to school for pictures. Will amused Mrs. Verde by being unable to look anywhere else but at her. He would never tell her that he kept her face in his heart to some degree almost through high school.

"Bastard! She saw, Tracy, Mrs. Verde saw. We got to do something. Today, Motherfucker!" This last was aimed not at CC but at Johnny Baldwin. Then Will said to Tracy, "You in or out?"

"Throttle down, Will, or he'll hear you. Don't tip our hand. I'm in. Let's hook up at the jungle bars, ok?" Tracy said.

"Ok."

They met at the jungle bars in a quiet, serious group. They all agreed it would be best to catch him in the bathroom by himself in the morning when he smoked. His JD buddies were not quite ready to openly defy the rules by blowing smoke into the hallway, but with how things were going, it wouldn't be long. The plan was to catch him before he got help or hurt someone. Mac had an idea and brought it with him. Everyone was impressed. Mac wanted to settle his personal score with Johnny.

The five of them walked into Mrs Verde's room. Will's forehead was bleeding, and so was Mac's lip. Georgios had what looked to be one swelling ear that would hurt like hell, not that the others could see it. He was black, and to the white eyes of the other children, he looked as if he sustained no damage.

"Will? Mac? What happened?" the clarion alarm was winding up in her voice.

Not answering her, Will walked over to Kim and said, "Kim, Johnny will not bother you again, I think." Then, he sat down in his chair.

But it wasn't over. Just as he was about to answer Mrs. Green, Johnny Baldwin burst into the classroom. He didn't look so hot. You could say he was having a really bad day. He looked as if he had been worked over by, yes, sir-ree, Bob, five or six of Mrs. Verde's big ones. He cursed and yelled and was beside himself. Tears streamed down his badly bruised and bleeding face, and even now, welts were starting to stand up on his exposed forearms.

First, Will stood up, followed by the other four and said "Just shut up. We're done. You're out." Will's voice was nervous, and he was hurt and shaking so badly he was sure everyone could see, but resolve was plain on all five faces. "The school may not be willing to do anything, but we are. Leave."

At this point, the five of them began to move forward. They all had their version of Mac's surprise, a 30-inch section of broom handle or equivalent. They caught him in the bathroom and beat him until he squealed like a rabbit caught by a pack of dogs. What sent Will over the edge was he sounded just like Kim had sounded the day he had molested her. "How do you like it, asshole?" He had asked over and over again. Johnny may not think it, but CC saved his miserable life when he asked Will to stop. Did he want to kill him?

Coach Curley got there in time to stop any further festivities, which was how they all thought about it from that day forward. Festivities. Hell, you would think so. After all, they emancipated themselves from an ogre. The authorities were uniformly silent. Oh, the Baldwins raised blue hell. They were going to sue. They didn't have a clean pot to piss in or a bed to put it under but they had a lawyer on retainer.

Will's grandfather later explained it to Will when he had just turned 18, "It was an odd moment." Will's grandfather, who only went three days of the first grade and couldn't read or write, had a way of speaking so that sometimes you heard the capital letters. "There we stood, members of the Klan, joined up with about the same number of some of the blackest sumbitches you ever saw. We all knocked on Baudin's (Baldwin's) door. He came out white as a sheet but red in the face as if the blood couldn't figure out where it needed to be. He didn't say boo. I asked him if he understood that he and his little bastard needed to stay low and quiet, and he allowed it as he understood. After he shut the door, I heard that wife of his start hollering about how he could let white trash AND niggers come to their door and threaten him, and then I heard a slap and....quiet. It was quiet until I heard they were just gone three months later."

"You got lucky, but you did well. I was proud."

Will knew he got lucky with the spider, too. *Well, it wasn't really a spider, was it? Nope, last I heard in zoology, a spider doesn't have the power of speech or bad attitude.* He had been pondering the spider more and more since his dreams of a more passionate nature just stopped. *Stopped cold. What is up with you?* Will asked himself. *Is your brain so determined to keep you from having what you want that it will even take away your dreams?* He suspected that it was indeed so. He was furious with his own subconscious.

Good grief, this is a waste of time today. Will was trying to do a budget analysis, which wasn't going well. *Hell with it. I will just work WITH Darryl tomorrow. I need to get out.*

"Sylvia, I am gone." Will headed towards the elevators. "I need to blow off some steam and will probably be late tomorrow." He hesitated and added, "If I am not in by 12, I probably won't make it in at all."

"Yes, I agree that he is clever. We witnessed that when we allowed him to 'rescue' us." Monica said to Crystal, who wasn't with her and Melissa when they left the bar. The pair had been hunting the group of men because they had been responsible for many sexual assaults in the Southside and Homewood parts of Birmingham over the past few months.

While the three Norns restrained themselves from feeding on humans as a rule, sometimes they got pissed off at the way scum got away with murder with little effort. Monica had walked into the ladies' room a few weeks before at the club where Will first saw them. She and Melissa overheard a very upset young woman explaining to a friend that the guys who had assaulted her were in the club, and she didn't want to go back through the club. Typically, she hadn't pressed charges or made a report or any noise. *Well, she won't have to worry about them anymore,* Monica thought with no small amount of ferocious pleasure. Feeling her canines involuntarily start to protrude, she returned to the issue of Will.

"We need to find out about his background, though. If we are going to change him, we need to ensure that we are not creating a worse monster. If he can kill an arachnid, he may be one who would become one. We can't have that."

"Well, here is an idea. If he can kill an arachnid without being changed, why change him at all?" It was an innocent question, but both Monica and Melissa looked thunderstruck.

Chapter 7

Separation

"You are needed in the southern counties. You and Melissa both will be needed. She has to do the glamours, but if anything goes wrong, she will need you to speed her out." Monica said addressing Crystal and Melissa.

"What happened?" Crystal asked.

"Melissa will explain in route. There are things I must handle with our business interests in America. Also, I want some one on one time with Will. This business with the arachnid has me concerned. We need more research for this!" Monica spent the last 12 hours in deep thought, but no matter how much she chased the rabbits in her imaginings, she could not come up with any set of circumstances that she believed explained how Will had been able to survive an attack by an Arachnid. Even a Level 1 abortion had more than enough strength to tear down a pack of pissed off male chimpanzees or most likely a grizzly. *...and he remembered the attack in detail.*

"Why don't you come with us? The three of us have not been together in months. I miss you guys." It was true that Crystal missed Monica and Melissa. It was also true that she could have been back a month earlier but had chosen to stay in Alabama for a bit longer. Only Will's surviving the attack had driven her home.

"I just feel like I have neglected you guys." It was true, though not for the reasons the other two had assumed. It is true that the people can not lie to each other, but they can make wrong assumptions about the meaning of words, whether spoken truly or not.

"Crystal," Monica was touched by the pain in her voice, "this little trip is one that needs Melissa's gifts of deception to the eye and your speed should she be found out by ill luck." She paused, considering the work ahead of her, then continued; "We will take company with each other when we return from our various adventures. I promise."

"Very well, this whole thing is tiring, though. I believed I had left fatigue behind." Crystal was mentally tired. She suffered from a malaise of the spirit. She was aware of it and so were the others.

"Six months, Crystal, and we will be at the end of the beginning for sure." Monica said, trying to comfort her. She also realized that she did not say the beginning of what. Her concern for Crystal was causing mistakes. Again, feeling as if she was failing but continuing on, nonetheless, "We will take our collective rest somewhere hot and balmy and tropical, I warrant this is true."

Smiling more for Monica's benefit and knowing that she will know it, Crystal put on a good face and turned to Melissa, "Let's be off, then."

"Crystal…" Monica began, "is there anything else of import that I should know?" Things she did not want to discuss troubled Crystal and it showed.

"Nothing of which I wish to speak for the present."

"Very well. Godspeed to you both."

As Monica made her way down the mountains and into the human territories, Crystal and Melissa moved towards the southern counties of the People's lands.

"Well, do you wish to inform me as to our mission or no?" Crystal was somewhat more upbeat than she had been. It was hard for her to remain too terribly down when she flies.

"Actually, I don't." Melissa was obviously pained to be saying this, but she went on, "you're mind is clouded by things I haven't seen in you before. I am afraid if you know what we are to do; you might give it away to a direct question without thinking about it. This way, you can truthfully say that you do not know what we are doing or why we are in a county we have not visited for 500 years."

"Good enough." Crystal was flying as she often did when she had a way to go and was too occupied with her own thoughts to take it as a slight. She was lying on her back, or appeared to be, with her arms under her head, gazing at the stars. Flying for the more powerful vampires is an automatic activity even more so than walking for humans. Flying does not appear to take energy and can be slept during with your waking up when you reach your destination. No one knows why. "I will talk to you when we arrive."

"Patricia, so good of you to see me without an appointment."

"Well it has been a while and there are things you need to make decisions on concerning your American taxes, your Alabama taxes, and such."

"The princes of this world do demand their due, human or not." Monica mumbled to herself, a bit louder than she intended. Patricia was sure she didn't hear her correctly.

"Excuse me?" Patricia said.

"The government, it wants its due and is it demanding or what?"

"That it certainly is. Now…" Patricia began.

After several hours of very dry reporting, Monica cut her off with, "What I want you to do is to have all the paperwork arranged to have these assets transferred to a trust based in Liechtenstein. I have found that once a venture begins to make money, it is often just too much trouble to own. Here is the name of the attorney to contact."

"Well, as long as you have worked with him before. Have you determined that he is competent in the area of transferring assets, trusts, and so on?"

Monica replied, knowing that Patricia was simply trying to look out for her interests, "Actually, he was referred to us by Diane, so that question probably needs to be taken up with her. You have her number I am sure. I want it complete by the end of the month which gives you…three weeks."

"Very good. If Diane referred him, that is good enough for me. Her family has extensive experience in these dealings."

"Too, I was hoping to see Will personally. Do you know if he is in town?"

"No, I don't but why don't you drop by his office? It isn't far from here."

"I know. I'd best be off." Monica left in her usual abrupt but not rude manner.

"Diane, nice to see you again. I was hoping to catch Will in. Is he here by any chance?"

"Actually, no, he isn't. He seems to have a bug this week. Nothing serious, I am sure."

"No, you're not."

"I'm not what?"

"Not sure that Will is alright. If it is concerning him, it concerns my money and me. He is the one in your organization that I trust without reservation. Tell me."

Despite being taken aback by Monica's intensity and as always by the off putting manner of her speech, Diane answered, "He just seems to have some sort of bug that he can't seem to shake. It keeps him home a lot and out of the office. When he does come in, he sleeps a lot. He just seems to be very tired and not overcoming it in a normal time frame. I am sure he will be fine, it just takes a while. It took me months to get over a strep infection. No big deal."

Will had taken the day off. He did not bother to call in, but that was his answer when Diane called to see if he was alright. Diane did not in the strictest manner work in Will's office, but their firms were joined so closely as a matter of method that more than once the question had been asked if the separation between them on paper was strong enough.

Will was home, staring out at Birmingham, musing on Crystal, soundly done up on his meds as he was sometimes prone to do when he was certain no one would call him or ask him to think too closely to the bone. He would agree with you that this was a dangerous road to be on; he would also note that 50% of the time the person making the observation was dead drunk by 10PM, five nights a week. At least he kept it within the walls of his own house and generally on the weekends.

It is no big deal. She was just a dream and I need to get over her or I will wind up just like I was before. If I had been born Japanese, I could have honorably chosen to take that path and all my debts would be paid. Instead, I have to stay here and take it.

Again, the answer presented itself to him in his mind, *Because, if you succeed, you live; if you die, you just lose. The battle's reward makes the battle worth it. If you can just find that mindset, that internal motivation, that go-at-it-ness, I know you would be successful.* Who speaks to him at these moments? Will would say God, but he wouldn't argue with you about it. Will would politely hear out your arguments and then proceed on his chosen path. Will was what the psychiatrists called, 'other directed.'

It is a vexing place to be, directed by things other than only the events at hand that you can see and touch or otherwise observe. Will was driven by feelings, convictions and in extreme moments, by voices he could only call God. Besides, technically, he was successful. He had money; he had time, friends he trusted, and business associates with proven trustworthiness. *So, why the funk? Because I no longer have wet dreams? Puleeze.*

Besides, the voices had a track record of always being right, so Will decided to follow them.

Will hadn't dreamed of her in weeks. He was beginning to get antsy. Meals were being skipped, and his home was beginning to become piled up with clothes, empty soda cans, and discarded food plates from the local sub shop. It was not very impressive.

Where are you? It was a question he asked over and over for the last three weeks. His sleep was erratic, again only this time there was no intervening angel of distraction to come and hold him in a warm embrace.

Will had spoken to Crystal of her embrace, had told her of how it healed him the next day, of how his spirit fed from her presence and gave him the ability to go on.

Perhaps it is simply that I am truly tired. We are fine and I can relax a bit. The only things wrong are what I imagine to be wrong. It is the weekend and I am going to do well today and tomorrow and begin a long weekend a day late. With that settled, Will began to firm up appointments he had earlier thought to reschedule. Getting up and dressing business casual, he made the short drive into the office missing Monica and Diane by only minutes.

"Sylvia," Will summonedhis assistant.

"Sir," Sylvia came in and sat down.

"Bring me the OEE files, please."

"You mean the cart or this month's notes files?"

Back in the People's lands, Melissa and Crystal arrived in the south and settled down some three miles out, walking the rest of the way. Their approach into town caused a stir.

"Highness…Miladies…" accompanied by several, "Get the Mayor…" and a few "What is wrong now…?" Not unnoticed were a few very hard stares. Melissa mentally marked them for later. If things are relatively quiet she intended to ask a few pointed questions later on.

Melissa asked for directions to the home of Dubois, son of Drake from the guardian that walked up and bows. His demeanor marked him as one who could be trusted. Guardians were generally female, but a few males were born with the mark of guardian. Very large, faster reflexes approaching that of an arachnid, and rather than appearing human in their normal, relaxed state they are hulking, armored beings with lost of nasty, sharp points on the striking surfaces of their bodies. Imagine a cross between a gorilla, a human, and a stegosaurus and you'll get the picture. Perhaps 3 births in 100 amongst the People were born guardians, and since it was a recessive trait, they didn't breed true. Also, a guardian seems to be instinctively incapable of betraying the thing or folks it is sworn to protect.

"I will escort you myself, if that meets with your approval, Highness."

"Please, lead on." *Guardians.* Melissa was letting her mind rove freely over the area, looking for impressions that might not hit her while she watched for danger. With the presence of a guardian, there was small chance of trouble and they were all on edge right now trying to figure out what was in the works. Rebellion and revolt rarely come about as a small initiative. It is by crafty opportunists taking advantage of many lines of disaffection in the populace that revolutions take place.

There is just so much we don't know about why we are the way we are, thinks Melissa. *Why blood thirsty vampires morph into monsters while the ones who restrain themselves grow more powerful as time passes and even when they do rage they only go part way into the change. Guardians don't drink blood and can stand the daylight hours but have to concentrate to appear human. Why?* As always, Melissa's mind has no answer.

The approach to Dubois's home was very difficult by foot. This locale had an odd prohibition about flying over the township, but it was understandable. There are jealousies amongst the People, like any human population, and the fliers versus those earthbound have a very visible point of contention. Not that jack is to be done about it as it follows no pattern that is discernible. You either can or you can't and it is almost always within the first year that you know. Birth vampires have a 20 percent chance of flying, changed vampires a 50% chance, no one knows why, but it is supposed that the gene is recessive in breeding vampires and dominant in humans.

Melissa knocked on the door of the home and was greeted by a startled Dubois, who immediately bowed to his queen's first associate, though it was clear his loyalties were divided.

"My Lady, I am unprepared to greet you…"

"Such was my intent. I am here for your daughter, sir." His look of surprise was mirrored by Crystal's face.

"My Lady, I don't under…"

"She can walk in the day light and has no blood needs, yet is not a hulking guardian. We face threats, sir, and Monica needs to know if her talents can help us face them. If she can be of no help, we will return her, but the Queen is most insistent and we must leave within the hour."

The child in question was named Circe, on a father's whim. It was clearly questionable if he even knew what the litany of Circe's gifts were. She was born to vampire parents, but could stand direct sunlight and had no blood needs, taking her food as a normal human. She had their strength and recuperative powers, and was lucky enough to fly. Those are not what interest Monica, though. The child was fourteen years old and rumor had it that she was strongly prescient. Her name was both prophetic and ironic.

"I knew you would come, but I thought there would be three." Circe said.

"Well, it is odd, but I am strangely comforted by the fact that you can't see everything." Melissa spoke kindly to the child. Crystal maintained her silence.

"You were followed and we are being watched. They intend to kill you and take me." She paused, and then said, "They intend to chain me and make me a prisoner!" Outraged, Circe's face took on the battle visage of a full grown vampire.

Interesting, Crystal thought. *She is precocious. Vampires usually weren't able to reach the rage stage until reaching adulthood. No blood needs with that speed of rage?*

Well, I suppose we will see.

Melissa spoke to the guide, "Guardian, protect this household and summon help now. Crystal, take the girl and leave town at speed. Fly as soon as you reach the town limits, sooner if you encounter resistance."

"What about…" Circe is now protesting, regretting her outburst.

"We will send for your things if needed. If not you will be returned when we can assure your safety and your family's safety."

"Let's go," Crystal is sympathetic with the father's turmoil. His only daughter, one he doted on, was being torn from his household on a moment's notice.

Settling the girl on her back with her arms under the girl's knees for support, Crystal began to trot, letting herself become accustomed to Circe's weight. As they passed the houses at the bottom of the hill, she began to pick up speed until she could outrun a cheetah. She loved to run as a child, being faster than everyone, even the fastest teenageboys in her village at the age of twelve. Her blurring speed was one of the few unadulterated pleasures of the change.

Running to the town limits has an unexpected benefit. The narrow streets, crowded like much of London, with buildings on buildings smack up against each other hide their progress from those who are set as sentinels against their success. These, not caring much for local custom, hover in a ring around the child's home.

As they reached the town's edge, Crystal leapt into the air and began their flight to Norn's Lair, their home and most likely soon to be Circe's home.

"I can fly, My Lady."

"Yes, but can you keep up?"

"Only one way to know for sure, isn't there?"

Indeed. Crystal was beginning to like this child. "That is true."

They were soon joined by Melissa. Crystal slowed their speed in order for her to catch up.

No fear in this child, of us or her future. She is precocious but is she safe? As usual, Crystal considered the stars as she flew. Circe wondered what she saw.

"There are severe problems in that county." Melissa continues as much to herself as to Crystal. "We would have been too late if we had waited two hours to leave."

"What do you mean?"

"I mean that it is possible that the majority of this county is for Draco and his cronies. If it weren't for the guardians remaining loyal…"

"Your glamour's didn't work? What…"

"No, not that. I didn't have a chance to use them before a crowd rushed me. The guardians beat them back giving me a chance to get off the ground. I stayed long enough to help the guardians get behind the stronghold gates."

"Things are unraveling faster than Monica thought."

"Yes. Yes they are."

"I just don't see how Will is going to make a difference. What can one man do? Even if he is some kind of super vampire capable of killing arachnids, what will it matter? He is still only one person."

"Crystal, I just don't know. I don't know what her plan is, nor can I even make any guesses. The future is just a blank wall to me right now."

"It is to her as well." It is the first Circe had spoken in a while.

"Yes, you're right. It is to me as well…" began Crystal.

Circe interrupted, "Not you, though it is true for you as well. It is a blank wall to Monica, too. That is why she sought me out." Her face is hard to read. She didn't have the facial responses of a normal person. She is just…there. "I can't see out past six months anymore."

"What do you mean, anymore?" Crystal asked.

"It is as if the future has simply disappeared. I hear that even many amongst the humans who are considered to have real powers of seeing have simply retreated into their mountain homes, shunning the cities. They can't see, either."

Everyone was quiet. When you had lived as long as the three had lived and seen all that they had seen and still not have enough insight into what course to take, it was troubling. They were silent the rest of the way, each lost in their own thoughts.

Chapter 8

Sylvia was ecstatic, mostly because she just got a huge Christmas bonus. She even hugged her boss, briefly. Will just wasn't someone you hugged. He flinched.

"Thank you, Will. This is much more than I expected!"

"Well, Sylvia, you stuck with me through everything and now that we are profitable and everything is just peachy keen, I decided I would spoil you a bit."

"Well, I know one little boy who is going to get spoiled, too." She pauses, considering, then to herself adds as she turns back to her desk, "Only 39 shopping days left 'til Christmas."

"We need to decide where we are going to have our Christmas party. I am thinking my house or Elizabeth's. You have been to both. What do you think?"

"I don't know. Have you talked to Elizabeth about it yet?"

"Yes, and she would rather have a combined party at her house and I tend to agree. I mean, last year I didn't get the Christmas tree out of the house until February!"

"Wasn't it awfully dry by then?"

"Yeah! And when I stuck a match to it, it went off like a rocket! Sylvia, it was so cool."

"Will, have the party at Elizabeth's. That way you won't have any…destructive temptations." Both Will and Sylvia laughed.

"Yeah, I guess…it would be something I really don't want to have to deal with and she did offer. Okay, we'll have it at Elizabeth's."

"Good deal. Want me to work out the details with her?"

"Please. Still…I need to do something at my house. I haven't had anymore than one or two folks over and I have been in it since September."

When your house burned down, something about paint thinner? She can't remember. "Well, you can do something in the spring. You do have a lot on your plate right now." Mostly, she had a lot on her plate but didn't want to say so.

"Sounds good."

The Christmas party was held at Elizabeth's and, like most social events handled by Elizabeth, it was a success. She was of old money lineage and was used to the logistics of inviting, seating and catering to the needs of several hundred of your closest friends for several hours.

Elizabeth made Will laugh when she put it to him just that way.

"Will, now I need you to sit down and make a list of the 75 or so folks you will want to invite to the party."

"75 or so? This isn't a coronation or a wedding, I just wanted a Christmas party!" He is laughing then adds, "Besides, I don't even know 75 people." It was a sobering thought, which turned out to be untrue.

Looking pained and put upon, Elizabeth looked at him with the air of a Jewish mother who was trying to raise a social retard. *Besides,* she thinks to herself, *I am Jewish, I am a mother, and Will IS a social retard. Well, at least he knows he needs to do something like this now. That is a start. Now I just need to get him to do it right.*

"Will," she is speaking slowly and deliberately, "how

many folks are you friends with at work?"

"Well, there is Sylvia and there are the contractors. I suppose seven or eight."

"How many clients locally do you have that pay you more than, say, six thousand a year for services?"

"Twenty five or so, I guess."

"How many folks at your church do you know?"

Sighing in defeat, Will muttered, "Twenty or thirty."

"And how many know you on a good enough basis that you would like to know them better in order to access their list of contacts for future business opportunities?", Elizabeth counters.

"Geez, everybody I know on a first name basis."

"Uh huh. See? Start making your list." She said in her most commanding voice.

He grumbled the whole way through the list making progress to the point that Sylvia bit her palm to keep from laughing out loud. *Lord, I never knew a man could bitch so much in the space of twenty minutes.*

"I am not a social butterfly; I am a technical consultant, emphasis on 'technical.' Wish I had never started this thing!" Knowing his reaction is inappropriate and out of character he pulls out the church roster, which he has Kelly fax him, then goes ahead and pulls out his address book. Grumbling as he turns in his chair, making the bearing squeal as if to mirror his frustration, he adds, "May as well get the damn phone books out and finish this crap now."

Sylvia heared him get up to come out to the outer office to retrieve the phone books exclaiming, again, "Good grief, I wish I had never started this party crap!"

She couldn't hold it and excused herself with a muffled, "I need to step out for a minute."

She thought she would burst once she gets to the hallway, but oddly enough most of her mirth evaporated into just a snort and a smile. *Well, it is a 'character' building experience. He is growing as a person.* Knowing how he would lump that in with the tired old job- hunting phrase of 'looking for a challenge', she was finally laughing because of the intern Will had hired this month.

He was young, newly graduated, and full of the idea that with a four-year degree he was ready to take the world by storm. He did have an impressive GPA, was active in a lot of extra curricular activities and a lot of what Will thought of as "yadda… yadda… yadda… look at me I am a well rounded person." That isn't what set Will off during the interview, though.

What set Will off was when young Seth Weldon said that he was looking for something to challenge himself. He wanted something to tear into with both fists, like the captain of a ship sailing into a storm and risking it all to stake his will and determination against the storm. He had just seen 'A Perfect Storm' and it just dove tailed so nicely with his personal self-image that he makes the very nearly fatal, from a job hunting perspective, mistake of projecting his internal mind set into the interview.

"Challenge? You are looking for a challenge? Let me tell YOU something, Mr. Full of Piss and Vinegar, you don't know anything about challenge or challenging events because if you did know anything you would sure as hell not be looking for it. I. Have. Had. Challenges. They nearly killed me."

"Sir?"

"Look, if you want a job here, let me tell you what I expect. I expect you to DO your job and as far as possible, know it so well, that you are able to ANTICIPATE any of these 'challenges' that you think are so thrilling so we can avoid them. We are not looking for challenges here; we are looking for opportunities to succeed."

"Understood." He needed the job, so he kept his mouth shut until Will resumed. With a flash of comprehension, it suddenly dawned on Seth that maybe being a business owner wasn't so hot. He knew from a theoretical perspective that you have to watch things but he was having an epiphany that the danger of bad decisions was real and that deciding to be a business owner had real, painful dangers. It is a train of thought he would come back to later. Right now he needed a job.

Seth continued, "I will make it Job One to minimize risk to the company from any activities I engage in or you ask me to engage in and to try to anticipate such things and bring them to your attention."

Will just looked at him, knowing he was being a bit intense, probably too much so. *He is still a kid, asshole.* He asks, "Got a family?"

"Not presently, Sir, though I am engaged."

"Yeah. Okay. We'll give it a go. Come in Monday morning, at eight. Sylvia will do the preliminaries if I am out of town. You never know with me."

Seth shook hands with the pensive Will, made his goodbyes to Sylvia and departed. Seth would later celebrate that evening with his fiancée at Bottegas.

"Well, Sylvia, your vote got him the job. Thanks for the pre-interview idea. That was a good call."

"Uh huh. You scared him to death, just about."

"Yeah, I know." Will paused, then continued, "I know. But it will do him good. Me, too. I really am not looking for challenges anymore."

"Oh, I know! And I totally agree. Take advantage of clear opportunities and leave the challenges to the hard heads."

"That's my girl."

The Christmas party was a success. Surprisingly, almost everyone invited had RSVP'd and actually showed up. Elizabeth said later to Will, "See, this wasn't so bad now, was it?"

Will agreed. He cemented some new acquaintances, renewed some old friendships, and made some connections with folks he'd met only briefly. While his motivations weren't entirely centered on the season, he made sure to make some comment about two hours into the evening that everyone should remember the less fortunate during this holiday season.

New Year's Eve didn't look like it was going to go as well.

"Hey, no, Sylvia, thanks. I appreciate it but I have plans. Again, though, thanks for the invite."

Sylvia invited Will to her home for New Year's Eve. She and some friends were having a small informal gathering, after which they planned to go to the top of Double Mountain and watch the fireworks display. She knew Elizabeth was out of town with family this year and, since Will wasn't especially close to his family and their being so distant, it was a good bet that Will won't be doing anything much. If anything, he may go to a club and sit around watching people get drunk and act like they are having a good time. He would act like he was having a good time, too. *He needs to be with folks he knows,* Sylvia thought. She was momentarily held back by the question of whether or not it was appropriate to ask her boss to a party at her house, then decided that they were past the normal bounds of employer-employee -have been long ago- and asked him. Will has friends. *He just keeps people at a distance for some reason,* Sylvia thought.

Even before...before everything was bad... he was distant. Well, he can only say no.

She is disappointed but not surprised. He went on about how he planned to be with this beautiful young thing, but his eyes were sad. Sylvia would bet fifty bucks Will is lying, but what can she say? "Yeah, right, you're the original Mr. Lonely, so quit acting and come be with someone you pay to show up every day?"

What he does do is idle New Year's Eve's day away as he does many other days. Walking around Southside, where he knew lots of folks and had lots of memories. Besides, Will loves the architecture. It isn't quite San Francisco in the numbers of Victorian homes, but there are blocks that could really be transformed into some stunning Painted Ladies if their owners were so inclined. Bad memories no longer burn quite as much, and it is exercise, so it isn't so bad.

It is cold as a witch's tit, though. Cold enough to freeze the balls off a brass monkey, Grand Dad would have said. Will laughs out loud, which is okay.

There aren't enough people around to think Will is drunk or crazy. In fact, he sees, as he looks around from his window shopping at Magnolia's, that there is no one at all on the streets.

Well, it IS bad weather for walking for most folks. Will is bundled up in a good camel hair long coat, Timberlands, wool socks, and thermal underwear. *It will take worse weather than this to keep me from a walk when I want one.*

As he turns back to his window gazing, killing time, he catches a scent that is almost forgotten. It is the perfume from his dreams, and it isn't until after it passes that he knows what it is. Then Will whirls around, only to see the empty streets, with the gray sky threatening overhead. The weather service promises an icy, if not snowy, New Year's Eve, and it looks like that promise is going to be kept.

"Crystal…?" he murmurs involuntarily. If you had asked Will about the dreams ten minutes earlier, he would have had trouble recalling her name, nor would he be able to tell you why he called out Crystal when what was on his mind was Baby Girl. It is the perfume that opens up his mind to remembering all the dreams he'd had.

Well, isn't that just spiffy? Now, I can mope over fantasy as well as spend the eve of the 21st century alone. Geezuz pleazus. His watch says it is time to split for the theatre, and his car is two blocks away.

The movie isn't important. Will doesn't remember what he sees anyway. He is taking too much medication now and dozes off in the movie.

Will knows point blank what he is trying to accomplish is to get away from himself and his own thoughts, and it just isn't working.

No matter where he goes, there he is. No matter how much money he makes, how safe he is, or what he has managed to do, he is still trapped by his own thoughts.

Sitting in the theatre, wrapped in the darkness that

promises to deliver him from his own mind in the temporary relief of 'suspended disbelief' and the deepening fog of the medicine he takes for his headaches (and sometimes just because), he smells perfume again.

God, if you're there, let the dreams come back. If you do, I will get off the Darvocet, I promise.

It isn't a light promise. Will means it. He is already frightened by the fact that when he goes more than two days without it, his headaches come in with a vengeance. It is called 'analgesic rebound,' but it is really just a nice name for withdrawal. *Quitting is going to hurt like a bitch.*

Let her be my drug, and I will quit; I promise. I need to anyway, and I know it. Let the dreams come back, and I will even finally go in for grief counseling again. Will sleeps through the movie, dreaming Crystal sits beside him, and he explains how nice it is of God to agree to bring back his dreams of her and why he has done so.

Crystal just smiles and looks at him sadly. "I was gone too long, but I had to be. Soon, Will. I am tired of waiting for myself. In fact, I will wait no longer." Then boom, she is gone, and a strong surge of air sweeps through the theatre, waking him. *I will keep my promise,* is Will's last thought as he leaves the movie, even before it ends.

Crystal flies, sometimes inadvertently breaking the sound barrier. When she does, she eases up for a bit. Sustained supersonic flight isn't good for her health or for her clothes. It isn't good for her health because AWACs, submarines, and other such craft make it a point to look for sonic signatures. Those unidentifiable are treated with suspicion. Sporadic booms are dismissed as freak lightening, causing superheated air to expand and collapse. No big deal, but her trip did make meteorologists scratch their collective heads over the weird electrical activity stretching from the Southeastern United States all the way up to where the Northern Lights began.

Crystal makes it to their northern lair in record time. As she strides into the great hall, she finds Circe, Monica, and Melissa sitting expectantly.

"See, my Regent, I told you she would arrive within the hour."

"Indeed, Circe, you did."

"How did…Circe. You know, that really weirds me out." Like Melissa, Crystal had picked up modern speech patterns more and more. Perhaps that is why Monica is developing a strong attachment to the young Circe. Their language is the same, more so now than the other two, mostly from Crystal and Melissa having to live in the lands of humans on assignment. It happens from time to time, but Circe is a new element. Melissa, looking on, idly wonders what it means for the future. *Well, Circe is the oracle, not me. Besides, your better class of fortune teller probably frowns on reading their own future.*

Melissa is wrong to think she is unobserved in her thoughts, as she discovers when Circe leans over to her and says, "You are correct. They do., But please don't worry. I am no Rasputin," which, of course, bothers the hell out of all three of the long time compatriots. Still musing, knowing she will be known, Melissa mentally adds, " *Yeah, and you KNEW saying that would bother the hell out of me, so why did you say it?* Circe doesn't choose to respond to these thoughts, however.

As I say, Crystal returns. She is not happy and is uncharacteristically demanding.

It is not that Crystal is not vocal; she is just less so than the other two. She goes about her business, giving the best advice and doing her best job at her duties. She tends to keep her own counsel unless asked and never speaks just to hear her own voice. She is not someone who demands things of Monica, which is Melissa's job.

Well, it is fine. I am here, and I sent her to care for him. So she does, and that's that, Monica thinks.

Crystal demands that she be able to meet Will in real-time. There is a brief discussion about how she wasn't supposed to meet him in the first place, just to watch over him and keep him safe. Monica's heart isn't in it, though. She is older than Crystal by millennia and has had relationships with human men before, as has Crystal, but never like this. She is affected.

"Crystal, what are you saying? Are you in love with him?" As the question formed in her mind it was rhetorical. By the time she is finished she realizes it is not. "Remember, he is a human, while you are not. We still don't know with certainty if this is the path to take." Monica never lets her heart run away with her head. She is certainly impressed with Will and is lonely, but Crystal is in pain. Touching her arm, Monica asks her, "Crystal, this isn't like you. Tell me everything."

"Monica, he sees me, me, the thing that separates me from every other woman on the face of the earth. If I were scarred and crippled, he would still see me, and I think he would still have cared." Crystal is near tears, but it just isn't her nature to let it go. This nature meant that when it did, it would be bad.

"Crystal, my darling, you can't know that. You feel that way because he loved you when you needed to be loved, but you can't know his heart. No one can know another's heart, ever. It just cannot be done."

Looking at Crystal, Monica carries on with saying what she intended to say before Crystal arrived, "Crystal, I agree, you should meet Will in the open and carry on a relationship with him in something other than just this 'torrid dream affair' you have been engaging in." Monica is smiling as she says it because Crystal had come in uncharacteristically demanding what she had already decided before Crystal's arrival, and now all her energy for argument was blowing itself out. She resigns herself to the idea Will and Crystal have something that might be more than just an affair, at least in Crystal's mind. It remains to be seen what Will is going to do when confronted with all the facts. *...AND allowed to keep his memory. Well, we will see.*

"Sometimes I am sad for you, My Queen." This is an unusual form of address for Crystal. "I am here to serve you in as much as I can. I will give you the best advice I can, and then I will let you make your decisions. You're good at that. You can make such a decision and move on. It doesn't cost you rest when you make a bad decision because you truly do your best. I couldn't and I know it. On this, though, you're wrong. I do know his heart, just as I knew my first husband's heart would be true."

700 B.C.

Epophaneia is newly betrothed. Like any young girl, she is excited about being married, having her own household, and having babies. Her husband-to-be is from two villages up the river. He was smitten when they had a trading day at summer's end. The year had been one of the best harvests in memory, though some of the older folks wouldn't have admitted to it.

Some of the younger men had tried new farming techniques brought in by 'some heathen' as the elders had named him, all but spitting when they said it. 'Shifting,' he had called it. 'Resting the soil,' he had called it. Why? They had planted beans here and wheat there and melons on the north side of the hill since everyone could remember. It was the way things were done, and the elders knew best, which is why the gods let them live so long, right? To lead?

Then, in travels, these fellows looked as if they had been burned in the sun, talking of bathing even in winter and all kinds of crazy things. A written language that looked to be one long, curling mark. How could you read if the letters weren't separated? Also, almost all of their band could read, which was considered highly irregular. All of them know how to read, which is a key sore point with the elders in Epophaneia's betrothed's village.

She is completely oblivious to all this, though. Not because she is a woman but because she is still a child in most people's minds. She is old enough to marry, but she is still a child to them. Epophaneia's family is the village's ruling family, and the next king will be the man to marry her eldest sister, as is the way here. Saying that it is a matriarchal society is too simple, but it will do. The king is determined by his marrying the Queen. Since she is out of the line of leadership, she never needs to be involved in such things.

"Epophaneia, you are such a sight. I have thought of you every day!" Brywnin is laughing as he catches her up and twirls her around. Their marriage is soon, and they both are obviously anticipating the event. Others on the shore are smiling, especially Brywnin's friends. They are young people who found their hearts were for much more than just beating. They are for loving someone and swallowing that person's presence whole.

"Brywnin, hold me!" She is flushed as well. She thinks of him every day, too, and just can't hold him close enough.

Brywnin McWalnm is a largish fellow, layered in muscle, tending to carry more weight than he should. He is constantly thinking ahead and of ways to improve things, and the advent of the folks from the east is wholly good in his eyes. The demands of making a living from the few warm months they enjoy and surviving through the harsh winters make things difficult. It is hard to think of things when you have to hunt and fish in the winter and toil in soil that only grudgingly gives up any food during the summers. Oh, they stay warm and are able to eat by fishing and hunting, but disease and want take a terrible toll every year. This year will be different. If these Babylonians are right about preserving more green things in addition to salted meat, roots, and fish for winter fare, they can get through with fewer winter deaths. Besides, they are right about the new crop yield. Perhaps they are right about that, also.

Witness Miriam's passage three seasons ago. *If they had come sooner, might she have lived?* Brywnin is thinking to himself now about how she woke up weak, took a fever, and died in a delirium. The shamans could do nothing, and he buried her two weeks later.

Mirium had never borne him a child, but he hadn't cared because she said the heavens must be preserving a special child for her. She had always smiled and had a laugh for him when he came in from hunting or when they worked their land together.

I was happy. Perhaps the gods have decided to forgive me for whatever sins caused them to take her from me and reward me with Epophaneia.

They are married for two years before the monsters

come. They sweep down from the northern shores of Pictland. Some warriors are said to have gone to a trading day scheduled at Pitwivbrak only to find the village empty and deserted except for thirty or so corpses left in the village common. The warriors leave in a hurry after setting all the dwellings on fire. If it is a sickness, hopefully, none of them going in or touching anything will minimize any risk. There is a good chance they won't get ill, and everything will be cleansed by fire. Upon returning home, a rider is sent to the next village to hopefully prevent them from getting in and getting contaminated. Disease often hides and travels in strange ways, and it is best to leave the cursed ground alone. Even the Babylonians thought it prudent to let the land lay empty and shunned for a generation.

Brywnin died in the ensuing battles, and their children managed to live under the loving care of their maternal grandmother. Epophaneia herself is taken and changed. If Monica hadn't found her when she did, she might have been one of the mindless ones. As it was, it was a long time before Epophaneia stopped wishing she had been and that Monica had taken her life as well, as she did the rambling crew of zombies she was making her way through northern Pictland with by light of the fall moon.

Epophaneia goes to the battlefield to see if her man lives, is dead, or is crippled from injuries. She comes up on him, wrapped in the corpses of those who had killed him. He still has his hand clamped to his sword, where he drives it all the way to the hilt through a monster with bony brow and teeth just as that same monster had ripped his throat out. He slew at least half a dozen of what appeared to be demons, his body bearing mute witness to the horrific battle through slashes and tears. He fought on through cuts, slashes, and chunks of missing flesh. He fed none of the monsters.

She begins her mourning, as she had seen her mother do for her father when he was slain, thinking to herself, *I am too young to be mourning you, Brywnin, too young!* Then she cries with a loud voice, "Gods, how am I to live without him? I wanted nothing but him! Oh, take me, too! Take my life, my breath from me, my heart from my chest!" These words are not spoken. They seem to tear from her throat, leaving it raw as she screams.

Epophaneia is disconsolate. Tearing away from her would be comforters. She will not hear their sayings or the words of how life is cruel; he is in hunting fields or on some epic battlefield awaiting Ragnarok or the battle at the end of the world.

"My world has ended! What is to become of me? My little ones! How am I supposed to live without my Brywnin?" She is rocking back and forth, holding the head of the man she loves, her tears doing the first washing of her dead husband's face.

Her mother walks towards her. She had not wanted her youngest daughter to face this alone as she had when her husband had been slain at the hands of the Northern men. She is stopped cold by her daughter's terrible oath. "I will not leave this battlefield until I have seen him once more. If the demons return, they will have to take my blood as well. Perhaps we will wait for Ragnorok together."

"There are still your two children, Daughter. What still lives of Brywnin still lives in them." Looking at her daughter, Epophaneia's mother feels her heartbreak. "They still need you to love them, and they need you to stay in this world."

Epophaneia takes long, hard moments to respond. She wipes her face, then wipes Brywnin's face with her shawl and finally looks up at her mother's sad face. She hadn't noticed before just how old her mother was. "I will wait for sundown, and then I will return home. We will bury my husband tomorrow, and you will help me, just as I helped you bury my father."

Epophaneia is dead, and Brywnin is wherever we go after we die. I did not ask for him to be taken from me. Crystal is looking at Monica with these thoughts hard in her mind.

"You named me Crystal, Monica when you saved me from the mindless ones in my homeland. You admired my singleness of purpose when you handed me a silver blade and bade me avenge my loved ones. Hear me now on this, then. Will only wants the kind of love Brywnin gave me some 2,700 years ago. If you change him and he fulfills his purpose, so be it. Must he be the Royal consort to you? Do you love him?"

Monica is silent for a moment, considering. The three Norns love each other as only women can do. She finally answers the only way she can, "No, I do not. How can I? I have been stuck here dealing with rebellion on every front, driven by things I cannot identify!" Her rage flares and quickly dies. These days, she just isn't herself. She has lived longer than any, save a few, and even some of those are questionable. Monica is many millennia older than both Melissa and Crystal.

Finally, Monica says, "Have I not agreed with your clear wishes? Go to him and stay with him. If we need you, we will let you know. As of now, I want you to stay in the human world. If you get the summons, I know you'll be here."

Crystal and Monica embrace. There are no words spoken after that, and they retire to their respective ends of the castle. Crystal leaves without word or ceremony. For the second time that day, the weather folks do the "what-was-that" dance and move on.

Will decides that, about 6:30 that evening, he is going to go by and visit his widowed Aunt Beth. Aunt Beth is a sweet lady who goes out of her way to help you, but sometimes she could worry the chrome off of a trailer hitch with her constant sniping and criticisms. Still, he loves her and knows she is lonely, so he decides to go by.

Besides, maybe making her feel better will make me feel better. It's worth a shot, anyway.

They sit together, watching the first hour or so of the absolutely dreadful stuff they run on evening TV when everyone else is out partying for all they are worth or home with family, agreeing that they just can't take the party scene anymore. Then they hear the neighbors across the back divide start shooting off fireworks. Taking their drinks out onto the back deck, they just sat watching the show.

Finally, Aunt Beth asks the question he always dreads, "Well, have you heard from anybody lately?"

Usually, Will goes on about how his folks are doing well, or at points in the past, lying about how well the business is doing and is now actually doing, knowing full well that she wants to know if he had heard from his ex. *Why she won't let it go, I just don't know.* Then again, he can't tell you why he doesn't just tell her how it eats him up to talk about it, even now. Tonight, he just decides to attack it head-on.

"Well, I heard from her some two months ago. She wanted to make sure I knew she was giving me a chance to change."

"Well, then, that's good news, right?"

"I suppose. She then asked me for twenty-five hundred dollars to go on an internship trip for medical school. I gave her the money, and she hasn't returned my calls since, so I figure that's maybe not so good."

Will says this all in a matter-of-fact way. He worked most of it out in his own mind. It still hurts, but he is past sharing his hurt with anyone. It is embarrassing. But he is also tired of hiding the truth from himself by hiding it from his family. Maybe if he just addresses it without letting anybody see inside, it will just go away. These thoughts aren't exactly conscious, but the results played out.

They are interrupted by the sudden sharp report of several rocket cannons going off on the street facing the front of the house. With wordless agreement, they get up and walk through the house, out onto the front porch to watch, passing the chugging washing machine in the kitchen and the blaring TV in the den. After watching for a few minutes and meeting some of his Aunt Beth's neighbors, Will makes goodnights and plans to return home to his Southside apartment.

He gets to his car door when he spies a small female figure walking down the street. *Extremely female.* The thought is without any crude undertones, and it is just such a pure reaction that he had none of the back-peddling thoughts that sometimes accompanied his appreciation of beautiful women. She just is. He finds himself walking out to the road to meet her and is ecstatic when she slows down and smiles at his approach.

"Evening, Miss. I'm sorry, but I just can't help myself. I realize you are probably way too young for me to be talking to you this way, but I just had to meet you. My name is Will." Here, Will does something he had never done in his life:

holding out his hand to a beautiful woman. He feels strange. She looks like…

"Well, very nice to meet you, Will. My name is Epophaneia, but you can call me Chris. Everybody does."

Chris. Crystal. Am I asleep on Aunt Beth's couch? A neighbor he had met earlier during the fall blows his horn in passing. Will remembers him, not because he can see him, but because he drives the ugliest Lincoln Continental he has ever seen. Will would have laughed if the poor guy hadn't been so proud of the hideous thing. Two tons, green, and long enough to land a fighter jet on. Two long scrapes across the top of the car indicate that some desperate pilot may have tried to do just that in some distant past emergency.

He waves, his eyes never leaving Chris's face.

"Chris, well, it is nice to meet you. You live here in the neighborhood? I don't think I have ever seen you here…"

"I'm new, just got into town. I have visited a few times, but I am here to stay for a bit this time, I think."

"Well, look, Chris, I realize we just met and everything, but I am suddenly struck with the idea of going out for a drink instead of crashing early. Are you planning on anything…I realize we just met, but maybe you could follow me to the Club and have a drink…"

"Well, in case you hadn't noticed, I had not planned on a lot this evening myself, just going out for a walk, but…yeah, okay. It might be more fun than walking around the neighborhood. Where did you have in mind?"

"The Latino Frog. It's…"

"I know how to get there. I've seen it in…passing." She smiles. He didn't know what at or about, but God in heaven, her smile made him redline about two-thirds of his gauges.

She adds, touching his arm briefly, "I'll see you there in 45 minutes?"

"Oh, it's not that far awa…"

"Will, a girl has to get dressed, you know." She laughs.

Gauges are 80%, Cap'n. I dinna ken how much more she can take! Scotty's voice to Capt. Kirk is sounding off in Will's mind now, making him crack up. "Of course! What WAS I thinking?"

"Well, then. 45 minutes. Me, in town just a day, and I already have my first date. See you there, Will."

Ten minutes later, Will is still standing there when his Aunt Beth comes out to see why he hasn't come back inside yet. He can still feel her touch on his skin, and he doesn't want to move, afraid of making it disappear. Her perfume also lingers in the air just a bit. He wants to enjoy it as long as possible in case she is just a dream, and he gets to Senor Frog's and her not show. Or maybe it wasn't a dream, and she just humored him. After all, he met her, got her name, and asked her out in the space of less than five minutes. *Chris is what everybody calls me, but my name is Epiphanes. What's that? Italian? Middle Eastern?*

"Will? You okay? And who was that? She looked very nice."

"Humm? Oh, she said her name was Chris. I asked her to meet me at the Frog, and she agreed."

"Well, I suppose that's okay." She has a look on her face that indicates that THAT was pretty quick.

"I know her family a couple of cul-de-sacs over." He doesn't, but Aunt Beth takes decorum very seriously, and he knows her well enough to read THAT look from twenty yards. "They know me, and I went by there earlier before she arrived. I guess they talked about me coming by or something. She's new in town, just arrived, she said."

"What's her family's name?"

"Wilson, Jon, and Mary Beth" just popped out of his mouth. He needs to make sure and remember it. *Which I will never in a million years do, and she will, and here we go.*

"I think I know who you mean. Well, I guess you better get going." She rubs his chin and adds, "You'll probably want to file down the sandpaper a bit before you go."

"I have my razor in the car. I'll shave on the way, but thanks." *She is a sweetie sometimes.*

Will shaves on the way. The shave isn't as good as a hot lather and razor, but if he manages to get a New Year's kiss, he will not give her beard burn.

Pulling into the lot, it is already packed, even though it is only something like twenty after seven by that time. *Well, at least it'll be warm.* The thrill of the cold weather had worn off since the afternoon.

He is worried that he might be late, but he isn't. His approach was waited for from the roof; the cold weather wasn't a problem. She waits for him to go in and get a seat, as she isn't quite ready. Glamour took time to get just right, and it is, after all, a New Year's Eve party.

Will walks in, gets lucky, and gets a table. Some folks walked by and seemed a bit aggravated that he had gotten their table, but there were no drinks or coats, so what could they say? Will offers for them to share, but it doesn't sit well with the guy, who moves on in a huff. *Some guys. I just don't know.*

The music is loud, the people are getting loud, and it looks like the waitresses are up for a good night. *I would still hate to have to do their job,* is his last thought as Chris walks into his line of sight.

Will is stunned. She literally takes his breath away and makes her way towards him. Of course, guys stop her on her way and introduce themselves, but strangely, he feels no jealousy or aggravation. She is clearly working her way towards him, and he finds himself content just to enjoy how beautiful she is and laugh at how she puts guys off balance.

She almost makes it to the table when a fellow interjects himself in her path and makes an introduction. Will turns to greet her, grins at her, and turns back to the table. She will be there soon enough.

She is dressed absolutely…well, Will was out of his mind. He sits very still, not because he is unaffected but because he doesn't trust himself to move.

"Chris, you really look wonderful." He hopes it isn't a stupid comment or that he is overworked or tired, but he is having trouble with neuron coordination right now. Will is captivated, mesmerized, and a hundred other things he doesn't even know in a thousand languages.

"Thank you." She smiles and sidles up next to him so that her arm and his arm are touching.

Thank you, God. This is better. She is real. And I will keep my promises, yessir, You as my witness, I will. He is sincere. Perhaps he will make it.

They talk about small things, not really anything of any consequence in the grand scheme of things. Where she hails from, what she does, and so on. Will doesn't much care to talk about himself. Frankly, he is completely caught up in trying to find out everything he can about Chris. Later, he sums it up this way: "As long as I was looking at her, just the barest of touches on my skin, her skin against mine, just her arm, I didn't hurt anywhere, and I didn't think about anything but her. I had read about drowning in a woman's eyes, but I had never done it. I never wanted that minute to end. It was as if she knew how my eyes felt filling themselves up with her, and she wanted to give me all I wanted." This, of course, led to endless ribbing from his friends.

When they part company, he hugs her goodbye, though he doesn't try to kiss her, even when the clock strikes midnight. You may believe me when I say he never wanted anything more. He walks her to her car, an unlikely Bronco truck. He briefly looks at it, shrugs off, and returns to looking at Chris.

He runs his hand down one arm, obviously with as much tenderness as his somewhat rough hands will allow, and then touches her cheek, just below her earlobe. Will touches her like she is a china doll, so fine she might break unless he is just so careful. God, I wish I could touch you so you felt my heart right now. *You ARE her. I don't know how I don't know why, but you are HER.* Realizing he may be overstepping his bounds, he stepped back.

"I'm…well…"

"I had a nice time, Will. Do I need to tell you I want you to call me?"

YES! "No, I mean, I'm glad. Because I want to." *How about when you get home tonight, so I can sleep hearing you breathe?* He thinks this is probably scary talk, but she affects him that way. He knows, right at that moment, he wants this woman sleeping next to him for the long haul. Quite simply, nothing else will do. *You're an idiot. Puleeze, what a sap. Go home before you embarrass yourself.*

"Well, give me something to write on." Will started to go into his truck but Chris grabbed his elbos and said, "Wait, I know. Some girls used to do this in high school," laughing, she writes her name and phone number down inside his left palm. "This way, if you try to pick up some other girl on the way home, you'll at least have some explaining to do."

This time, she hugs him, and he lets himself feel her over his entire length squatting down a bit so that her breasts against his chest, her hips and thighs against the inside of his thighs, with his face in her hair. He can feel her breath on his neck, warm and a little moist. He steps away when he realizes where her stomach lies and that she is going to be physically put on notice of how she affects him if he doesn't do something soon. *Also, damn it, I am shaking.*

She has that knowing look in her eye, though, and is touched by the realization that she is in the presence of a male who will protect her at any cost, even against himself. It is something in the pores. She wonders if he knows how other males react to it.

"I will call you Friday."

"I look forward to it."

Later, Crystal thinks to herself, *He is safe, and I can trust him. I wonder what his reaction will be when he finds out that Crystal and Chris are the same and that his dreams are real.* For the first time she really is worried. *He will be angry that I played with his mind. Still, what choice had I?* Then, *This sucks. I guess now I need to decide whether sooner is better or worse.*

While Crystal is pondering how and when to break it to Will that Chris and Crystal are the same, Will is lost in his bed, with his sweater balled up against his face. Chris's perfume is in it, and he can't help it. By tremendous force of will, he makes himself wait until Friday to call.

It is a strange call because she just doesn't seem to be there for some reason, distracted by something. She answered the phone, and they talked, made a date, and hung up.

What was up with her today? Should I have not called? Then, *I can't do that, overanalyzing everything to death. I just can't do that.*

He looks forward to seeing her again, but he also knows he is overreacting to her because she looks like Crystal. *I must have seen her walking through the neighborhood sometime in the past, which is why I had those dreams. I need to get over it, or I am going to screw this up.*

It is 2 AM on Saturday morning, and Will just can't sleep. He is 'other-directed,' as we've remarked on before. He is excited because she is a beautiful and striking woman and she is evidently interested in him. What bothers him about all this is that it seems to him that he is being led blindly into something here, and he can't see what it is. *Else, why the dreams?*

He believes in God, and he also believes that every person born on the earth has a specific reason for being here. He believes that people have free will, but he believes in very few coincidences. All his life, Will has believed he has a special purpose and that there is a special person out there who is supposed to share his life. It is just too damned convenient the way his dreams of her are validated in some way by her actually walking into his life.

Then tonight, Will dreams of a dream he'd had when he was a kid. He had forgotten all about them for the most part. Occasionally, he would think about them but not dwell on them.

I haven't even thought about it...should I even be doing this? Do I really want this grief in my life? It will end badly. It always does. She was beautiful, and it was her. Either that, or I am just making...what? Plugging her into the empty places in my mind? After 29 years?

1970

"Momma, I don't feel well. Can I stay home today?"

"Will, you're just being silly. God, you're just too sensitive for a boy. This is sissy behavior. You need to stop this nonsense and go to school." Will's mom, like lots of moms who have too little money and time, just isn't very available. Working two jobs didn't make it easy for her to worry about the concerns of an 8-year-old boy who just thinks about things too much. *I don't know where he gets it. Now, he's obsessed with dreams.*

Will isn't sick; he wants to stay home and go back to sleep. Occasionally, he has dreams for three nights in a row about a girl his age he can't be close enough to. Last night he dreamed of her again, only this time she went missing, and he couldn't find her. He wakes up weeping. In his eight-year-old logic, he thinks he has to go back to sleep so he can find her before she gets too far away, and he never finds her!

Will just figures there is a special place, maybe an entire world, where your mind goes when you fall asleep, and he thinks she lives there. Later, he will wonder if perhaps she lives in that world somewhere and they met there. If he could just find her, he wouldn't have to only visit her. They could be together day and night, every day!

It is always the same and always different. He goes to her house, and they sit on the porch or at dinner with her family. Sometimes, it is the Wild West. Other times, it is in a large stone hut with a thatch roof. Once, they had to run from creatures, large, deformed spider looking things, attacking them. He'd sent her on with her family, and the men folk had stayed behind to protect the home. After the battle, he is not able to find her and wakes up with a wet pillow.

What is the same is how his holding her hand is like feeling an electric current flow into him, or perhaps the feeling one has when thirsty and the cool water is cascading down your throat. Even as an adult, he sometimes wants those dreams to come back when he thinks about it. He wants them to come back just so he can feel that way again, just for a night.

Chapter 9

Choosing Sides

"She is insane. We cannot stand by and allow our destiny to be controlled by those it is our right to rule." Sven is Lord Draco's successor after he was slain in the Lair of the Norns. Sven escaped the same fate only because he had been delayed by a bunch of trivial had-to-dos that couldn't wait.

They may have been trivial, but they saved my life. I'll need to think about that later. Right now, Sven is trying to convince this idiot about their joint destiny and rights.

"Do you wish to stand against her as Lord Draco did? Don't be stupid. Besides, why, why would I want to go to war? She lets me alone, and I don't bother her. I have lands and wealth and a family and am quite content. The last time I had to deal with those three, she asked my opinion concerning folks like you. Besides, she hasn't levied a tax in 300 years."

"Folks like me?"

"Yeah, divine rights nuts. We live as long as we want. I have more wealth in the human lands than I have here because THEY understand that commerce is a more powerful engine for building influence than slaughter." Here, Roger reaches his hand up, scratches the back of his head with a perplexed look, drags it down and across his face with a loud rasp that indicates he may want to shave, then adds, "Well, some do anyway, most, in fact. You, on the other hand, want to set fire to the planet. Start a world war against 8 billion humans. By the way, in case you haven't been keeping up with current events, fire kills us quite effectively, and there is nothing better than a fusion device to start a fire. I don't want to fight; I will not fight, and if I am forced to choose sides, you may find yourself arraigned against me."

Roger is beginning to be red-faced, but it is anger at the situation more than anger at Sven. He goes on, more mildly, "You will lose. I have too much to lose to war, no matter who wins, you or the Norns because the humans will win in the end, and our world will end, period, in a ball of fire. Don't you get it? All my children will die, and all of yours as well."

Sven looks at his long-time friend. *There is no persuading him. You either see the future as it should be, or you didn't, and you do not. Roger, you are satisfied and just do not understand that to have power requires the use of that power. It is sad.*

This is also why we will need to thin our ranks once we take control. We can't have disloyalty in the people.

Sven can't answer who 'we' are unless it is in the royal sense. Then again, he is the type who would enjoy the distinction.

"Roger, can I at least count on you to sit on the sideline? We will not draw you into the fight; just do not declare for the Queen if it comes to that. Can I have your word?"

Roger and Sven are both of the People, so the answer is known to be truth or lie. Roger will not insult their past friendship by trying to dissemble now.

"Sven, there is nothing I would like more than to sit on the sidelines and not be involved." Roger had told the minimum truth. He was not disappointed in his hope that Sven would hear what he wanted to hear.

"Good! Good! I will send news when I have some, Roger. Give your family my best." Sven is sorry that after this is all over, he will have to do away with Roger, but it is, after all, his choice not to stand with them. He is too powerful and too influential to make an enemy of for now, and his leadership in standing aside will draw others who want to ride the fence to his position. *Whether you like it or not, Roger, you will aid our cause by leading people to the sidelines and off the battlefield,* is Sven's last thought as he crosses over the pass into the next valley. Sven is not blessed with flight.

"Guardians!" Roger calls out as he enters the great hall of the manor, "to me. Now!" Roger had told Sven the truth when he'd indicated that he would like nothing better than to sit on the sidelines. It is true. That doesn't mean he will.

"Lord Tamerlane." The guardian on sentry duty is naturally the first to arrive.

As the rest of the manor guardians assemble, Roger begins to lay out the ground work for them.

"Each of you has sworn to me and my family, correct?"

"It is so, Lord Tamerlane!" Everyone assembled knows that they have entered into the formal language of cementing a guardian's loyalty to a course of action. While one can swear allegiance, there are enough cases in the past of guardians using independent thought as to what that oath means to often cause consternation on the part of a Lord. Why, once a guardian sworn to protect her master had locked him in the castle to protect him from going out to battle. She had then gone out to the battle, took down the opposing force and brought back his enemy's head. He had raised blue hell about trying to move her somewhere else until he realised he was a household joke.

This had been amongst some clans who were patriarchal in nature. The fact that most guardians are born female is one of those things the male segment of these areas just ignored unless they were in their cups, and then it is just a bitch session. The sexual dimorphism between human males and females carries over to the people, with the exception of the birth rate of female guardians. This particular Lord was one who was brave to the point of stupidity. Later analysis would indicate that his forces were outmatched 5 to 3. The unexpected savagery of this single guardian and the fact that you really cannot effectively bring an army to bear on a single opponent in a well-chosen escarpment not only saved this Lord but probably his entire army. Though it was well trained, they had by design refused to do as others and retain certain levels of guardians. Fortunately, so had the attacking force, deciding insanely that this single guardian could not be allowed to live as an embarrassment to their clan.

I wonder what the end of that story was. Roger snaps back to the issue at hand.

"You all swear, now, that these conversations will only be revealed to the person or persons I give you permission for?"

"We so swear, Lord Tamerlane." Thunderous voices.

"One of you needs to volunteer to go to Queen Monica."

A guardian steps forward to volunteer. Her name is Salome.

"Salome? Who named you this?"

"My father, Lord, it was a good name at one time. He thought I might make it an honorable name again."

"He had a lot of faith from the outset, then. You know who Salome is?"

"Yes, Lord, I do. There is a Hell, and she is in it."

Lord Tamerlane just looks at her for some seconds then goes on to the group at large. "I, Lord Roger Tamerlane, is he to whom you have sworn duty and allegiance, correct?"

"It is so, Lord Tamerlane!"

"Then your allegiance is also to those to whom I swear allegiance. Do you agree to this?"

"We so agree, Lord Tamerlane!"

How the entire planet doesn't know every time a group of guardians swear, I don't know. They rattled the windows when they all thundered out in unison.

"Then know this, I this day in your presence declare for the Queen Monica and I pledge my life and all yours to her cause. Do you all agree to this as well as to the idea that this knowledge does not leave our ranks until I, Lord Tamerlane, reveal it?"

"We so agree, Lord Tamerlane."

"Salome, take news of this to the Queen. Reveal it only to her or her two sisters. Pack now, leave now. You need to tell her that it is my desire to remain undeclared publicly for now."

"Yes, Lord." She turns to leave. Lord Tamerlane stops her with a hand on her elbow and asks her a question.

"Guardian Salome, why did you volunteer?"

"I am the fastest, Lord, both in the air and on foot."

"Very well."

"And," she is almost smiling, with a definite twinkle in her eye, "I have never been beaten in a footrace. I hear the same is true of the Lady Crystal."

"Do you intend to ask for a race?" *Good Heavens, a guardian gone insane. What now? What next?*

"NO, my Lord, I would never assume such an affront to my Queen or her ladies!" her face registers a stricken shock. She steps back and bows from the waist, "My Lord Tamerlane, I meant no offense. It is just that I have heard that the Lady Crystal often engages in sports and, like me, has never lost."

"Ah, I see. Should she give you the chance you should like to try?" Oh, he is feeling much better now. Much better.

"Well, my Lord, it would be impolite to refuse."

Humor in a guardian? Now I have seen it all. Next thing my youngest son will want to accomplish things and be a productive member of the family. Why, he could even want to go live elsewhere!

"Just as you say, Salome. Go earn your name's honor."

"My Lord." Salome leaves to prepare for her departure. She is not to return but is to stay and serve Monica and the Norns.

Chapter 10

Monica

"Monica, there is a guardian here from Lord Tamerlane. Her business is for the two of us alone, preferably you, but I was told I would do if you were not available." Melissa's tone is dry. She is not being used to being conscended to in her own castle.

"Huh. Well, then, let's get to it."

Seating themselves in the great hall of the Norn's lair, Monica on her dais and Melissa in a chair somewhere near halfway up the wall to Monica's left in order to observe, they await the guardian's arrival.

"You'll be able to see everything clearly from the wall chairs." *And to react should this prove deadly,* thinks Monica.

The three queens, as some called them, or Norns, as some had called them in the past, were powerful and deadly. Still, it is a guardian's nature to be deadly. This one, though not large, looks extremely, wickedly dangerous. Not large is relative. Salome stood at 6' 9" and some 315 lbs. *...and it looks as though she polishes her killing points.*

Feline. She looks feline, somehow. Monica is watching Salome's slow, respectful approach to the dais. Without prompting, the guardian stops further back than would have been acceptable.

"Why stand you so far away, guardian?" Monica is mild. Her reaction to the guardian's answer is not.

"Because to come two inches closer would put me within reach of your highness's person should I mean you harm. The Lady Melissa would not be in time to aid you, My Queen.”

Alarms went off in both women’s minds, and Melissa was down at Monica’s side. Almost immediately, the room was full of huge guardians, and Salome fell to her knees.

“Why would you speak so, guardian?” Monica is angry, feeling violated. *We let a traitor walk into our manor? Why the hell did Circe not warn me? Are we already too late?* Monica and Melissa assume the back to back stance of being under siege from unknown directions.

“I speak so because I have sworn to Lord Tamerlane that I would warn you of the danger threatening you from Sven, Lord Draco’s successor. I am also, at his request, formally pledging service to the Three Queens.”

“Well, you nearly caused a brawl between you and the manor guardians.”

“My purpose was to make you see how vulnerable you are. I simply walked in and announced myself and was shown to your great room.”

“My Lady, I realize your power has grown great. However, so has your overconfidence. Accidents happen, and assassins are known to plot against you. You must take care.”

“Indeed.” Monica’s voice was mild, but she intended to have a talk with this fellow about making his regent feel like a fool.

“Lord Tamerlane also expressed his wishes that you do not acknowledge his loyalty at this time. He feels that he can gather more information if he is anonymous for the time being. He has Sven’s ear and hopes to capitalize on it.”

“Sounds like a good plan. Is there anything else?”

"Lord Tamerlane has heard stories, My Lady, about harnessing elfin magic. Steel was thought to be protection against elfin magic. He thinks that it is possible that there were people who were thinking to master it and use it against both you and the human nations."

"Magic? That is just plain ignorant. There is no such thing as magic."

"We fly, My Lady. Is that not magic?"

"Actually, that is a bad argument, Salome." Monica is pacing around the chair she received guests in, her robes flowing out behind her as she traced the intricate carvings of a long-dead Turkish boy.

He had been so talented. It is a shame that I can find no other examples of his work. There were artists who would be numbered amongst the grand masters of Europe but of whom there was no record, simply because Monica had collected every single work for her own.

"Why?" Salome almost forgets to add the usual honorific but manages to get it in just in time for there to be no need to notice the lapse, "Highness?"

"Because no one can explain the bumblebee's flight. It should not be able to fly, yet it does so and beautifully."

The people have science. Much of it is quite advanced. One of the benefits of long lives is the chance to truly learn all that is known in a particular field. No one has solved the mystery of bumblebee or human flight, though.

Yet bees do have wings. "Do we know the source of these rumors?"

"No, My Lady, we do not. This information comes through Sven's confidence in Lord Tamerlane. He will try to ascertain their source."

"Well, good enough. Not much hard information but it is good to know of Tamerlane's loyalty."

"Melissa, we have need of your glamours again."

"Indeed. I wondered how long it would be. Frankly, I had expected to go out sooner."

Monica looks at her, somewhat put off by the tone, a mixture of puzzlement, irritation, and worry. "Melissa, what is wrong?" There is concern in her voice, and as she puts her hand on Melissa's arm, Melissa turns to her.

"Crystal is in trouble somehow. I can feel it."

"But Circe…"

"Circe doesn't see everything, Monica, not everything."

"It is true that the future seems closed, but…"

"I am telling you, my queen, Crystal is in danger from some quadrant that is hidden from us and must be hidden by power and purpose. The fact that the seers can no longer see out past the next…five and a half months now…proves that it must be by design, yet no one, not even the seers themselves, thought of that possibility."

"Yet you did. Why?" Monica is concentrating her vision on the far-off, rolling hills at the edge of the fields where they had built an artificial hill upon which sat the Norn's Lair. She can't see it from here, but just past those rolling hills the land dropped off in a steep cliff that fell for thousands of feet. It is almost impossible to get to the lair without flight. The cliff sides are more than just treacherous; they are lined with false paths, deadfalls, and permanent glamours set by Melissa. Only those who mean no harm can see through those glamours. If you meant trouble, you had to be able to fly.

"I think it is because I am not a seer like you and Circe. My sight is simple intuition, but strong nevertheless. It is only those who are of the sight who are blinded."

"Then that means that whatever, or whoever has blinded them, wants no interference in what is planned in some six months. Well, at least we have a date now."

"We still don't know what has been planned and we still don't know what is happening with Crystal, Will's status, or who is behind Sven."

"Yes, but perhaps the date will give us an indication of WHAT is being planned. We just need to look at all anticipated events for that period and see if there is anything or things that stand out. As for Circe, I am considering returning her to her family. If she cannot see, of what use is she here? She is young and needs her family. I am no mother." This last is delivered by a woman whose patience has been tried in the last few weeks by the presence of a young woman with definite ideas of her own.

Melissa is amused inwardly, but she takes pity on her. "Perhaps she can spend more time with me. I will take her with me on this next foray. Her head is steady, and she can still see weeks into the future; perhaps she will be of some use to me as I collect information…do a little pre-glamour prognostication."

"Do it." Monica is relieved.

"Circe, you are to come with me." Melissa enters Circe's room unannounced and comes up on the girl, concentrating fully on a circle drawn upon the wall. It has a series of runes drawn through out the central portion.

"Nothing. Still nothing. Past June 30th, I can see nothing. Just a blank wall." Then, "My Lady."

"This, My Lady, is making conversation tiresome, for me at least. You will refer to me as Melissa."

"As you wish, My…lissa." She tries to correct it in mid-phrase. It comes out badly, but both think it is worth a small smile.

She is an engaging child. I wonder why there is friction between herself and Monica. "Think you can see why I am here?"

"You want to be able to run various ploys by my sight to make sure there are no 'unforeseen' consequences. No, I don't read minds, but I can extrapolate backwards by reading the future. Of course, when the future affects the present, it affects the future to some degree so that I can never really see all of it. I think it must be because it is hard to see yourself. Because now that I have explained this, you will not ask me do I read minds."

"Interesting." She is mulling over an idea. *Perhaps the reason the seers are blinded is because whoever is planning whatever doesn't want the future changed by affecting the present. No, that can't be right. Besides, I am having trouble following my own mind after itself. It's close to the correct way to approach this thing, though. It is close.* Again, here is that intuition thing rearing its head.

"So, where are we going? Are we going home?"

"No, Circe, this time we are going to Sven's province to the east. We'll be disguised as changed people who cannot fly. We'll set down on foot at the border and walk in."

"Walk in? How long a walk? From the border? How big is Svenia?" *She's a chatter box. That is the irritation to Monica.*

Monica watches as Circe and Melissa disappear into the

thunderheads, beginning to pile up on the east.

Probably snow and lots of it.

She looks forward to it. The world seems so clean and quiet when it is blanketed by a thick layer of snow.

It even looks like a blanket, a blanket made from the wool of spotless lambs. Perhaps that is why purity, cleanness and safety are tied to the color white.

She is always this way when both her 'sisters,' as she thinks of Crystal and Melissa, are gone. The Norn's lair is empty save for the guardians, and they are not conversationalists in any sense of the word.

Salome might be.

The queen, lonely, goes off in search of the diminutive (relatively) guardian. She could have summoned her but wants to see what she might have chosen herself to occupy her mind while her eyes, like all guardians, constantly measure her environment for threats to her charges.

Chapter 11

News Items

While Will gets to know the sweet Crystal, the world begins to look stranger and stranger from an economics point of view as well as a news view. In fact, there is the curious phenomenon of news stories being pulled at the last minute on the orders of network executives and entirely new, oddly undocumented news items being run in their place. There is a decidedly odd flavour to changes from the usual fare of footage and on-the-scene comments collected by high-paid anchors.

There is one item, though, that gets plenty of coverage and plenty of on-site commentary. The United Nations Security Council convenes an impromptu session in New York. This in and of itself isn't so unusual. What has all the anchors in a tizzy is that all five of the Security Council heads of state choose to attend rather than just send their usual surrogates, such as the Secretary of State for the United States. For the first time since the Council of Yalta (where the world was split in half between the democracies and the Soviet Bloc countries), the US and French Presidents, the Queen and Prime Minister of Great Britain, the French President, and the Secretaries of Russia and Red China are assembled in New York City.

There is no announcement that the trips are being made other than the horrendous traffic snarls created by the impromptu security measures needed to make sure that the leaders of 90% of the world's economic power are safe. Once they are in meetings behind doors guarded by the world's best troops (a hand-picked group of 82nd Airborne, SAS, Spetznaz and a few others barely known outside their own countries; although pointedly, no UN troops are used), an announcement is made. The world is expected to believe that a low-priority, low-key meeting is taking place to cover some minor points of departure for economic relations in the 21st century.

While Generals patrolled the halls from time to time, Colonels looked to the troops, all hard-eyed young men who looked each other over coolly, knowing that sooner or later they would be asked to kill each other, wondering whose training was superior and knowing there is only one way to find that out for sure. In the middle of all this, you have idiot talking heads running around asking stupid questions designed; I am sure, to confuse the average viewer about what is happening until the execs can decide how they want to spin it so it means what they think it SHOULD mean.

A week later, there is a press release indicating how pleased everyone is with the outcome of the meetings and how the 21st century is sure to be one of unprecedented growth, both in economic and cross-cultural understanding.

ITEM: A few enterprising reporters ask the secretary of state in a follow-up news conference to either confirm or deny that NATO forces are on defcon 3 status for the duration of the conference and the following week. Their contracts are not renewed.

ITEM: Raw research dollars allocated by Congress to defense contractors suddenly increased by 75%. A few liberals start to raise a bit of sand, but quickly hush while the hawks in politics decline to pat themselves on the back publicly. Things are just quiet. Rush Limbaugh comments that the quiet on both sides of the aisle indicates that someone is terrified and that someone has the power to shut people up.

ITEM: Immigration worldwide grinds almost to a halt, not because people don't want to travel, it just becomes prohibitively expensive and governments begin to actively discourage it with safety announcements. "It is a tragedy. Tourism is the main industry of many countries," says the Honet Travel Centre, a Hong Kong Based Travel trade group. "It is as if governments no longer want the tourist trade."

ITEM: Over a three week period, two smaller ships, a Coast Guard Cutter and a Carnival Cruise Line cruise ship, disappear off the coast of Florida. The only thing in common is the reported presence of a Greenpeace launch with the unlikely name of USS Davy Jones stenciled across its bow.

ITEM: Greenpeace, usually tolerated by governments everywhere, is put on notice that all ships have the authority to fire on them without warning should they approach closer than 1,000 yards by day and on visual contact by night until the USS Davy Jones and her crew are apprehended for questioning. When asked if these measures aren't a bit extreme in light of the peaceful nature of the organization and the fact that Davy Jones isn't registered with them, the deputy secretary only answers with a simple "Yes."

ITEM: The US Government contracts with the government of China to absorb and purchase all the excess silver their mines can produce. In a surprise unrelated move China officially recognizes the island of Taiwan as being a sovereign nation to itself. All US mines went into 24-hour operation last month when the United States, Britain, and France announced their plans to look again at using metals as the backing for hard currencies. Silver futures are up this week and are expected to continue to climb.

ITEM: As tensions on the high seas continue to mount, all ships in US waters have been instructed that no night time distress calls will be answered unless answered by groups of three ships. Any attempt to approach US military ships in anything short of full daylight will be taken as an act of aggression and responded to accordingly in a swift and unhesitating manner. Similar edicts have been issued by most other sea powers, with the most notable exception being Russia, who is in a struggle against some northern provinces who have rebelled against any Moscow-based government. While it is known a rebellion is in progress, few details are to be had as the Russian government is not allowing journalists to travel north of St. Petersburg, the former Leningrad.

ITEM: Roswell, New Mexico "The government is at it again," says several residents. "Last week, the roads were bumper to bumper with military trucks, and I guess fifty to a hunnerd planes came into the base over in the hills." When asked for comment, the US Airforce had this to say, "Well, it is the end of the month, so supplies were brought in, some by truck, some by air. Also, we had some personnel changes come due." Looking sheepish, he added, "I guess it was just one of those statistical flukes like a triple witching hour, and everything seems to happen at once. We sure didn't mean to upset anyone. We just had a couple of normal activities all come due at one time."

ITEM: Finland: Several small towns were closed due to an outbreak of what the CDC is calling a cold weather version of a weak eboli. While it is considered serious, the World Health Organization and the CDC in Atlanta both indicated that this is not anything as serious as the equatorial version of the disease. "We know the vectors for this outbreak and are moving to eliminate them quickly. The villages should be habitable within the month," said a grim-faced 20-year-old technician. He added, "This clean up will be finished by the weekend, one way or the other."

When asked to elaborate on the clean-up procedures, he declined, citing the recent trend for terrorists to use bio-weapons.

"Chris, please." Will is leaning his forehead up against the cool glass in his 30th-floor office in the AmSouth building downtown. The view is spectacular and worth every penny. It is just an easy place to be, and he gets more work done.

"Will?"

"Yeah. Look, Chris, I am not going to be able to make dinner tonight. Something has come up."

"Everything okay?"

"Oh, absolutely. Just OEE and Browning want to have a conference tonight. Apparently, they have just been awarded some Fed contracts." Will likes to talk to her about what he is doing. Chris has a brain, and her spin on things sometimes helps.

"Well, do you want to come by later or just punt?" Chris had an accent when she moved in, but she is picking up Will's colloquialisms.

"No, no, absolutely not. But I will be late, perhaps very late, so go ahead and eat. I will just swing by when we're done if that's okay."

"Sure, no biggie. As for dinner, I think I'll just crash until later. Rocky's delivers until 2 AM, right?"

"Well, yeah, but it may actually be that long, so don't wait for me."

"I may or I may not. Either way, I'll order you something if you'll call me just before you leave."

"Good deal. Get me a Philly cheese with no onions and

light sauce if I haven't called by midnight. If it's cold, it'll just be cold." In the background, she hears Sylvia announcing Mr. Browning's arrival with his crew. "Listen, Angel, got to run. See you soon."

He called me Angel. She morphs in her bed for the hell of it, and laughs, "Not exactly, nope, not exactly."

"Mr. Browning, you have no idea how good it is to see you." Will isn't exaggerating. He is truly glad to see the old man. Will, like many in the dot com world, doesn't have time for many friends so the few he has are all the more close for it.

"Same here, son, same here. Business good?"

"Great! We have so much that it's practically falling out all the windows. We're getting folks who prefer to wait for us rather than have it farmed out, even to people we recommend, so…" It is an enviable place to be, and Will intends to enjoy it for as long as it lasts.

"Well, it is about to get busier for you."

"Do tell? And here I thought you just wanted to discuss your roses again."

Will and Mr. Browning share more than a passion for business. They are both avid rose collectors.

Well, we both will be once I get past the next two years.

Will had planned out a compound that, in addition to his home, would also entail a rose garden, a pecan orchard, and possibly both an Italian and Japanese garden. As he had told Sylvia in dreaming one day at lunch, 'My house is going to be a refuge where I can rest and be at peace. I want it to be perfect, a place where I can think.'

"Yes, we are suddenly faced with the task of producing

the next generation of shielded, secure computers and computer networks. The idea of building a computer that is immune to EMP was also broached."

"Really? Now, there is an idea. How do you think such an animal could be built? Electronics being what they are, EMP is always fatal to machines in operation, common knowledge. What news do you have?"

"EMP has no effect on data being transmitted via fiber optics, but it does kill the converters on both ends that take an optical signal and convert it to electrical pulses. There is also the problem of shielding entire areas from EMP because not everything can be built in a hardened fashion, nor do all crises allow for the time needed to bring equipment online."

Besides, you can just hammer someone with another EMP, Will thinks.

This is old hat to Will, so he just sits and waits for whatever nifty, neat, spiffy new thing the old man is going to spring.

"Will, we want you to work with Felix Dorcai. He heads up research over at the plant. He has several patents on optoelectrical interfaces and has a few ideas to run by you."

"Well, Mr. Browning, I am all ears. How does this affect the EMP issue?"

"It is no longer an issue." Felix Dorcai interjects and makes it count.

"No longer an issue? What does that mean? EMP fries everything within a hundred or more miles. Planes fall out of the sky."

"Well, the entire computer is composed of optical circuits."

"Yeah, but the interfaces…"

"Are optical in nature. The circuits, the RAM, the CPU's internal cache…are 100% optical. Circuit speed is 100% of the speed of light within the matrix of the optical circuits."

"How…?"

"Well, for the RAM, instead of charges, we use color change flip flops caused by the interaction of light on the RAM substrate. We call it cRAM."

"cRAM?"

"Stands for chromatic Random Access Memory. Faster than SDRAM and never loses its data, even with power loss. It just picks up where it left off when the power comes back online."

"So, where do I fit into this?" Will's mind is blazing.

A CPU and RAM running at the speed of C on board. RAM that doesn't lose the info on a power loss? That has been done, but the speed increases this method promises!

"I suppose the heat discharge is minimal?"

"Yes. Now, tell me what that means if you see it." Felix is, in his own way, assessing Will. He isn't disappointed.

"It means that you can take clock speeds up to almost any number you would care to deal with without heat sink worries."

Felix is pleased and goes on to explain what they need without further prompting from the Senator. "We need you to build us a wide area network that will be truly secure from prying eyes. Now, as you know, optical links are inherently secure due to the fact that if you intercept the data stream, it is a broken circuit, either through damage or monitoring."

"Well, that is BASICALLY true…"

"Right. The problem is, we have to work closely with a few Federales on this, and we need reporting, secure circuits, and someone who is paranoid enough to sit and think of all the ways we can be compromised in our communications and head them off at the pass. Remember the laptops at Lawrence Livermore?"

"Yes, but I don't see how you can guard against stupidity and treason on the part of someone who is sufficiently determined."

"True, but we don't need it to be perfect and unbreakable, we just need to be able to stay ahead of the pack long enough to complete various phases until we move on to the next phase."

"Ah. 1960's mentality. It's a good idea, but we'll need to add a few twists to it. Like blind alleys."

The senator's aide, Kyle, broke in with "1960's mentality?" at precisely the same time Felix said, "Blind alleys?"

Will chuckles as he answers, "Kyle, in the 1960s, some people worried whether the nuclear devices we had spent so much money on would even work because we were using technicians trained on-site to put together pieces of the devices which were sent somewhere else for final assembly. They were told they were building TV sets, or radios or what have you. It didn't really matter what they were told as long as they didn't know they were building ignition devices for nukes. Blind alleys are my variation on that theme. We set up so many bullshit devices in the pipeline that no one who is watching can figure out which ones work and for what. Maybe 60% of what goes in the machine will actually work."

"Great idea!" Felix is animated. "Damn, fine idea. Mr. Browning, we need to do that." He then considers Will. "You are under an NDA with us?"

The senator breaks in here, "Actually, he isn't."

"Well…" Felix is sputtering here a bit. His former boss has been a real horse's rear end for this kind of stuff, and since his leaving, all the NDAs he had signed were now being used to make him keep his mouth shut. *Here I am, jabbering out of control, and now I don't know what I said that I shouldn't have and…*

"Felix, relax. Will is trustworthy on just his word, as are you."

Felix just looks at Will and says, "Okay. As I was saying, the computers are immune to EMP because the light is immune to EMP, at least within the tolerances needed for the things to continue to work…"

Later that evening, as Will and Chris sit looking out over Birmingham, eating a late dinner and enjoying a slight mutual buzz, he explains the whole thing to her.

"What concerns me is all this carrying on about building an EMP-immune computer and communications system. I am pretty sure it violates the whole MAD theory. If they want communications to survive EMP, it is because they are expecting to need it too, which is, as that gifted thespian, Eddie Murphy, has pointed out, 'some scary shit.'"

"MAD theory? What is EMP anyway?" Chris lets him talk since he is so excited. She isn't sure how big this OEE contract is for Will, but it is big enough to fire him up. Way up.

"MAD means Mutually Assured Destruction. The Soviets, the Chinese, and the West-mostly the US believed that if everyone knew they would both be destroyed in a nuclear exchange, then no one would pull the trigger. EMP is short for Electro-Magnetic Pulse. A nuke puts out these hugely powerful pulses and fries the hell out of everything solid-state electronic for hundreds of miles. Vacuum tubes aren't affected as long as they aren't active when the pulse comes through…I think." He has never worked on tubes, so how could he know? "Point is, if they are looking to build communications immune to this they are expecting to have to need it. Not good, not good at all."

Chris is leaning back in his arms on the deck, enjoying the view and Will's warmth.

"Well, let's just enjoy the positive things for now. You said the…PCs? Would it be a lot faster?"

"Orders of magnitude faster. See…" He goes into a tirade of excitement over these computer things which she knows very little about. Apparently she is nodding in all the right places because he just plows on.

Well, he is excited and he listened to me the other day when I went on and on about Shakespeare in the Park. It was amusing to watch Will struggle to keep up with Chris and another couple, obviously, theatre people, rhapsodizing over the performance of the actress playing Titus's daughter. He certainly enjoyed the play but had no reference points from which to discuss it.

At least until we ran into the actress herself. Then, he certainly knew what to say. It isn't a jealous thought. He was just Will being Will.

Will was enthralled by what was billed as Shakespeare's bloodiest play. He even insisted that they sit in the nobility section. Crystal's thoughts about how the nobility section isn't what it used to be she kept to herself.

Will's eyes never waver from the play. When Titus' daughter is attacked, ravished, and her hands severed from her, he is sitting on the edge of his seat, his face unreadable. After the play is over, they go back behind the stages to see Tritono, the student who invited Will to come out.

His enthusiasm is total. "Tritono! My God, Man, that was great! I had no idea. That was so cool. I thought, yeah, I'll try it…but…I can't wait for the next one!"

Tritono is glad at his new friend's excitement. It pretty much goes that way: people either love theatre or hate it with few fence straddlers. "By the way, this is Laurie, she was Titus' daughter. Laurie. This is Will. He works out with me at the Y from time to time."

"Pleased to meet you, Will. What did you think?"

"I both wanted to be the one ravishing you, and I also wanted to fly to your rescue so that your attackers prayed for hell. It was most disturbing." Realizing his response is a bit intense, wondering what the hell is wrong with him, he turns beet red and tries to compose a way out of looking like an idiot. "What I mean is, you pulled me into the story so completely that the emotions I had seemed real."

Laurie thinks a minute, then smiles at Will saving him the trouble of almost certainly making worse what is a true compliment. "Then I guess I did my job. Thanks."

Will is looking at Chris' face. At least as much as he can see from his vantage point sitting in the chaise lounge on the balcony with his arms around her.

"I just bored you to tears, didn't I? Sometimes, I forget that not everyone likes computers like I do."

"No, not at all. I am interested, I just don't' know some of the lingo is all. Sounds exciting, if you like that field."

"Very." *But you know what? Being here with you and having no worries is much better.* He pulls her closer to him and they sit there, looking at the city for a while.

"Sylvia! You vision of loveliness, you ravishing heartbreaker, you! How you be this fine morning?" Will comes in this morning in very high spirits.

"Okay, I guess." Sylvia is looking at him with raised eyebrows askance, one hand on her hip. She spaces her words far apart as one who is looking hard at a crazy person. "Did we, by any chance, overdo our meds this morning, perhaps some illicit mind-altering substance?"

"Naw, we just landed a big contract from OEE that will double our sales this year. I don't have the final numbers yet, but we'll be spending some time over there, probably the majority of the next month. So get ready!"

And here I thought I could slack off this week. She sighs and begins calling some of their vendors that they move work off onto when more interesting or profitable work comes in. She has to move three or four contracts today and tomorrow, she is sure and wants to go ahead and get a heads up on a few.

She calls after him as he enters his office, "Will, you want me to arrange for dinner to be brought in?"

"Nope, got plans. All work and no play makes Will a very unhappy camper. You have to let go, Sylvia. Enjoy life. I know, let's knock off at four. Whatcha say, little lady? Ah say, whatchu say?" It is a terrible Foghorn Leghorn, and he lets it go at full blast.

"Well, okay. Do I still get paid? If not, I need to stay."

"Sylvia, as many hours as I know you spend thinking of things away from here, I think I'll survive. You still get paid."

"Cool!"

"Salome, can you please go and get Melissa and Circe and bring them to the conference room? Thank you so much." Monica agrees with Melissa on instituting the newer patterns of speech that indicate a partnership between the regent and the staff rather than a ruler/ruled relationship. The authority is never questioned, and the perceived loyalty does indeed seem to increase. Melissa is quite a treasure on these little things that seem to count so much from time to time.

"Of course, My Lady."

While Salome goes to fetch the other two, Monica ruminates on the meetings she had with the NATO Security Council. Of course, the Security Council knew of the People, just as had the secret societies of medieval Europe. It is just good business for the People to be on good terms with the current ruling class of humans.

A source of aggravation for some of the Chinese rulers, though, is that the mongoloid races (not to be confused with someone who has 24 chromosomes rather than the human norm of 23) are, for the most part, unable to convert.

Not a thing we can do about it, either, except to keep that jealousy powder keg wet with technology and a closed mouth policy towards how they handle their internal affairs. Still, I do not see why the population doesn't rise up against their leaders when they butcher millions. Not even the people would put up with such rulers. She then realizes her thoughts aren't accurate as Hitler strode across her mind's eye.

Whatever. I will return to this line of thought later.

Circe enters the conference room ahead of Melissa and bows before the Queen. Melissa does much the same, though it is clear she has an equal place.

"Monica, how are things in New York?" She has been unable to meet with the Security Council as they all had in the past. It is unsettling, and they are all three stronger together, but events are speeding up and they still are not sure from what quarter the threat is coming.

"It is clear that the leaders of the Security Council are as much in the dark as we are. They have no intelligence concerning what has happened and why we are blind to the future. They are also concerned that their own field ops intel has been compromised by whatever or whoever is responsible." She pauses, goes over to the windows, looks out on the plateau's plain where the wildflowers are now in full bloom, and rests her arms on the window seal. It is full daylight, but the polarized glass protects her from the sun.

"You are more worried than usual, Monica. Why? We have faced many challenges over the years, but this one has you…afraid." Melissa finally uses the word out loud and with hesitancy.

Why shouldn't she hesitate? Monica asked herself. *We are immortal and cannot die except through exceptional force or stupidity. Besides, if one doesn't indulge in too much stupidity, exceptional force can be avoided. Wish to Heaven that psychotic Sven could understand that.*

She adds out loud to herself more than to Melissa, "I just wish I knew what was driving him. It isn't wealth or power. Does he have a reason to hate us? Have the Norns ever done any harm or offense to him?"

Then she addresses Melissa directly, "Have we done anything, ever, to your recollection, to Sven?"

"Not to my knowledge, Monica. Crystal and I have had

this conversation, as have Circe and I. We are dealing with unknowns that we can't intuit or see."

"Hellfire and damnation!" Monica exclaims and then slams both of her small hands down on the window seal, crushing the bottom and shattering the bottom third of the glass. She is instantly burned badly on both hands. Her screams as she leaps back bring the guardians running.

"Melissa, we have to find the answer. I can't see, no one can. Whatever is coming is accelerating its plans. I can feel it. I can feel it in my heart. I can almost see it, but it sees me and moves."

Melissa isn't entirely sure what Monica means, nor that Monica is entirely awake now. Her eyes close and her smoking hands, while they will be healed by the evening, are probably making her delirious as her body tries to cope with the pain. The senses in the transformed body, like speed and strength, are enhanced.

"Salome, see to the repairs, please. This is your lady's favorite place for recollection."

"Yes, Melissa. It will be done by the morning."

Melissa escorts the wounded queen to her chambers, where she is administered to. While the guardian sees her wounds and gives her painkillers, Melissa decides that it is time she just went on a hunt.

Returning to the window, not sure why she is driven to do so as Salome hasn't had time to fix it, Melissa finds that Salome manages to surprise her again. The repairs are well underway.

"Guardian, you are dedicated to us. Why?"

"Because your hearts are good and you want only peace. Guardians want only peace. We are built for war, but quiet is what we long for. Perhaps it is because most of our waking time is spent caring for those who sleep during our watch. You get used to it."

"Perhaps."

The Norn watches as the small guardian continues to effect repairs, doing the work herself and clearly thinking about each step as she goes. The window will be much stronger after than before the damage. For no particular reason, Melissa decides not to ask why, possibly because she thinks Salome expects her to ask.

"I am leaving, Guardian. Please let Monica know when she awakens."

"Shall I tell her anything else?"

"No. Tell her nothing other than perhaps randomness may yield results where methodical steps have been blocked."

"Very good, Melissa."

Later that evening, when Monica returned to the area as Melissa knew she would, Salome relayed Melissa's message.

"She didn't say anything else?" Monica to Salome.

"No, Milady."

"Well, what is one more bizarre action? Perhaps it will do some good. We are down to five months now, we have intrigue amongst our 'friends,' the human world has lost its mind, sinking ships even in broad daylight out of paranoia that some rogue vampires are killing crews, arachnid births are up, and Melissa decides to take a break from it all. What next?"

Circe walks into the room. Without preamble, she

addresses Monica.

"Monica…I mean, Lady Monica…" She is white-faced and trembling, totally out of character for the self-possessed pre-pubescent girl that had arrived.

"Circe?"

"I know now why I am blind, I think, as are all the other seers. I know now why we can't see the future." She sits down next to Monica's feet. "There isn't one."

Chapter 12

Loki is Removed

"Salome." Monica walks up to Salome in the west wing, where she is eyeing the edges of the cliffs. On this side, they simply drop off into a black emptiness. The foot of the cliff face is nearly 3,500 feet below, almost straight down, and clouds that had rolled in off the sea obscured it.

"My Lady." Salome bows.

"What are you doing?"

"Simply looking at the edges here. What are our defenses? I see none."

"Melissa is our defense here," responds Monica.

"I don't understand."

"Melissa's glamours are permanent. She can set glamours that last indefinitely."

"Ah. Impressive. They last forever?" Salome has heard talk of such but never actually knew it to be true.

"Forever is a long time. We know she has set some that are still holding and have been for…350 years, I think."

"But glamours can be…"

"Walked through or ignored. In most cases, this is true. Not with Melissa's. Her glamours affect all 5 of the senses, not just sight. Some have walked off cliffs she set, fallen six inches, and suffered the trauma of falling hundreds of feet."

"Interesting."

"Also, there are deadfalls, false trails, traps, etc, both real and made by Melissa. Only those with good intentions can see the true path to the plateau."

"Then I will quit worrying over the edge."

"Unnn…Chris!" says Will, jerking himself awake. He is about to roll out of bed and onto the floor and only catches himself by slinging his left leg violently to the right. Sitting up, covered in a light sweat, he finds himself trying desperately to sort through a confusing mental mosaic of spiders, Chris, flames, and earthquakes. The phone is ringing, interrupting his sorting. He answers with a grunted hello.

"Sir?" It is Sylvia.

"Yes."

"Will you be making it in today? Your eleven o'clock appointment is here."

"What? What time is it?"

"11:15."

"Geez, mentally. I overslept. Ask them if they can give me another 20 minutes, and I will be there. I can't believe I did this. Wait…tell them I have a flu bug and simply didn't wake up. Hell, it may even be true."

"Hang on…"

After a brief 45 seconds, Sylvia is back on the line. "That is fine with them. They also indicated that they would be perfectly okay if you wanted to reschedule for tomorrow, same time, but 20 minutes is okay as well."

"I'll be there. I want this one squared away. Tomorrow, I will be at OEE all day. The old man thinks there is a security breach or a leak, probably just someone talking out of school who needs to be reminded of his NDA. I know who I think it is, but I am going to double-check everything before I hand the old man his ass-chewing suggestions for the week."

"Very good. I'll have the caffeine ready when you get here. Jolt, okay?"

"Nah, I'll have that caffeinated water if we still have any."

"We're out, but I can get the new guy to go get some if you want."

"Skip it. Jolt will be okay for this morning. Let's get him to lay in a supply of that other stuff when he makes a run."

Will's arrival is met with amusement. *It helps to be good and known as a bit eccentric.*

About half an hour later, Will is closing another contract with a new company to maintain and provide systems administrative duties for a small law firm in the financial district. They want services to begin on the 27th of March.

"Very good. We'll plan to see you on the 27th."

After his 11 o'clock appointment leaves, will says, "Sylvia, see that copies of these are sent over with an invoice for the first quarter. It is a law firm, and you know me."

"Get lawyers to pay upfront, I know." A law firm that had some thirty-odd lawyers one day and filed for bankruptcy the next had stiffed them.

"And get me an appointment with Felix for dinner tonight. I need to talk to him concerning our little project."

"I'm on it."

"Where's our 'I like a challenge guy?'"

"He went to pick up some stuff at Office Max." Sylvia chuckles.

"We really need to start ordering through the website. It saves us 5%. Well, since he is already out, call him and get him to pick up some of that caffeinated water stuff."

"Okey dokey."

If there's anything funnier than okey dokey in a Brazilian accent, I don't know what it is. Will smiles to himself and walks into his office to check his email, return calls, and start the rest of the day.

Two days later, a not so friendly meeting takes place at OEE.

"Loki." No friendliness in the tone. The room's temperature drops into the frostiness zone. Felix, LB, and Loki, along with their respective counsels, had agreed to meet. They are seated in the executive conference room of OEE and, to use that old tried but true and in this case nowhere near trite phrase, the shit had hit the fan.

"LB" Not in the least apologetic, Loki had agreed to come to this meeting only with counsel present. He knows he is busted, but that is okay. He had been taken care of by his part-time employers. Or it will be, soon. The delay had been something to sweat over, but now he is in the chute and there is nothing to do but to hang on.

"Loki, you're probably going to jail, one way or the other. I don't much care, but since I am trying to minimize the damage you have caused us, we are willing to try to work a deal. We simply want to know who you have been working for, what information you gave them and when, and you are out the door."

Loki's counsel breaks in, "You have no proof that my client is guilty of any wrong doing…"

"Look, Son," LB cuts Loki's attorney off, "I don't have

time to play with you or play any of your legal games. We are here to propose a settlement that I think we can both live with. Your client is guilty as hell of corporate espionage and theft. The fact that he most likely is working for the NSA simply clouds the issue of how much trouble he is in. We want to settle this and make it go away in order to fight the NSA on a different battleground on a different day. In effect, we want to give them this victory in order to have an accurate assessment of the damage done."

Loki and his attorney, Felix and his, and LB all fall silent. LB's attorney interjects in order to take control and make the offer. "Here is the offer. You give us your contacts, what has been passed, who initiated it, and the dates, phone numbers…everything, right down to any notes in your planner you may have made, and OEE will pay your retirement, beginning immediately. In return, you simply go home, play golf, and leave this field altogether. You are young enough and…greedy enough, I think, for this to be a good offer. You see, we have analyzed your bank records. You did this for what, $350,000 so far?"

"Don't respond to that," says Loki's attorney. He looks PO'd. Apparently, Loki hadn't clued him into his culpability in this matter. He continues on, "If you have made illegal, unauthorized access to my client's…"

"We have and who gives a shit. Sit down and listen to the rest of the offer." LB's temper is high, and his face is flushed.

"Sir, if you please? Let me do my job." LB's attorney is only mildly unhappy with his client's outburst. It is to his advantage as he can now deny knowing about the inappropriate nature of how the information was gathered. LB sits back.

"Point is, we want to know how much more you have been offered. We will match it, begin your retirement, and forego all criminal proceedings against your client."

A pause, then Loki's attorney responds. "I need a few minutes with my client."

"Fine."

LB suggests more than a few minutes. "Why don't you take 20 minutes? I need to make some calls and do a bathroom run. Damn, prostate makes me need ten minutes to piss anyway."

"Put with your usual tact and aplomb," quips Felix. He is sure Loki will bite. He is a greedy little creep and just wants retirement with money anyway. He favors Loki with an eat shit-and-die look and steps out.

"I can't believe the gall…" Loki begins in a not-so-convincing voice.

"Loki, are you guilty of what they are charging? You said you were accused, but these guys are believable, and I think they have proof."

"No, I'm not guilty. Besides, you're my attorney. How dare you…"

"Spare me. I have listened to your tortured explanations of what has transpired here. I'm pretty good at seeing a lie. I am your attorney but you really strike me as arrogant and stupid."

Calls to his house in the middle of the night, dropping in unannounced and yelling at his assistants, have pretty much worn the charm off of a hefty cash retainer.

This guy is a car wreck waiting to happen. You have just been offered a golden goose and for all your professional accomplishments, almost certainly not as great as you imagine, you are too stupid to see it.

"Loki, take the deal. They want to see you in prison, but you are, I think, in the middle of something perilous to your life. If you are passing information to the NSA illegally, you can go to jail. NSA has been known in the past to leave people hanging. Take the deal."

"Well, I am walking away from a lot of…"

"That money is gone. NSA would only pay you if you finished doing what you started. That is done, finished. You are no good to the NSA if you're fired and just in case you haven't been keeping up on current events, here's a news flash for you: You have been fired and you no longer are employed."

"But they can't. I own 2% of the stock, and my work is critical to…"

"Apparently not critical enough for them to not want you retired and not working. Again, how much?"

"Another $750,000.00 once all the documentation on…"

"Don't need to know that. Don't want to know that. Okay, here is what I am going to tell them is acceptable, and my cut is 20%, which is a hell of a lot less than it would take to try this case, and you would probably lose anyway. You'll take…"

LB returns from his duty as Loki and his attorney finish a spitting conversation.

"Sir, they are ready." Kyle, L B's personal assistant, adds, "Loki's attorney looks pissed off."

"Pissed is a normal state of mind for anyone who has to

spend more than 10 minutes with Loki. Well, let's see what the son of bitch has to say."

LB is under no delusions that Loki will agree. He expects to have to destroy the guy in a criminal proceeding. He is happily disappointed.

"Here are my client's terms. First, he will take a full retirement salary beginning immediately. Second, the amount of cash in question as a lump sum is five million dollars. Third, you will execute an agreement I will draw up today that you will not bring any charges, criminal or civil, against my client and it will be executed by noon tomorrow. Lastly," and here Loki's eyes widen with understanding of what his attorney thinks his circumstances are, "you will provide 24-hour executive level protection to my client until such time as we are sure his life is in no danger from… all sources, even if that term of protection turns out to be the rest of his natural life."

A look from LB's attorney to LB, LB nods in the affirmative. They need the information, and it is an acceptable price if nothing more than to just make sure the damn project is still secure and get Loki out of the picture.

"There will be only one change to all this," LB adds. "He will have to surrender his stock in exchange for the lump sum."

"But the stock is worth…" Loki is not getting out without a little pain."

"Done." Loki's attorney doesn't even consult with his client. *This guy really doesn't know how much trouble he is in. I wonder if he'll be alive at Thanksgiving.* "It is a good deal. Take it."

"Very well, I agree." Loki is defeated, but he isn't bad

off. He hasn't really lost that much anyway on the stock, maybe. He doesn't keep up with it that closely anyway. If he had, he might not have said yes to the spook who approached him one day at the car-detailing place.

Chapter 13

Crazyman

There was once a man who had to go away for a while. He had tried to keep from 'falling apart,' as his dear old mum had put it. She is sure he got it from his father's side of the family, as no one from her side would have ever been so crass as to give in to such a weakness as mental illness.

As she explains to her son, whom she loves, despite his complete failure to uphold the British ideal of keeping a stiff upper lip, she stayed with his father purely out of duty. She had willingly married the man after all and given her word. All her friends pitied her but assured her that her reward would be in heaven for staying with such a man. It wasn't easy being a righteous woman, but she carried on, regardless. She just hoped her son appreciated all that she had given up and all that she had done and all that she had sacrificed (without any hope of thanks, it was true!) so that he could grow up in a home and know motherly love, even if he did have to be saddled with an addle-brained father.

I am having a severe mental earthquake. Thoughts are running through my mind that, while I am going to take advantage of them, I am struck by the horror or the joy of whether they may be true. What if the fact that I feel like I am all alone in the world is because I really am?

If anyone had asked James to name a specific point in time when he began the slide into complete withdrawal from reality and an eventual stop in Bryce's mental institution in Tuscaloosa, Alabama, he would have indicated that it was this mental earthquake. James' concept of reality was fairly vague. He is trapped in the loop of what 'real' means. He isn't sure that he, himself, is real as defined in Webster's. He is diagnosed as schizoid, autistic, and any number of other maladies, all of which have failed to respond to drug therapies. Electroshock therapy had actually seemed to work, but that was misleading.

What really happened was that James learned to keep his mouth shut and try getting the hell out of the institution his mum had had him committed to.

'Another shock treatment, doctor? Really? You know, it is quite amusing, but I have had no visions, nightmares, or odd trains of thought that I couldn't reconcile with what I see in front of me since the last treatment. It's a miracle how just doing a reset of the old noggin can help one gain a better perspective on things. What? Why, yes! I certainly do see how it would be upsetting to others! Yes, I do feel terrible about the way I have behaved, and I can…' He is subjected to two more sessions anyway - kind of like kicking an errant child in the ass on the way out and then being released.

Deciding that Britain is just too close to Mum, James had gone through the passport process; when asked if he had any illnesses, he had responded that he was just as loony as a cat done up on catnip, did that count? His interview just laughed and said, "Aren't we all?"

He tells her one morning he is going out for a few beers down at the pub, goes to the airport, shags himself to the States, and walks out into the masses that occupy New York. Some weeks later, he'd called home to speak with his mother only to find out that she had passed away. His sadness is colored by a strange apathy that he feels guilty about. Still, he just can't seem to bring himself to feel anything like what could be called real grief. He is migrating down to Florida for the winter, as the homeless tend to do when he is picked up in Alabama and committed to the care of the state again.

Nobody asked, though; at least no one that qualifies as being 'real' asks. He pretty much keeps his mental gymnastics to himself. He is inside Bryce because he'd had a particularly bad spell of intrusive voices that make him scary enough for a 7-11 clerk to call the law and report a 'lunatic wit' wild eyes scaring the payin' customers off.'

James isn't sure, but letting the doctors inside his head is a really bad idea in his estimation. If he is right about the definition of 'reality,' it is most likely a very, very bad idea. Instead, he spoke to the little voice that sometimes passed the time with him from outside his window at night after everyone was asleep. He isn't sure how he can hear through the thick plastic that is his barrier to the outside world, but he quit trying to place the daily pageant of events that filled his days like some bad acid trip into any kind of order years ago. Just about the time he thinks he has things figured out, they screw the pooch with another round of drugs.

The voice is soothing and sympathetic. He wonders if it is the voice of his mother as a young girl. The idea that it is further evidence of a deteriorating mind enters his thoughts. However, it is dismissed because that bitch's constant haranguing shows up later, telling him that he is crazy and such a disappointment to the family. He responds that isn't it a shame that she had been brought back from death as a captive of his insanity and made to bear mute witness to the continued decline and embarrassment of the family name. As the only male heir to either side of his parent's family, his demise was the fate of both families' names. This had sent his mother's voice, or that part of his mind that wouldn't let her remain at peace, screaming back into his subconscious.

I can only hope that I am not completely crazy and that you are actually awake and trapped inside my head with me, bitch! Yes, there was more than a little blame pointed in her direction. It is probably one of the few things that James and his doctors agreed on.

What if the idea of God being me and being in me is because I am talking to myself? What if there is really only one intelligence in the universe, and we are all simply multiple personalities of that intelligence? I don't really believe that-what would I do if I somehow proved it true? It would mean I have seriously been arguing with myself for years when I could have simply decided that part of me was crazy and ignored it. James was still laughing when the orderly came with his daily dose of Haldol.

The laughing isn't lasting. The Haldol always makes him feel as if part of his mind is covered in big, soft, gauzy pillows and strapped down. It is not totally unpleasant, but it makes him feel as if he is missing important connections in the daily events. When he comes down off the first hour or so's intense buzz, he is depressed. He doesn't know, but what if, during that period, he might have missed the pattern he was always searching for? Sometimes, he would catch glimpses - in a television show, in a musical score he sees in a music video that is also in a horror flick from years past - of some overriding pattern that, once seen, would free his mind, and he will see the universe in all its complete totality.

I feel as if my insides have turned to stone and are trying to wiggle out through my mouth, and I cannot stop crying. He also begins to notice that when he has these fits of depression, it is as if some part of his mind goes over to the side and observes.

Now, please notice, James, as you go through this breakdown, how it acts as a release of pressure. It is actually quite therapeutic, don't you agree?

James does agree, and more than once, he notices that his crying spells seem to leave him tired but washed out, feeling cleaner somehow than before. It is as if something is moving through his spirit, or maybe he is realizing terrible things on a subconscious level that his conscious mind simply can not handle. He'd discussed it with his doctor, a resident from Norway who had come to UAB to become a psychiatrist. James asks why she would come all the way to Alabama to go to school. The good Doctor Inga explains that UAB is one of the top 5 research hospitals in the world. 'Huh. Interesting,' is James' reply.

"You see, doc, I may not be crazy, and you may not actually be sitting there. You and I may be parts or personalities of the single intelligence that is the counterpart to entropy."

"James, you're saying that you and I are a part of some being that is so lonely it makes up or chooses to suffer from multiple personality disorder?"

"Yes!"

"Well, can you not see how this is part of the reason you are in here?"

"How is it so different from the Greeks' idea of the divine fire to which we should all aspire to rejoin and be absorbed by?"

"Well, I can see where this line of thou..."

"I would say prove me wrong, but there really is no way for you to do it. If I am delusional, it is a delusion that is internally consistent and has no handle to crack itself with from the outside. If I am indeed sitting here arguing with you, I know what track you will take and have an argument prepared to keep myself playing this game because I am so alone in the universe. Interesting, isn't it?"

"Yes…though what exactly you are…"

"What I am referring to is the fact that I am mentally ill. The question is, am I ill because I am right or because I am wrong?"

After the doctor leaves, James sits quietly, laughing at himself, the doctor, and the world. He figures the doctor will up his medication and most likely engage in a little medication herself after dealing with him. Half of what he tells them is made-up material designed to throw their diagnosis off the mark.

Tonight they'd given him Darvocet for his headache that he feels coming on. Dr. Inga agrees to give him a strong enough dose to really work up a good buzz. She is pretty cool that way.

Guess she figures a good buzz once in a while does me good. I agree.

Looking out at the greenery surrounding Bryce, he begins fooling with some of the exercises he'd designed under the assumption he is correct and begins to concentrate on a fellow lounging up against a pole. Sure enough, the guy turns around and looks directly at his window.

Crazy? Maybe so, maybe no.

Will's head knows that everything is okay, but his body is jonesing in the worst way to get well. He decides to ride out his headaches for a while and see if the rebound headaches will pass.

They WILL pass if I can just hold on long enough. It's their kicking the hell out of me as they go by that hurts.

He laughs at himself at this and then grabs his pillows

and scrunches himself around them in a fetal position as another spasm wracks him, seeming to emanate from his mid spine and radiate outward along his nerve beds. He is pretty sure he can now trace all the major nerve beds in the human body, even without having studied anatomy.

He and Chris had agreed not to see each other. Well, actually, Chris had suggested and then insisted, and what could he do? He had begged one woman to stay in his life and lived through it. No way was he going to go through that again. 'Okay, no biggie,' had been his response. There is hurt in her eyes, he is pretty sure but then why had she done it?

Again, the tremors have him rolling up in his bed covers until he is down at the foot of the bed with his head hanging off. He is looking at the small dresser that faces the footing from an upside down position. Seventy-two hours is what the doc says I should plan on…24 to go. He has been here for two days, taking off Thursday and figuring he will be worthless all day Friday.

More like a paraplegic, still, it is my fault.

"Shit!" The really crazy part of this thing is his emotions. He feels like the world is going to end, even though everything is okay. If it weren't for something called cognitive-emotive therapy, he'd probably be running through the hallways now.

Maybe if I called Chris, she would come over. We could sit and watch the neighbors on their evening walks and...

Will is suddenly wrapped up in his spine again, only this time with stomach cramps that seem bent on displaying his liver to the world.

...along with a delightful assortment of other essential organs, I'm sure...

Will manages to get up and over to the bathroom room before losing control of his bowels and bladder and vomiting at the same time. Sliding into the side of the bathtub, his last thought before unconsciousness…

…Ms. Lopez is NOT going to like this…

Fuzzy images intrude onto his brain.

"Go away. Will doesn't feel like participating today. It's his day off."

"Will." Chris' voice is calling him.

"You aren't here. You went away, remember?"

"Yes, asshole, I remember. What were you trying to do, kill yourself?"

It isn't Chris's voice. It is his ex's voice. *Oh, this just keeps getting better and better.*

"Hi, how are you? How's the cat? How's the new sap?"

"Fine, dead, and it didn't work out. They found you covered in your own puke and shit. What? You party overtime again, or were you trying to kill yourself? You know I really don't have time for…"

Will allows her drone on for a few minutes, wondering, not for the first time if perhaps there aren't really aliens amongst us.

"If you must know, I was trying to go for days without my meds for migraines. It got ugly, but I was determined to just grit it out through the rebound headaches, no matter how bad they got. They got real bad."

"Oh, and you thought you could get through it alone? Why didn't you tell your doctor or me? Someone should have been with you. God, you are SO hard-headed!"

"Yeah, well. I didn't buy the farm, so you can go back to your life now." At this, he turns toward the window. He expects she will be gone when he turns back around, but he is wrong. She is still there.

"What do you want?" He is curious. The sight of her stirs nothing in him but a ghost of the anger he felt in the past, nothing more.

"I was worried about you. They called me because there was no one else to call, and you've no family here in town…"

"I have Aunt Beth. Besides, I'm okay now. Thanks for stopping by."

He has to do it this way; he just has to. No way is she going to get next to him again. Will doesn't know why she is here, but if she hadn't come to see him before when he had his breakdown, right after the breakup, she wouldn't come now, at least not without a good reason. I can do without knowing why, too, thank you very much.

She stands, starts to say something, and then simply leaves. He told himself for the rest of his life that it had been for the best. As it turns out, it was.

"Sylvia."

"Yes, Will?"

"Any calls?"

"Everything is handled, Will." Then she adds, "Everyone says to enjoy yourself on your little impromptu tryst with Chris." Her voice is sad but caring, and he knows that it isn't just a job for her. He is like family to her and she is covering for him to save him face.

"OEE?"

"OEE is fine. They discovered who was funneling info out. It was a…" he can hear her fumbling with papers and switching over to the keyboard, "…wait, it's in my email." More noises of logging in. Finally, "Yes, here it is. A Dr. Loki."

Loki, Norse god of mischief. Fitting. "What actions are they planning to take?"

"None; currently, Loki claims he was working under the direction of NSA and has claimed that OEE is conducting dangerous, illegal research into human genetics."

"This is all BS. OEE is doing some strange things, but genetics is as far from the truth as you can get."

"So, what were they working on?"

"I'll tell you when I get out. They are releasing me this afternoon. You know, I probably should have waited to try to kick this thing…" Will is beginning to feel tired again.

"Hindsight and all that, I know. Still…"

"Un-huh."

"It was good to try. I know you have been struggling with this for…"

Later that afternoon, after his consult with his doctor, Will sees he is in for more than just a little bit of inconvenience. He gets on the phone with Sylvia because he doesn't know how soon he will be cut off from the outside world.

"Let's talk when I get there, okay? Walls have ears, and so do phone lines. My paranoia meter is off the scale, and not just because I have been partying. Some of these orderlies look a little too capable of things other than cleaning bedpans. I think it is safe enough to call Mr.

Browning, Felix, and Kyle and fill them in on a few things. There is a file on a disk labeled 'Wonderland' under my desk. It is taped to the inside of the machine cover of my desktop. You'll need to pop the top and shoot the file to Felix. While it is sending, get them all on conference now and tell them I think everything is open to the spooks. Do it now, no hesitation; we may not get another chance."

"Done. Bye." She doesn't hesitate. She is up and through his outer office door, hitting the releases on his desktop even as she is in the act of sitting down. As she slides the disk into the bay with her left hand, her right is calling up Eudora and attaching 'wonderland' to a message to Felix Dorcai. She thinks a minute, and then decides to use their offshore email accounts that use a much higher encryption bit length. She creates LB an account, writes down his password, and emails the information to LB's new account. She will get his username and password to him by hand delivery.

While uploading the file, she waits for the video conferencing server to find the three gentlemen over at OEE. They had to wait a moment while Kyle retrieved L.B. from a meeting.

"Yes, this is Browning." His face swims into view on the video conference call on her screen. She is faced by a spectrum of men from ancient, middle-aged, and early twenties. "Your Will's assistant, no?"

"Yes. No time for pleasantries. Will believes that all aspects of the projects have been compromised. I am emailing a file called 'wonderland,' to you now, Mr. Dorcai. I have also created all emails in a secure offshore email server and will deliver the usernames and passwords within the hour. Will has been hospitalized against his will at UAB. He thinks they may release him this afternoon but is unsure.

He seemed to hope you would have some suggestions."

As it turns out, they are unable to effect Will's release until after he is transported to Bryce Hospital in Tuscaloosa. He endures sitting in a common room, in a hospital gown with his boxers hanging in the wind, with a number of other "patients."

Imagine a place, if you will... Rod's Serling's voiceover came into his mind, really creeping him out. Then, *Thanks, Mom, for nagging me to always have clean underwear, 'cause you never know when you'll be in a mental institution with your skivvies blowing in the wind.* Will snickers to himself, and notices a nurse watching him with tiny, beady little rat eyes or maybe hawk eyes. *She looks ready to pounce if I do something. What does she expect me to do?* He decides that laughing out loud at this situation, a sign of healthy mental strength in the world on a normal day, is a very bad idea right now. *Just relax, OEE is on the way.*

Sylvia picks him up the next day. Will can't help himself and curses the administrator on his way out. "You will be hearing from my attorney, you son of bitch."

"Our actions were entirely within the law."

"That's as may be. So will mine be. Asshole." With a final burlesque three-finger salute, the second in 5 minutes, Will leaves Bryce. *I need to get some new material for these special occasions.*

As they travel up I-59 towards Birmingham, Sylvia wants to know if he wants to stop and grab a bite of real food. "Sure, as long as it is outside of Tuscaloosa County and a good ways towards Birmingham. They were about to drug me! My god, I could have been a bumbling vegetable for months. How can they do this to someone?"

"Well, it looks as if a doctor interviewed your ex. She signed the papers on you…"

"Fucking BITCH! I told her what I was…"

"…after your maid called her when she found you in the bathroom passed out. The doctor who sent you there has left town on business. We can't seem to locate him. Mr. Browning released you because he knows the probate judge for Jefferson County and got him to rescind his ruling. He told the judge you were trying to stop on your own, got sick, and passed out. The blood workup supported the idea, so the judge agreed. What did happen?"

"Almost exactly that. You know, I'm not hungry. Let's just press on to Birmingham so I can change and go see Browning. Heaven knows what kind of cluster fuck this is going to be."

After a few miles of silence, Sylvia asks, "What was it like in there?"

"Bryce? Like any hospital, except there were locks on the doors. I am convinced some of the orderlies were there for the first time…they stayed close to me and seemed not to know where things were. They weren't very happy when you and Browning's goon squad showed up to pick me up. I guess they were more afraid of too much attention than we were of getting away."

"Before I get any deeper into this thing, can you tell me more about what is happening with you and OEE?" Sylvia looks concerned.

"Not yet, but soon, I am sure, soon." Will stares out the window, thinking back to Sylvia's arrival to pick him up.

She walks in, heading up a column of OEE security that looks like the front line of an NFL football team, only instead of being suited up for a ball game, they are suited up in Armani suits with bulges under their arms where no bulges should be.

"We're here to pick up Will..." Sylvia begins explaining to the nurse on the desk when Will hears her voice and walks towards the nurse's station. An orderly tries to intercept, but despite his weakened condition, Will manages to skirt around the corner before the orderly gets to him. He hugs Sylvia while her entourage immediately surrounds them.

The nurse sputters and is clearly unhinged over this invasion. "You can't all be here! Only two..."

"Fine, I am releasing myself." Will is taking charge now, and he IS leaving. "Tiny, reach over and hit the release." One of his escorts reaches through and hits the button on the desk, pissing off in the extreme and scaring the nurse, while another opens the door to the exterior. As Will walks towards freedom under the glaring eyes of two maybe-not-orderlies, he flicks a three-finger salute. Sylvia follows, and three of the OEE security guys bring up the rear.

The nurse is still yelling something about release forms. Will figures he will have his attorney sit in for him on that.

As they ate the miles towards Birmingham, Will continued, "You know the worst part of being there, even for a few days?"

"Not a clue."

"There was this guy who seemed to know me."

"Yeah, he kept saying, 'I know you, I know you. You're the one who sees. You're the one who sees. Tell them I'm not crazy.' Over and over like some mantra."

"Maybe he thought you were someone else."

Perhaps, only why did he keep saying she left because she was scared that I would open the world to her mind and she would have to see who she was and all that other crap? Have I met him somewhere?

Whatever. "I'm going to close my eyes. I'm glad you guys came, you and the goon squad."

"Aren't they just? I really didn't expect six when Mr. Browning said he was sending a security detail with me. I think if they had tried to stop you from leaving, those boys would have cut a hole in the wall."

"They may have had to if the two orderlies had had more backup. I don't think they were expecting an armed troop."

"Armed?"

"Armed, those bulges under the big guys coats aren't their lunch pails, you know."

Sylvia is silent and after a bit, Will is asleep.

Chapter 14

Journal, From the Journal of Will

October 31, 2000

I must say for one of illegitimate birth, I sometimes lead an interesting life. My new girlfriend, oh dear Lord, she is such a hot filly, by anyone's standards, that she makes me wonder if I shouldn't have my heart checked. She walked about the apartment all day (she claimed), nude, and left me a note with a Polaroid. 'Think about me until I get back tonight,' an inscription on the back. *Yes, Ma'am, will do.*

This new contract with OEE has really been a Godsend. I have achieved my goal; I am out from under all my past debts and have cleared every debtor listed in my bankruptcy. I am in the unbelievable position of only working 40 hours a week or less when I choose, and I have a sweetie who makes me forget about it all when I am with her.

Still, it is troubling to me. She seems to think it would be a good idea for me to find my bio dad. In fact, she seemed just a little insistent. Well, why SHOULD I be able to understand what goes through her mind? She is a woman and my track record there is not so good. Even Mom got a bit flaky when I started asking about my father. Actually, sperm donor, not father, would be more accurate. He had a wife, and my mom was a young woman in love. A whisper from an aunt has it that I actually have two sisters and that my paternal grandmother actually blamed my mother for it all, calling her a home wrecker. Well, of course, my mom is a home wrecker! After all, according to my ex-father-in-law, if a woman puts it in front of a man, he can't help himself. It is just the way men are built. At least that is what he said after Terri came home for 3 weeks after finding out that her husband had been having an affair for 4 ½ years with his secretary, with his mother's approval. God, what a red-neck family they turned out to be.

Well, hell, if you stop and think about it, it's a good thing that 'real men' don't have to worry too awfully much with that whole 'frontal lobe' thing. Damn, things can get in the way of what men are about if you aren't careful.

This father thing bothers me. I think it would hurt my adopted father too much if I started looking for bio dad, hereafter referred to as BD. It is also weird how much Crystal is insisting. Just more proof that I have been correct in my lifelong conviction that everyone is psycho; it's just a matter of where the seams in the mind lie that determines whether or not a person can be a productive member of society.

Crystal's family is a mystery as well. She says that all her close family is overseas, up in the fjord countries like Finland and Norway. You know, she has absolutely NO accent. With that blonde hair and being from there, you'd think she had an accent. Maybe I can get her to fake one sometime; it might be fun. I thought the night I met her that she had said she had family over in the Pelham area, but I must have been mistaken. No biggie. I am lucky I can keep up with the time of day. Well, not now. Everything has calmed down a lot.

OEE. What a blast. I go to work when I get ready to do so. I leave when I get ready to do so. I am what is called an SSIR, or Senior Scientist In Residence. What this means is I am paid to think up shit, next-generation stuff. I have a laboratory that is larger than all the square footage of my old offices in the old building. Our funding comes right off the top, and we are not required to produce anything but pure science. Eight of the programs are required reading for all of us. Felix's project is off-limits to everyone. He says if you know about it, you have to be part of it. Like I say, everyone's a psycho.

My office and Sylvia's office freaked when I told her she would have an office and an assistant herself-are quite comfortable and palatial. Felix told me they had 9 SSIRs on staff and never had a loser. Then he had to be a smart ass and say so-don't-be-the-first-but-hey-no- pressure. He said he was kidding. Maybe he was.

My new house is a blast. Never in a million years did I, as a kid, think I would be living in such a place. Mom and Dad freaked completely when they came for a week. Mom asked me three times how I could afford such a mortgage with my troubled credit from a few years ago before it sank in that I don't have a mortgage. She still doesn't get it. Her final comment was that since it was paid for, I could probably use it to borrow money when I got into trouble. Not IF, but WHEN. I stood there, understanding the urge to beat my head against the wall.

Sylvia is as nervous as a long-tailed cat in a room full of rocking chairs. She point blank asked me how secure her job was because her workload had been so greatly reduced. Hell, I guess I will find her a project to occupy herself with. I admire the work ethic but don't know how to explain that part of this gig is a reward for her staying when I couldn't afford to pay her. She really can't seem to understand, either, that she can't be replaced. How the hell am I supposed to train someone else to know what my habits and eccentricities are? The woman balances my chequebooks, pays my bills, makes sure I am where I need to be on time, handles my cleaning, makes my travel arrangements and basically keeps me on track. Maybe she can help me with some of those community projects I have been doing, and we can get serious about a few. Yeah, that sounds about right. She'd be good at it, too.

Anyway, all is right with the world. I have no complaints.

Not that I didn't have some serious complaints some weeks ago. I began to get nervous because my headaches had really escalated again. Darvocet is wonderful stuff, but addictive, physically and mentally. It was clear that I was beginning to take too much, so I decided to just grit my teeth through the weekend. I was stupid to try to do it alone, I know, but damn it, you can't just ask people for help on some things. What was I going to say? Ima druggie, watch me while I puke? I don't think so. Besides, if I were absolutely addicted, I couldn't have forced myself to sit through what I did with a full bottle of that shit in the house. It's gone now, believe it.

It didn't go well. I wound up in a mental hospital courtesy of my ex, I think. It is a bit hazy and even the administrative office hasn't been forthcoming with many details of exactly how I got there. Somebody's ass will pay. What I can't figure out is how I wound up there so quickly. Even my attorney is mystified as to how they were able to get a judge to sit and have a committal hearing on a Saturday evening. Summation? The facts don't add up.

She came to visit me. She seemed concerned. If so, why did she have me put there? She hates that place and has said so. I asked her, but she wouldn't talk to me. She gets weirder and weirder every time I see her.

Another really off-the-wall thing: Who were the goons who showed up with Sylvia? OEE didn't know who they were, and I could have almost sworn they were with us when we pulled into the driveway. Now, neither LB nor Felix knows who they are. Everyone who has had anything to do with the project at OEE has denied knowing who they were. LB looked a bit puzzled but not overly so. He assured me he would look into it. Yesterday, he called me in and told me point blank that no one, even among HIS contacts, has any knowledge of who they were. I don't think the old man likes it much when he can't find out stuff.

Still, he has been away from there for some years. Perhaps he is just falling out of touch was my thought. Felix killed that idea. Apparently, the old man is pissed that he isn't getting his questions answered. According to Felix, LB is revered in the intelligence community. If it's a case of they can't tell him, they tell him so. This 'no one knows what you're talking about' routine has got LB doubting his sphere of influence's reach. At least, that's what Will, yours truly, is pulling out of the conversations with Felix. I guess we'll see.

Chapter 15

The Test

"Senator, the world really is going to hell in a handbasket."

"I know, Kyle."

"This is a question between me and you. I realize what we must say to the press and why. But tell me how things really are. I need to know because I need to make plans to care for me and mine."

"They are about as bad as they can get. Trade has all but stopped completely between the EC and the US, all our forces have been withdrawn to guard our borders, and Congress is reacting to this like a child pitching a tantrum. Some knew about the People, and others didn't, and they wanted to know why. A full third want to unleash nuclear hell on the People, in spite of the fact that with a few exceptions that have been dealt with, they never venture into human territory. What they want to do is analogous to declaring war on China because a few criminals came into the US and committed a few murders. I'm not discounting the crimes, but we wouldn't go to war over it, normally."

"Why weren't we told? Seems that something this monumental needs to be known…and prepared for."

"We are prepared as to why, those of us who knew, we all decided…unanimously, not to inform the world. Actually, it is more accurate to say that centuries ago, this decision was made, and everyone who comes into this knowledge in an official capacity makes the decision not to reveal it. Look at the congress now; practically bursting at the seams to run and raise hell, thinking it will make them the next big oompah of the whatever. What it will do is cause a bloodbath. If I were still in the Senate I would move for marshal law, now."

"Isn't that a bit drastic?"

"Sure. Marshal Law is, by definition, a drastic measure for dreadful times. But consider: How long do you think it will be before the new age kids, who dress all in black and sport the 'vamp' look, will start being hung from street posts as sympathizers? Make no mistake, these are VERY dangerous times."

"What are we doing to prepare? I must admit I am uncertain as to how to prepare OEE for what may arise from these things. Our stock is giving me whiplash; we can't get the product to the EC, and our folks over there are cut off from returning by our own government...I just don't know what to do."

"Well, luckily for you, your job is to serve as my assistant and not make decisions. I don't say this unkindly, and I appreciate your candor. It saves me the time of acting like I am considering your thoughts." *Unlike Loki, I really do not see how he can be so smart about resolving the mysteries of the physical world but be so clueless about his own self-interests or that of the people around him. He makes my head hurt.*

"Sir?"

"What we have to do," LB goes on, choosing not to answer him directly, "is to treat this situation as we would any other war scare. We also want to put down as misdirection any news of what is actually happening. We need a plausible reason for all these activities."

"What? We act as if we don't believe the reports about

the People. That the Administration is lying?"

The Senator begins laughing. *It is a damn fine idea; put the dumb shits in Congress on the defensive.*

"No, that wasn't what I had in mind, but I want to take some time to consider it. It is a good idea. We can probably do a takeoff on something like the H.G. Wells scare…yes, it might just work. Let's get our media people in here for some groundwork. We can probably lay it off on the administration's continuing efforts to misdirect people's attentions from that idiot's sexual escapades, too."

The Senator is now smiling to himself as he adds, "The man couldn't keep his britches up in a scissors factory."

Associated Press: 15 August 2000

In an unusual move for an avowed non-partisan electronics icon, famous for its comeback from the brink of bankruptcy and its gift for backing underdogs successfully, Outer Edge Electronics, headed by the former Senator LB Browning, attacked the Administration's measures as posturing bordering on insanity. Addressing the issue of motivation on the President's part, Mr. Browning elaborated at length, "This man's willingness to sacrifice lives to get the attention off of him is well known. Look at the aspirin factory he bombed in the Kosovo area when we had intelligence that made it clear it wasn't a munitions plant. Look at how he allowed a young woman to absorb all the impact of an affair. He even allowed a Buddhist nun to go to jail for activities that directly benefited him personally. Need I say more? I just shudder to think what activity he is trying to mask with this new craziness. I can only guess that it must be pretty bad to go to these lengths. I want to encourage Congress to look hard at the idea of hearings on whether or not this president is fit to continue to act as the leader of this country. Vampires, indeed, this is lunacy."

The White House Press Secretary indicates that they have no response at this time but that one would be forthcoming at Thursday's press conference, where the President will be presenting an update on what has come to be called "The People Question."

A one-sided conversation, heard in the office of the Chairman of the Board of OEE:

"Yes, Will, I am sure we have been compromised, both from internal sources and external sources. Our IP traces are all ending up in D.C. and in Silicon Valley."

There is a pause as the Senator listens, and then he responds, "No, not at all! I have my best people on this, and they are not slackers themselves; they, in fact, cannot come up with a scenario that doesn't involve someone giving them critical access…"

Another pause and a severe furrowing of the brow, "Yes, they assure me that all VPN access to the network have been revoked and remain revoked. What? No, I didn't think to ask that specifically. I would have thought that…" Opening a drawer and almost dropping the phone, he says, "Well, hell, Will, you are the security freak. Just come on over and let's all go through this together. I don't feel like running message football. Besides, you will be better able to communicate directly. Can you be here today…though tomorrow is better for me." LB listens and then says, "Good enough, 10 AM."

After hanging up, Will leaves his office and says, "Sylvia, I need to punt my meetings tomorrow morning."

"Troubles?" She had expressed doubts about the profitability of one contract sucking up so much of the company's time and resources, thinking it was perhaps a better idea to spread out the income from many smaller companies so that if one fails, they aren't hit so hard. Will agrees with her but moves ahead nonetheless. He likes her thinking but explains that OEE will finance going after those smaller clients.

"Yes, but not of our making or oversight. It looks as if the old man may have pissed off someone big enough to give even me nightmares. Security is like access; to some degree, you are relying on the percentages to work in your favor. Otherwise you couldn't have a network at all connected to the outside world. I think they have some spooks looking into their activities and scoping their networks.

"Spooks?"

"Yes, government agents. I think his attack on marshal law and some of the other Bizarro World festivities have made the government sensitive enough to act."

"Well, do we really want them looking at us?"

"They already are, Sylvia. By their definitions, we are a threat. We are a computer security firm that relies on in-house solutions and does custom encryption algorithms. They try to get in every day."

"They get into our network…and look at everything?"

"They try. They generally get as far as the firewalls, and then I do a reverse DNS lookup, log back into their IP, and send them a 'screw you, get out' message. I am considering setting up reverse IP mail bombing runs…of course, I would need to set the servers up overseas…humph; this will take a bit of planning once I get through OEE's security crisis. Browning might have some insight into the response we can expect.

"I am sorry, Chris. Will is over at OEE today and will most likely not be available until late. Can I give him your number?"

"He has it; just tell him to call if he can't make it tonight."

"I will do it right now," Sylvia says as she begins opening up her email client. "Take care."

Sylvia's email client begins acting kludgy until it won't respond at all. She swears under her breath even though there is no one there to hear her. *Well, it is 5 'til. I will stick a note to his monitor and fix this tomorrow.* Sylvia, in one of her rare lapses, doesn't consider that Will is most likely going to check his email and voicemail remotely from OEE. He didn't get the message.

"Definitely not your run-of-the-mill hacker break-in. See, you can see where they have modified the logs, remotely by hand editing to remove the reverse IP traces. This is why I have these logs archived off site. Just let me retrieve them, and we'll begin doing an analysis. Wait, let me check my messages first; we may need to break for dinner…"

Will is checking to see if Chris has called about dinner. He has no email or phone messages from her, though there are plenty of others, mostly trash. *Well, okay, I guess she got hung up. I would have thought she would've called, though.* "We're a go, guys. Let's start doing the byte head boogie."

He didn't call. Crystal begins to worry to the point she decides to do a flyby check on him. Will is not only someone she cares about. She is responsible for his safety. Until they determine his status, they can't change him. Things are really confusing now.

She arrives at his offices, hovering right outside his suite's windows. There are no lights on or any visible activity.

Offices are empty, and his car is gone. It would be nice if I knew how to get in touch with Sylvia. She is sure that Will might consider this behavior obsessive, but then again, he is only subliminally aware of his own existence sometimes.

She decides to do a quick walk-through of the office. She isn't afraid of being seen or caught on camera.

After a quick walk through to be certain that no one is still working late, Crystal begins to look through his messages. She knows this is probably frowned upon by your better class but can't help it. She is worried. Not returning her calls isn't like him.

She finds a message indicating that Will thought he would be at OEE all day as the situation looks grim.

OEE? He left at 8 this morning. With a lot more rambling around, Crystal sees that Sylvia had later blocked out Will's whole day for the electronics giant, moving several appointments, several with notes indicating serious displeasure on the part of the move.

Well, Will hasn't called me nor, she looked down and checked her beeper, a device she is absolutely in love with, *paged me.*

She is beginning to worry a lot now. Will has hinted at how much trouble it is to deal with the government, and he makes his living, making people's info safe, not just from the criminal element. His networks are all but bulletproof, even from government snoops whom he dearly despises. 'The technical term,' he once explained with an intensity that might have bothered some folks, 'is jack-booted Nazi.' He isn't popular in the intelligence community, even though he is one of their most highly paid and respected consultants.

I am going to check at OEE. Besides, I am curious about their company if anyone asks. She then thinks about how to explain why she is snooping around his biggest client if she gets caught or if something goes wrong. She couldn't come up with a good line and decided to go anyway. *I just won't get caught, and I don't have any other ideas.*

Glamour time. Crystal disappears into the background and begins to walk the admin offices, straining her senses up to full alert. The complex is covered in a din of noise, normal for a manufacturing outfit. All her efforts did was make her head hurt. *I will just begin an expanding circle and see where it leads me.*

She winds up some forty-five minutes later in front of a legend on the wall. IS Department…data processing… She guesses and gets lucky and decides to head for security instead. *They will have cameras monitoring the place, and it will save me time. At least it will let me decide what looks interesting.* She decides that since he hasn't called or paged, and she can't get a lead from the intuition that sometimes came on strong as to what to do next, she will simply scope this place out. It felt right but not intuitive. *Whatever, I am overthinking myself these days.* She smirks slightly. *You are corrupting me, Will.*

"Will, you want pizza or Chinese or what?" The question comes from Felix, the CTO of OEE. It isn't necessary for him to be there. However, like most folks with a globular intellect, the chance to learn something new and nifty just can't be passed up, especially when that something is how to safeguard his research department's info and ideas.

"I dunno, can we get something from the Chinese place

with chicken wings? It is the closest thing to fried chicken, which, for some reason, I've been craving the last few days."

"We can do better than that if you don't mind Hardee's. It's closer, and they have fried chicken."

"Well, whatever you guys want to do is fine. I'm not picky."

"Hardee's it is, then." Felix is in the mood for a mushroom and Swiss burger. He buzzed the girl, who agreed to work late in case they needed any help. "We decided to do the cholesterol thing. There is a fifty in my top drawer. Take it and run to Hardee's and pick up…"

Crystal is in the corner of the security offices, using a truly weak glamour.

I probably don't even need to use one. She is amused to find that the guard is so truly exhausted that he doesn't notice her in any case. He was in front of the monitors in his chair, head canted back and mouth open, snoring to wake the dead. She thinks about goosing him, vamping out, and then disappearing to leave him with the thought he'd just had a bad dream. Her better judgment wins out. *He's too old.* Then she spots Will in conference with a bunch of guys in a room filled with what could only be the big mainframes he told her about. *South tower?*

The South Tower turns out to be the next building over, even though it took her three false starts to locate it. Apparently, someone thought it was cute to have a South tower, South building and South complex. She is becoming somewhat irritated about this little foray she had started. She looks down at her pager and thinks, *Still hasn't paged me.* Then she says to herself, somewhat wryly, *Aren't we becoming somewhat possessive of his time? Then, No, I am doing what I was sent here to do. Guard and watch over Will.*

That bit of rationalization out of the way, she walks up the stairwell so as not to mark her approach with the sounds of the elevator.

"She did what?" Felix and Will are in a spirited conversation about women, exes, and all things female. Will is telling Felix his war story about his marriage, deciding he is getting tired of telling it. He is finally healing enough that it doesn't seem worth the trouble. *This is a good thing. Besides, I have enough work to do for twenty years. Why keep beating it to death? I did what I could, and shit, move on.*

"See, that is why I never got married." Felix is expounding on his bachelorhood by choice, as he calls it. "My money is mine, my house is mine, and when I go home, there is never a fuss."

"Yeah…I suppose. But don't you want folks around you on the holidays, and don't you want a family someday?" Will is talking around a mouth full of chicken. *Man, this is good. I won't wait so long next time.*

"I have thought about it, but I never seem to be in the right place at the right time, I guess. Besides, I am no lady killer. The kinds of women I like don't like me. It is a bitch, but it's true. Besides, doing what I do, I don't have time to see to put into a relationship."

"I suppose. Still…"

"What? Look at you, divorced only 2 years and already head over heels in love with some girl you barely know."

"Yeah, but she's…"

"What? She's beautiful? She's different? Will, are you saying or feeling anything for this girl that you didn't feel for your ex-wife when you first met and got all crazy for each other?"

"No, I guess not, but…"

"Then give it some time. Build your business back to where it is huge and not just successful. Let your mind reintegrate itself. They say getting divorced is at least as stressful as burying your spouse. At least with death, you have fond memories and can have the illusion that they are waiting for you on the other side. With a divorce, you have to sit and watch your sweetie turn into a goddamn spider and try to bite your head off."

"Thanks for the imagery…" Will is laughing now because it was a pretty good analogy. *Now, every time I see her, I will see her in some black-and-white take-off of The Fly. Only instead of seeing a human head on a fly trying to get away from a spider, I'll see myself running from a spider with that bitch's head screaming at me for being such a loser, a failure…*

"Will?"

Focusing in on Felix, Will responds, "What…?"

"I dunno, you went somewhere there for a minute."

"Yeah, I did, didn't I? Thought I was through with it, too."

"Huh?"

"I said, 'Let's get it on and get through with it, too.' By the way, where DID that word picture come from?"

"Word picture?"

"You know, what you said about turning into a spider and biting my head off…"

"Oh. My brother, Ned, read some story or some such

and quoted it to me. Something like there is nothing better than a divorce with custody issues for turning people into insects."

"Ah. But a spider isn't…"

"Spare me the technicalities of zoology. A spider is an arachnid, not an insect. That was my personal embellishment."

As they finish up their late dinner, the conversation wanders back to the reason they are all here, which is the security issue. Upon returning to the lab, Will comments after a half hour or so, "I'm looking at these logs that show signs of tampering, Felix. They have been tampered with during the last week."

"So? We knew they were possibly being tampered with from the memo you sent over. What I need to know is, can you stop it?"

"That's not the point, Felix. They have been tampered with during the last seven days. We pulled the plug on dial-up and IP access on the 14th, which would have been…12 days ago."

"This means that whoever did the tampering had to do it from a console, damn it."

He is taking this well, Will thinks to himself. He revises his opinion when he sees how badly Felix's hands are shaking.

"Will, you'll have to excuse me for a few minutes. I need to call the old man."

Closing the door, Will hears the tale end of Felix's comment, "…and wake him up. Now."

Will, Kyle, and the other techs retire to the break room.

Felix indicates that he will page them after his conference call and they can decide whether to call it a night or continue on. "Besides, Will, if they are doing this from the inside, it is no longer your issue, but a physical security issue for us to resolve."

It turns out that the Senator, aka 'the old man,' agrees with Felix's position that showing signs of tampering internally removes it from Will's domain of responsibility. Felix and his assistant stay long enough to draft a memo to various department heads, insert a reminder into Browning's calendar, and lock up.

Will heads home, and when he hits the I-20/I-59 and I-65 intersection, locally called 'malfunction junction,' he remembers that he'd had tentative plans with Chris for this evening. *Well, they were tentative, and it was probably too late to call. I'll just hook up with her tomorrow.* He turns off onto Green Springs towards his apartment.

Crystal is watching as he turns up the hill.

I guess he just forgot. OEE is his major client. No biggie. She is bothered about Felix's advice to him, though. Not because she thinks he is wrong but because she fears he might be right. *Still, what does it matter anyway? I can't figure out what to do and what is right because none of it may matter once we get past the deadline because there might not be anything here to worry about. Shouldn't I just be selfish and grab what happiness I can now because, now more so than ever, there is no guarantee for tomorrow?*

Crystal finally decides that perhaps Will doesn't really know his own heart. What to do? It is clear he is a passionate man who needs a woman in his life if only to cool his passions, but does he want her, or is she just a place marker?

I am well over two thousand years old, and here I am,

worrying like he was my first love. I'll outlive him, most likely, and will feel this way again some other time. Feeling like her head is screwed on straight for the first time in a while, she returns to her apartment in the border area between Pelham and Hoover.

"Let's hear it." Browning is addressing Felix with no preamble. The idea that someone internal is giving someone outside internal information is not entirely unanticipated, but the clearances required for the information and the machines that seem to have been compromised were supposedly cleared with only twenty people in the company. Project Mind's I is a company black bag operation so closely held that those involved even agree not to discuss it with their spouses and maintain intelligence discipline even if it means sitting in a prison cell for and extended period. The buildings and assets used don't even show up on the company books. They are instead held by a Liechtenstein holding company, New South Financial Services, supposedly looking to set up and operate here to market offshore financial services to wealthy Alabamians. It is a shock to many, but Mountain Brook has the third-highest per capita income in the world. The marketing effort is real; it just isn't the primary reason for the start up.

"Well, the project has had some files altered. Will says they were altered to prevent showing that copies were made. He has EVERYTHING on those machines logged. He can even tell you all the keystrokes made from each individual console for the last week."

"Is that a good thing?"

"Well, you picked him. My instinct is that he is a good people. I think he understands what we are trying to do; he doesn't understand the math enough to know how close we are."

"Did he have any suggestions as to our next course of action?"

"He did, actually, and they are fairly draconian but effective, I think."

"Go on…"

"We need to call a halt to further access under the guise of upgrading the equipment for now. The only two people I am sure of are in this room right now. If it were you or I, the project would be screwed in any case. You have the contacts while I have the ideas. Will indicated that you and I need to sit across the table from each other and assure ourselves that it is neither of us. Once we do that, call him and he will have some ideas on catching the bad guy.

"Are you sure it isn't me?" the Senator asks.

"Yes." There is no hesitation on Felix's part.

"Call Will then and ask him how soon he can get a game plan together.

OEE is a house of hell the next day. The board meets, and the usual calls for someone's head to roll go right up there with duck and cover in terms of effectiveness. LB Browning had made more than a few enemies amongst the board members when he called their bluff some months ago. This security lapse reflects directly on him and his choices of advisors. Some on the board look at OEE as a private reserve for living the good life, doling out favors, and using it as a cash cow to finance more than a few folk's political ambitions. LB's quiet accumulation of stock proxies over the last several months is an ace he'd rather not play until absolutely necessary.

"There is a good side to all this, folks."

Silence greets this, and he adds, "I just haven't managed

to find it yet."

After a few comments are offered as to his state of mind and thinking to himself that he is sure Iacocca never had to take this much crap and didn't make as much per share, LB says, "This is an internal security problem. We cannot guard against betrayal. There is no safety from it. We just have to make the price high enough that it isn't repeated."

"Do we have the person identified yet?"

"No, nor do we have any good plans for doing so yet. I am informing this board at this point because I feel it is necessary. We are trying to come up with a plan for identification. I do not have any further information, and we don't even know to what extent we have been compromised."

"Are all our projects compromised?" This comes from one of the few people in the room the Senator is comfortable having an unguarded conversation with.

"Almost all, though there are a few projects that by design have no outgoing contact with the rest of the world. Those have not been compromised."

Will instructs LB and Felix to refrain from disclosing the extent of the espionage, preferring to let them think they had gotten away with the most critical part due to the extreme measures that had been taken previously. He has no ETA on the plan for ferreting out the perpetrator, he'd explained, because he has no motives. This will be detective work and not just chasing bits across a network. In-house security is instructed to cooperate with Infosurge at every instance. Privately, the personnel records of all connected with Mind's I are handed over, as well as lots of records that he has no legal right to have.

Felix objects when told his personal finances will be

investigated, but LB calms him by saying his own are to be looked at as well by Will. They are looking for patterns and breaks in patterns, trying to see the mosaic of activity of the folks involved. 'Whoever did this is not stupid. That was good work they did. I almost didn't have everything backed up to my systems. If I hadn't, you would have not been able to catch it. It would have looked secure. Frankly, had I not been paranoid about going the extra mile for a friend, we still wouldn't know.'

This scares the hell out of me and Will, too. LB is done thinking about this today. *Maybe Will can have something by the weekend.*

Chapter 16

The Battle Continues

The thing you need to understand about Will is this: He is a guy who likes to see things finished. The fact that things just seem to go on and on is what drives him bug shit. Life isn't a series of accomplishments, it seems, but more a series of interrelated, run-on sentences from a narrator that just will not shut up.

This isn't to say that Will has anything approaching a death wish. He just wishes that more things in life cleaned up a little more neatly. It is so core to his personality that he often gets aggravated with folks who just can't make up their minds. God save him from getting behind someone in a fast food restaurant who can't decide between a Big Mac and a Fish Sandwich. Once, he'd finally suggested a guy flip a coin as they both tasted like shit anyway.

"The point to fast food," he'd gone on to explain as one would to a child who simply refuses to learn out of hard-headedness, "is to shut the little bastard up in the pit of your stomach so we can get on with what needs to be done today. I am sure I speak for all of us when I say, 'hurry the hell up or get the fuck out of the way so people who have things to do can get them done.'" The guy had nervously ordered the fish, which he dearly hated, and moved on. Will's sympathy would most likely have been as sincere as the fish sandwich.

The situation with OEE is beginning to develop all of the earmarks of a war in which long lines of trenches developed along certain well-marked paths. The government tries a new ploy to get into their networks to find out what is going on or to simply try to tear something up. Will's group marks the attack, does a reverse IP lookup and traces it back to some installation. They then slam their system with some variation of a denial of service attack or a mail bomb of increasing sophistication. At the same time, the legal department enters formal protests and files briefs against the government. The government almost always denies the attacks saying someone is spoofing their attacks using their IP numbers. The fact that these so-called teenage 'hackers' can gain access to all kinds of supposedly classified computer networks on government sub-nets does nothing to help their case.

Besides, Will thinks that *anybody capable of such attacks is a full-fledged cracker, not a hacker. Though I doubt the stupid sonsabitches who make policy on such things ever take the trouble to know the difference. Also, Such talent gets put on the spook payroll in a hurry. Without fail.*

The thought isn't entirely applicable or clear, but Will has been running on triple Shots-In-the-Dark for the last week and is beginning to wear down. In case you ever want to try it, a triple Shot-In-the-Dark is three shots of espresso in a tall cup of coffee. One of these babies and your heart will sound like a chainsaw in a pissed-off beehive, guaranteed.

It is fun at first, squaring off against the Feds best. Like a game of chess against an equally matched opponent, the game is satisfying. Unfortunately for Will, the Feds retire a player and send in fresh talent when Will begins to wear him or her down. He, on the other hand, has only a handful of talent, all of whom are playing against a number of skilled crackers.

There is one thing to this situation: if we do win in the long run, it will turn us into the best group of crackers on earth. The thrill of this thought shared amongst the group lasted almost a month.

"We need more help, Will. We're wearing out faster and faster, and they keep pitching." This is Ken Maya Moto, one of Will's best crackers. "We're down to the bone, and I think one or two are planning on quitting. Mark came to me this morning and showed me an offer of employment with NSA."

"Think he'll take it?"

"Look, you know me, loyal to the end, mostly because I have an irrational hatred for government. I think Mark is the same way, but he is young and looking at his paycheck."

Ken isn't kidding. He is a formally self-proclaimed anarchist, though he admits somebody has to be in charge of the water works and such. He continues, "They offered him three times what you are paying him. I suspect others on the team have had offers, too, and are trying to make up their minds.

"How long before somebody bites, do you think?"

"Well, not more than a week, I'd say," Ken says, shaking his head.

"Okay. I will try to have a plan of action by Friday."

"What are you thinking?"

"Ken, I don't have a friggin' clue, not a clue."

"I am somehow not comforted."

"Hell, cheer up. They could pass a law tomorrow outlawing what you and I do. Then we could go work at McDonald's."

"What part of 'not comforted' did you not get?"

Will ignores this last and finishes up with, "Hold the fort. I'll be back at 6."

"Sylvia, we need to do some brain storming, and I think I need Felix here."

"Will you need L.B. as well?"

"No, I think not, just Felix."

"Okay." Sylvia is curious. Will isn't a man who is unsure about a course of action. It is mostly 'go here, do this, buy that, call them, tell them this or that.' Something is up on the OEE project, and it appears that the boss has no idea what to do about it. "Will there be any additional prep for this meeting, Sir?"

He hesitates as he turns to go into his office and finally responds, "No, I don't think so, Sylvia, not for now, anyway." Way more cryptic than his normal style. It is as if he wasn't really there in the office.

"Very good; I will do it now." This last is said to a closing office door.

This OEE thing is getting dangerous. Will doesn't realize how much NSA fears him and OEE thinks Crystal. She knows from experience over the last many years that a government fears nothing so much as a man who cannot be bought or intimidated. Such men are dangerous to the status quo, which they equate with the natural order of things. It is like heresy to a fanatic believer, punishable if need be, by death.

Which I must prevent and it would be easier if our relationship hadn't become somewhat strained! She can't explain exactly why it had. It just seems that both want something but can't figure out what, even to the point of being able to explain it to themselves, much less to each other. *I will just have to deal with that later. Right now, I need advice on how to deal with this. Monica and Melissa need to be apprised of the situation and so I go.*

Crystal leaves word on Will's machine that she will be out of town for a few days and then heads to Norn's Lair. "Will, I will be gone a few days, perhaps even a week. There is a situation with…my family back home, and I must go. I'm sorry I didn't have time to see you before I left, but it really is an emergency. Maybe we can talk when I get back?"

Sure, why not? I would love to talk and be able to understand why it's so goddamn hard to have a conversation between two people who are nuts for each other. Will had checked his messages from another security meeting at OEE.

"So what you're saying, "Will, is that you believe…" Felix's voice drones out, and Will comes back in on, " and that, I think, is all there is to it. No worries, at least for awhile."

"What…?" Will is flummoxed as he loses focus on Felix's suggestion as to how to deal with the situation of NSA trying to buy his folks out from under him. "Felix, I'm sorry, but you'll have to repeat that last. I'm pretty punchy right now."

Felix eyed him and nodded his agreement.

"I can see that you are. What are your shifts like now?"

"We work four-hour shifts and sleep four hours, doing an honest heads up if we're not rested enough yet."

"Christ! That's no good. We have had people working that shift on projects before and it always led to losses. You need more personnel, Will."

"I agree, but the budget L.B. approved when I bid on the project…"

"Well, the hell with that. This is my fief, and I am telling you, make an estimate now, and we'll refine it as we go."

"The budget needs to triple. We need more folks, we need to pay more to get them here, and we'll need to pay them more to keep them here. Also, we may as well hire the trouble makers out there. They are less likely to want to fall to the dark side, anyway."

"Not a problem. You should have brought this to me a month ago." Felix didn't normally scold Will, but in this case, it is justified.

"Won't you need to get approval from L.B. on this?"

"Not at all; we were shocked at the low ball anyway. This is at my discretion, and you have leeway to go over your current budget by a factor of ten, as long as it is clearly justified."

"Huh." Then, "Well, that is all right."

"I will leave you to it."

Sylvia walks in on Will doing a Snoopy Christmas dance in his office. "Will?"

"Never mind, for now, Sylvia, just call Ken and get him over here ASAP."

Chapter 17

Thunder Woke Will

Thunder wakes Will. Rolling over and laying his head on the still sleeping Crystal's side, he sees the fat raindrops slapping the bay window of his apartment. Birmingham is gone, swallowed by the storm.

Not wanting to wake Crystal, Will lies in the darkness, thinking how sometimes darkness is warm, safe, and comfortable and how nice a woman smells in his bed. She had returned from home, reticent about the emergency.

The strobe of the lightening made everything stand out in bright blue relief. Sometimes, the blanket in the chair is a blanket, sometimes an older woman, sometimes a large blue-black reptile like this world has never seen. The only one that troubles him looks spider like and appears to move. One of Will's hands dives to the lamp and another to the Star 9MM hidden under his pillow for the unexpected midnight guest. The light reveals all kinds of horrors: his laundry, past due; his desk, covered in correspondence he just can't seem to deal with; and his walk-in closet, a subject he is leaving for the maids when they come on Monday. There is no spider present.

Dreams, man. That is some bad shit to be thinking of during a perfect morning.

Will is convinced by two close friends he had confided in that there could have been no spider. One even asks him for a hit of whatever the hell it was he'd been on-it sounded like some wicked stuff. Did he smoke it or chase it with Crown?

Crystal begins to stir. "Bear, what is it?" She notices his

high state of agitation and whirls in bed, whipping her hair around as she checks out the room and Will. The bedclothes add to this whipping motion.

"Nothing, now, I just thought I saw something impossible. A bad dream is all."

"OK."

"Go back to sleep, Babe."

"Well, I kind of need to go, full day."

"Okay, I just wish you didn't always have to go before sunrise. Just once, I would like to see the sun come up with you."

As she rolls over on her right side, facing the bay window, she replies, "You and me both, Bear, you and me both. I have about an hour and a half. Hold me, okay?"

"You got it." Will tucks himself in behind her, snaking his right arm under her neck, cupping her left breast while his left-hand rests on her belly, right below the navel, just high enough not to touch anything sensitive.

As Will is about to drift off to sleep, enjoying the thunder, her hair in his face, and the way her butt nestles in his lap, Crystal asks, "Will, what was it you thought you saw?"

Now, Will is beginning to enjoy how his body always reacts to being nestled close up to Crystal. Not that he has any intention of acting on it, it is just nice. He replies, "A big ugly, hairy spider with the voice of an angel."

Crystal's reaction isn't what Will expects. Again, there is that disconcerting speed Crystal is capable of. She also screams a strange word, "Guardians! To me!"

A commotion erupts on the roof of the apartment,

sounding like storm troopers suddenly on the move.

"Will, don't move."

"Okay. You're acting a little bent, Babe. It was just a dream." Will is still fuzzy with sleep so he figures he hears her wrong. *Spiders must freak her out.*

Crystal notices that one of the side windows is open and the screen removed. Carefully leaning out and trying to look in all directions, she sees that a guardian is giving her a negative or 'no sign' signal. She pulls her head back in and turns to Will. The guardians had been Will's constant companion since the mental hospital episode. Will told Crystal about the escort he thought had been provided by OEE and how OEE had denied any knowledge of who they were. A few guardians is the answer to any human threat is her immediate reaction.

"Crystal?" Will knows she is upset by his waking her up with his nightmare, but this is about two steps from abnormal.

"I'm sorry, Bear. I hate those bastards." She then adds a none verbal grunt, shiver and stomp.

Okey dokey. Mental note to myself: Don't do any spider jokes on Halloween.

"Well, it's gone now. See? No nightmares." Will offers his ear for inspection.

"I guess." She still jerks her head in unexpected directions as if to catch an errant spider trying to slip out the door or window.

"Babe, come lie down. I am sorry I bothered you with that stupid nightmare."

"No, I overreacted."

"I'll say, pretty fast reactions."

"Umm?"

"Reactions, you're quick. You were a blur, and I don't usually miss movement."

Rolling back to face him, Crystal asks, "So, you had a dream about spiders before?" She is awake and needs to leave soon. Thoughts of a more cuddly nature flee.

"Yeah, but it was just a dream. No big deal, and I don't want you to whig again. Let's just doze." *Besides, I might get you to stay today.*

"No. Really, I want to hear."

"Okay. But you asked."

"I asked."

"I had this dream, see, where this spider…hell, it looked kind of like a spider-was singing to me in the sweetest voice I think I have ever heard. It was like a drug. I began to think, it's okay; it's just a dream. With that voice, I am sure it will change into a wench soon enough. See, sometimes, I can control my dreams. I thought if I just looked at the thing and remembered that I was in a dream, I could control the situation."

"Interesting."

"What?"

"Nothing. Go on."

"Anyways, the thing never changed and something, I don't remember what exactly, made me think this was no dream. I am about to get eaten by a spider with an angel's voice."

"What did you do?"

"Well, I rolled out of the bed and let it get tangled up in the sheets."

Arachnids have the fastest reactions ever measured. Things that fight arachnids die, period. "What then?" she asks.

"Well, while it was tangled up in the sheet, I sprinted downstairs, got my shotgun and a can of gasoline-I may not be remembering this correctly-hang on."

After a few seconds of recollection, Will remembers, "Ah! Now I got it. I think, uh, I rolled out of the bed and got my shotgun. While it was tangled up, I blasted that thing all to hell and gone. It was great! I felt high. There was a singing it seemed like in the base of my skull like I had reached my moment, my place in the natural order of things. It felt almost a little like the first time I had sex."

As he takes a breath, Crystal urges him on with an expectant look. *Man, she is hard to figure out sometimes. Dreams,* Will thinks.

"Pressing on! The thing started to reassemble itself. I had just blasted this thing all over my headboard and Play Station, and the pieces began to crawl and ooze back towards each other. It was putting itself back together. Unbelievable."

Crystal is thinking, *This must be why even a guardian has had trouble with these things, such hardiness. We'd heard it, but no one believed the tales. Who could blame us?*

Will finishes, "I was finally able to sprint downstairs, get some gas-or was it turpentine?- poured it all over the thing and set it ablaze, burned my fucking house down."

"So you killed it?"

"Yup, I did." Will is proud. Then, *It was just a dream.*

"How do you know?"

"Because I stood there long enough to actually see parts of it catch, burn and disappear."

"But it was just a dream."

"Well…yeah. It had to be." Will is troubled but doesn't elaborate. Some days, it is a dream; some days, he believes it really happened.

"But your house really burned down."

"I know…the do…" He hesitates here and then continues. He almost says doctor but doesn't want Crystal to know how bad he has been. "It was what's called a night terror. You're still dreaming and seeing, but your body is no longer disconnected from your brain. Kids get them all the time, but you usually outgrow them."

"Okay, Bear. Let's just sleep."

The sun finally checks in to wake Will. Crystal is gone.

"Morning, Will." Sylvia, after all her years with Will, is finally using his 'Christian' name as she calls it. Will figures it is because of her upgrade in pay, office, and how she can now set her schedule as he does. The two of them have an administrative assistant they share, though Will gets first priority. Sylvia is now his senior media research assistant and her function is to read all the technical journals and earmark what Will most likely needs to see first.

"Morning, Sylvia." Will, looking at the stack of periodicals, says, "You know, you used to create less work, I think."

"Humph. I threw away two-thirds because I knew you couldn't get to it all. These are the ones I think you really have to read."

"Okay." He thinks he should finish by noon, plenty of time to go scout the new fields on the north side of the complex where a new lab is to be built. He and Felix are going. Felix wants him to walk the sections of the first floor and get his input on the drawings. "Could you or Marlene call Mr. Dorcai and tell him it should be between noon and 12:30 before I get there?"

"I'm on it."

A Hummer is such a beautiful vehicle, thinks Will. Will is in awe of where the Hummer can go. Felix's vehicle is equipped with a snorkel. They go through a creek that is over 3 feet deep. *Gotta have one,* Will says to himself about a hundred times that day. Will and Felix drive the Hummer over to the back side of the area where they are building the new lab.

The area is marked out in what Will thinks of as pole bean lines and bright orange flags strung across the Alabama red clay. Usually, floor plans walked outside appear to be smaller and this one is no exception.

They find the carcass of what might have been a medium size dog. It looks shriveled. "Nasty thing that," says Felix.

"Yeah, it must have been here a while. It's already dried up and shriveled away. It's so dry it doesn't even stink anymore." Will turns away, no longer interested.

Felix wasn't through. "I suppose. But it doesn't add up." Felix likes chasing rabbits, and sometimes they turn up interesting information. "It rained yesterday and last night. Its fur should be wet like clay. It's dry."

"Well, the sun is hot…"

"Yes, but the clay around the dog is still wet. There

ought to be a scrim of clay that was dry, anyway," says Felix.

Will gets more interested. "Okay." Felix is Will's boss, more or less, so if he wants to chase a puzzle, they'd chase it.

Felix is looking around for a stick to move the corpse with. "That's the ticket," he says as he finds one.

They turn it over. Not only is the fur dry, but it is not being matted into the mud like something that had been there days would be. The mud is wet and the fur only marginally so. The dog had been laid here after this early morning's rain.

"Look here, Will." Will bends down to look and mutters a nonverbal grunt of surprise.

"Don't you just love a puzzle?" Felix is grinning a little. He likes unsolved things.

"Weird," Will agrees.

The underside of the dog had been ripped open a bit. The blood is still fresh.

"This dog may not have been dead for more than two or three hours because we've had rain since then."

"But how did it get so shrunken?"

"No clue." Then Felix adds, "We've had a couple of these things around. The general consensus is that this area has some unusual atmospherics."

"Remind me not to fly a kite or anything then. Atmospherics, huh?"

"Yes."

"Sounds like bullshit to me. But it is curious as hell."

"I agree, but let's move on to the lab again."

After they walk the area, Will and Felix return to where the dog carcass lay. It is gone.

"Maybe he got to feeling better?" Will had meant it to be humorous, but it falls flat in the increasing brightness of the afternoon sun.

"Any word from Crystal?" Monica asked.

"None, Milady." Salome.

"Circe was right. For some reason, saving Will rather than killing him was the correct action."

"Indeed."

"Are you always so terse with words?"

"Yes."

"So, we have more fluidity to this than we knew."

"I don't understand."

"Before the decision to execute Will, the blind date was July 22. We then decided that Will may be the culprit, even if unknowingly, and had to be eliminated."

"Yes?"

"Now," Monica muses, "we have spared him and protected him, and the blind spot doesn't occur until December 17, 2000. What does this suggest?"

Salome's is interrupted by Circe's entrance. "My Lady, Salome. I hope you are both well."

"Circe."

Salome's response is a silent bow from the waist.

"I believe what it suggests is that there is some agent carrying out a plan. The plan will eliminate all seers. Since you never know where or in what circumstance a seer might be born it is a safe assumption to assume large segments, if not all, of humans and People will be eliminated on the date of blindness. The manipulation of Will's fate has changed the clock, though. I am guessing this will bring some rage and probably a retaliatory response." Circe's tone is adamant.

"Agreed, but what?" Monica.

"Alert Crystal about the extended date, but just do it with the normal dispatch, I think," says Circe. "Waiting changes nothing."

On the shores of Lake Purdy, Crystal meets with a dispatch guardian, a fairly large one standing at 8 feet, nine inches. She is pregnant.

Chapter 18

Crystal Reveals Herself

Will arrives home a bit late. Crystal drops a bombshell in his lap. She reveals her true nature to him. She isn't who she claimed to be, and he is somehow special, too. Destined is the word she uses.

"Destined." *She is crazy. Well, of course, she is crazy. I really do need just to be alone with no significant other.*

"Yes."

"You're sure?"

"You killed an arachnid by your own account. If one notices you, you die."

"But honey, angel, Babe, that was just a dream. I went to counseling, and it turns out that…"

"It turns out that you don't want to really see the world around you for what it really is just like 90% of the rest of the human race."

"What do you mean? I believe what my eyes see, but this is crazy!"

"Really? What about witches? Telepathy? Legends? Unexplained things like ships disappearing for no reason?"

"All fairy tales?"

"If they are ALL fairy tales, then why do humans burn witches at the stake and make an outcast of anyone who believes in things outside the norm?"

"Well, I don't know about that. Ignorant people overreact to what they see as threats to them. I don't know why people are the way they are. Hell, if I knew that, I could figure out what is going on with you."

"I am trying to tell you that I am one of the People and that there is a threat to everyone, and for some reason, you are a key player in what is to come."

"Crystal, there is no threat to the planet. The UN is more closely united than ever. I mean, with the exception of this virus sweeping across northern Europe, everyone's at peace."

"It isn't a virus and the world isn't at peace. Besides, your holy writings predict it. Peace, peace, then sudden destruction. That's in Thessalonians in case you want to check my math."

"Come again?"

"The world isn't at peace. The ones who would oppose our rule are invading the northernmost reaches of human territory and spreading through conversion."

"Crystal, baby doll,…" Will is concerned for her and he loves her, but he is now worried that she may be dangerous to herself. She is losing her mind. He feels no fear of her, but for her. "Okay, just calm down and come sit by me. Start from the beginning."

She does, and it takes awhile. She explains that there are two major groups in the world: People and humans. People and humans have common origins. Humans can be converted, but People can not and live forever. How long is forever? No one knows. Seers are also real and are accepted amongst People but not amongst humans. Now, all the seers are blind, and a rebellion is brewing in the People, leading those who would enslave the human race and turn them into nothing but cattle. There is a smaller group coming exclusively from the ranks of human to People conversions called arachnids. Arachnids suffer from homicidal insanity down to the last one. They are savage, murderous, desert-loving creatures inhabiting most of the Sahara desert. Being immortal, they don't die but are unwilling to tolerate other living things, even to mate. Unless some of the academics are right and they are all male, which explains why they don't mate. Who would want to?

"Un-huh. Okay. This isn't funny anymore," Will says. "I am going to have to go now."

"Will, don't leave. I am telling you this because I have no choice. You were the only one to ever kill an arachnid, human or not."

"Is THAT what this is about? Damn it, this isn't funny, like I said. I had a damn dream, and I don't need any crap…you know, I really didn't expect this from you, Crystal."

"Of course you didn't! I am only telling you because Monica and Melissa have insisted. We are out of options. You think I wanted to drop this on you?"

"I didn't expect you to go to this length to play a practical joke. I lost my house in that fire and lots of other shit I will never be able to replace. Geez, I guess you're even now for me freaking you out over the spider thing. Man, I guess I am an idiot; after all, I didn't even see an inkling of the mean streak in you." *I am gone now. She is crazy.*

"I am not crazy, and you didn't dream it, you hard-headed jack nape!"

Jack nape? "Oh, please. I suppose you will tell me now that the spider was real and it tried to kill me."

"Yes." They are standing face to face now in the center

of her apartment. She is beginning to get a bit pissed now. She'd gotten irritated before with Will, but now it is close to edging over into pissed. "I didn't stutter, and I was clear when I said you need to keep an open mind."

"Yeah, but not so clear my brains fall out." He turns and heads towards the door. "You need help."

He makes it so far as to place his hand on the door handle when he hears a rumbling noise behind that sounds like thunder speaking his name.

"Will. Stop. Close the door and face me."

Closing the door and just facing it, he considers that this is just more of an elaborate joke she is playing. The short hairs standing up on the back of his neck argue that he needs to just open the door and get the hell out. His mind, ever that great tool of rational thought, argues that he should turn around and let the trick play out a bit more. He turns.

Crystal is standing there covered in what appear to be multicolored scales and hunches over a bit. *Helluva, good costume. How did she get it on so fast?* He walks towards her, all the while his lizard brain is screaming, 'Get out, now!'

"Baby Doll, when you decide to jerk someone's chain, you lean into it, you know?"

"Will, touch my face and see that it is real."

Touching her face is disturbing. The costume doesn't appear to have an ending. His eyes keep looking for the end of the makeup or a zipper.

Or something, I can't see the joke. I'm dreaming again. I like the other dreams better.

The corners of her eyes crinkle as she smiles and says,

"Now, you have seen the real me." The thunder sounds sad.

Will, looking at her, sees how old the soul in her really is. She is immortal, but changes in the People as they age are communicating to Will on some level he is incapable of verbalizing, un-definable, but visible. "Angel?"

"Want to see your Angel?" Crystal asks. Then she says, "Okay, Will, here is your angel." She turns into the glorious creature that seduced him in his tower office before joining OEE.

"The dreams, which was you? You're real?"

"Yes."

"Why didn't you say so? Why the games?"

She switches back to what she calls her real face and asks, "Would you have wanted me this way? Besides, I took the picture from your mind, and it was so close to what I looked like as a human that I added a few sparkles."

He reaches out a tentative hand, touching the hard ridges in her forehead. She allows him to do so, though she can feel her battle skin reacting to his nearness. Her lips involuntarily flare, revealing a wicked set of fangs, more like a big cat's jaws than Bella Lugosi's. Will pulls back.

"No, no. Go ahead. I want you to understand," She rumbles.

Reaching for her face, noticing for the first time that she now towers over him, Will says, "You're bigger than before."

"Yes."

"How? The mass has to come from somewhere."

"I don't know."

He looks her over, circling her, running his hand over territory that he runs his hands over in passion, totally confused as to how such a small, delicate thing could transform into this killing organism. He rejects his own eyes' reports.

"I am dreaming again, aren't I?"

"Will, you were never dreaming. Me, the arachnid, it was all real."

Will, mind reeling, remembering other things at other times, remembering Monica and Melissa, he says, "The mountain! The keep! I tried to kill myself! Dear God in Heaven, I threw myself off, and they caught me…"

"Yes, you did. You remember it all, now."

"Monica, she…" his hand flies to the side of his neck. "She bit me. Why would she after I saved her and…"

"She wanted to know the blood of a brave man. She was never in any danger but wanted to see what action you would take."

"She could have killed me." Now, he is backing up again.

Crystal follows, smoothly flowing into the diminutive blonde form he'd fallen for. "Will, we don't do that anymore. They only wanted to know you. It is our way."

"They BOTH bit me?"

"Yes, but not even enough was taken to slow you down. It probably helped you, but no one knows how long it will last."

"Helped me?"

"You'll be immune to most diseases for some time."

"Immunity. How long?"

"It varies. Are you okay?"

Will walks over and sits back down on her sofa. He is relatively sure it is safe. He is beginning to believe.

Crystal sits down beside him. "I know this is hard to accept."

Will says, "Do the change again." His head is slung back on the back of the sofa as he looks at the ceiling. The woman's softness hardens against his side, and the sofa seat sinks in as if with a great weight and Will finds himself sitting with his arm around a killing thing. The killing thing still has sad eyes that love him. It changes back, restoring the illusion that he is just sitting in his girl's apartment with his arm around her, engaging in conversation.

"So, this is why we never see each other in the day."

"Yes, sunlight is hell on the skin."

The comment is so out of context and applicable that it breaks Will up.

"So the spider was real." Will knows he is repeating himself and he dearly hates to do that. He is stalling for thinking time, and he almost never does that. Clearly, Will is nervous and hates it when it shows.

"It was real."

"If they are so badass, why didn't it get me?"

"We don't know. We thought maybe you just got lucky, but Will, it just doesn't happen. Not with an arachnid."

"They kill your kind?"

Crystal looks at him, wondering if he knew how he'd said it, then moves on. "Yes, Will, they kill my kind.

Guardians, too."

"What's a guardian?"

"A guardian is of the People but built more deadly. Bigger, stronger, faster, and with lots of sharp, killing edges and points."

Bigger and meaner. Yippee. "Okay, remind me to stay away from those guys."

Telling him about the guardians can wait. No, skip that. Tell him everything. "Will, there are guardians here with us now."

"Where?" He gets up to check the back rooms. As he walks down towards the hallway, six large forms shimmer into view when Crystal signals them. Will's reaction is to fall into a stance and back towards a wall. They ignore Will and bow to Crystal. One addresses her.

"Lady Crystal." Again, that thunder almost making the bones in Will's head rattle.

"Dallas. Please meet the good Will."

Will is still in his stance as the giant bows towards him, addressing him as 'Sir Will.' He only now notices that the creature looks female. Well, that is if you ignore all the points and edges.

Dallas continues to Crystal as she straightens, "Lady Crystal, you are correct about his reflexes. He is unusually quick for a human."

Crystal says, "Will, you can relax. They are here for you."

"They're here for me?" *They've come to take me away, haha.* Will is seriously looking for a hole to bolt through.

"Not here to take you somewhere. They are your protectors. If you are who we think you are, you need protection. We can't allow anything to befall you if you are who or what we think."

"Yeah? Well, if I can kill arachnids and arachnids can kill big Mama here, then why do I need protection?"

"A cogent argument, My Lady," says Dallas. Then, "What's a big mama?"

Ignoring Dallas' question, Will objects, "Besides, I am just human."

"You're not just human. Well, you are, but you're not just an ordinary human. You have faced arachnids and lived; you have, on occasion, faced as many as five other humans and cowed them. You don't quit when others would have given up and just slunk away, and you inspire others to want to see you win, and they help you when others would be laughed at. You do more than win; you inspire others to try to do the same. You may not be what you want to be, Will, but you are more than ordinary. I suspect that if you were what you wanted to be, you would be like Enoch of Christianity. The fact that you aspire to such but don't talk about it marks you, too."

"Enoch?"

"Look it up. The point is that you're needed in the fight of history. Because of your nature, I suspect you need to be in the fight of history, too."

He cranes up at Dallas. "My, you're a big one, aren't you?"

"Actually," Crystal answers, "Dallas is fairly typical of a guardian."

"What do you want me to do?" Will asks.

"You'll need to become one of us."

"You need to bite me? Change me into one of the Undead and cursed to hell?"

"We're not demons, Will, just different and not subject to hell by default any more than humans."

"Lots of legends disagree."

"Yes, well, they record me and my sisters as three furies, too."

"Furies? What's a fury?"

"Fury, f-u-r-y. Look it up. It's a type of angel."

"I will. Anything else I need to know?"

"Will, I wouldn't do this or ask you if it weren't necessary."

"I know." He DID know. He just keeps expecting to wake up. "Look, I need to go. See you same time tomorrow night, I suppose?"

"Definitely." They hug and kiss goodnight.

"Some set of chaperones you have. Glad you didn't tell me at first. I might have been nervous."

"Not you. Besides, you wanted to so bad you could have probably done it in the middle of the legion field for a crowd."

He sniffs, then brags, "Well, obviously that IS true..." He kisses her again and looks at Dallas, "Stay."

Within minutes after he leaves, Crystal says to Dallas, "Don't lose him."

"He wishes us not. He said stay."

"Not really worried about what he wants. Besides, I

think he meant, 'Stay out of sight. You make me nervous.'"

"As you wish," Dallas says as she and the other five fade out.

When Will arrives home, he checks to see if he has messages. The staccato dial tone indicates that he does.

Why do I even bother to check? I always have messages. Then, *At least they're not all from bill collectors anymore and that, boys and girls, is an improvement. I'll check them later.* He sits down and turns the television to the WB network. Buffy the Vampire Slayer is on.

Neat, just what I needed to see. He had left Crystal without spending the night. *Too much weirdness there to concentrate anyway.* Sarah Michelle Gellar moves across the screen, arguing with Charisma Carpenter and the Willow girl talking about Darla. *Yeah, the one who created Angel. That's what I need. I need to get tag-teamed by the entire female cast of Buffy.*

He watches about three-quarters of the show and then thinks about what a fury is. As the WB continues to run in the background, he pops over to the bookshelf and pulls out the F volume of Britannica. Will is a technogeek, but sometimes he just likes books.

He looks up fury and finds the following synopsis.

Fury: An order of Angel. Specifically, a female entity taking revenge upon men for wrongs committed against women.

Whoops. Not a real clear thought, but having seen Crystal's change and her buddies, it isn't real pleasant.

The rest of Buffy is a blur, and he doesn't even recall seeing Angel. About ten minutes into Andy Griffith, he thinks to check his messages. Nothing major other than Felix wants to do another walkover of the lab space tomorrow. *I will sleep, and then in the A, I will feel better and all this will be remembered as a dream and I will KNOW it is a dream tomorrow. That IS the ticket.*

Will wakes about 4 AM and in the ensuing rush through the gym and getting on over to the lab, he doesn't even think about all the weirdness of the day before. Like the rest of the human race he is remarkably selective in what he remembers. He would have occasion to think about this trait in detail in the future.

Going through the day's business, he almost forgets about his decision to talk to someone about yesterday when he and Felix found the dog. It doesn't look dried up; it looks sucked out, like some cricket by a spider.

Okay, here goes nothing. Or perhaps everything...up in smoke.

Will decides to tell Felix what is going on. Excusing himself, Will goes to find a restroom and thinks carefully about his decision. While relieving himself, he asks the empty bathroom, "How the hell do I ask him about this shit. I have no proof, and I am probably crazy anyway."

Only the bathroom isn't empty. Dallas answers him, "Sir Will, we can prove the veracity of your statements if you so desire."

Dallas scares Will, who proceeds to miss the urinal a bit while trying to cut himself off in mid stream and pull his pants back up. He feels vulnerable as hell and can't seem to get everything working at once. His reaction is to again back up to the wall.

"Show yourself, Dallas."

She shimmers in. "Will."

"Damn it!"

"You said you had no proof, and I offered a solution."

"But while I was taking a leak? Don't you have any sense of propriety? Get out so I can finish!"

"As you wish." She shimmers out.

Will stands there a few minutes without being able to finish and finally looks around. "Dallas, show yourself."

Nothing. Good, Will thinks as he turns back to the urinal and finishes. *Right as I was taking a leak. I ought to cuss her out, but that's probably a bad idea.*

He walks back out and calls her name. "Dallas."

"Go back inside the restroom, please. We want to be seen by no more than necessary."

"Good idea." Will is about fifty feet away from Felix.

Felix hears thunder in the distance and thinks Will had muttered something to himself. It sounds like idea or some such. *That kid is always thinking about something.*

Back inside the restroom, Dallas appears. *Beam into my location, Scotty.* "You had an idea?" No preamble.

"Yes. If you want to talk to the wizard, we will reveal ourselves, but I suggest you do it somewhere remote."

"Remote."

"In case he, as you call it, freaks? Becomes hysterical, though I doubt he will do so. He is a wizard, after all."

"Felix? He is just an engineer. He's no wizard and he doesn't believe in all that stuff."

Dallas just looks at him. *Why argue with someone about the color of the sky? Things are what they are,* she thinks to herself.

"Okay. I will do it. I will just say, 'Guardians, show yourselves' or something like it, okay?"

"As you wish." And THAT is how Will decides to tell Felix.

"You said your ex was the wife from hell, right?"

"Pretty much."

"You said when she got mad, it was almost impossible to calm her down, right?"

"Un-huh."

"So, the woman you chose to make your life perfect…correct me if I am wrong here…after being married to what you termed an 'impossible, bad-tempered, shrill, insane bitch,' unquote; turns out to be not only the inspiration for the legend of the Norn, three hags who interfere in the affairs of men, but also the basis of the Furies legend, an order of angels whose sole function was to reap vengeance on men who have done women wrong."

"Un-huh." Will looks sick.

"Who is also a vampire?"

"Vampiress, but yeah." Will now had his head hanging in his hands as he sat with his knees hanging off the side of the new lab's tenth and, in this case, top floor.

"Well." Felix muses for a minute. Then he continues, "You love her?"

"Well, I thought I did. Then I find out she is some demon/vampire/angel thing out to do something which she says is my destiny to take part in."

"What else?"

"What else? What else does it take?"

"You are not saying you believe her? Will? These things don't exist. I had heard that you'd had some problems, but I think you should seek some help…"

"Guardians, show yourselves." Will cuts Felix off in mid-sentence.

"Will, are you sure?" Guardians know humans don't generally react well to the sudden site of guardians. They chose to shift to their more human guise. They still stand head and shoulders over both men. Will understands her, but Felix only thinks he hears thunder out of the clear sky.

Felix sees 6 forms, marginally feminine, shimmer into view. They are off to both sides of the men, behind them, and two appear to be standing against the support beams holding up this edge of the floor. The fact that they appear to be standing at 90° to the pull of gravity has Felix just about gibbering. "Will, what…look…she is…Is it a she? Yes…no offense…"

"None taken, human male," her voice, thunder rolling across a mountain range.

"Felix, meet the girls. Girls, meet Felix. I can't pronounce all their names, but the only one who will address me directly is called Dallas."

"Well," says Felix as he stands up and offers his hand to the one named Dallas, who takes no offense. "You sure do appear to be a very healthy young lady."

Dallas only looks at him and then says, "I have no response to that, but it does seem to be a consensus amongst Will and his friends."

"Felix, relax. Don't pop a hose on me. They are here to 'guard' me."

"From what?"

"That is for the Lady Crystal to discuss. We are simply Guardians, sworn to the Three Queens." This evokes some rumbling from the other five women, but they manage to repress whatever they have been about to say.

"Don't get them started on the Three, Felix. I will fill you in later."

"Please do. How do…" Felix is looking at the two standing on the columns in defiance of gravity.

"I do not have a clue. I asked, thinking it was perhaps some tech…" he holds his breath, blows it out and straight up his face as he sometimes does when exasperated by cupping his lower lip over his top lip, and continues, "They either don't know or won't say. It has to be technology of some kind, though they say it is just ability with 'People' who can fly."

"People? Fly?"

Thinking this could take awhile and wanting Felix clear-headed, Will asks Dallas to step off the edge.

"Don't!" says Felix as he realizes the woman is about to step off the edge of the building, no doubt plummeting 100 feet to her death.

Except she doesn't. She stands there on nothing.

"Hey, Will."

"Yeah?"

"Ever do acid in the '70s?"

"Nah. Did smoke some weed, though."

"This must be what it's like for Alice going down the rabbit hole, huh?"

"Pretty sure."

"So," Felix asks, "what now?"

"Not a clue. Crystal is supposed to be back by the weekend. She wanted to give me time to think about what she has offered."

"What will you do? Offered? Offered what?"

"She wants to make me into one of them."

"I must have had acid and am now having a flashback. And tell her to stop that. It makes me have vertigo for some reason."

"Dallas, if you please."

Dallas steps back onto the 10th floor. "As you wish."

"She wants to make you into one of them."

"One of the People, a vampire," says Will.

"I want to wake up now. Really."

"It's real, Felix. Madness all around, but it is real."

Looking at Dallas, Felix argues, "But you can't be a vampire. It's daylight."

"We're guardians. We have no blood lust, and we walk in the sun. We guard the People's homes during the day and sleep at night, like you." Here, Dallas smiles, trying to be friendly and put Felix at ease. The action only accentuates the amount of muscle she carries as her face bunches in what she hopes is a smile that will put the man at ease. She has so much muscle under her skin that areas on her face and skull move with the smile that humans can't move. There is also a disturbing movement in her ears.

"Oh. Okay." He looks to Will. "So, what does this mean?" He is still fully convinced he will wake up any minute now.

"I don't know yet. I'm still committed to OEE. Girls, you can go now." The women shimmer into nothing.

"They are gone?"

"No, just out of sight, they would stand out, wouldn't they?"

"No doubt, but Will..." Felix asks, "what the hell is going on?"

"I don't know for sure. But I needed to tell someone."

"No doubt."

"So, what's next?"

"Beats me, but this thing is real. I just assumed that with you guys working in the edge of technology and the senator being on some major defense committees in the senate, I thought he maybe had…shit, I don't know. I thought that maybe he had…"

"What? Spit it out, for Peter's sake!" says Felix.

"I figured maybe he has some experience in dealing with the…unusual."

"Oh my god," says Felix. He is laughing hard. "You're talking about that area 51 crap, aren't you?"

"Well, it's no crazier than this thing you just saw. I figured maybe there was more than one kind of craziness out there." Their feet are slung over the edge again. By now, the sun is dipping below the horizon, and they can see the traffic beginning to build on the interstate. Rush hour is, as in most other major cities, creeping back towards noon. In Birmingham, Alabama rush hour now officially begins about 4 PM. Will figures that in another ten years, gridlock will begin about 1 PM.

"I suppose that is the only rational way to look at it, but good grief! Vampires." Felix shakes his head, snorting again.

"Yeah, tell me about it. Vampires. Furies. Guardians. Next thing, we'll have fairies and witches and all kinds of things. Even gravity seems to be put on hold."

"Nope, I just can't buy it."

"What, specifically, can't you buy? Not that I would blame you. It took me weeks."

"You can show me all kinds of stuff, but I just can't buy the gravity thing. It is the cornerstone of everything I believe in!"

"Okay. Vampires are good; screwing with the gravitational constant is bad."

"Yeah," Felix said, waving his hand in the air, trying to emphasise his words somehow, "Something like that. Want to get smashed tonight?"

"Thanks for the offer, but I will pass. I have given up drinking permanently."

"Why? Not that today wouldn't tempt me, too."

"One, I have decided to return to what I claim to believe and two, I don't need the DTs adding to everything else I am seeing. I've already had to deal with the idea that I am just so far around the bend that I can't see it from here. It's also why I had to do a show and tell on you. If I see this shit when I am sober, what would I see when I am drunk or high?"

"Good call. But consider this…"

"Yes?"

"What if you are crazy, and I am sitting here telling you you're crazy and need help, but what you're hearing is what you want to hear?"

"That is where I give up. I just hope I get clear enough to enjoy the drugs they will no doubt pump me full of when I get to the hospital again."

They sit for a while, not speaking, just watching the interstate fill up with the rush hour animals.

"Well, at least we won't get bored for awhile," says Felix.

"Yeah."

"So, when can I meet this Crystal."

"She'll be back this weekend."

"Lunch is out of the question, I guess."

"Yeah."

"Dinner, then. Nine o'clock?"

"That's when we usually do it, so yes."

Both men got up and began heading to the elevator.

"So, which Chinese did you piss off?"

"Huh?"

"Which Chinese did you piss off? You must have pissed one off somewhere. Only a native Chinese hoodoo man could have slapped you with that curse so convincingly."

"Which curse?"

"May you live in interesting times, of course."

Chapter 19

Laying In Bed

Laying in bed, Will begins staring at the ceiling. Will, his brain whirling with thoughts over what Crystal revealed to him and how Felix is taking it, realizes that his life is forever changed. Legends are realities and the world as he knows it all of a sudden is filled with possibilities he had dismissed.

Only, they hadn't been dismissed. Each day is filled with the unexplained and each day, people are in the process of rationalizing away the miraculous and unexplainable.

Why? Why would we spend this much time denying what is really there? To what end?

Will is thinking back to what Felix said about not being able to accept it. What was it he said? Something about you can tell me about fairies, trolls, and vampires, but don't screw with my gravitational constant. But isn't the definition of irrational denying the evidence of what is directly in front of you?

He isn't going to sleep and acknowledges this by getting up and shuffling to the refrigerator for a can of soda, Vault Zero. Will is exhausted, wishing he could pass out but knowing it is no good. Sitting down in his recliner in the darkened living room, he begins summoning the strength to reach for the remote. He flips to CNN, which reminds him that the election for the presidency, which was held last week, is still not over because they are fighting it out in the courts.

Idiots. Will decides that TV is a bad idea. *Can't watch the damn thing without there being 900 commercials that make you hungry, anyway.* As his TV time decreases he finds his eating decreasing as well, a welcome side benefit. *I'll call Crystal. She's a night owl.* Smiling at this thought, he reaches for the phone with considerably more enthusiasm than for the remote. Then he hesitates, wondering if she is back in town yet. *Only one way to know for sure.* She answers on the first ring.

"Hello, Will." It is his little petite blonde's voice, the one who makes him sweat.

"Hello, Angel."

"Am I?"

"Am you what?

"Still your Angel?"

"Yes." He doesn't say, 'of course.' Of course is often a lie.

"I am glad. Can I come to see you?"

"Yes." Then, "Crystal?"

"Yes?"

"How did you know it was me?"

"Who else would it be? Especially at 2 AM?"

"Good." The amount of information one word can convey is an amazing thing.

Five minutes later, Will's doorbell is ringing.

"Who the hell can that be at this hour?" Will asks himself as he walks to the door, stopping long enough to retrieve a Walther .32 from on top of the grandfather clock in the hallway. It is Chris. Crystal.

"How did you get here so fast?"

Crystal just looks at him, letting him think for a moment. He is exhausted. "I didn't exactly have to take the interstate."

"Silly me. Come in," he says as he wraps her in an embrace. He says, "I don't really want to talk for awhile, okay? I just wanted to be with you."

"Talking was the last thing I had on my mind."

Will wakes up. All the blinds had been covered with thick blankets. Crystal is sleeping beside him.

She stayed. Leaning over to call in and tell Sylvia he'd be late, real late, Will notices how still Crystal's form is. There is no movement in her chest.

She's not breathing! Will immediately panics. Not now! Shit! He immediately gave her CPR, breathing into her mouth. She is not responding. She wakes, groggy as hell but aware. *Thank you, God.*

"Will, what are you doing?" Crystal asks.

"You weren't breathing, are you all right? Open your eyes." He wants to see if her pupils are even. *Or something. I need to get her to a doc.*

"Will, Baby. I'm okay. You were mistaken."

Will is sitting on his knees beside his woman in bed. Leaning over, he kisses the side of her neck and mumbles into its hollow, "You scared me, and I thought you weren't breathing. I... all I could think of was I can't listen to her when she sleeps now. Too many great revelations lately, I guess."

I know. I don't have to breathe anymore, and I forgot to set the glamour.

Arriving late, Will greets Sylvia at somewhere past 1

PM. Listening as she berates him for missing an appointment, nodding in what he thinks must be all the right places because she finally looks satisfied and returns to whatever it is she is currently working on. He realizes that he has no idea either what she is concerned about or what she is working on when Felix pokes his head in and asks for a few minutes if he doesn't mind. He does not mind and follows Felix out into the hallway. Felix is clearly on his way to meet with LB, or he would have stopped and visited.

Okay, this is a bit out of touch. Oh, for Heaven's sake, it is Friday afternoon. I will catch up on Monday.

Crystal is in the middle of giving Salome instructions and updates for Monica and Melissa. Salome is extremely quiet for her.

"Salome, what is it?"

"What is it?"

"What is wrong, I mean."

"The war is spreading in the Northern European countries."

"Interesting, there has been no news of even the viral cover story."

"Human losses are verging on cataclysmic. Monica and Melissa both estimate that the human kings can keep things quiet for no longer than two weeks. This is a maximum, hopeful number, my Queen."

"What do they expect will happen?"

"Five days, My Lady; they expect only five days before irreparable damage is done to the cover of silence."

"Inform them that I have broken my own cover of silence with Sir Will, and he is making his decision even now.”

“My Lady, I will do so. Do you think he will accept your challenge?”

There is no other way to put it. It is a challenge. Definitely lose your humanity or humanity possibly loses its existence. It is a challenge and a daunting one at that. If he doesn't accept, I don't know what alternatives we have. Then we will have a choice about giving him a choice.

Saturday evening:

“Will it be any different after you change me?”

“Will what be any different?”

“You know,” and he is oddly hesitant with Crystal this evening, “this,” then, “what you and I have. Will I still be me? Will I be different?”

Looking at him, Crystal realizes that Will is overcome by popular myth, thinking he may be volunteering to be replaced by another soul altogether.

“Yes, Will; no, Will; and I do not know Will.”

Will sits in silence. Crystal continues, “You will still be you; you will be different. I hope so much that you still love me the way you love me now.”

How can such a tiny, fragile woman change in the link of an eye to something so monstrous? What will I become compared to her?

“Everything is magnified, Will. Strength, speed, some argue intelligence but I think it just speeds up a person's ability to be stupid sometimes, and emotion.”

“Then I shall surely die from loving you.”

They don't talk for a while after that.

Monday morning:

"Felix!" Will calls as he walks into Felix's office. *Wizard.*

Dallas' name for Felix sticks in his head, though the strong urge not to tell him of her nickname has no rational explanation. *Perhaps the time of rationality is passing for me.*

"Will, how are you? Still, breaking physical laws? Come to tell me you have fairies living in your back yard now?" His tone is jovial, but is there just the slightest nervous tick in his jaw?

I do believe my friend Felix has been doing a little self-medicating. I wonder what with?

"I am well. Just wanted to drop another bomb in your lap and I need you to tell me if I need to prepare the old man ahead of time or just go for it."

"Will, a day without a 'bomb' from you is like a day without sunshine. What is it now?"

"I need to take off for some personal business and I need to be gone about three weeks."

"You don't need me for that. L.B. has given you free rein anyway. Truthfully, don't even bother. I will square it with him if the need comes up. If he asks, I signed off on it."

"Thanks, Felix…"

"Yes?" Felix could see Will had a look.

"When I get back, I will need to be assigned to the night shift, I am fairly certain."

"Godspeed, Will. Also…" Felix falls silent for a few minutes. Will doesn't interrupt because he had found long ago that when people fall silent it is an unconscious attempt to get you to fill that silence with information. Finally, Felix says, "Be SURE what you're doing, Will. Be SURE. You have become more than just a friend."

"Thanks, Felix," Will takes his leave.

The ride to Crystal's home is a haze. She decides that since she is apparently going to be spending the foreseeable future here in Birmingham, she will buy a home. Owning her own home is the only way she can make the customizations that make it safe for her to live without drawing undue attention to herself. Will helps her pick out a nice garden home in the Southlake subdivision. One of the more interesting modifications Will suggested is blinds that are controlled by photoelectric cells. As the sun goes down, the blinds automatically open. The thinking is that a house with the blinds closed ALL the time will draw some comment.

Will gives up listening to the radio as he can't seem to hear his own thoughts as he rides down I65 South towards the Valleydale Road exit. Reaching over, he flips the noise box off and sighs as he feels the welcome silence sink into him. This must be where the 'silence is golden' saying came from.

Sometimes, I think your bones must get tired of sound or something.

As he turns up Valleydale east towards the Southlake entrance, Will finds he is beginning to feel unreal. The feeling is like the one you remember while an auto accident is taking place, only he knows it for what it is. This may be a kind of mental shock.

Well. Shit, just ride it out and see where the yellow brick road leads, I guess.

He turns into her driveway and looks at the drawn blinds. Will is thinking that if he goes through with this, this may be the last sunrise he sees. Yesterday Felix had been adamant in his advice to be sure, but hell, how could he be sure? He is either in love with a woman who is crazy; he is crazy, or about half of all the things he believes in his life are crazy.

One of either what I believed or what I now believe is crazy from the perspective of not being true but being held to no matter what. Will didn't know if that was true or clear, but it was the best he could do, even to himself.

Will turns away from the sunrise, rests his head on his forearms as he leans again against his car, an SLK 320 he had bought as a birthday present to himself and looks at the quiet house. He is realizing that his lover, the little petite blonde, is in there and is technically dead. The thought is disquieting. Then he laughs out loud.

Well, every relationship has its challenges...and she does look so good in anything or nothing...

The thought is unfinished as the front door opens. No one is there. Clearly, Crystal is inviting him in but can't come to the door.

The sun is so harsh on the skin, dear.

Will is still caught up in a feeling that his brain has been covered in gauze as he walks on in.

If this were a horror flick, I would be sitting in the audience saying stuff like, 'Look at that fool. You could color my ass gone.' Either that or I would be laughing at some of the black women talking to the screen, trying to warn the guy.

Will is walking, approaching the door. He hears an 18-

wheeler leaning on his horn out on the interstate and wonders idly why some idiots in cars want to argue with 20,000 lbs. of rolling metal. His footsteps seem preternaturally loud, even when he is stepping across the grass, ignoring the walkway. All his senses seem to be at about 1200% normal. Smells, sounds from the freeway, even the next door neighbors dog snuffling about the base of their privacy fence seem to be pressing in on him like some great weight. Nothing, however, is as loud as the deafening silence that is emanating from Crystal's house.

Reaching the door, Will tries to clear his mind of that gauzy feeling. It is no good. He is standing in the doorway, still in the sunlight. A thought comes to his mind about the moon shots. There is sometimes a 400° difference in temperature between a shady area and one that is sunlit on the surface of the moon. The difference between here and in there may be much greater along lines he knows he cannot foresee right now. He also realizes that any perceived differences are illusions. The world is what it is, regardless of how you choose to see it.

He steps into the shadows and looks for his heart and his fate.

Chapter 20

The Transformation Part 1

"Will, are you sure?"

"Yes, Angel, I am sure. We have no choice."

"I wish I were sure of the 'we have no choice' part of all this."

"It will be okay."

"You understand what you are giving up?"

Will laughs at his lover. "Baby Doll, you have explained it to me over and over again. I KNOW."

Crystal had explained that Will would never be able to go back, and he would never be able to have human children again. He will never be able to walk in the light of day. No conversions have ever been able to stand the daylight. She also explains that many times he is going to feel a bitter coldness in his bones that no amount of heat will relieve. Will is going to have to grin and bear it until it passes. Cold spells never last very long but are most unpleasant.

"Well, then, Will, sit over in this chair. Because of your success against the spiders," Crystal is calling them spiders like Will, "we are going to restrain you."

"Sure. Got it. 5 by 5, Babe." Will is sitting down in the chair as the guardians begin strapping him in. These are leather restraints reinforced by chains across the back. It is a dull color, but it smells like steel.

"It is Toledo steel," notes the guardian. "You will not be able to break it."

Toledo steel? Well. Toledo steel is a secret lost to

humans. I wonder what else I will see while I am following the yellow brick road over here.

"Will." Crystal.

"Yes, cutie-pie?" Will is about to take a ride he has no real way to get ready for. He is nervous, and his banter reveals it against his wishes.

"You understand that if it looks like you are going to change into a…" and she can't even bring herself to say it.

"You mean, if I 'spider-out?'" Will finishes for her.

She smiles. "You are insufferably cheerful at times, did you know that? Yes, if you 'spider-out,' do you understand that I have already given these guardians instructions that cannot be countermanded? These are guardians."

"Yeah, I know." Some of Will's insufferable cheerfulness evaporates. "But there is no choice. There really never was."

"Hold your head back." Crystal secures his head by wrapping another of those thick, leather, chain-reinforced restraints over Will's forehead. He is now sitting in a heavy, metal-reinforced, oaken chair that looks as if it weighs 500 lbs. Will's neck is arched so that his head is against the backing and exposed to Crystal's bite.

She rubs her hand down the side of his face, feeling the very slight stubble of a fresh shave. She is thinking that he will never grow a beard again.

"Here we go, Bear."

Crystal straddles his lap as she changes into the feeding form, placing her knees and shins along the length of the tops of Will's thighs. Will feels her weight change, marveling at how the known laws of physics really are a short list.

Crystal's weight now becomes painful as she takes on a sharper and more pointed profile.

Will is afraid but is more afraid of showing that fear. It doesn't matter. Everyone in the room can smell it. Crystal leans in for the bite. The only sign that Will is afraid is a single bead of perspiration forming at his hairline in the center of his forehead and a small creaking in his restraints as he tightens up.

This is going to hurt like hell.

There is a sting against his neck.

At least they're sharp.

Will makes an odd sound, something like a cross between a hiss of pain and a chuckle. As Crystal sucks harder and harder, the pain reaches a crescendo and begins to ease off. Will begins laughing out loud now as he realizes that he is gaining an erection so strong it feels as if it may lift Crystal off his lap. The restraints are creaking loudly as Will's muscles bunch and relax, bunch and relax.

Crystal is draining hard now, tasting the blood of her lover, seeing some of his past as she consumes his life. Will's emotional landscape and his inner demons become hers as his hot blood begins to course through her usually cold veins. Humans are creatures, both physical and spiritual, existing on at least two planes of reality. Much of what makes someone unique is carried in their blood.

He is past conscious thought now, caught up in arousal so strong he feels like the top of his head is about to come off. Impaling herself on his manhood, she drains the last of his life's blood. Crystal is now making small noises herself and has morphed back into the petite blonde she was in life. Her pleasure is greatest in this form.

Will is arching his head back now, not out of pain but because he doesn't want Crystal to stop. His hands reach up to take her by the wrists. There is barely enough slack in his restraints to reach her. His head breaks free of its restraints. Snapping his head to the left, he has her head pinned between his neck and shoulder.

The guardians move in. Will raises one finger as if pointing to the ceiling. Conversions are physical events, so they settle back down a bit.

He comes, and as he does, the muscles in his arms bunch so hard he bursts free from the waist up. Crystal now begins a back flood of blood into Will that will result in his change. Wrapping his arms around her, Will hugs her close as she begins to feed his nearly empty veins with a small amount of her own blood.

Only Will isn't satisfied with a small amount. Crystal tries to withdraw but finds herself caught in a grip she cannot break even in her transformed state. He has her face held hard against his neck. Her teeth remain buried in his carotid artery. The backflood she initiated has become a vacuum from which she cannot break free. Crystal tries to cry out for help from the guardians, but her voice is muffled by Will's neck.

I have to get loose. He doesn't know he has to stop!

Will is indeed changing. His forehead, already visibly armored with bone as a normal human, begins to bunch and plate. Clearly, Will is going to be a warrior-class male. Not a guardian, but one of the more fierce People. As she comes to completion herself, in spite of her fear, Crystal feels Will release his grip and stop pulling her. She leans over and hugs his face to her breasts, relishing the way his newly hardened face feels against her skin.

He is going to make it. He is going to be okay.

"Oh!" she cries out.

And we are going to have to learn a few new things. Together. She also realizes he could have killed her.

Even as crystal is thinking this, Will begins to talk. His voice is deep and rumbling, as would be expected. Crystal steps back to see more clearly what she has created.

Will is now one of the People, more heavily armored than most. Crystal is horrified to see the sores begin to blossom along his ribcage. Will appears to be past consciousness again. He comes back and speaks to them all, "God in Heaven, this hurts!"

"My Lady, he is an arachnid, step aside! He must die!" This is spit with such venom. Crystal wonders why Will is not struck down by the words. She will have an opportunity to think about this again.

Will is still restrained in the chair from the legs down. He manages to say, "Guardian, tie my arms back down."

Never having had experience with someone making a coherent request while going through an advanced stage of arachnimorphia, the guardian is swayed just enough to give it a bit more time. Will is again restrained, except for his head. The guardian seems to know that the sight of Crystal may aid him.

Will is sweating so badly that it appears he is melting. He is soaked, sweat beading up in the hair on his chest and around his butt in the wooden seat. His feet, formerly well seated on the stone platform on which the chair was mounted, now slide around helplessly as he tries to gain somewhere to push while he strains against the pain. Water is pouring out of his scalp, down the sides of his face, and into his eyes, burning them.

Anything is welcome if it helps take my mind off this pain. It feels like my joints have all been separated.

Will can also feel a searing in his brain. The feeling is like someone slicing through his brain from many angles.

His neck, thick from years of lifting, is beginning to swell even more. There is no clear delineation between his neck and his chin now. The sound of bone cracking and rearranging fills the air. It is clear that Will is not to be one of the People. Crystal is crushed, and she is wailing. She signals for the guardians to burn him, burn her lover, her best friend. She thinks it is better he die than become some mindless thing.

She turns away, thinking she cannot bear to watch, but continues on in a 360-degree turn until she is facing him again. She owes him. If he is to die, she is to live with the image of his death.

The guardians are opening panels in the room, pulling out what look to be high-tech water hose nozzles. Made of burnished brass, they are flame-throwers. Nothing of an arachnid can be left to live. Salome thinks, *Especially this one. He killed an arachnid as a human. What could he do after the change?*

Monica and Melissa enter the room, both in armor. Neither says anything as they walk over to Crystal.

"He isn't going to make it," says Crystal.

"Crystal, let's go and leave Salome to her duty."

"No, I should watch. I owe him that much." Her voice is barely understandable as the pain of losing Will tears its way out of her being. She is standing now only because Monica and Melissa are supporting her.

Monica asks, "Crystal, do you think he wants to want you to see him this way?"

Knowing her mentor is probably right, Crystal agrees and allows herself to be led out. The last thing she hears before the metal doors slams shut is the ignition of the flamethrowers.

My Bear is going to die.

Inside the room, the guardians back against the walls and aim their weapons at the body in the chair. It is no longer recognizable as human.

Salome looks to the other guardians, nods a signal and pulls her trigger. Will begins to burn. The Will creature, as Salome is thinking of him, begins to writhe. One arm falls off, and then a leg separates at the knee. The appendages continue to move as if trying to flee the fire.

Crystal is being supported as she walks down the hallway. Wracked by the pain of her own culpability in Will's death, she realizes she can't go on. Breaking free from her friends, she is racing through the halls. Neither Monica nor Melissa is capable of catching her on foot inside the castle. Resorting to flight, they are within sight of the distressed Norn as Monica is struck with a sudden knowledge of what Crystal means to do. Crystal is heading. for the huge front doors to the courtyard. It is 1:00 in the afternoon.

Crystal clearly means to use the sun to commit suicide. As the plans were laid for the transformation, the thinking is that if Will is indeed an arachnid, he will at least be confined to the keep until more strength can be brought to bear.

"Crystal, don't! It's not your fault!"

Crystal ignores her friend, her dearest of friends, for

thousands of years and flings herself out into the burning daylight.

Monica and Melissa both come to a halt, barely keeping them from falling into the killing light. They can do nothing but watch their friend burn. Guardians stand helpless as they watch the youngest queen die.

Chapter 21

The Transformation Part II

This isn't going well.

Salome is concerned that the Will-creature isn't being consumed. Parts of it are, but it appears to be mounting a more effective campaign of self-preservation than usual. That portion that would have corresponded to the torso and head region is using the chair as an effective shield. It crawls up under the chair and sacrifices its appendages to shield what the chair can't.

It is aware.

Salome holds up her hand for the guardians to stop. All but one does and has to be nudged by another guardian. This is the guardian who spoke with such passion about Will's need to die.

Staying well away from the thing with her heels pressing against the wall but her nozzle still pointing towards the dying creature, Salome looks at the creature. The mouth is moving, and a sibilance of voices is coming from it.

Laughing and crying is the voice of a child. Will's family might have recognized this voice as the voice of the Will-child, the little boy who would grow up to die at the hands of a guardian vampire. Another voice intrudes. It is the voice of the man the Will-child became. It calls the name of his ex-wife and says goodbye. A rumbling comes through as well. If asked, some might speculate it to be the voice of the Person Will might have become had he not succumbed to whatever it is that causes arachnimorphia.

The form, smoking now, charred and blackened in some

places, bleeding and leaking a clear fluid in others, releases its hold on the chair and falls to the floor, rolling out from under the chair. The guardians flinch, thinking it is an attack, but Salome again signals restraint. She is curious as to what the Will-creature is saying.

For twenty minutes, Salome is enthralled. She hears what she almost takes to be babbling until she realizes it must be a language she's never heard. During the middle portion, a set of voices roll out of Will, freezing them all in their tracks until another voice says -

"Free them."

The guardian who was so bent on killing Will early on, isn't mollified and screams at Salome, "Do your damn duty and give the order or I will do it anyway!"

"No, and you will not. Something is happening here and I want to see what."

Fuming, the guardian crouches down, back to the door. *It will not escape.*

Salome is completely shocked to hear her own name issued from the Will-creature's mouth.

"Salome." A whisper so full of pain that even the battle-hardened guardian is tempted not to listen and simply burn it into numbness anyway, curious or not.

"Yes?" This is new territory, speaking to the remains of a failed conversion.

"Listen to me; I don't know how long I will be able to speak."

Salome remains quiet. It is clear that the Will-creature is allowing itself to gather its strength.

"I am not arachnid."

Salome continues to simply look at Will.

"I am something else." The form is rising and falling, beginning to breathe more regularly.

Because Will realizes what is happening and has thought about the possibility of arachnimorphia, he begins to fight the change. He feels his brain moving into strange parts of his body, and he begins to hear the voices he often hears just as he goes to sleep, arguing with each other. He sees what is happening because he knows that those voices are just facets of his own mind. As he falls to the ground, different parts of his psyche take control of his mouth, and it sounds as if many people are speaking from his single body.

Will feels a burning sensation begin up and down his sides. The sensation is like a hitch in the side one gets from running, only this one is not in one spot; he feels as if there is a white-hot wire running from his armpit down his sides to his groin. Voices begin to come from everywhere. It seems the voice of a child, a man's voice, thunder.

Not thunder, one of the vampires, Will thinks.

Will hears a man call his ex-wife's name and realizes it is not others he hears but himself. There is a sensation as if he has become some burning liquid, intent on getting as far away from itself as possible. The emotion is that of wanting to not only be oneself but to not BE.

There is the sound of a woman crying. *Is it her?* In his extremis, he knows he is still not free from love for his wife. *God, maybe she is right. Perhaps I am not a man.* The woman calls him by his pet name, Bear. Will turns his head to see her.

It is not his ex, but his forever, Crystal. She is crying. Will begins to say, 'Don't worry, it isn't as bad as it really is,' and to laugh, but she turns away. It doesn't matter; his mouth isn't working anymore.

The guardians are all turning away with the exception of Salome, who is simply staring down at him with hard, unmoving features. Still, her eyes manage to convey a great weight of pity. *I'm sorry,* they say.

Will is wracked by a spasm so strong that he feels the restraints cut into his flesh, even along his waistline where they have tied him to the chair. His eyes see the other two Norns begin escorting Crystal away. The guardians have all pulled what are obviously guns of some type from lockers in the room's walls. The guns have hoses attached, and Will, in a single instant, both question and understand what is about to happen. *I think I want my money back,* is his last thought before the flames jump to him and begin to eat him away. First, he smells bacon. The nerve endings are all burned away on the skin in an instant. In the next, the flame reaches down to those nerves that scream no matter how much morphine is administered. *Game over,* he thinks.

Will leaves for a bit, his mind shattered by the pain. He awakens into what, for a second, he thinks of as hell. There is a wall of flame everywhere and on every side.

Not dead yet? Looking down his left side, Will sees that his leg has fallen off at the knee, and his arm is sloughing off like some dead bird's leg, suspended only by a single thread of skin. A blast of purple hot flame from a guardian's gun burns it through, and it strikes the floor with no sound.

All of this is unfolding like some silent film. Flames have burned away all his hair his ears, and burned down into his ears. *Why am I not blind?*

My mind has come loose from its hinges. Will hears screaming. My God in Heaven, what ARE they doing to that guy? Then he realizes he is hearing his own voice in his mind and with his mind. This part of him observing these events has separated itself from the rest of his mind. Will is able to think.

Racing ahead, Will begins to think and calculate. A hundred, a million perhaps, theories are postulated, evaluated, and tested against the lab of his mind and what is left of his body, and he finally knows the arachnids for what they are and what they intend to do. Death is not a choice now.

No matter how scarred I am, nor how crippled, I must live.

Suddenly, Will is falling through space. It seems to last a lifetime, as things do during times of great physical stress, and being burned to death qualifies. Finally, Will strikes the floor. As the guardians move about the business of destroying him, so much has been burned away that there is not enough to keep him in the chair.

I needed that. He thinks as he sees his leg, burning, some two feet away. As if and almost certainly in response to this thought, the limb begins to twitch and work its way towards what is left of Will. Everything begins to move in towards Will as he climbs under the chair, thinking to gain some moments and regain his voice, not realizing he is talking out loud all this time anyway.

As he moves under the protection of the chair, he sees the guardians. One motion to the others. They are arguing. One of them wants to hear him out. He knows he should know this thing's name, but it just won't come.

Those others inside him begin arguing. Will is overcome and disappears inside what is left of his own mind. There is a mutiny afoot. *What is happening to me?* After some time, Will re-asserts control. He no longer has a brain, strictly speaking, but many nodes are distributed throughout his body. Each has its own agenda and way of escaping. Had Will not been able to take control, he would have died. *We would have died. There are many of us now.*

Suddenly, there is a presence in his consciousness, like blackness. Watching it invade his mind is like watching some accelerated film footage of fungus eating its way across a forgotten loaf of bread. *Welcome, human. Are we not beautiful? We will consume you and make you one with us, and you will only know a cold certainty of the beauty of death for eternity.*

"NO!" Will screams.

Relax; there is no pain. Man is born to suffer. His mind is our meat. Once you become, you will eat. This is said in a sing-song voice that, again, reminds Will of some girl at youth's peak.

Coldness begins to invade Will. He feels what was his mouth open and screams at the guardians. The coldness thinks, and Will knows its thoughts now, what with them being bonded together at the seams of their minds like two metal sheets being melted into each other; *these guardians are ours now. This one is strong! He will be able to freeze armies.*

Rather than fight, Will relaxes. As a child, he remembers suffering from 'night terrors.' The doctor tells him that it is nothing more than the Pons in the brain failing to disconnect the spine for sleep, but Will is never sure. As a child, he awoke many nights to find himself paralyzed, a prisoner in his own skull, while the room filled with all kinds of terrors and delights. This is the same.

Just like it. Nighty night. As Will disengages and just

relaxes, he senses pain and withdrawal from the coldness.

What are you doing? Those guardians will kill you if you don't allow us to fight!

So who's arguing with you? asks Will. *I am just relaxing here. You motherfuckers want to be in charge? Go to it. My faith is in my God and in myself. I may be destined to die here, but I will not take anymore with me. Nor will I live as a monster. You have no authority over this body, and I WILL NOT BE A SLAVE. I AM MEANT TO BE A KING, AND I HAVE THE POWER TO KNOW THAT WHICH IS AND MAY BE, SO SIT IN THE STINK OF YOUR OWN CHOICES, UNBORN ONE!*

With that, there is a tear in his mind as the unborn thing tries to withdraw. Will isn't through, though; he strides through the thing's mind, pulling things unknown to humanity, or perhaps forgotten, out by the roots. Even as he looks at some of this, he knows his rational mind will not retain it. *Now, I understand the balance in justice. We are that balance!*

Will's last act before releasing what he will remember as something that exists without having been born is to command it to free the guardians.

"Free them." The unborn thing goes screaming into the blackness, wailing about betrayals and opportunities lost.

"I am something else," says Will to Salome.

"Lord Will?" Salome is unsure.

"I am an arachnid, but I know what is wrong with them, and I know now what they plan."

"What...?" The guardian who is bent on Will's destruction fears greatly for Salome's life. She puts the barest of pressure on her trigger. *Better that I be imprisoned than Will escape.*

Salome's movement across the room would have been almost invisible to a human. It is barely a blur to the guardians.

Snatching the weapon away, Salome shoves the bigger guardian against the door hard enough to make it rattle in its frame. The guardians outside send one of their number for reinforcements.

"Go. Notify the Queens as well!"

Inside, Salome is arguing with a screaming hulk.

"He is aware, and he remembers who he is!"

"It's a trick! We must finish him before he completes his…!" Before she finishes, Salome lifts her in one deceivingly slender left arm, reaches across with her right arm, opens the door, and slings the offending guardian into the hallway, slamming it behind her. She turns back to the others, who are simply staring at her.

"You others will leave me with him and set up a perimeter. Inform the Queens that I will try to ascertain what Will's status is."

They hesitate until she barks, "Now!"

Opening the door, the first to leave turns looks at Salome, and says, "You are going to die."

"Not yet and not today," Salome says. She closes the door after the last and turns to Will.

Will is sitting up. At least, there appears to be a layout of body mass that would suggest he is sitting up. The mouth that had spoken to Salome is on top of the mass leaning against the chair and two legs are extending out from the bottom of the main mass. He hunches over and a crunching noise fills the room as the mass appears to bend and break halfway up what looks to be the torso.

It looks to be disappearing into itself. Salome's state of mind is what it almost always is, unflappable. To watch Will roll into himself is going to give her nightmares, though she doesn't know it now.

The outer covering is no longer black or red or running in places with whatever that clear fluid is. That discoloration has been replaced with a covering that is almost completely white. As Salome watches, the sphere begins to elongate and exude extensions, five in fact. After a few minutes and answering, bangs on the door to say that she is alright. Salome is looking at a roughly humanoid shape on the floor. Some 40 minutes later, it is clearly human. An hour later, it is clearly Will. He sits up.

"Salome, where is Crystal? I made it. There is nothing I need right now but her." He takes a deep breath. "I need her and about 400 lbs. of red meat.

Monica is looking at him, clearly torn up over something. *What? I made it, didn't I?*

"Monica? What's wrong? I made it!"

Chapter 22

Aftermath of Changing

Well, that was not worth it. Nope. I live forever, and Crystal is dead. Then again, am I really me? Is this thing that has taken Will's place really Will?

As Will becomes acclimated to his new condition, he finds, much to his delight, fleeting as it is that he is not bound by the rising of the sun. He is truly an arachnid, but somehow manages to maintain the integrity and identity of his mind. Being an arachnid, he is able to walk in the light of the sun. Will is still unable to come up with a set of thoughts that explain how he can transform from a 220 lbs. human to a killing machine with a distributed central nervous system weighing as much as a Bengal tiger and being many orders of magnitude more dangerous. He tested his strength against one of the bulls on the agricultural compound to the south of the main keep. Will is astonished to find that he barely notices the bull's struggles. Finally, the bull simply quits struggling and goes limp. Will turns loose and steps back from the animal. It simply lies down. Observing guardians pick the animal up and carry it back to the barn. Fear of Will's arachnid form drives the poor animal into shock. Will hears later that the bull isn't good for much for months.

Looking out over the plains surrounding Norn's Lair, Will is struck by how quiet the land is here. There is nothing moving across the fields. Even the guardians by the gate seem preternaturally still. The sun is coming up over the eastern edge of the crest on which the castle and attendant buildings sit. Automatically, the metal louver blinds begin their twisting to a closed state, blocking out the killing rays.

"Will, how are you this morning." Queen Monica joins

him once the blinds are fully closed.

"Fine, I am fine. Is it always this quiet in the mornings?"

"No."

The pause goes on until Will finally notes that something is required of him. Having no idea what to do next, he simply breaks the rules and asks. "Okay, what now?"

"I have no idea."

"Well, then, no worries. Just beam me back to Alabama and buzz me when we know what I have done to myself."

"That is as good a plan as any."

I really hate phone menu systems.

Will is fuming now. He is trying to get through to Felix. No one seems to be able to find him. It will not be possible for him to talk with him once he is airborne. Oh, he could call, but there is no way he will, not with absolutely no way to secure the line. Talking on the nifty, neat cell phones from 30,000 feet is like screaming your business to every security agency on the planet.

Hell with it, I will call him when I get there, and he can come get me.

The flight home from Germany is uneventful. From Norn's Lair to what the guardian calls the Holy Roman Empire is calm as well, though why the guardian calls Germany the Holy Roman Empire is anyone's guess as far as Will is concerned. History is so full of interweaving and revisions according to the vision of the victor that truly, the only thing you can know for sure is that at this location, at this time, something happened and we're pretty sure these folks were there.

"Felix."

"Will! Buddy! Where are you?"

"At the airport. Can you come get me?"

"Yes, but it will be…30 minutes, okay?"

"Sure, no worries."

"…and Will?"

"Yes?"

"You okay?"

"Doing great."

"Well, I only ask because it's daylight."

"I know. It was a weirder trip than I thought."

Weirder than you thought? Okay. "Good to have you back, Will."

I was only gone for three days. "Glad I was missed."

Will is being brought up to speed on all the events since leaving with Crystal. As Sylvia continues on with her litany of things that simply must be handled by him, he becomes alarmed and excuses himself, shutting his office door. He picks up his headset and punches up Felix' extension.

"Felix here."

"Will here. Felix, how long was I gone?"

"What do you mean, how long were you gone?"

"Why, almost three months. Your infection had laid you up pretty good, didn't it? Will?" Will had hung up.

"Why didn't someone tell me, Dallas?"

"I don't know, Will. It honestly didn't occur to me."

"Do you think I can just disappear for months and not cause problems?"

"It was only ninety days, Sir Will."

"That's three months!"

"I am to guard you. I don't have to be shouted at. Ninety days is nothing to get excited about. You…ah. Alright, I see now." Dallas hunkers down to Will's eye level. "Your temporal perspective will be much different after a bit, Sir Will. When you live hundreds of years what you see as an extensive period of time goes through changes. It was a mistake. I apologize, both for myself and the Queens, as I am sure they won't mind my doing so."

"Hell, I guess when you put it like that, it was an honest mistake. It just feels so weird. What was I doing those three months?"

"From what I understand, you were in the transition room the whole time. No one wanted to move you for fear of upsetting the process. What you did has never been done."

"Dallas, I remember being in the transition room. I went through the change, your buddies tried to flash fry me, and Salome talked me through. I put myself together in about 45 minutes, got happy about making it, and was told that Crystal committed suicide." Will's face clouds over here as her face fills his heart.

"Will, you were in the transition room for 11 weeks. We didn't know if you were going to make it at all. There were days when it seemed that you were just gone. Twice, we gave up on you and almost removed your body, and you would speak…" Here, Dallas looks distant, "A few guardians even refused to work the room. There were…" she trails off.

"Were what?" Will asks.

"Sometimes, it seemed that you and your guardian had company from time to time."

"Who?"

"We do not know. The seers not only didn't see them coming, they couldn't' see where they had been."

"Something new, then."

"Yes. Again, something new." It is clear Dallas equates 'new' with 'dangerous.'

Chapter 23

"My Lady," Salome says.

"Salome," Monica greets the small guardian as she always does. She has given up on bringing a guardian into their circle of friendship.

I think perhaps they are more hardwired in their brains than we are. It is an errant thought. Monica knows it comes as a result, like the rest of the things she is wondering about, of being exposed to Will. Right now, she wants to know about Will's status.

"No news, my queen."

"And Circe, any reactions out of her? Any warnings?"

"My Lady, Circe is a bright spot in all this. She says the cataclysm has been delayed an additional two years because of Will's conversion."

"He was a major player in their plans, then. We were right to change him."

"So it would appear, My Queen."

Circe knows as they escort Will through Norn's Lair that he will emerge as a powerful warrior-class vampire, rivaling even the guardians in strength. She is taken aback by his calmness on the outside because she can feel all his internal noise. He is in a full blown panic attack inside, but his exterior even has the People around him fooled. Except for me, but even my eyes insist he is completely nonchalant about the conversion.

Circe is watching as they pass by, the human male encircled by giants and led by two of the queens, Monica and Crystal, down the hallway to the conversion room. It hasn't been used that any of the guardians can recall for such a thing. As he passes by, Circe sees.

Will is standing on a hill in what appears to be a desert country. His back is morphing, and his forehead plating is beginning to beetle up. Suddenly, he is surrounded by guardians, and they move forward into a wash of what can only be arachnids. Their nightmare shades cover the sands as the groups engage. Will's forehead suddenly depresses even further and …

"Circe?" A guardian was touching her elbow. "Are you quite all right?"

"Yes, certainly, why wouldn't I be?"

"My apologies, but you looked as if you were about to faint."

"No, no. I was just thinking about things. He looks to be holding up well, scared and all."

"Yes, he does; fast for a human, intelligent, and honorable. He is unusual."

The vision is not returning. She is straining her not inconsiderable talent to see. No matter how hard she is trying to retrieve it, it is not coming. She finds something else instead. The temporal blindness isn't there anymore!

I can see! Will IS the key. He... and here she sees the end of the road again. The blindness is still there, but it has been pushed back some 25 months.

A reprieve is good; a lot can be accomplished in two years. I must inform the queen.

"My Lady, I have good news."

"So I am told, Circe, so I am told. Well?"

"The blindness has been pushed back two years."

"That IS good news. Perhaps we can figure out a way to actually determine who and what is behind this and perhaps where they are."

"I have a suggestion along those lines, My Queen."

"Proceed."

"Well, it occurs to me that since I can't see what has been happening out the past two years, perhaps I should begin looking at the span between here and there. I am thinking that their seers will see this, too. If I can determine who is angry over the delay perhaps that will lead us to the more directly culpable."

"Excellent idea, Circe. Move forward with it."

"As you wish, Lady Monica, I will do so now."

Salome is saddened by the loss of the youngest Queen. Guardians' emotions aren't so pronounced with the exception of protecting their charges. Salome still misses Crystal, though.

We never did get to our race and now we never will. Is there an after life even for the undead? Salome is ignorant of it if there is. She only knows that she and every guardian there will meet the same fate as the queens right down to the last one.

Chapter 24

Journal

February 1, 2001

My Angel is gone, and there is no reprieve. God has seen fit to match me with first an untrue wife and then to take from me my long-sought heart.

I have anything I want, I only have to reach put my hand and take it. It is all like dust in my mouth, dry and with no taste. Food doesn't satisfy, I drink and stay thirsty, I sleep not to rest but from simply passing into unconsciousness. She haunts me.

It is her scent. No flames of hell could torture me more nor make me happier. It fills my heart until I can't seem to breathe and yet I continue to live. Her scent is in my head, her taste is in my mouth, her skin is on my fingertips, and I imagine her heart beating next to mine. My sleep is wracked with feeling her next to me with her breath in my ears. My days are filled with her face in my mind as I walk through things I no longer care about. Now, I can't even look forward to the peace of death. I can't figure out if God hates me and has taken her from me or loves me and sends her spirit to me at night.

Then again, this thing I have become. Is it something she would want? I am a killing machine that thinks of nothing but another life.

The People who are rebelling against the Norn are even worse. They are ungrateful. Essentially immortal, they fight amongst themselves for power over things that mean nothing. They know no disease, no aches other than cold, and hunger cannot kill them. Yet, they continue to spread misery, death, and poverty rather than use eternal life to make paradise.

The arachnids, now, are to be pitied. Insane, mindless beasts, they are controlled by something. I am convinced that the mind that they were before is trapped down inside them somewhere. Maybe the legends of demons in hell were close to the truth, only instead of being in hell tortured by demons, hell is being trapped inside a demon's shell.

I watched an arachnid from a distance before killing it. The things don't know what they want to be. Maybe they are seeking a form that doesn't torture them. Who knows?

Tomorrow, I travel to the Sahara Desert. There seems to be reason to think that the rebels have found a way to ally themselves with the arachnids. We will see if I am what Monica supposes. There is an area believed to contain some 40 or so spiders. Monica is insisting on sending an entire battalion of guardians with me. I see no reason to risk such a number of folks. If I am what she supposes, I will win. If not, I will die. No point in getting them killed, too.

My work at OEE goes on. The more obvious attacks have been dropped in favor of subtlety. Well, maybe that's a strong word. It is the government we're talking about here. It is interesting to see the technology progress as OEE and the government grind into each other. The kids in the hole are beginning to warm to the work, sometimes sleeping by the machines for days. We have increased physical security about as much as we can, I think. Kyle has even gone so far as to recruit a corp of retired or inactive SEALs and others to build an internal security force for OEE. Hell, call it what it is: a private army. We call it Attitude Response for some reason. OEE has interests all over the world, and with the troubles in northern Europe, we aren't able to depend on the US military to protect us anymore, so we do it ourselves.

I met one of the young men yesterday and was surprised to find that he has obtuse mathematics as a hobby. His name was Siggy. He's a newlywed. I like him. He is to be head of security on Felix's pet project, whatever the hell it is. I am now wondering just what it is. The old man is now even talking about going out into Arizona and basically building a company town and closing it off for the duration of the final phase. Again, of whatever the hell it is they are working on. Stay tuned.

Chapter 25

A Game Plan

"Well, there are a few issues that need addressing. Will is on his way to test himself against a number of arachnids in the central desert. We can only assume he will be successful for the purposes of this meeting." Monica is trying to come up with a game plan that will satisfy sympathetic human leaders and her own loyal lords, minimize the resentment of the losers, both human and of the People, and put in some measures that will prevent a repeat of the way World War II grew out of World War I. The need for speed in moving on these things is suffocating.

"But what if he isn't, My Lady?" Lord Roger Tamerlane is skeptical of Will's chances. He has seen arachnids in battle and only escaped because a bridge had collapsed. While the river swept the thing downstream, he and his guardians had fled. It had been a nightmarish journey driven by guardians nearly insane with fear for their lord.

"Then we will come up with a different course of action. Right now, I don't have a backup to Will."

"Very well," Tamerlane isn't agreeing, he is admitting he doesn't have an alternative to futility. *But I guess doing something better than nothing* is a thought he would never admit to.

"The cover of silence that masks knowledge of our existence from the masses of humanity holds. The United Nations was always in our favor. We just had to convince junior leaders in the US and Britain that it was in everyone's interest for us to remain in the background. We don't need another bloodbath in addition to the one that will occur here.

Humanity's best course of action is to avoid the rest of the battle."

"What about the infected areas of northern Europe?"

"If Will is what we think, then he and a smallish-I am speaking relatively here-force of male guardians will go in on point, backed up by Lord Tamerlane's Coyote brigades." The Coyote brigades are composed of only truly large, fast guardians who have faced or been involved in actions against arachnids.

"Does the UN really think that they can keep us secret from the human hordes?"

"Doesn't really have to, human capacity for self-delusion is easily great enough to do it for us. All the UN has to do is laugh it off and go on about their business, ignoring questions concerning us. Oh, a few will pursue it, but we've measures for them as well. A trip to a psychiatric hospital and professional destruction will be more than sufficient to dissuade the pushy ones."

"I have to agree with you there, My Lady." *Humans may not be able to decide which they like best, fucking or fighting, but they understand their money.* "Make it a financial proposition, and they will let it go. What about Sven and his ilk?"

"I have thought about it, agonized over it, actually. I'm figuring that if we don't finish this now, it will just come back and bite us again later. I have decided that total extermination for the rebels is the only choice. Their lands will be divided amongst you and the other Lords. The only thing I ask is that a portion of your increase goes towards reclaiming the great desert. It is becoming a self-sustaining system that grows and may become a great danger itself someday. Do you agree?"

Here, Roger responds without seeking agreement from the rest, but he is right to do so. "In principle, there is no objection. Of course, we will want to go over the details between now and the time Will returns. When do you expect to know the outcome?"

"Within 2 to 3 weeks."

It is hot. Even the guardians, normally fairly sanguine about physical hardship, are complaining. The Bedouins hired to guide them into the deep desert, are still insisting they travel at night to conserve energy and water.

The guardians resist for the first week out of habit. Will, ignorant of the desert, thinks maybe listening to their guides is a good idea. He goes along with the guardians at first but now is leaning towards changing the game plan for the trip.

"Dallas, the girls are suffering from the heat. We are shifting to night time travel."

"We prefer to be called guardians, Lord Will."

"I know you do. Now, we will continue through the rest of the afternoon, and tonight, we will build camp for tomorrow and begin again tomorrow night."

"We will be behind by nearly a day, Lord."

"Yes, but if the girls start passing out and possibly dying from heat, we will be under-strength when we get there, and all could be lost. Besides, I still maintain they know we are coming. If we are a bit late and they are anything like us, perhaps the waiting will make them antsy enough to make mistakes." *...and why this damn Sahara heat is affecting the Guardians is another thing that makes no sense.*

It isn't as if they hadn't gotten the best equipment available. The deep Sahara desert, though, will simply punish and grind any vehicles built. Even the Rovers are unable to do anything with the daytime heat, edging over into overheating territory if you try running the air conditioner.

"This shit isn't getting it." Will is hot, and leaving the windows down as they crawl over the crests of the dunes is like standing in front of a blow dryer on high. Running the air conditioner is no good because the things are designed to drop the temperature of the air some 15 degrees. Dropping from 118☐ to 103☐ just fails to get anyone excited.

Will instructs the English-speaking guide, who immediately translates it for the rest of his companions. The looks of aggravated relief suggest that they have already had this conversation with enough fools to have it memorized.

Dusk, on day 12 of their trek into the desert, wakes Will with a question.

"Dallas, we should have flown in. We could have dropped in on chutes."

"What if the plane had crashed?"

"Yeah, but we could have been there in 10 hours instead of 10 days."

"I never thought of it, though I wasn't in charge of the logistics planning for this trip. Salome is. I am sure she has her reasons, though I could not tell you what they are."

"Okay."

The morning of the 14th day of driving they arrive at the edge of an area that is different from the surrounding desert. The wind, kicking up dust from the top edges of the dunes they had just come across, seems to just stop at a line that meanders in both directions for as far as they can see. The ground on the other side of the line looks to be covered in what looks to be a yellowish talcum powder.

"Lord Will, we are here. Please do not cross that line until we are prepared."

"Okay, I won't, but why?"

"That is arachnid land. You cross the barrier, they come."

Will turns to instruct the Bedouin leader on avoiding the barrier but finds one of Dallas' lieutenants doing the job. The guardian is holding one of the pit bulls brought along to guard camp at night by the neck. The dog is pulling back from the guardian away from the line in the sand. Will doesn't hear all the conversation, the wind is picking up enough to even confuse his new hearing. One word gets caught.

"Watch…"

Will thinks the guardian says, 'Watch and remember,' but he isn't sure. With that sentence dying in the wind, the guardian picks up the pit bull and pitches it perhaps twenty yards over into the powder-covered area. The animal lands, stands up and immediately begins to sprint towards the line. Even from where Will stood, he could see the fear in the animal's eyes.

From the north and northwest, there is movement. Will is reminded of early morning cartoons where the Tasmanian devil is whirling towards some victim chew toy. A cloud of sand moves towards the dog from the two directions until it is clear the one from the north will get there first. The northwest cloud then begins angling in towards the first cloud.

Still sprinting, the dog is within ten feet of the barrier when the first dervish catches up. It is quick. One second, the animal is a killer dog, and the next, he is dog meat. It is so fast that the human eyes can't follow. Will sees it all. The animal is slung upward, beheaded and gutted in three motions. The animal never even saw the blows coming.

Then, the two creatures square off for maybe two seconds, seeming to lapse into what can only be called a formal stance and fly into each other like a couple of lawnmowers. It is like looking at two huge mutated crabs, perhaps 3 feet across the main section of their bodies, with numerous arms of differing structures. They are silent, just as they had been when attacking the dog. Then, a simple challenge in voices Will recognizes. The voices are still beautiful.

He looks around to see the guardians, each holding back a Bedouin from crossing the line. Their faces seem to be in a state of rapture. The guardians look wary, amused and deadly.

The creatures close, and after perhaps ten seconds, one is down, dead, and disappearing into the gullet of the other. The dog also disappears. The thing then looks towards the barrier line, considering.

I see now why 'spider' is both apt and irrelevant to this thing, Will thinks. *Insectile hatred is the only thing behind those eyes. Hell, even an alligator has enough emotion to care for its young.* Then, the thing disappears into the sand.

Silence returns long enough for the humans to regain control and begin packing. Abject fear and leaving now is their agenda. A guardian tries to stop them by morphing all the way into a battle state. She isn't going to hurt them, of course.

The human leader looks at Dallas, shrugs, and says, "Fine. You are a demon, too. Better you than those."

Will interjects, knowing she isn't going to hurt the guy, "Dallas, we are here. We can find our way back without them. Let them go."

Turning to the leader of the Bedouins, Will continues, "Go two days' drive back and wait for us. If we are not there in four, go on and notify the office that hired you."

Will and the guardian's pitch camp well away from the line in the sand. A single guardian isn't a match for an arachnid anyway, and nobody wants to roll over in her sleep across the line. They know that tomorrow will bring a battle, and no one knows what will happen. Oh, a dog isn't enough to set the spiders off. An armored convoy, though? Will is pretty sure they will come from a good piece to the disturbance they planned for tomorrow.

I wonder if I will be able to sleep. Will thinks.

Will's question is answered by the sun shining through the door to his tent. *Okay, the answer is yes.*

There are no Taps as in a military exercise from the past. There is not a lot of discussion, though more than once, guardians simply stop and look at Will. Most had not seen him change. This is Dallas's idea. 'He is disturbing, My Lady. I feel parts of me reacting to him as an arachnid even as my brain is telling me to answer his questions.' The guardians are efficient, and the camp is broken and packed within the hour. After some 45 minutes of testing equipment and reviewing the plan, they are ready to proceed. Will doesn't need to be part of the other's preparations. He will either survive or he won't. Failure here puts them back at square one and no backup plan.

I will not fail. This thought isn't one of a ball player psyching himself up for the game. Will is confident of his victory. He hates the spiders like no other because he understands what they are, why they are the way they are, and the decisions they make on whom to follow. He intends to cross the line and kill spiders until there are none left.

Besides, if they had left things alone, Crystal would still be here. With that thought in his mind, Will crosses the line without giving the guardians time to follow. *No point. I am what Monica hopes or I am not. No point in Dallas getting killed, too.*

"Sylvia, please begin making backup copies of all Will's documents concerning OEE." Felix is trying to be cheerful. He doesn't understand Will anymore and Sylvia has become strange as well. She seems to have multiple personalities lately. One minute, she is the super efficient assistant Will brought with him from Infosurge, and then she seems to go away and be…well, somebody else. Her speech changes, her mannerisms are totally different…and she just seems sad.

Well, who wouldn't be? I wonder when I will start showing the strain. Sylvia at least doesn't have to deal with knowing what is going on with Will. *Maybe she is looking at Will the way I am looking at her.*

Now there is a neat image, all of us sitting in a circle looking at the back of the other watching the other go slowly insane or change so completely we are looking at a stranger's back. This is…

"Felix?" Sylvia is touching his forearm to get his attention because he quit hearing her.

"Yup, you caught me woolgathering. What?"

"I asked if I could bring them over in the morning or do you need them right now. If you want, I can simply put them in our safety deposit boxes unless you just want copies yourself."

"Well, we need them put in something other than an Infosurge lockbox."

"These are all owned by a trust based out of Lichtenstein."

"Perfect. Better than an OEE box even. Good. Just let me know that it is done. Let me point out. I DON'T want to know where the boxes are."

"Yes, I know. Just like Will."

This is amazing. We don't do anything wrong, and we still have to watch the government. It is better than home but the federales are doing what they can to make it JUST LIKE home. Sylvia is making copies, filling and labeling boxes, and thinking to herself that it must be working for a government that makes people bad.

I don't think Felix knew what he was asking when he asked me to make and file copies of all OEE-related papers. She works all day and hopes to finish today. Being maybe 70% done at 4 PM Sylvia decides to push on and complete the project.

Besides, I will just go home and watch TV. "Phfft!" It is a sound of disgust at the thought of watching the mental gruel that is well-chewed by mamma networks and regurgitated for consumption by the audiences.

I wonder what these trips are about. First, he goes to...Norway, is it? His girlfriend gets killed in an accident in the mountains. Poor guy, now he is in Africa in the Sahara. Well...

Finishing up around 11:00 PM instead of earlier, she gets home by midnight and crashes on the couch. As she passes out she knows she will be late getting in tomorrow.

Even as Sylvia is passing out on one side of the world, Will is striding across the sand on the other. He calls back over his shoulder, "I am ordering you, Dallas, to take no action that will endanger any guardians in any way."

"There will be multiple arachnids here momentarily! Perhaps as many as fifty! You are our charge!" Dallas is beside herself. She is also unsure that she can stop Will even if she can get to him in time.

Will responds in a steadily deepening voice. Striding across the sand, he feels his humanity slipping away as his body becomes plated in armor. He is striding through sand that is clinging to his two feet, and then the sand is replaced by a hard-packed talcum-like powdery surface that seems to settle almost immediately, almost as if the dirt itself wanted to attract no attention here. Will ceases to notice the retiring quality of the soil as he sees his two feet grow to three very different appendages. One, still recognizably human, aches almost unbearably, but the pain is fading. Will is standing on four legs, all tipped by wickedly sharp triple-pointed hooves. Will turns to address Dallas, just as he feels his mind split along the lines it usually does.

By the time he finishes his turn to address Dallas, he is telling the truth when he says, "Dallas, Will is no longer here. This is our war, not yours. This day, we will avenge Crystal and every death that has occurred here. Watch and report if we lose this battle or the second one."

The thing addressing Dallas isn't even remotely human. Standing perhaps 6 feet high, it is even longer than that. Will has become a bladed, insectile centaur, standing on four feet and holding four bladed appendages. He appears to be dancing some exotic Indian dance. He opens his mouth, and a sound comes out.

It sounds like he is singing, thinks Dallas.

As Will continues, his arms begin a winding motion, as if he is weaving the air into something that the eye cannot see. Dallas hears a noise from one of the dunes to the rear. Thinking for a split second that one of the spiders has gotten around them, she springs over to the hill side and snatches up one of the Bedouin tribesmen who has come back. He is looking over towards where Will is beginning his dance of death as the arachnids close in and scream over and over, "Shiva! Shiva! Samaharamurti! The angel of Death has come!"

"Yes, Felix, everything is archived and stored. I even made multiple copies of everything on CD."

"Good girl. Whoops. I mean, well done. It's that sensitivity training crap I had to go through for CEC. You are not a 'girl,' or if you are, I am not supposed to comment on the fact. It's all very confusing."

Sylvia is laughing, "God, what a crazy place the US is. They are trying to train out of the American male any admiration for women…and the women seem to encourage it. I AM a girl and thank you for noticing. What's CEC?"

"Continuing Education Credits."

"They want to be sure you keep up with the latest 'crap?'"

"That must be it. Bye, Sylvia." Felix is cheered up as he heads to meet LB.

"LB." Felix.

"Felix." LB.

"Kyle." Felix.

"Felix." Kyle.

Felix meets LB and Kyle in LB's office. With greetings out of the way, the meeting begins.

"Felix, bring me up to speed on where we are with the security project with Will and his team."

"The team is getting better. They are slamming the break in attempts at the NOCs rather than at the mainframes, always a good thing."

Felix is proud of Will's team. They work twenty-hour days, sometimes 30-hour days, with no rest against the feds best. Make no mistake here. It is the feds and every hacker they could put the squeeze on trying to break through to OEE's in-house skunk works. Now, working eight-hour shifts, the team is beginning to look like a group of humans instead of a bunch of zombies.

"What's a knock?"

"NOC. N-o-c. It stands for Network Operations Center. It is where we store the routers, bridges, and other telecom equipment. It is better that we catch them there because we can shut the door physically at the drop of a hat without having to worry about what it will do to internal communications."

"Oh, okay," Kyle says.

"When will Will be arriving, Felix? He is to be here, no?"

"Actually, no. He is in Africa doing some research in the dunes of the Sahara."

"The Sahara Desert? Why?"

"I am sure that I don't REALLY know, LB." *And I can't really know. I know what I saw. I know what Will told me. But to suppose that I really know what is going on is lunacy.*

Will is on to something huge and is simply going overboard on the security issue. I have to trust him because the old man trusts him, and he has never done us wrong. So. I can't really say what the case is. Ergo, I bow the hell out of this chain.

"LB, I don't know. He has done an excellent job of dealing with the hackers from NSA and the threat is understood now."

"Well, good. But…"

"But, as you say, I am really getting snowed under with the…Project. I think it would be a good idea for Will to report directly to you from now on."

"Felix? Is everything okay with you and Will? I thought you were fired up about working on this project."

"Right as rain, LB, it is just that Will has proven himself more than capable of overseeing these projects, both the network security project and this…environmental project in Africa. I am just in the way."

"Well, I see no reason to object. The boy is trustworthy and we did groom him for the job, though this soon wasn't anticipated."

"He can handle himself quite well. In fact, I can say with complete confidence that he is extremely suited for handling the unusual."

Kyle is watching Felix from the old man's left. Felix looks nervous and that's not good for someone sitting on the projects he is sitting on. He starts to bring it up and, point blank, asks him what is wrong, but LB stops him with a single uplifted finger.

We'll talk in a bit and you can tell me what's got your wind up, but not right now. LB's eyes are making it very plain that Kyle is to be quiet. He does so.

"Felix, I will follow your advice on this. Have Will report directly to me. If I am unavailable, tell him he is to debrief Kyle here in depth."

Smiling strangely, Felix nods agreement in Kyle's direction and walks out. Neither LB nor Kyle hears Felix chuckling to himself as he makes his way back across the hallway to the elevators and back to Sylvia.

"Sylvia?" *Felix again?* "Yes, Felix?" *What's the deal with his being here three times in one day?*

"On the projects Will is working on, please let him know that he is to report directly to LB from now on."

"Okay, will do."

"And Sylvia?"

"Yes?"

"Can I call you sometime?"

"Well, you do…oh."

Felix is silent until Sylvia responds, "I'm sorry, Felix. I do have a boyfriend, and he wouldn't like that at all."

"Oh, well, I had to try."

"It is okay."

Felix leaves awkwardly. But he brightens later. *A boyfriend. Well, a boyfriend won't even slow me down. I am a patient man. Besides, it took her a bit to tell me no, so…still. You need to be careful, Felix, my brain buddy.*

This is what Felix sometimes referred to as conscience, or maybe the part of his brain that is purely logical. He can never decide, and he knows it is because it is interwoven with the rest of his mind. If she says no, she means no.

Yeah, but no now may not mean no forever.

True, but you need to understand that she said NO, NOW. Later is later and doesn't have a lot to do with right now. Besides, something is wrong with you thinking about her now anyway. You've got a Project to work on, remember?

Yeah, okay. You're right.

Well, the old man doesn't want to know right now. Then, *Works for me.* Kyle is thinking back to the meeting earlier that afternoon where Felix Dorcai withdrew from direct supervision of Will's projects. *Or he knows and has something else in mind.*

Kyle is up to speed with the fact that he works for one of the primary architects of America's war against the Soviet Union during the Cold War. LB has even clued Kyle into the fact that there were months that the so-called 'Cold War' was pretty damned hot all along the division line between West and Eastern Europe. '3700 casualties, Kyle, and not one network carried the news. Think about it.'

Kyle did think about it, and it bothered the hell out of him because it pointed to a level of control not even the most laughed-at kooks believe in. *Not a helluva lot to do about it, but it would be nice to know. Then again, maybe ignorance is bliss indeed, and the less the masses know, the fewer of them you have to kill in order to maintain your power.* It is a working theory, anyway.

Well, you hired me to be your assistant, Old Man. You're holding stuff back from me? Okay. But I am beginning to think that we are not just making a buck here and trying to keep the government off our backs while we do it.

Come to me, Will thinks. *I will grant you the peace you have been seeking.*

Will opens his mouth and thinks to bellow this in a loud, deep voice. What comes out is a sweet voice, perhaps some gifted child who will certainly sing opera; only this voice is understood by those who use it. It is the voice of a beautiful death, where all suffering is gone.

As he gears himself up to fight the horde, he is reminded that Napoleon thought he was sure to win, as did Hitler and the others. *Should thought about that myself before I crossed the line.* What passes for Will's face now grins in its fashion as he steps into the path of the oncoming arachnids.

The four-bladed arms begin a pinwheeling motion. Will steps forward into the first wave? From the guardian's perspective, Will appears to be where he was and where he is simultaneously, like a double image. Four spiders fall, severed in half, the stumps spouting the fluid that passes for their blood.

Will steps back, in one place again to take stock. Being basically animals in battle, the other arachnids fall on the carcasses of the others. Some of the dead aren't as dead as others, inflicting mortal wounds on those who would be diners. Within minutes, Will is simply taking out those who are busy consuming their brothers.

If this is as hard as it gets, this shit will be over soon, Will thinks.

These must be the weak ones. Battle strategy dictates they would test you out, reserving their best for last.

Perhaps. Still...

Still, what? This didn't even take ten minutes to kill nearly 50 spiders. THIS is what has put the fear of God into the People and the human leaders? I don't think so.

Will is suddenly slammed to the ground hard enough to

impact him into powdery soil and then slung into the air. He hears the crackling sound of his body's natural armor beating against itself.

I knew there was more to this than...

Will hits the ground and turns to see what just kicked the hell out of him. He sees nothing. He looks to the guardians who are watching from across the line. Dallas is looking around and it is clear that whatever hit him, she doesn't see it, either.

Will is backing out now, turning suddenly in a random fashion, hoping to catch the thing. He isn't hurt, his armor protects him completely, but there had been enough force to move him.

I didn't hear it. I can be slipped up on. That's a BAD thing. He crosses back over the line and moves back towards humanity when a wall of dust erupts along the line in the sand and races in both directions.

A challenge, Will thinks. Okay, but I think today is a draw.

"Besides," Will says out loud, "if the thing could have killed me, it would have."

"I agree," says Dallas.

Besides, I don't know if it was a challenge or not. They got their asses kicked, I got cocky, and the suckers snuck up on me. No big deal.

"Success!" Monica is talking to Melissa.

"Scores of arachnids, dead at the hands of a single individual. Never before."

"Well, it did go fairly well." Will is wondering when the subject of the mystery mauler should come up. He decides to allow Dallas the opportunity to discuss it and invites her to tell her story. She is telling everything but decides not to bring up Will getting ass slapped across the desert by an invisible foe.

I guess it will have to be me, then.

"Monica, the arachnids went down with ease, but…"

"Will, if I might interrupt?"

"Sure."

"Perhaps we don't want to bore the Queen with all the messy details of the trip. You slew nearly 50 arachnids single-handedly. The trip was a success by any measure."

"Dallas is right, Will," says Melissa. "The details are clear. You faced one as a human and lived. You faced dozens as an…as a Person…" here she stammers a bit, "and lived. What else is there?"

The younger Queen is clearly uncomfortable with the discussion. She is about to say as an arachnid but catches herself, only it is more of a fumble, really.

"My Lady," says Will, "I know some are uncomfortable with my status as a person, owing to the way I don't change into the typical person…or even the same battle state twice in a row, apparently, but my mind is my own, and I am your ally."

"We know this, Will. We know," says Monica.

But you are still uncoble. Here, Will just looks at the floor. *Things are what they are. Perhaps time will remove the looks of distrust and disgust.*

Chapter 26

Lost Soul

Where am I? She is looking down at a machine she has seen but can't recognize. A man is looking in through the doorway and calling her Sylvia for some reason.

Why? Then, *So, what IS my name?* She panics and passes out.

"Sylvia? You okay? Felix is concerned. Sylvia looks for a moment as if she were going to pass out.

"Who are…" Sylvia hesitates, and her vision clears. "Felix?"

"Yes? Are you quite alright?"

"I am now. I don't know what that was…" *Weird. I haven't felt that since…magia…abuela. Shit.* "Is nothing, Felix…" her accent was extremely pronounced now.

"Well, okay…" Felix leaves, concerned. *She is a grown woman.* Felix has a hard time interacting with Sylvia. She has become different in his presence. He thinks it is because he asked if her could call her. It is not.

She is dazed and confused and aching in every bone in her body. She tries to look down and see her legs, but she can't seem to focus on her legs. *Hurts.* Sylvia's vision seems to blink back and forth between in the office and standing on a sidewalk.

She is trying to focus on the last thing that happened and discovers she can't remember anything, period.

A homeless person wanders by, and she reaches out to him or tries to. Her arm doesn't seem to respond. He takes no notice of her and continues his meandering down the sidewalk.

Unconsciousness takes her.

"Will, I understand you need a leave of absence?"

"Yes, Sir, I need to see about some family business in Europe."

"Europe is a dangerous place right now."

"Yes, LB, it is. But this is imperative."

"I know, and you have my blessings, but Will, can't you discuss with me the nature of your troubles?"

"I really can't, LB."

"You know, Will, Felix was gung ho about being over the security project. All the technology involved is just right up his alley. Then you disappear into Europe for three months. I am really sorry about Crystal. Then you're in Africa for some ecological study for a bit. I realize that I offered you free reign but don't you think this is a bit excessive?"

"Look, you bought me out when I didn't particularly want to be bought out, but it was a good opportunity. You told me to check out some new things and just run with whatever looks really important. I need a leave of absence to do that. Do I have it or not?"

"Of course you do, Will. I just need to know what you're working on."

"Okay, what is the Project?"

"Excuse me?"

"The project, Felix's pet project, what is it?"

LB looks at Will and then turns, reaching over himself

from left to right to punch up his assistant.

"Kyle, Will is about to begin a leave of absence."

"Very good, Sir." Kyle is waiting for further instructions. Then, "Anything else?"

"Make sure he gets whatever he needs. You can coordinate with Sylvia. He will be working on some company projects in absentia."

"Will do, LB."

"Have a nice trip, Will. Have a good time."

"LB." Will leaves.

After Will is gone, LB picks up his handset and calls out to his receptionist.

"Secure line to Felix, please."

"Yes, Sir."

It takes a bit longer than usual and LB is about to walk out and see what the delay seems to be when Felix picks up.

"Felix, here, LB, just had to run," and he puffs out a chest full of air, then continues, "to a land line. What's up?"

"How much does Will know about the Project?"

"Nothing. I mean, he knows it exists, but he doesn't know anything about it. Why?"

"Well, I don't know, Felix," and here the senator lapses into a long drawl that earmarks his getting pissy about something. "Do you think maybe he should know about the damn thing? Why? He isn't part of it, so…"

Felix cuts him off, the second first in the last thirty seconds, "Whoa! LB, hang on. Will was in charge of the network security project, remember?"

No, I didn't. "Felix, you are correct and no, I didn't remember. I just had a visit from Will, and he clarified that he was going on a leave of absence. In any case, he knows now just how sensitive I am about the Project, and he also knows that I am not ready to trust him with any info on it. All of which adds up to, I don't know what, now."

"Well, let's just let sleeping dogs lie, for now, LB. When did he say he would be back?"

"He was unclear. He also made it clear that while it was important, he didn't want to go into any detail with me on it. He…what's funny?"

Felix is laughing. He stops and answers the senator, still with a chuckle rolling around underneath his words, "Can you blame him? You want to know what he is up to. He doesn't want you to know…yet. Will uses the Project to tease a little data out of you, and you gave it to him. Now he both knows how important the Project is to you and that you don't trust him with what it is."

"Hell, it isn't that I don't trust him. You just don't want…"

"Too many eggs in one basket?"

"Precisely, although this looks like a sly-stupid decision now."

"Well, don't worry about it too much. Will probably understands."

"How can… doesn't matter. What do you think of taking him into our complete confidence and promoting him to a full directorship?"

"Kind of changing gears, aren't you? First, you don't want him to know what we're working on then you want to promote him to a position of Director? What's going on, LB?

Sometimes, you wait too long to give me information, you know."

"Things are deteriorating, and I am worried that our efforts may be in vain, Felix. We need another ten or 12 years to bring the project to a point where we can make some changes, and now things seem to be falling apart. By the way, you sure you don't know what Will is working on?"

"LB, I really don't."

"Good enough."

"Monica." No, my lady, Queen, whatever. Will is tired and beginning to lose a bit of his respect.

"Will." He is unexpected, un-summoned and unusual in his manner.

"I am tired of waiting. Where are these people who have turned on you? Why don't we just march in there and take them out?"

"Well, there are quite a few things to consider before…"

"I don't mean to be disrespectful. I really, really don't. But enlighten me. If I am to do this thing, then I need to be brought up to speed on what I am, what you are, who we are facing…the whole ball of wax."

Monica lets Melissa do it.

"Basically, Will, the People are what humans have called vampires for centuries, or are at least the source of the vampire legends. The truth is close enough that the People let the name stick, kind of like the Mormons allow themselves to be called Mormons when their actual name is Latter-Day saints. Mormon is from the name of a book of scripture, the Book of Mormon. It is simpler just to let them call you Mormon rather than spend 30 minutes explaining the name when you can concentrate on more important things.”

“It is believed that the People are an offshoot of Cro-Magnon man, the most direct progenitor of homo sapiens. Cro-Magnon man may BE Homo sapiens, but some scholars disagree.”

“Got it,” says Will. “Go on.”

“The Neanderthals were wiped out either through a catastrophe or planned attack. Histories are sketchy and this happened so long ago that even the few vampires old enough to yell down anyone else in the house can’t really remember it. Evidently, immortality is no proof against stupidity.”

“We do not know if they were wiped out by disease, some sociopath person or groups of persons or even if the disease that wiped out the Neanderthals may have been the disease that unlocked the Cro-Magnon’s ability to become a vampire. Will, we just don’t know.”

“Well, what DO you know? I mean, I am pretty sure that discussing what we DON’T know in an infinite universe is a losing proposition.”

“Well, yeah, I guess it has to be. Anyway, what we do know is that some small percentage of conversions results in an arachnid, a vicious, almost certainly non-sentient being that cannot stand itself or its own kind or anything else.

“But it has enough sense to hate itself?”

“I see your point. I will have to think about that another day. There are others, the guardians, who are built like armored cars. They have very strong protective instincts and are employed by People to guard during the day hours. A few guardians are born males, but they are generally useless and suffer from an analog of the double YY chromosome disease you see in humans."

"But I thought they did a study of the top business leaders and found an inordinate number of them have YY make up."

"Actually, they found that the YY males tend to be taller, more aggressive and of lower order intelligence than the majority of Y males. We know that Y males are more successful at reproduction. If they weren't, you would be a double Y."

"I suppose. Please continue."

"We think that here is some inherent ability in the human genome for great things…witness the People and the Guardians…but also the same weight for possible destruction. Look at the arachnids. "Let me put it this way. Was Hitler a great leader?"

"What?"

"Was Hitler a great leader?"

"No! He was a monster! He murdered millions!"

"Was he a worse monster than Stalin or Mao?"

"Sure! Certainly. The Chinese and Russians were our allies. Why…"

"Okay, so explain to me why Hitler was worse than Stalin for killing 6 million Jews when Stalin executed more than 8 million Georgians?"

"Stalin killed…?"

"Mao killed maybe as many as 200 million people during his reign. Which is worse?"

"Why doesn't anyone ever talk about it?"

"Let's leave that to history. Were these people great

leaders?”

“No.”

“I disagree. They were great leaders. They were just evil.”

“I don’t getcha.”

“Will, what I am trying to say is that there is power in the human genome that is untapped. Hitler was a great leader…for good or evil, he was great. He chose to be evil, but that didn’t have any effect on his effectiveness as a leader. The human genome is a thing of power.”

“Okay. Let’s say I agree. So what? What use is it to know this?”

“There is a missing piece to all this and I not only don’t know what it is, I don’t know how or where to look for it. You know what Circe said to me the other day?”

“Yes, I do. I am just waiting for you to bring it up.”

“Excuse me?”

“Skip it; my sense of humor is just a bit odd some days. No, I don’t know. Tell me.”

“She asked the question, very tongue in cheek, about why she and the other seers were blind. Was it because they were all dead, everyone was all dead, or because the universe wasn’t here. She feels like she should be able to see the lands of the People and the humans even if every living thing were dead.”

“But she can’t see.”

“Nope, not a thing, Will, she cannot see a single thing.”

“Which is why we are blind to the arachnid areas? Everything is dead there.”

"Oh, no, she can see into the arachnid areas."

"But I thought everything was dead."

"See, that is just it. She can see into areas that have at least SOME form of life, and even the arachnid areas are teeming with bacterial life. She is saying that it may be possible the seers are blind because all life, not just humans and People, but all forms of life right down to the simplest, are dead."

"Dear Lord," says Will.

"I agree," says Melissa. "I agree. I wish He were here because I think we need His help. I can't imagine that what we are looking at is anything other than the Apocalypse."

"The apoca-what?"

"End of the World. Ragnarok. Armageddon. Every major religion and thought system in the history of man has looked at the end of man in some way or another. We see it. Well, Circe and the other seers see it. We have to stop it because it is apparently going to sterilize this planet and not just kill off people. Everything dies, and earth is a rock."

"Okay, so, the human genome, yes? Okay. You think there is some kind of answer there for what we are facing?"

"Possibly, we don't really know. Circe walks around in a daze half the time, asking sly-stupid questions that feel like they ALMOST apply but she can't seem to remember the line of reasoning for the question. There seems to be some link between you and this event that wipes the slate clean, so to speak."

"Well, I don't know about that."

"Yes, you do. You do know. Your conversion is the only one known on record where someone successfully averted becoming one of the mindless arachnids.”

“To sum it up, humanity is not only composed of different races, but also different populations that have to live in different environments due to the predator-prey relationship that CAN exist between the humans and the other races.”

“I thought there were only two, the People and humanity.”

“Where would you classify the arachnids? They were human once. The guardians aren’t really People… the point is that we are at war with a rebellious group of People who want to slap the humans down permanently. The arachnids are helping for some reason.”

“Can’t the rebels see the end of the road the way Circe does? Surely they have seers, too.”

“Will, they don’t believe us. They don’t believe the seers. They see the seers as weak and spineless, refusing to join their cause,” says Circe.

“Hardheadedness is its own cure, eventually.”

“I agree. I just don’t want the whole planet being burned down.”

There is a knock at the door.

“Milady, Lady Monica requests your presence in the throne room. It appears to be quite urgent. There is apparently a guest with important news.

“We’ll be right there.”

Melissa is getting up from her seat as is Will. Together, they walk through the door and turn left towards the throne room.

"I don't know if we're fighting super spiders or super bio-teacher now. I mean, I am familiar with genetics. We have even used some of the principles of genetics in the creation of evolutionary algorithms for encryption purposes. I just don't know how you can say that there may be more power there. Okay, so I can see the benefit of creating biological weapons to use against the spiders, but this thing you are talking about sounds like it might be years before we can come up with some information that could be useful. We need to act now."

"I agree," Melissa says as they enter the throne room, "but I am thinking that if your conversion put it off over two years, perhaps other actions can push it further back until we get some decent intelligence on this thing that we can't name carrying out actions that we can't see."

"I will do my best, but I am only one. There has never been another like me and even I got slammed the other day by something I couldn't see."

As they walk towards the dais upon which Monica sat, they turn to look at their guests.

Those must be what old vampires look like. Yuck. Will thinks.

Monica almost smiles. "Yes, Will, these are fairly mature examples of People."

"Honored, Lord Will, but I am afraid you are laboring under an incorrect assumption."

"What is that?"

"That you are the only one. You are the only one living."

War

"Will." Monica nods her head to Will. She has

summoned him in what are the wee hours of the morning for him.

"Monica." He is not disrespectful this time. She has asked him to speak familiarly with her, and he is doing so. "Is all well with you?"

"Yes, but I have decided on these rebels."

Will waits silently.

Monica continues, "We know where what we believe to be 90 percent of their leadership."

"Really? Where?"

"County Draco, Circe's homeland."

"My Lady." Circe walks in. She looks very sad and very small.

"Circe, come sit with me."

The young woman walks over and sits beside the Queen. Her dejection is evident in her shoulders' set.

"Circe, what's wrong?" Will is astonished at the young girl's change. She looks as if she is about to be physically ill. Pale, hair somewhat straggled, and her hands trying to take control of each other in her lap. She doesn't respond, so Will turns and looks at Monica.

Monica meets his eyes, and her pain is great, almost as great as the child's. "It is her homeland that is to be invaded and…expunged. It seems that…"

"My own father has betrayed the Queen." Circe is calm in her voice. There is a quietness that will not last forever.

"Monica, are you sure? Are you positive?"

"Yes, Will, we are positive. Circe herself has found him out."

"How?"

"By being a seer and looking in the quiet spaces between what is and what may be." Circe's voice is very small. "He wants to be more than he is; being my father and my mother's husband and just a…normal man isn't enough."

It almost never is, thinks Will.

"What is to be done?"

"You are going in with the Coyotes as an advance guard. We don't know the status of the area."

"Arachnids?"

"Not that I can believe, no. In case they have found some way to keep the bastards on a leash, you will go in first with Dallas and Salome. Salome is to hang back a bit with you. If the arachnids are there, you are to engage while Salome brings word."

"Good. I want this over with."

"Well, I don't know if this will make it over with, but it is a needed action and is such that we can temper the range if need be."

"You expect them to initiate peace negotiations if it goes badly for them."

"No, I expect them to bag for their lives WHEN it goes badly for them. I don't know what I will do."

"When will we leave?"

"Salome is with Dallas. They are coordinating now. I want this to be done and over with." Monica is staring out the window towards the now green fields around Norn's Lair. She is looking at the very spot where Crystal went up in flames.

Why can I not mourn over my sister? She is dead because of me to some degree. Monica had lived long enough to truly understand that an individual's actions really don't control other people's lives, but she still feels responsible for allowing Crystal to be Will's guardian. *But who else would have done it? Not me, I am the Queen, most recently head bitch since I have just consigned dear Circe's entire county to death, but what can I do? She found her father to be a traitor. The child never hesitated. She also knows her father will disown her…she has seen it.*

Monica turns to Will. "How are you doing, Will?"

"Good, I guess. Why?"

"I mean, are you holding up with…everything."

"Oh, the change gets weirder and weirder. For some reason, I turn completely white now when I change."

"Why is that weird? Your changes are never the same. At least, that is what Dallas has reported." *So what else is added to the mix of the thing that is Will that would make him say it gets 'weirder and weirder?'*

"Well, that is just it. See, when I first started changing, I was pretty much following the line that the arachnids usually do: insectoid, bladed, and generally bug ugly. Now, though…"

"You not bug ugly?" Monica is smiling a little.

"Well, no, not so much. Instead of changing into a big spidery-looking thing, the changes are becoming more mammalian. In appearance, they are, anyway."

"So why is that so weird?"

"It looks like there is a war inside me as well. I think maybe I am fighting on some level to NOT be an arachnid."

"Well, that is good then."

"I suppose so. I just don't want it to make me weak in any way. We need to win this battle with the rebels and their spider buddies first. Then I will deal with whatever the hell it is I am."

"Sounds like a reasonable approach, so what about the white thing?"

"Well, see, usually, to some degree, I can sort of 'aim' my changes unless I get spooked, and then it gets really vicious, and I am not there for a bit…that I can remember. Dallas says I answer her and talk to her, and I remember everything from now, but in this form, I don't remember much of what goes on in my battle state."

"But you answer to Will, and you remember everything as a changeling from your human state, but as a human, you don't remember everything from your changeling state?"

"Right."

"Will, change now and let me talk to you as a changeling."

"Okay, but it means I will have to eat again."

"We are not without the ability to feed you. Change and let me see this thing you say is weird."

"Okay."

Will closes his eyes and feels the familiar blink/tug inside his mind that indicates he is morphing. It is no longer as painful as it had been at first. Since the day he had been thinking about 'runner's high' and how the body dumps endorphins into the blood stream under stress, his changes are increasingly pleasant. He thinks maybe his brain had picked up on the idea and the power of suggestion causes his brain to do the endorphin thing. He is pretty close to the right of it.

When a vampire changes, there is usually a crackling noise as the bones restructure and shift. It is even more noticeable in the guardians. Will's change is marked by a hum that seems to come from each individual air molecule in the room. Almost sub-audible at first, the tempo and volume increase until there is a thrumming vibration that sounds like long horns blowing, filling the room, and he slides into his new form. Today is no different, but all clearly insectile characteristics are missing. Monica only says one word when he is done.

"Beautiful."

I think those Old Ones may have been right.

Reorganization

"Felix, I think it is the only way to protect our interests. If they get antsy enough, they will send in the federal agents and take the database and such, and we will be screwed." LB is about apoplectic with rage. He had been sitting on intelligence committees for years, and now he is the target of the very machine he had helped build to combat the Russians and Chinese. LB now knows how a dog owner must feel when the thing turns on him.

Betrayal, fear, and not a little bit of being tach'ed out on the pissed-off meter are just a few of the emotions he is experiencing as he continues to talk to Felix and read the paperwork that the NSA has just delivered to him. The delivery agents probably hadn't even gotten off the parking lot. LB doesn't have to read the whole document to understand their intent. *Prepare to be boarded and ass-*

cored.

"How can we do it? I don't mean why, I mean how?"

"Well, assemble all the departments' heads. We may want to do a wipe down of all hardware and just do a single back up."

"Okay, one hour?"

LB paused, considering. *If an hour isn't enough time, we are fucked anyway.*

"Sure, also, get Sylvia there as well. She is Will's second so since he is not here, she will fill in. Also, I won't have to explain to her what is happening. She is the one who acted so quickly before."

"Sure thing, I will do it now." He is cheered at the thought of a reason to see Sylvia again. *Sad, you're really sad. Whatever. Oh, and note to my subconscious: Shut the fuck up.*

"And call that son of a bitch, Loki. I want his ass here if they walk in. He'll walk, but at least he will sweat, too."

"Okay."

"Hang on…" *Not enough time. They know we have measures in place. They would know that from my own damn protocols. Okay, do the unexpected.*

"Felix, do you have enough design data in your laptop to start over if necessary?"

"LB, are you kidding?"

"No, Felix, I am not and answer me now."

"Could be, I am not sure."

"When was the last major backup done?"

"Hang on…"

LB can hear Felix in the background putting the question to someone and asking if the backup is a full, verified, tested backup or it is an incremental backup.

"LB, it was done two days ago."

"Can you run with that if need be? Can you get back up to speed if a meteor turns your lab into a smoking hole?"

Felix now realizes where this is going. "LB, are you sure it is that bad?"

"Felix, I designed these protocols for the purpose of combating domestic enemies. We have, I am positive, been targeted as a domestic enemy of the United States. Take the backup, get in your car, go by the bank and…scratch that. Leave your personal finances alone. Kyle!"

Felix hangs on, raises a shaking hand to his forehead and listens as LB tells Kyle to bring him his attaché that he thinks his personal checkbook is there.

Felix hears a few more noises, clearly the snapping sounds of someone opening a briefcase, a grunt that might have been the word 'good,' then footsteps approaching the phone. He hears the door to LB's inner office close which surely indicates Kyle's leaving the office.

"Felix, take the backups now, and leave. Call me this afternoon. About an hour from now should surely be enough time for me to get some cash for you."

"But…"

"Listen up! Here is your schedule for the day."

Shit. "Okay."

"You writing?"

"Writing."

"You will walk over to the storage area for backups and put the thing in your pocket. Will it fit in a pocket?"

"Yes." If Felix had had time to be amused, he would have been. Backups of multiple terabytes would fit inside a thin bikini crotch cup these days. That's what happens when you become pure management. You lose touch with…

"Felix, you with me?" LB.

"On my way, walking down the hall now."

"Okay. Let me know when you have them in your hands."

"Walking that way now."

"Alright. When you have them, you want to begin a wipe-down procedure for all the machines. I want them clean."

"Okay. Will do. Hey, Brandon!" Felix is calling out to one of his crew in the lab.

"Yes, Sir?"

"I need everyone to log off the network."

"Okay."

"I also need you to walk to the Cisco's and turn them off."

"That will leave us out of touch with the other labs."

"Right, do it."

Brandon is walking away, signaling to several of his compatriot technicians.

"LB, I am in the backup room. I have a box of drives in hand."

"Very good. Now begin…shit. They will be able to pull a lot of the data off anyway, won't they?"

"Not when we get through. I would like to stay and see to the wipe-down procedure myself."

"Nope, I want you out of there as soon as you can instruct…what's that kid's name I met last week? You know the one with the hot rods all over his wall?"

"Brandon. He is unplugging us from the hardlines now."

"Good. Can't you tell him what to do?"

Yes, I can. He will also quickly pick up on what is happening, but that can't be helped. "Yes, I can. Talk to you soon?"

"Yeah, about an hour now, I think. Just tell Br…no, call Sylvia with where you are in about 45 minutes. I am on my way to see her. I don't know about the lines in her building now."

"Okay, talk to you soon."

"Brandon, are you done with the routers?" Felix's full attention is now on taking down OEE's entire data mining and research databases to a single data backup.

"Yes." The routers, all Cisco 7500 series, now sit quietly in their racks. Brandon had even had the sense to unplug the network connections from them. He responds to Felix's raised eyebrow as he fingers a dangling RJ45 jack.

"Well, if they can find some way to reboot the routers remotely or if someone forgets and cycles the building's power, they are still unconnected to the outside."

"Smart. Now, are all the machines loaded with Wipeout?"

"I believe so, yes."

"I want you to walk through the lab and instruct everyone that we call it a day. Go do it now and come back to me."

"You want me to send everyone home?"

"Yes, with the exception of one or two guys who will help you format the drives after running Wipeout. Do it now, Brandon."

Brandon looked as if he were about to say something. "Don't think too hard right now; just do what I asked. We will talk on the other side of this thing.

"Okay."

Felix walks to the window of the storage room where he had picked up the drives and looks down on the parking lot. He isn't entirely surprised to see several vans of LB's Attitude Response Team pull into the lot and take up positions at the parking lot's corners.

Oh, boy. LB is upset. This is some bad shit.

"Felix, I made the announcement. Everyone says you're their hero. What now?"

"I have to go. You, after everyone but your help is gone, will begin running Wipeout on the machines. Use the DOD seven pass option and wipe those babies down completely." Felix had considered the Gutmann scheme but decided they did not have time.

"Okay."

"You will then run blast.exe and format the drives."

"Okay."

"My machines, you will do the same thing and then

take…walk with me, and I will show you."

Felix and Brandon walk down the hallway to the good-byes of the support staff. Some obviously have wonderful plans for the rest of the morning and afternoon's unexpected break. The scientists and techs are also jovial about going home.

"Don't you guys get too happy about it? Just be more tomorrow to do." *I think.* Felix is cutting up with them as if nothing is wrong. Maybe nothing is.

Walking into his office, Felix goes to a closet, reaches in, pulls out a heavy block of metal, and turns to Brandon.

"Brandon, wipe it down, blast it, and format it. Then, pop the case and lay this on top of the hard drive."

"What is it?"

"It is a 3 lbs., 50,000 Gauss magnet. It will trash my hard drive completely. There is no way to recover this machine after you're done. Do NOT fail to carry this out, understood?"

"Yes."

"Get to it."

As Brandon walks out, he is disturbed but determined. *As am I,* thinks Felix.

Brandon walks down the hall, steps into his office, and dials out.

"This is Brandon Chaney. I want to speak to…"

"Beautiful." Monica is staring at Will in his changeling state.

"What?" Will is looking down at the Queen. She is even more diminutive looking from his changed state. It is only now that he realizes that he is looking down at her from what must be eight or nine feet. *Something new. Again. Yip-fuckin-yee.*

Will looks over at his warped reflection in the silver urns that flank both sides of the doors leading into the room. He grunts to himself.

"I need a mirror."

"Follow me," says Monica.

As they leave the room, Will stops and turns around thoughtfully. He is distracted by the sound of hoof beats in the hallway.

"Will, that is you."

"Yeah, I know. It just startled me, is all."

"Come on."

The small Queen and her escort walk through the castle in search of one of the few mirrors in the place. Will is struck by an idea.

"Why don't you ride?"

The Queen laughs, "Why not?"

Will kneels, and Monica climbs on. She is dressed in all black as she sometimes does. She indicates that he should turn at the third left door.

"There."

Will is surprised at his image. There is nothing spiderlike at all. He is almost nine feet tall, a human horse centaur with four arms. His skin is a uniform snow white. His face is his own, and he is glad. His belly is armor-plated, but the plate conforms roughly to the layout of human stomach muscles.

No freakiness here. Now, this is what I'm talking about. This thought would return to him later.

Journal

February 11, 2001

Well, tomorrow I go to war. They say Salome is the fastest guardian and can keep up with a cheetah. I saw her sprint to the north gate. I don't think she could keep up with a big cat. I think she would smoke its ass so bad it would give up speed as a bad job. If there is anything sexier than a woman running, I don't know what it is. She morphs back into an almost human form. She claims she is faster! Crystal used to run like that. Never mind. Some things are what they are, moving on.

Salome is to come running back here if the spiders are in Circe's dad's county. I am to kill spiders if they are there. If not, we are to execute the traitors. I have an idea that execute may not be the right word because I don't know. They may decide they don't want to participate. We'll see.

My changes are becoming stranger, but at least I am not as bug ugly as the other arachnids. Today Monica told me I was beautiful. Imagine that. I am finally beautiful. Don't hate me because I am beautiful, nyuck, nyuck.

Moving on. Oh, yeah, the latest change makes me wonder, no bug parts. Apparently, there must be something to this horoscope thing. I am a Sagittarius, and today, I morphed into a white one with four arms…still have that eight-limb thing going, though why that would be, I don't know. Other spiders have different numbers of limbs and apparently, it changes even in a single organism. I still can't get my head around a set of laws that would explain it. Also, the energy it requires! I have to eat more than my own weight in beef after an engagement. Even in my human form, I have to do it.

Oh, and here's today's puzzle. How can a man who weighs over 200 lbs eat over 200 lbs. of beef, get on the scale and STILL weigh 200 lbs.? It is a mystery. Folks here at Norn's Lair don't really want to talk about it, either. Why?

There are too damn many things people don't want to talk about in my life. LB and his 'Project,' the People and why they can do things that violate the last 500 years of science…

As Will is making this journal entry, he is struck by a thought. After tooling around making preparations for what both he and Monica hope is a limited engagement that's what they said about Vietnam, too, he decides it is worth writing down.

Yeah, but they were doing this before all these Rationalist Humanists came running to tell us how the universe should be. SO? The universe is what it is, and you can't violate physical laws, right?

"Felix, you haven't left yet?" It is LB, but he sounds happy enough despite Felix's apparent inability to leave the office quickly.

"Walking out now."

"Good. I just got a call."

"And?"

"It was your boy, Brandon."

"Huh."

"Yeah, he seemed to want to be sure you weren't wacking the Project."

"Yeah, well, I guess that is a good thing. What did you tell him."

"I reamed his ass about going over your head. So, don't say anything to him. I will be sending Kyle to make sure he doesn't freak out in any other ways. Just go on and get the hell out, okay?"

"Leaving now. You still need me to call you?"

"Actually, no. Meet Kyle in the parking lot with the Attitude Response unit on the corner facing this building."

"Be there in a sec."

"Kyle." Felix is getting tired. *I am tired, tired of doing everything but my work. I have to run around like some damn criminal because some pencil-neck bureaucrat thinks we are getting above ourselves, and I am tired of crazy ass hallucinations that I can't talk about, tired of subterfuge.*

"Felix. Take this. Go for a trip or vacation where you have never been. There is a plane and pilot waiting for you at the Shelby County Airport. Go now. Don't call. Someone will find you."

Felix turns to get back in his car and head for the airport, but he stops and turns to Kyle.

"Kyle?"

"Yes, Sir?"

"Tell LB to be careful, okay?"

"It is my job to be careful for him, and I will be, but I will also give him your message. You do the same."

Felix gets in, slams his door and is soon merging into I65 South. He is followed by several Attitude Response Team vans.

"Sylvia." LB walks into Sylvia's office. She is not expecting him.

"Mr. Browning." She smiles, offers her hand, and shakes hands with him.

"We have a situation."

Again, she smiles and responds, "We almost always do. That, I think, is the natural state of affairs for those engaged in breaking the rules and making the world a better place."

"Felix already talk to you?"

"Felix? No. Why?"

"We are carrying out a dead man switch scenario with certain projects until we can safely move them outside the US borders."

"Sir." She is puzzled. She has been helping will with the security project but she knows nothing about the project. LB gives her just enough information for her to carry out her next few days of duties.

"I will be thrilled if you can finish, but don't be surprised if you have visitors with court orders telling you to vacate the premises."

"Will they be trying to arrest me? Or you? Or anyone?"

"I don't think so. My questions to them were pointed, and they answered negatively to all so I should be on good 'legal' ground, but I am afraid we are about to enter an arena where 'legal' and 'doable' aren't the same. They may try to just take our technology and try to work it out in the courts later. Meanwhile, they still have open access to our science, which cannot be patented or protected in any case except as a trade secret."

"What shall I do now? Will is not here."

"Didn't Felix have you to make copies of everything Will was working on earlier this month?"

"Yes, Sir, he did. I put them…"

"In a safety deposit box, yes, Felix told me. I don't need the details. You are on leave of absence as of now, without pay."

"Sir?" Sylvia, like many women, values security above all else and now she is afraid for her job.

"Kyle, please come in here."

"Sir."

"I have just informed Sylvia that she is on a leave of absence now, without pay, until we can ascertain Will's status and the status of this department. She has argued the point and I really don't have time to talk about it further."

As LB is talking, Kyle is pulling the blinds closed.

Sylvia is upset. Her disappointment turns to confusion and then quickly to understanding as Kyle hands her an envelope. "You're suspension should last at most three to four months, Sylvia. Please understand that we are just trying to work through this as quickly as possible."

The envelope is full of $100.00 bills. "Perhaps it is a good time to go home."

Looking at Kyle, she realizes he is not talking about her apartment, but home, to where her family is in Brazil.

"I think I will do exactly that. Go home, that is. When should I check back with you all to see how the…inquiry is going?"

"Give it a month, Sylvia." LB is talking again. "Give it a month.

Sylvia is walking down the hallway to the elevator. The elevator doors open and Will's escort from the mental hospital steps out and quickly surrounds her.

"Please, Sylvia, come with us."

Like I have a choice. "Do I have a choice?"

"Certainly, we are here to care for you. We do have suggestions, though."

"Which are?"

"Take your clothing and your cat and go to the airport from here. Your affairs have been handled and your landlord is being notified."

"Look, this is all well and good, but Mr. Browning is really going too far. Are you telling me that you have already packed me up? And it is all sitting outside?"

"There is a car waiting with your belongings to take you to the airport. I am sure Will is going to contact you once you arrive home."

The trip to the Birmingham Airport is a strange one. Sylvia's bodyguards are eerily silent. *Men in black.* The thought occurs to her, but she dismisses it. *Men in black don't wear Armani, I am fairly certain.*

She is in trouble and she is hungry and most likely, in that order. Last night she got lucky and managed to defend herself from a would-be mugger. He might have had more on his mind, but if he did, he no longer does.

He must have been drunk to go down so easy. I got lucky, very lucky. She is in the city, which she found out is Atlanta about twenty minutes ago. Her memory is still entirely gone.

She is wandering around the city streets at night in the

February air, but she isn't cold. She thinks she should be, based on the way everyone is dressed. *Maybe once you reach a certain point you just can't feel it.*

A few fellows begin to approach her, but when she is afraid, she feels her fear crawl across her face. *Well, at least they have heart enough to leave me alone. No challenge in it? God, I am so tired I could sleep a thousand years.*

Someone offers her a ride after her honest answers about not remembering anything. Says he knows a guy who can help.

"Oh, yeah. It happens a lot. Let's go see this guy."

"He is a shaman?"

"Hah?"

"He is a doctor?"

"Yeah, I'll give you a ride to the hospital. Little bitty thing like you needs to be taken care of, what witcher memory gone'n all."

"Okay."

They catch the Interstate, I85 North. After a brief conversation, the guy naturally tries to put the moves on her. Why some guys think they can put the moves on a girl in a car doing 85 miles an hour is one of life's great mysteries. It doesn't work out.

The car slews to a stop just underneath the Jimmy Carter Blvd overpass and she hops out. She has forgotten everything, everything except how to shine a guy on who won't take no for an answer.

She begins walking back towards the exit ramp that will take her up to Jimmy Carter Blvd while her ride goes on towards the next morning where he will tell everyone about the bar fight he was in where he got his nose broken. The story will grow as he tries to rationalize what happened until someone tells him over the weekend that his old lady got tired of his shit and she racked him good so shut up and take it like a man.

This enrages him to the point he really does get in a bar fight where he kicks some fool's ass really good. Not mollified in the least, he decides to go home and spread the happiness a little further. He beats his wife for the last time. He is drunk and after the Friday Night Fights are over with, he passes out on the bed. The little woman promptly walks out to the garage and gets the four rolls of Duck tape and straps him to the bed. She then gets a soda and falls asleep on their living room couch.

She is awakened the next to some god almighty pissed off ape raging in her bed. She calmly looks down at him and says, "David, you have hit me for the last time. I told you last time it better be the last time, didn't I?" she is scared to death, but she figures he is set to kill her anyway.

"You damn scoozy ass cunt! You better let me up from this bed or I will kill you! You know what? I'm goanna kill you anyway! You bitch! I'll…"

"I know. I know you will. That's why you're tied up in the bed." Here she reaches behind the door and pulls out the 24 inch Tennessee Thumper he had brought home one night. She walks over to the bed and looks down at him.

"Never again, David." Crack! She smashes the bat down on his left shin, sending him into cursing and crying and twisting like a wild animal in a death roll, but it is Duck tape and it holds.

She is horrified at the sight of blood welling up under his skin and is almost overcome with shame at what she has done, what she is doing. He has done this to ME time after time because he enjoys it! How can he enjoy it?

She feels her hands raise the bat again. She isn't home. She is simply sitting by watching as her body takes its revenge on the man she had thought she was in love with, the man she had trusted to take care of her, the man she had thought she wanted to be the daddy to her kids.

He is begging her to stop now, and she does. She is going to walk out now, with just the clothes on her back. She knows he will try to kill her if he gets loose and she is in the same city. He is sweating and that's not good for the holding power of the tape. She sees this and knows it is deaths knell for her unless she either gets out now or finishes the job.

I am not a killer. It is time to go.

She leaves.

At least we don't have kids.

She is still hungry and has found nothing that really satisfies her. She is walking down Jimmy Carter Blvd. For no particular reason, she turns down Cheshire Lane and comes up on an establishment called the Piper Club.

She walks in through the front door and is stopped by the guy at the door. Point blank she asks if there is work available. He looks her up and down. It isn't a sleazy looking over. There is no personal interest there, just one you would see on a horse trader's face looking at a possible new acquisition.

"Most likely," he responds. "What's your name?"

"I don't remember."

"Okay, we'll take care of that later. Have a seat over there while I get the manager."

She sits and waits for the manager.

Chapter 27

Here I am

At least I am eating now, though I doubt that James would appreciate my appetites. But they deserve it. She is thinking about how odd it had been to be attacked, for the fourth time in three weeks and come to leaning against the dumpster outside the abandoned building she had been squatting in with her attacker in her arms with his throat torn out.

She shoves him off her lap, makes a slight noise of disgust, and walks on into the building. Going up to the fourth floor, she climbs out the window at the end of the hallway, walks three windows north, and climbs through.

As she walks through the crumbling ruin of an apartment, or possibly a small office-it is hard to tell- she passes in front of a mirror. She looks. Her face is covered in what can only be blood. She raises one hand to her face, touches it, and leaves a smear that trails away from her mouth. She had tried to clean the mirror as her reflection is all smeary and indistinct, after many tries, she gives up.

Involuntarily, she licks the corners of her mouth, and enjoys the salty sweet taste of the mess there. She thinks, *I feel like I am full. Good.*

Another line of thinking blazes across her brain, but she dismisses it. *If I am to be miserable from not eating, maybe my brain just gets tired of dealing with the issue* and says, 'Hey, you're not hungry right now. We'll deal with it later."

Like most humans, rationalization comes naturally to her.

"He is on his way, then?" LB is discussing Felix's departure from OEE with his assistant, Kyle.

"Yes, Sir, he is. And furious, too, I might add."

"I imagine he is. Felix has spent his entire life, or at least since he was fifteen years old, chewing on this project. Now, he finally gets within shoutin' distance of knowing whether or not he is right and NSA gets wind of it and comes running like a bunch of raiders after catholic gold."

"Sir?"

"Ah. Sorry, it was a historical reference. The Vikings used to raid the Christian countries in search of Church gold."

"Oh, I see."

"I doubt it, but that's okay."

The old man is worried. I didn't think he could get worried.

The thought must be on Kyle's face as well as in his mind because LB responds, "You know, Kyle, I always looked forward to old age, before."

"Before what?"

"Why, before I got old." LB laughs, but there isn't much humor there. "Yes, I looked forward to holidays with grandkids running around, sitting for hours with the woman I had loved for 50 years still with me, and just puttering around my property. There is a lot of satisfaction in having a well-kept yard that you have seen to yourself. Did you know that?"

"I suppose I did." Kyle fools with a few rose bushes that he suspects could turn into a full-fledged rose garden, given time and attention.

"When I was younger and chasing after the 'enemy' in the Cold War, I despaired of finding the woman in whom I could cool my passions."

"Well, traveling the world and fighting would make it hard to be a good family man."

"It does, but it is a choice you make and it is a damn bad choice to make." *...but it is a choixe some have to make so others can make good choices.*

There is really no response that can be made here, so Kyle keeps his peace. He considers himself lucky in that he had never been caught up in anything approaching a serious romantic relationship. Kyle is a career lieutenant, and always will be. Intelligent, but not overly clever; dedicated, but not overly ambitious; in need of material success, but not to excess, Kyle is the perfect second in command. LB sees this in Kyle but has long since lost the pity he feels for such as a young man. 'People are what they are,' he had once said. 'Why should you feel sorry for a shark? It is happy being a shark.'

"Besides," LB continues, "I just want this crap to be over. They never let you rest and they never let you alone."

"They? Sir?"

"The rulers of this world, son, the ones who give us about 20 more feet of chain to run on than you have in the slave countries. They line our collars in felt, upgrade our gruel to burgers and tell us aren't we glad we are free?"

"I am confused."

"Of course, you are. Your education is so full of half truths and outright lies that I am amazed you have the abilities you have." *And I can't set you straight on lots of things because if you know, they may kill you. Unless you are like me and agree that for now, ignorance is the best place for humanity to be. Soon, though, soon...*

Chapter 28

New Age

At the dawn of the 21st century, the history books of the Western industrialized nations waxed poetic about how they had overcome the evils of the Soviet Empire after defeating the Nazi threat in World War II.

The truth is, the victory of the Western industrialized nations is not in defeating the competing economic systems but in bringing about the indentured servitude they claimed to oppose in their own populations and making them like it. Marketing, they say, is the key to success, not building a better mousetrap. If you can make the mouse like it, you can keep using the same old crappy designs.

The democracies are, in truth, ruled by an oligarchy of wealthy interests who know the value of giving good government, at least good enough to the people in order to keep them working in the factories and concerns that are about the business of concentrating wealth into the hands of that same group of folks. Where they shined, truly shined, is setting up the argument so that if you attacked the status quo, the way things are done, you are attacking freedom and free enterprise. By defining the argument and the terms in which the argument is discussed, they assure themselves victory. The only problem with not having an outside enemy to unite against is human nature. An author once wrote that the Good Book should have said, 'Yea, and wherever two or three of you are gathered together, somebody is going to get the shit knocked out of him." Those are good words for a bad state of affairs. A balloon that is released into a vacuum quickly ruptures.

"Well, we can't just have people running willy-nilly

over the borders without being regulated. This has got to stop, and if they don't cooperate, then we will damn well make them cooperate."

"How?"

"Oh, say, a flat 30% surtax on monies wired out of the country to any jurisdiction that won't play ball with us."

"The G7 countries will raise blue hell with that."

"I don't think so. This e-commerce thing is eroding their tax base as well. We are losing hundreds of billions of dollars in revenue and it has got to stop."

"Yes, but what about your accounts?"

"Don't be silly. I am not talking about myself or your family's interests. We can't have the populations at large using the tax havens. This revenue is what we use to maintain an orderly society and the services people have come to expect."

"I don't know what I was thinking," a dry response that went unnoticed.

"We'll make sure the appropriate loopholes and exceptions are in place, of course."

"You'll also make sure we have a six-month window to take advantage of them, I am sure."

"Don't we always?"

"I suppose. Have you spoken with the governors yet?"

"Yes. They agree. All seven agree."

"Very good."

"What about the European situation? Have we a solution yet?"

"No, not one that is acceptable. We are running out of time, too. Those bastards really put the hat on us, there."

"Yes." *Well, what do you expect? Making common cause with a bunch of blood-thirsty freaks of nature? God, I would love to put a bullet right in the back of your WASP who wishes he were a Jew's head.*

"So, our business here is concluded, no?"

Dismissed, am I? I hope one of their rogues comes for you in the middle of the night. I bet you will piss your pants yellow and squeal like the pig you are. He had seen photos of some smaller communities in Scandinavia that had been marked as 'expendable' as a concession to some of the more blood-hungry elements of the Rebel People, which were invariably home to elements the national governments wanted to be eliminated. Streets that were utterly silent were littered with the corpses of the victims of People bent on drinking blood until their throats overflowed.

"What's the big deal? If it weren't for these folks, it would be soldiers with machine guns. Dead is dead, right?"

Remember that. Dead is dead, so what does it matter if it comes at the hands of old age or some fiend? I may even want to watch it. The fucker may turn on me and take me, too, but I think it would be almost worth it to see you scream your guts out. I hope it fucks you while it's killing you. He had been in a meeting with the Joint Chiefs and their European counterparts where a video was shown.

People were running in terror, power lines being yanked down by forms that were human only in varying degrees, some not even remotely so. An entire town is gutted in 20 minutes. The lucky ones die in that time. Others live for hours. The audio is turned down, but laughter is clearly in what passed for faces amongst the raiders.

The minority whip is impassive in his narrative, counting it as a necessary concession for furthering their collective interests in this situation.

One of the Joint Chiefs, an African American, looks at the slightly overweight congressman in horror and then with death in his eyes. The fellow sees he is observed and nods with a grin toward his observer, knowing his look is reflected in his eyes.

None of the older generals in the room believe that this situation can be contained. If the people at large knew that their governments agreed to any of this…no army could kill everyone down to the ground. They need to get in front of the wave that is coming.

This fool has no idea what he and his like have started. We'll be lucky if any significant civilization survives.

"Well? Any thoughts, gentlemen?"

"We have no response for you at this time, Congressman. We'll be in touch."

"Look, we need to coordinate with the G7 countries. The meeting is in 37 days. The Joint Chiefs will have to have a plan in place for the integration of People rule for the proposed European concessions."

"When we consult directly with the President, we will contact you. Believe me, it will not be longer than 48 hours."

"Well, then, I will look forward to hearing from you by 5 PM Wednesday."

"You do that."

After the congressman leaves, the black general of the Air Force looks to the others and asks, "Do you all realize what we just witnessed?"

"Everything the conspiracies and religious fanatics feared coming true?"

"Pretty much."

"There is no way the President signed off on this, no way."

"Oh, I am afraid it is very true," an unexpected voice from an unexpected source.

"It is very true. Both the president and the minority whip have signed on for a brand of eternal life."

"Mr. Vice President." No introductions are necessary. The Vice President is more of a celebrity than most, having inherited the office courtesy of a plane crash. The fact that he is of the opposition party makes him even more of a target of the President's allies, especially in the press.

"The President will introduce legislation and call for a constitutional convention asking that we adopt the United Nations Bill of Rights in place of our current Bill of Rights and…" he holds up his hand to cut off the interruption he sees coming from the chiefs, "he wants to implement the old Section 22 of the Disarmament Code over three years."

The Joint Chiefs go ballistic. Profanity fills the room.

"That sorry motherfucker…"

"He IS the President, though…"

"Maybe we should have discussions of a more frank kind elsewhere." This suggestion on the part of the Air Force General stops the conversation. Almost as a unit, they all agree.

"I think it is time to inspect Colorado Springs, Gentlemen," says the Marine's general.

"Tomorrow, 8 AM?"

"Oh, I think I can wrap things up and be there by midnight, myself," says the Marine.

"Will."

"Lady Monica."

"Are we returned to formal terms now?"

"No, I just finally realize that you feel the weight of all you carry on your shoulders, Monica. You deserve the moniker 'Lady' applied to you."

"Thank you. How are you holding up?" Monica is concerned for Will. Despite the Change and his new nature, Will is still human at the core. Humans are ferocious, but they pay a price for their ferocity, sometimes in blood, sometimes in a piece of their spirit.

"Well, enough. Nightmares are horrible, then I wake up and realize they aren't nightmares but memories."

"Should I be more worried than I am? I don't know how else to put the question. You are opaque to me for the most part." Will's ability to hide himself from other people is another anomaly in his change.

"I am fine, Monica, just…tired, and I can't seem to get the images out of my mind. You know, many of those people we took out think…thought…they were doing the right thing."

She absentmindedly pushes the hair away from her forehead and considers Will. Then she says, "I know. Over the last few millennia, I have consigned thousands, Will, literally thousands, of people to death who were sincere in their opposition to me. I had to.

"You have no idea what it would be like under some of

the ones who see the People as having some divine right of lordship over the rest of humanity. I know what I am talking about because I have lived under them."

"I know, I just…I am different now. I don't know if I can even claim to be remotely human anymore, and then I think of Crystal…" Will is silent, thinking of his lover and then goes on. "Maybe it is better she never saw me for what I have become."

"You are wrong there, Will. You are ever so wrong."

Really? Do you know how much I enjoyed doing what I was doing up there? Would you like to hear about how I mowed down entire regiments of their soldiers, cutting through them like a threshing machine through wheat? Their weapons didn't even harm me, but a few times, they found their mark.

"Crystal would have been proud of the fact that you cannot do what you do and not be affected by it, I think. Don't you know that all People have to fight this thing? It is just the next level up from what normal humans fight every day."

"What, the urge to be a murderer?"

"No, a predator, Will; humans are predators. It is in their nature to hunt, fight, and take territory. The intellect is the offset and what sets us apart, though some are set further apart than others."

"Why is it…" he hesitates, then starts again, "Why is it that I can not remember half of the crazy shit you say I tell you when I am in my centaur form, but I always remember EVERY time I take out a person but not an arachnid? There just seems to be no rhyme or reason to it."

Circe walks in on the tail end of the conversation and

asks one of her off-the-wall questions, "Maybe it is because of the same reason I can see into the arachnid areas, but not into an arachnid mind."

"Explain," says Will.

"Well, there is a connection between me and all other living things. It is, I am convinced, the way seers see and why we are not always right. We don't actually see; we just see the connections between all living sentient things. What we 'see' is a consensus on what WILL happen based on where the collective mind is going. There is room for true randomness in the universe; it has to be."

"This relates how?" asks Will.

"You are connected to the humans and the People you engage in battle with. It costs you to take their life, and this is a part of you. You are not connected to the arachnids other than you went through an unusual change. I don't think you ARE an arachnid, Will. Never did."

"You know, I just don't know what is going on with all this shit. No, hold on, Circe. No…skip it. My head hurts and I have to go run it off. None of the medications work on me anymore, but the headaches came with me. Isn't that nice?"

Will walks out of the foyer double doors into the sunlight, knowing the others can't follow. He is unaware of his change into centaur form. He knows he will have to learn to watch that when he returns home, but here it is a so-what thing. He finds himself needing clothing fairly often, but folks here at Norn's Lair don't see clothing as a necessity anyway, more like a guideline.

"Will."

Of course, there is Circe. She can stand daylight, too.
"Yes?"

"You can't just keep ignoring your situation, you know."

"Well, being where I am, doing what I do, I hardly think I am ignoring my situation. Monica only has to call me, and I go."

"That isn't my meaning. You are ignoring the things down inside your mind. You see things inside, and I can't get to them. Nor can anyone else."

"I don't know what you're talking about."

"I know. That is why we are having this conversation. You need to see the things inside your own mind that are there for you to use. I think…" and here she peers at the now towering Will's form, "…I think you are mourning things lost that perhaps weren't yours to lose."

Crystal was never mine to lose? "Circe, don't say that. If she were never mine to lose, that meant I never had her. You can't imagine how cold that leaves me. Besides, she WAS mine for a while. She died when she thought I had died. When this is all done, I intend to…" But he left the sentence unspoken.

"Will, do you know the legend of Circe?"

"You mean you're legendary?"

"No, I mean the Greek Circe. Do you know it?"

"No."

"Well, see, she would write your future down in its entirety, so she kept that part of the bargain."

"So?"

"The only way she let you actually READ the thing was to tear it into shreds and throw it to the winds. You had to chase the pieces."

Everybody on this fucking hill is crazy as a shithouse rat. "Okay. You're going somewhere with this; I can just feel it in my bones. So get there already."

"I tell you what I see of the future, but you interpret it. Sometimes, you should let your future be what it is and not what you worry about. So, let me repeat myself- I think you are mourning things lost that perhaps weren't yours to lose."

"Okay. I will deal with that later. Now I need to run off this headache."

Being an oracle is not so much fun as I thought it would be. Then, *Father, I would not have had you die this way, but you were wrong! You would have turned this world into one great slaughterhouse. Normal humans are good enough at that without our help.*

Circe turns and goes back into the keep with the sound of Will's hooves in her ears, trying to work off a headache.

Nope. We are not going to participate.

"Mr. Browning, you better than anyone should be able to see the inherent dangers of pursuing this course of action." This is the NSA's local counsel. He is all smile and all teeth, and LB knows it. LB also knows that the attorney, Mr. Wright, knows he knows it.

"Perhaps, but why are you all upset? Have I not allowed you open access to all our facilities?"

"After you made it a point to wipe down entire networks and your chief scientist is missing."

"Hardly missing, Felix is on a leave of absence. He will check in soon enough, I am sure."

"Certainly, that is true," agrees Mr. Wright. "Does he

have the information we are seeking on your activities here at OEE?"

"What activities would that be?"

"What some of your folks refer to as the Project, of course. We want to know the nature of this research."

"You know, we do a LOT of different things here at OEE. I really can't have my fingers on all the buttons at one time. You will have to see Felix for the things he is working on. As for something called the Project, I don't know what you are talking about. There are hundreds of different research initiatives going on here. Walk around. See for yourself."

"I am sure that won't be necessary, LB. Your former associates were clear about your capabilities. I would find nothing here that would help me or the NSA."

Glad you think that, though I am not so sure, best to press the issue, I think. "But I insist! Where would you like to start?"

"I think…" *I will start with a search warrant for Felix's house,* "That I am through for now. Thank you for your time."

On the way out of the parking lot, Mr. Wright gets on the phone to his office.

"Have they got it yet?" Then, "The search warrant for Dorcai's house!" Wright pauses, then "Good, I am on my way." Wright wants to be there.

"They are getting a warrant for Felix's house, LB."

"Yes, I figured they would. Assholes. Okey dokey. Felix is going to be pissed."

"Do it?"

"Yes," LB orders Felix's house burned down. He can't remember if Felix had put everything he cared about away yet or not. *Too late now and I can't take a chance on his thoroughness. Sorry, Buddy.*

Wright pulls up to a smallish home for the area in Hoover. It is a smoking ruin. He gets out, calmly closes his door and walks over to a firefighter.

"What happened?"

"Somebody was too much of a rocket nut, I guess. Place went up like it was full of rocket fuel. It burned out quickly, though, which is good."

"The police here yet?"

"Yes, over there."

Wright walks on over to the detective, who is standing there with a piece of paper wadded up in one hand, almost as an afterthought.

"Detective, I am Jim Wright, local NSA counsel. Is that the writ of search?"

"Yes, for what it is worth now, but yes. I'm detective Spiegel."

"Well, let's see what is left."

"Heard you talking with the fellow over there in the red hat. I think you're wasting your time. This was a seriously hot fire. Even the cars in the garage, though mostly untouched, are warped on their frames by the heat from this blaze."

"There was an explosion?"

"No. No explosion. It seems like it was more of a jelly thing sprayed on and set on fire. Burned through The walls and even ate down through the foundation. Whatever was in the trunks was incinerated, though the fire didn't burn long enough to eat through the paint on the cars, and no, I don't know. If there are or were any skeletons here, they are gone now. He could have had bodies in here, and we couldn't tell it, now."

Well, shit. Okay. "Alright, call me when you get through with your investigation."

"Sure, will do. In about ten minutes. I mean, are you seeing this place? This fire lasted ten minutes."

"Yes, I see it. I have to go."

On the way to his office, Wright calls his liaison at the NSA.

"Mr. Wright."

"Yes, I was just at Felix's house. They…"

"We know. It is on the news. We will call you soon." Click.

Rude bastards.

"Kyle, come on in."

"Sir."

"You know, let's drop the 'sir' shit. We are in more than an employee/employer relationship now."

"I agree, LB. Sir."

"Good. Now, you have only one job today. Walk around and do a morale survey."

"Morale?"

"Yes, morale, the news has been blasting the airwaves with news of an impending investigation of OEE and their connections with the so-called rebels in northern Europe and we need to see how our folks are doing. Everything is great when I am there, but I suspect the gristmill really starts to turn when I leave. Maybe you can get more than I."

"I will do it. Where will you be this evening?"

"Oh, just call my cell."

As Kyle goes through the day, he is disturbed to see many of the folks who were so hard at it last week actually sitting. *Well, can't really blame them for that. Most of their working data is just so much magnetic slop right now, with the hopeful exception of Felix's copy.*

"Yeah, it is ALL gone," an overheard conversation relayed to Kyle's ears, "years of research. Even the backups are missing."

"The backups are gone?"

"Everyone, the guy who runs backup central, isn't saying a word, either. Says he doesn't know where the backups are, and he is waiting for someone higher up than me to tell him what to do. Stupid fucks, I KNEW we should have had paper copies of all this stuff somewhere."

"You think maybe they do somewhere?"

"If so, they are almighty quiet about it."

"Well, wouldn't you, with the NSA breathing down our necks?"

"They aren't breathing down MY neck. I just work here."

"Yeah, but you cash the paychecks, don't you?"

"What's that...?"

Kyle hears these and others and has enough to know that

while morale is declining, it is holding strong amongst the ones who head the projects, most of their close advisors, and a surprisingly large number of flunkies.

Good. The old man will need to hear this. His morale is what I worry about. We need something, though, a bone. Maybe a rumor will do the trick?

"Yes, LB, I think we should leak something down through the folks to keep them calm, but something that can be denied. I will mix it in with enough bullshit that if he rolls over the NSA, his credibility will be destroyed."

"Okay, I thought I had left all this shit behind with Reagan and Gorby."

"It never lets YOU go, though, right?"

"Right."

Kyle moves on about his business, thinking that it looks as though the project just got delayed indefinitely, if not permanently.

"Brandon?"

"Yes?"

"This is Kyle, LB's assistant."

"Yes, what can I do for you? If it is a missing file or a restore, you are out of luck."

"Actually, I wanted to give you a piece of information."

"Okay."

"We will be doing a full restore on Monday week."

"Well, that's good because I have about 300 plus techies wanting to bite me in the ass about every thirty minutes. It makes a guy feel unloved."

"I guess so. Anyway, Monday week, spread the word."

"Will do."

"And Brandon?'

"Yes, if it doesn't work out, I need you to be willing to take the flack for a fuck up."

Brandon is silent. Then, "Now, why would I want to do that?"

"You will be compensated in your severance pay for your trouble."

"I don't want to lose my job. I like what I do."

"You were there when Felix wiped down all the drives, correct?"

"Yes, but I was following…"

"Yes, following orders. I understand, and I sympathize; believe me. But you knew that Felix was trying to hide evidence from the NSA."

"Felix is my boss, damn it. I…"

"Well, whether Felix is your boss or not, when you agreed to help him wipe those drives because the NSA was breathing down our necks, you became involved with knowledge in the possible obstruction of justice."

Brandon is so mad his eyes are watering, *Bastard.*

Desperate thoughts and plans fly through Brandon's mind, but he sees no options. He is young enough to be intimidated by someone like Kyle. He swears to himself that one day soon, there will be payback.

"What do you want me to say?"

News Items

Atlantanewsnet.com February 19, 2001: Adding to the grisly string of Columbian necktie murders, another crew was found hanging from the Omni's parking deck today, bringing the death count to 37. Police Commissioner Emerson said today that they have several fairly strong leads but refused to comment further. When asked if it was true that all the victims had ties to organized crime and invariably had extremely violent records, he responded with, "Does that make their murders any less wrong?"

Well, a growing number of the Atlanta communities are answering in the affirmative.

Atlantanewsnet.com February 20, 2001: Witnesses to what may be a Columbian necktie-related case say a young woman was pursued into an apartment house by several gang members. 'She didn't appear to be afraid. I thought they were playing a game from her expression. Then one of the guys came by, and I got worried about her.'

Another witness said she heard screaming coming from inside the building but didn't bother to call 911. 'We hear that shit all the time in this neighborhood. If the cops come, they want to question YOU in front of the neighborhood so everyone knows it was you what called.'

The Birmingham News: OEE has come under fire from top congressional hawks and doves alike in what has come to be called the Project investigation. The odd thing about it is that the agency responsible for bringing the investigation is being mum about why they want access to OEE's records. When confronted about the ongoing investigation, NSA local counsel refused to comment. This week, he made the statement that he had no information about the nature of the Project other than the NSA, in an apparent concern over national security issues, wants access to OEE's research conducted on something referred to as 'the Project.'

'This is all the information I have at this time.'

Alabama's senior Senator, John Baker, has taken the position that the probe is a fishing expedition set to take the heat off the president for his 'hysterical' position on the European troubles. "You can't just say we 'think' you may be doing something wrong and go in and search, which is exactly what NSA is doing. There is no basis to have granted any of the search writs issued in this case, and OEE has done nothing but move to protect itself and its interests from an agency that is being misused by the President." The Whitehouse had no comment at this time. Also, there is still no word as to the whereabouts of either Felix Dorcai, senior research fellow, supposedly in charge of the Project, or the head of OEE security, former head of infosurge.

"The southern counties are clean, Monica. It is time I returned to the US."

"I agree, though I will need to see you from time to time. We still have the cutoff in some two years, Will. We will still need your input on this."

"I know you say you do, but I honestly don't know what you need from me. I am not a seer. I'm just the clean-up crew, me, Salome, and Dallas."

"You are a hell of a lot more than that," says Monica. "You are part of the family, like a…" *brother-in-law, but I can't go there because you will freak.* "You are of my family. Now, Will, you are of my blood. Remember that."

"I remember, Monica. Every ten minutes or so, I remember." Will leaves.

The guardians watch Will leave as only Will does and

turn to the lady Monica, "Should we go with him again, Lady Monica?"

"No, to what end? Anything he couldn't handle would kill you, too, most likely, right?"

"Almost surely," says Dallas.

"I don't know, I still haven't run against him," says Salome. She is a little piqued that Will wouldn't run against her in a footrace. She thinks it would cheer him up, but he will have none of it. 'You should have run against Crystal,' he says. 'She was beautiful when she moved…and she could MOVE.'

Salome is tired of it. Does everything in this universe make him think of her? *Good grief, it has to get old. She's been gone months now, and he is still not over it. Eternity is a long time to grieve.*

She stretches her legs by herself. Salome doesn't bother to wait for Will to try to run off one of his headaches. She tries to match speed with him, he sees her and slacks off and quits. 'Don't want to race,' is all he ever says.

"Will! You are back. Good! Leave! The Huns are at the gates!"

"So I gathered from the news services, any word from Felix?"

"Nope, not a blessed thing, and it cracks me up. NSA is just all up in my ass about it, too, didn't think he could hide this good."

"Maybe he is more than hiding."

LB thinks about it a minute, then says, "No, I don't think so. NSA is really having a bad case of ass rash about this whole thing. If they knew where Felix and the rest of it were, they wouldn't be doing wholesale proctologic exams up and down the east coast, and everywhere the boy has been in the last five years."

"You know, LB, you have this flair, this knack for explaining things in such a way that I have disturbing mental images for days. Do you work on it, or does it just come naturally?"

"I am just having so much fun, right now, with my replacements that I just can't stand it. Hang on." Here, LB picks up the phone and dials out.

"Director's office, please," A pause, then, "Tell him it's LB."

"Hey, Big Fella, How are YOU?"

A response from the phone that even Will could have heard without augmentation.

"Now, now, I just called to see if I could be of any service and to let you know I still haven't heard from Felix.

Lower, less intelligible sounds in response are heard.

"Well, I may have something for you. I may have seen my security chief, Will, earlier, can't be sure, of course." Here, LB looks to Will to see if he agrees or is up to going ahead and stepping into this mess right off the bat. Will nods affirmatively.

"Well, hell, speak of the devil and in he walks."

A short bark out of the phone expressing less than warmth and caring for LB's welfare is heard.

"Yes, Will just walked in. Let me put you on speaker."

"Will, I would like to introduce you to the Senior Director for the National Security Agency. His name is Dick

Payant, but he will answer to Dick. He LIKES being called Dick."

"You know, LB, you might want to play this a different way. We will get what we need, one way or the other."

Before Will can respond, LB loses his happy face and waves Will to silence. "Let me explain something to you so you can go back and explain it real good to the stone stupid son-of-a-bitch you work for, okay, DICK?" It is clear that LB thinks Dick is more than a nickname. "I and OEE have neither and severally done nothing wrong. We have given no technology away. The fact that you are shitting bricks over what we MAY…POSSIBLY…JUST MIGHT…be working on means that this gentleman across from he has done his fucking job, despite the efforts of your best, half of which I trained for you.

"You have no evidence, you have no reports, all you have are the mindless ravings of a lunatic environmentalist nut case I should have canned when I got here, but I didn't out of some idea that he was better than he was.

"If you keep coming, I will fuck you up and end your career. Keep pushing, if you must, but remember how many others your boss has thrown to the wolves to get his ass out of the fire."

"Now, goddammit, LB, you had better…"

"Dick, why'd you even take the job? I told you not to. You knew it would end up with you doing shit like this, if not with me, then someone else. Why'd you take the job?"

"LB, I didn't have a lot of choice. I figured I could minimize some damage because I trusted myself more than the second choice." Now the two men are talking as old friends again, as reluctant enemies as men often do before the shit hits the fan.

"Are you? Are you able to keep it down somewhat?"

"You have no idea what is coming, and I am out of time on this quarter. Give us what we need, LB. One way or the other, we will have it." Click.

LB and Will just sit for a few minutes. Neither is in any hurry to break the silence. Kyle does it for them.

"Sir, will you be taking lunch here or going out?"

"What do you say, Will? Let's eat here, okay? I will bore the hell out of you with pictures and stories about my grandkids."

"That sounds good."

The lunch is good. The kitchens send up something with chicken and rice. It doesn't have a name according to Kyle. It is just something the chef, a twenty-year-old girl from Raleigh, North Carolina, comes up with. She never fails to make people talk about her food.

I will miss her when she goes back to school, thinks LB. He then sets about the deadly serious business of boring Will with pictures of and stories about people he's never seen.

The next day, Will is trolling the halls, getting debriefed by Kyle, picking the brain of Brandon for any gleanings of information Felix might have accidentally let slip. He doesn't know what he is looking for, but at least it is different from la-la land *and brother. Sometimes, that kind of relief is worth just about anything.*

"LB," Will asks when he runs into the senator outside the cafeteria, "what's the word on Sylvia?" Will had asked that she be sent for. He is a bit worried she might decide to stay gone. It had been a strange journey from bankruptcy to here. He can replace her no more than he can replace an arm.

Actually, that doesn't cut it anymore, Will thinks to himself. Seeing Will's intense interest in Sylvia's status, LB again realizes why he confided so much in Will over the years. Will is a stand-up kind of fellow.

"We have no word yet. But it is too soon to worry."

"I don't know whether it is or not, too many great escapes and changes lately. The mind starts to get tired and begins making stupid mistakes. No word on Felix, either?"

"Nope, but then I didn't expect there to be. He is doing what I told him to do." *Hopefully, he is.*

"Yeah, well. Do we have a hearing yet?" Will asks.

Their case is in the Atlanta appellate court. The District Court in Birmingham had ruled, not unexpectedly, in favor of the NSA being able to just waltz in and look at everything.

There is precedence for being able to declare an invention as a national security issue, but never one man's ability to create. They are trying to say that Felix is a state asset due to his inordinate ability to understand certain things. The ACLU finally comes to Felix's aid in absentia, a turn of events that left LB scratching his head for all of ten minutes, but he is glad for the help. *They are a bunch of liberal crazies, but no one is better at getting the court system all bollixed up in itself than the ACLU, and this one had set their dogs to raising hell.*

"One has been agreed to, but no date, not yet. I am to do a news conference this afternoon and I am going to recommend to Felix that he stay in hiding."

"Can you do that?"

"Oh, they will lean on me and threaten me with

obstruction of justice, but I will make it plain that justice is not being served and that I am working in the interest of justice, yadda, yadda, yadda. Relax, Will, I do enjoy a measure of immunity to things due to my position as well as a few measures I have taken over the years. Not very egalitarian, but it is true.”

“Okay, you ARE the boss and might I say, I have never been so glad it was someone else in my life?”

In Atlanta, where the courts sit glaring at OEE like a cat that is hell bound on taking out the bird in the window, another confrontation almost gets off the ground.

“So, girl, you think you are so special? All of us here are dancers, so don’t you be getting’ no fuckin’ attitude wit’ me.”

She just looks at the woman, at least a head taller than her, though it is hard to tell in the heels they are both wearing, wondering where this is going. She kind of expects her to take a shot. She just can’t figure out how expensive it is going to be when she beats the shit out of her in the club. She sees the manager making his way towards them with mixed emotions. He makes it.

“Just calm down, I don’t need this shit, not tonight.”

“I didn’t…” she begins.

“I know. Go in the back and calm the fuck down, Alexandria. You, you’re up in two.”

“Got it and gone.” She is, too.

“So, Brandon, what do you want to do this evening? I need to pick your brain because if there is anything Felix might have said to you as he was making his run for the border; I need to know what it was.”

"But I'm telling you, there was nothing. He whizzes in one day, yanking the hell out of RJ45s and telling everyone to run some kind of disk utility called 'blast' and do a backup, backup was first. I'm telling this badly."

"No biggie, breathe in with the good air, out with the bad. Relax. You're not in any trouble with me or Mr. Browning. We both think you did a hell of a good job in executing orders under a hell of a lot of pressure and very little time. We are also very pleased with how you confused the hell out of the NSA folks."

"No, you don't understand. I really tried to tell them what I know."

"Which only cracks me up and makes it even better. I guess old Felix was even wilier than we thought because now the old man himself is wondering if HE knows what the project is about." Will is looking off into the distance now, noticing for the first time that the grounds over by the new labs have become extremely barren. *Not a single plant left? Why'd they do that?*

Brandon is taking his attention back at the grunt point, as in a grunt of complete frustration. "Look, I will have to get with you on this in the morning; I have plans in Atlanta tonight."

"What?"

"We're going to something called the Piper Club or something." He looks embarrassed, but only a little.

Will just looks at him as if to say, 'and?'

"It is a strip bar."

"Never been to one myself. I guess…purely in the interest of pursuing this picking your brain, I should tag along."

"Well, it really is…you probably wouldn't have a good time. It is just a bunch of 19 and twenty-year-olds."

An old guy like me wouldn't have any fun or maybe you guys wouldn't, huh? Oh, this will be fun. "Yeah, but what would your mother say if I let little Brandon out to play by himself?"

"Well, I am sure she would be grateful for your concern…" *this doesn't look good at all. Brandon is thinking maybe his security chief is seriously considering going with them to Atlanta.*

"You know what, Brandon, you are exactly right."

Relief, "Good, it's just that…"

"A trip to Atlanta to see some babes is JUST what I need. Hang on; let me see if LB wants to go." *LB will never in a million years want to go, but this is fun.*

Poor kid is nearly crapping his pants. If he had any balls, I would just agree not to go, but if he hasn't the cahoneys to JUST SAY NO, then I am going. Besides, I have never been to one. The phone is ringing in LB's office.

Brandon tries to take control here, but Will brushes him off with, "Brandon, relax; the old man will love it! He will be off'n his rocker by the end of the evening. You need to help me watch him if he goes getting all sloppy drunk like the last time he, Felix, and I went out, though, 'kay?"

Brandon just raises his hands to shoulder height and drops them to his side in defeat.

Too much fun to be legal, thinks Will.

"LB, yeah, how are you? What? No, I enjoyed the hell out of it. Sure. Love to. Listen, Brandon…yes, that's him…well, he has invited you and me to go to some bar in

Atlanta. Oh, it's a strip bar, he…"

Will stops and turns to Brandon, "Topless only or totally nude?"

"I don't know about this one, topless for sure, Atlanta style? I don't know."

"He doesn't know for sure…yeah, okay."

"Well, is he going, too?"

"Nope."

Thank goodness, one old guy is enough.

"Man, Brandon, this is going to be great; I can just feel it. We can talk on the way and party when we get there, right?"

Oh, yeah, right-o, this is unbelievable.

Brandon had been telling the truth. Will is able to find nothing out from repeatedly rehashing the events of the day Felix had taken French leave, as they are beginning to call it. French leave equals AWOL, which applies. He isn't on OFFICIAL leave, but everyone with three brain cells knows he damn well has permission.

They get into Atlanta at about 7, just in time for the first crew of the night shift to begin working.

Will, Brandon, and company sit down, some seats back from the main stage, and out walks the first dancer for the evening.

"Guys, hang on to your drinks 'cuz I don't want to see them anywhere else! Here is…"

Chapter 29

The Calm before the apocalypse

"Well, let's look at where we are," says Will.

"Should I send up for lunch?" asks Kyle.

"Certainly," says Will.

While Kyle orders some sandwiches from an Italian deli down the street, Will is organizing the paperwork in front of them in order to get ready for a long day of discussions concerning the current situation between OEE, the federal government, and how all this relates to the European situation. If asked by the man on the street why OEE concerned itself with foreign affairs, LB would have most likely said something like companies often must be the lone voice of reason in foreign affairs.

"Philly cheese or turkey and Swiss?" asks Kyle.

"Turkey and Swiss," says Will.

As Kyle is completing the order for lunch, Will comes across a card Sylvia thought to buy him one day just because he was feeling low. *Sylvia, I need your butt here.*

"Is there any word on Sylvia's whereabouts?" Will asks as Kyle hangs up the phone.

"No, no word as of yet," says Kyle.

Will picks up a sheaf of paper work and walks over to the table immediately next to the large glass windows facing out over the rest of the complex and signals for Kyle to come and sit with him.

For the next nine and a half hours, Will and Kyle go over the security measures for the corporation, talk to several of their corporate attorneys and generally look for ways to cause the NSA hell. *We really are not just fighting for survival as a company here,* thinks Will as he looks across the table at Kyle. *I just wonder if it matters in the larger scheme of things. After all, I still have not heard back from Monica as to what our next step will be concerning the arachnids and the rebellion.*

While Will is wondering about Sylvia's whereabouts, Sylvia is in the process of fitting back into the flow of things in her native Brazil. It is not going well.

"No, Uncle, I have no plans to return to the United States," says Sylvia. " I'm done with that place. Besides, it's not much different from here. You still have to watch your back, and you have to know whose palm to grease."

"Well, then that's very good. You belong here with your family," says her uncle.

"LB, have you thought about just moving all your operations overseas?" asks Kyle.

"I have thought about it, " says LB. " but I decided against it because it is clear to me that in spite of all that shit we're catching from NSA, American laws still provide us with the greatest layers of protection."

"I suppose," says Kyle. "But have they protected you?"

"No, I don't suppose they have. But, I don't have to worry about the NSA executing the judges that rule in our favor."

"I don't guess I can argue with that."

Felix, in the meantime is breaking all his old habits and moves into the heart of San Francisco, a locale he knows that no one will look for *him* in. His attitudes, which are not to say his prejudices, make this Mecca of the gay lifestyle a fairly safe place for him to be.

He has a couple of close calls and very nearly falls into the trap of assuming that he is not important and hasn't been observed in the past. Felix is almost apprehended at the airport in Miami. He is saved by an agent's allergies. The agent's sneeze is unique in that he always mutters the same profanity after sneezing. This agent has done so numerous times in Felix's presence just before LB decides to pull the plug and put Felix on the road.

I have got to think five and six steps ahead of these assholes, thinks Felix. *Otherwise, I'm going down, and OEE is going with me. Besides, this is my research, and I'd just as soon see it flushed down the tubes as to see the NSA get it and bury it.*

Felix is not terribly optimistic at this point. He doesn't know where to go, that they will not have some chance of anticipating his arrival. Then he sees two men gazing into each other's eyes. While it certainly isn't Felix's cup of tea, it does give him an idea as to a destination where he will be able to hole up until he gets some kind of word from LB as to what to do next.

The apartment Felix takes is in an intensely urban area specifically because everyone knows of his horror of and aversion to living in a city. The linoleum is curling up in the kitchen, the toilet is lined with some kind of scrim he is unable to get off, and the phone jacks appear to have been installed prior to World War Two.

Thankfully, there is a corner grocery right underneath his apartment.

I can keep going out very far to a minimum anyway. That is, after I get back from Los Angeles.

It had been prearranged that once Felix gets to a place where he feels fairly safe, he will contact LB or Will by e-mail. He is driving up to Los Angeles tomorrow to go to a copy shop to buy time on a PC so he can check his e-mail and see if anybody has dropped him a line to his public e-mail address.

Felix's apartment is furnished, so it's nice enough, he supposes, but the natural noises of the city and traffic and car doors slamming provide an all-night long cacophony that finally rouses him some few minutes after 4:00 a.m. the next morning.

Bleary eyes, aching back, and a really bad cup of coffee from McDonald's see Felix off on his trip to Los Angeles. The journey, like any other in the West Coast megapolis, is simply mile after mile of asphalt and concrete overpasses. Finally, he spots a copy shop on the Interstate. Thinking it looks random enough, Felix pulls off onto an exit ramp and turns right onto a service road.

The copy shop is fairly empty. Felix pays for access and quickly logs on to the free mail Website. There is no mail for him yet. *Well, I suppose no news is good news.*

The next morning, back in Birmingham, LB has been up since 3:00 a.m. He is faced with making a decision that will affect hundreds of workers in Birmingham and thousands of OEE employees and affiliates worldwide. NSA is bringing pressure to bear that cannot, at least today, be borne by the corporation. *I can bear it, but my employees cannot.*

"Kyle, please notify my counterpart at the NSA that we will comply with their request for full disclosure on all projects currently pending at OEE. Please note that we have no good intelligence on the whereabouts of Felix Dorcai, our chief technology officer. Also, we will make available to them at their pleasure all travel itineraries that have been filed by Mr. Dorcai with accounting.

"And this is to be my formal notice of resignation as chairman of OEE. Obviously, I will retain my majority stock ownership until an appropriate buyer is found. Now, let's start looking for a capable CEO to step in and take my place. I am tired of this shit." LB lays down the tape recorder and proceeds to finish his coffee. *It will look as if I'm finally succumbing to old age. Good.*

Kyle knows about the pressure on LB to allow a technological audit by various security agencies in the United States. He also knows they do not have a legal leg to stand on. Apparently, they do have the power, though.

"But what about the project?" says Kyle to an empty room. The room does not answer.

"Sylvia! Baby Doll, how are you?" Will is damn glad to be talking to this former assistant. "Are things going ok in Brazil?"

"Yes, Will, things are fine. How are you?" asks Sylvia.

"Missing you, Sylvia. I am just not as organized without you."

"And that's supposed to be a news flash, right?" says Sylvia.

"Not exactly, but it would be nice to think that I had some organizational skills if only a few," says Will.

"I understand that OEE is having some fairly severe legal problems right now. Not entirely unanticipated, am I right?" asks Sylvia.

"That is correct. Apparently, there is some project, which is only known as the Project, that no one but Felix seems to know about or have any data on. When the NSA and some other fools got hold of some preliminary info, they apparently went off their rocker and wanted to declare the whole thing a national security issue and shut it down."

"So, what will you do?" asks Sylvia.

"The old man, LB, is going to resign and give them keys to the facility. OEE is going to drop its lawsuit against the NSA and, in giving them keys to the entire facility, has gotten personal guarantees from the NSA director that they'll make a decision within five working days as to whether or not national security interests are involved," says Will.

"Well, that sounds very nice… if they don't just decide to declare the whole thing a national security issue just for the hell of it anyway," says Sylvia.

"Our confidence is fairly high that we will prevail," says Will. "But that is not why I'm calling. Sylvia, I want you to come back to the States and work for me again."

"Will, I do enjoy working for you. But I cannot and must refuse," says Sylvia.

"Why?"

"It is just too dangerous, and I'm tired of fighting governments. If I have to stand against a government, I intend to do it with my family and my father in my homeland," says Sylvia. She is very sad. Will is more than just a friend; more like a brother, actually. She is sure he will understand.

"Stay safe then, Sylvia. The world is more dangerous than you ever thought."

"Goodbye, Will." She breaks the connection with a click.

She is right to want to stay with her family. Besides, Kyle is becoming fairly adept at juggling both LB's schedule and mine. It is easier for one man to handle our multiple schedules. I just like having her around. She HAD a native wit that Kyle just hasn't got. Then, She'll be safer by being further south anyway.

"Brandon, I need you to set this up for me." Will has discovered that Brandon, in addition to being really talented at coming up with nifty neat explanations as to what backups are available for the project, makes a good organizational assistant as well.

"I'll handle it," says Brandon.

Brandon hesitates and looks at Will. "You want what?"

"Brandon, I know you have worked here long enough to know that we do a lot of shit in this place that doesn't make sense, unless you have the whole picture. Correct?"

"Well, yeah, but ... you want them to leave two living steers in the slaughterhouse when they lock up tonight?" asks Brandon, who is beginning to get used to such bizarre behavior on the part of OEE executives. The number of businesses and concerns that were connected to OEE often seemed unconnected and random until you realized that there claims about being dedicated to research across all disciplines was not just hyperbole.

"That is precisely what I want you to do, Brandon," answers Will.

"Alright."

"LB?" Will is setting up a meeting with LB and the remaining senior scientists from the various projects at OEE. He intends to bring them up to speed on the true nature of the European crisis.

Monica is not being consulted on this. Will is pretty sure she will object. This is by design. It is better to ask forgiveness than permission.

Monica has ruled for millennia; the likelihood that she is beginning to exhibit habits and predictability is a near certainty. Will takes it upon himself to consult with some of the best minds he knows before implementing his plan. In Will's mind, the players in this game know all the rules. Like chess, you can have your opponent in check or checkmate 10 or 12 moves out without him or her knowing it or even having the ability to see it once you explain it. They need to find out if they are in check.

If we are, we're changing the game.

"So, LB, the plan is to divest yourself of the larger part of OEE stock, resign from the chairmanship of OEE and for that, you maintain a fairly large minority position in OEE, take a substantial cash severance package, but you do so being free from any non-compete or nondisclosure agreements that may exist between ourselves and OEE to date. They have agreed to drop all pending actions against yourself and all OEE executives, including the missing Felix Dorcai, in return for you allowing them to have free walk-through privileges in the Birmingham facilities for two years," says Will. "Does that just about sum everything up?"

"Sums it up admirably, Will," says LB. "Of course, I'm fairly certain they will take measures to create new situations for Felix, though, to give them a handle on the boy. We'll need to find ways to keep his exposure to a minimum. I don't worry about his loyalty. What I worry about is his innocence regarding such matters."

"I don't know that I would call him an innocent after all this shit, LB," says Will.

"Yes, well, Will, I've known Felix longer than you; he is better than he used to be, but he is still a substantial risk unless he has someone to hold his hand. I've decided I am going to laterally promote Kyle to the position of Felix's right-hand man. Kyle is a Good Man, and I can depend on his reports and observations to be fairly accurate and relevant."

"Okay." *But that makes for three schedules he will need to be juggling. Yeah, Sylvia Babe, I do miss you. Looks like I will do more than I thought I would, too.*

"Well, it is about damn time," says Felix as he is sitting at another randomly chosen copy shop in the Bay area.

The following is an e-mail to Felix from LB:

Felix:

The wicked witch is dead. Come home. Thanks for tracking the trash out, so make sure not to step in any on the way home and drag it inside.

Felix is whistling on his way back to his apartment. Mostly because if today is not the last day he will see that piece of crap of an apartment, it is at least one of the last three days he will spend there.

"That was Felix, Kyle," laughs Will. "He is fairly fired up to return to the land of grits and honey."

"Where is he?" asks Kyle.

"San Francisco."

"Yes, but Felix hates San Francisco…" says Kyle.

"Yup, isn't it a hoot? Mr. really-ain't-got-no-use- for-gays holed up in the Mecca of gaydom."

"I don't know, Felix. Will has taken to making a run to

Atlanta it least every Monday and Wednesday nights," says LB. "He says he's been holding some sort of an outreach program or something or other. He was kind of vague about it all, so… I don't know. He will fill us in if it is important."

"Okay. Now, bring me up to speed on how we're supposed to salvage the project from all the concessions you guys made to NSA while I was hiding in Buttfucked, Egypt."

"It's really very simple. You, Felix, are the Project. Without you, there is no project. In my mind, it is time to throw off all the dead weight that is keeping us from concentrating 100 percent on the project. Since the majority of what OEE works on is completely unrelated, I want to hand it off to someone else. I'm going to retain my stock ownership and use the dividend income stream to finance this thing through an entirely different corporation."

"Are you still going to own a majority ownership?" asks Felix.

"No, I am not, although I will still most likely be the largest single stock owner of the company. The main reason I'm doing that is that OEE is finally to a point where it doesn't really need me. I'd just as soon take my time and play on the Project 100% of the time."

"So, I guess Will is fired up, too?"

"I'm sure he is. But he doesn't seem as fired up as I thought he would be," says LB.

Felix asks, "So where is he tonight?"

"It's Monday, so I suppose he's headed to Atlanta."

Will is headed to Atlanta. An outreach program is hardly his goal, though. He is on a mission to see an angel.

Arriving at the Piper Club, Will decides against

allowing the valet to park his car. He hears horror stories about the valet's motor skills from time to time and wants no part of it. This causes him to park on the back end of the parking lot, but that's OK. He notices he doesn't hit anything when he parks.

"Wassup, Reuben?"

"Nothing that'll get me in trouble, Bossman," says Rueben.

"She working tonight?" asks Will.

"She sure is. She's a strong one, that little girl, ain't she?" says Rueben.

"She is surely something," says Will. He pauses a second, looks down at his shoes and sticks his hands into his pockets up past the wrists, considering. Not finding anything satisfactory, he just almost repeats himself, "She surely is something."

Will walks on into the club, pays his cover charge, and makes a right-turn detour into the men's room. He finds Herb, the bathroom valet guy, on his stool, taking care of folks as usual. From the looks of his tip jar, it's going to be a very good night for Herb.

"How you doin', Big Man?" asks Herb.

"Doing pretty well, Herbert," says Will.

"You here to see your lady?" asks Herb.

"She is the only one I come to see, Herb. You know that," says Will.

"Man, you are so in love with that little girl," laughs Herb.

Will just looks at him. What is there to say?

Hell, I may be and what to do with that? I don't have a clue. I just know that I can't see her or talk to her enough to ease this hunger and my chest whenever I think about her.

Will watches her do her first stage. He watches her and wonders at the fact that she causes absolutely no feelings of jealousy in him, *which is probably a good thing since she is a stripper dancing in a strip joint.*

The waitress, Julie, walks by and pokes Will in the ribs, "What are you smiling about? You're just happy to see me, right?"

"Yes, Dahlin, that is exactly what I was smiling about," laughs Will. "That and how fine you are looking today."

"You'd probably say that to all the waitresses, wouldn't you?" says Julie.

"Now, Julie, you know I only come up here to see you," says Will.

"Un huh, what about Suede?" counters Julie.

Will sighs and says nothing in response to her. Julie indicates that she'll be back with his soda in a minute. Under his breath, where no one can hear him, hopefully, Will says to himself, "The girl is going to be mine. If it takes me the rest of my life to win her heart, I am going to do it. I will make her remember our time together."

It isn't a conscious thought yet. Will isn't even aware that he has spoken aloud. But in the coming days, Will realizes why men will give up half their kingdoms for a woman. It is because she is the one that makes his whole being hum, like some crystal vibrating because of an oncoming earthquake. He may have thought he loved in the past. He is wrong. Will knows that he has to feed this passionate hunger; he has to satisfy this hungry passion.

What if I go through all this and she doesn't remember me? What if she just says no? It is an ugly thought. Will isn't really happy about it. Then, *Fuck it. I am not going to sit by and let her get out of my life without pulling out all the stops and trying my dead-level best to win her heart. That is for wimps and weaklings, and I am neither, not having faced what I have faced...and lived.* Will wonders regularly why he still dreams of Crystal in sleep when all he can think about in the daylight is Suede.

The trip home is a slurring, stop and go, cursing at times nightmare of bright headlights and monsoonal rain, both of which are blinding. Just past the Anniston-Oxford exit on I-20, Will's car pulls over to the side, idling. The backup lights flash as the vehicle is put in park. Ten minutes later, the lights are turned off, as well as the engine. An hour or so later, Will pulls back onto the interstate and continues on home, sometimes driving five or ten miles below the limit.

"These facilities are exceptional. I cannot believe that an hour or so from Birmingham we could find acreage at $200.00 an acre."

"I know, LB. Two thousand acres for $400,000 is unbelievable," says Felix.

"And I think we are far enough from major cities that security should be manageable," says LB.

"Yes, and Will is pretty fired up about returning to the country and near his hometown again," says Felix.

"His hometown?" asks LB.

"Yes. I thought you must know. Will is originally from Childersburg," says Felix.

"Well, at least he will know where everything is," says LB.

"There he is," Felix is nodding to a slim fellow as he is walking across from the impromptu parking lot that is basically a square area cordoned off with bright yellow nylon rope layered in crushed gravel. Engineers from Johnson Ruston are here to walk over the property with LB and Felix. While there is no real reason or pressing need to adopt an accelerated construction schedule, all three men want to press forward and get some real, tangible progress under their belts. But Felix and LB agree that they really did not know how much property 2,000 acres is until they walked it personally.

"I'm wondering if perhaps a microwave relay is not a better way to go than trying to stretch a T3 or T1 landline all the way from Birmingham to Rockford," says Will. "In fact, I am almost certain that a landline is a bad idea."

Will is heading up the communications aspects of the new facility in Rockford. They haven't even gotten around to naming the new company yet. Suddenly, Will is struck by an idea. *Maybe we should leave it unnamed for now. If we do not name it, it will be harder to focus on. Then again, no, that's a bad idea. I mean, it isn't like they don't know the three of us are working on this thing anyway.*

Rockford, Alabama, is probably hard-pressed to come up with 2000 folks who would claim residency in Rockford. It is the quintessential small town: one street, one red light, and the town hall is in the back of the local post office.

And it is perfect. We will probably be the main employer in this town by the end of the year. I think I kind of like that, thinks Will.

They- that is, LB, and Felix, and Will-have already made significant donations to the local library in terms of books. None are more than 18 months old, so it is quite likely that the tiny little town of Rockford has one of the freshest libraries in the state.

"Yes, we will be running all our internal communications on IP telephony services. What? Oh, yes, we will." They will be supplying their own phone switches and other equipment. All the vendors have to do is get the bandwidth to the property.

It is a lot more fun building a business when you're not saddled with a bunch of damn debt, thinks Will.

The rest of the day he intends to spend walking over the property. There is a need to be certain that none of the communications lines if they choose to go the landline route, run close to the stands of pulp wood pine that cover a significant part of the property. *Hopefully, we will use the microwave route and will not have to deal with the issue of trees.*

I'm guessing we'll need full communications in ninety days. "Let's shoot for an up-and-running end date of… May 26th?" says Will.

"I'm sure that is a reasonable date. We usually only ask 45 days, so that should be more than enough time," says the AT&T rep.

"Let me know when it is 90% done so I can order the switches and in-house telephone equipment," says Will. *Well, everything is ticked off of my checklist for today anyway.*

Brandon, one of the employees who made the cut from OEE, makes the decision to move to Rockford rather than commute. He figures, if nothing else, he will have fewer places to spend his money. He thinks it will make saving up for a house easier. Besides, this project thing is beginning to look interesting.

The offer to bring Brandon on full-time is entirely unanimous. LB, Felix, and Will all have firsthand experience working with Brandon when he is under pressure. The team needs that kind of talent because they're fairly sure that the pressure is really going to mount in the future. Unlike most people, Brandon doesn't spill his guts or start covering his ass before he knows what the situation is or even if there is a situation.

The only one to object to Brandon is Kyle. His objection is overruled in an unusually rough fashion by LB.

Trouble there? wonders Will. *Not my problem. Kyle is a funny bird, anyway.*

Brandon is also very confident of his ability to contribute to this project. With this attitude, he rolls into Rockford and begins the search for a home or apartment. It doesn't take long to find a small home within 10 minutes of Rockford, a shotgun house but fairly well maintained with a few additions built on to create a reasonably comfortable living area. It is a straight shot to Rockford if you turn left and a straight shot to the property if you turn right out of his driveway. The place doesn't have city water; it has well water, but not bad. The water is sweet; a filter and UV system cover the rest.

Construction begins the first week of March and continues through May. Given Felix's assurances that they will be entirely adequate, metal buildings are erected in half the time it takes for the construction of traditional brick-and-mortar buildings. A second layer of ICFs, insulated concrete forms, is applied to the outside.

They're walking the property for about the fourth time in as many days when Felix begins breaking it down in his mind.

"Let's think about it, LB. Like this, if my calculations are right and we rolled too many quantum states the wrong way, whether we're talking about brick and mortar or metal buildings, it becomes quiet irrelevant."

"If you did the calculations wrong, how bad can it get?" asks LB.

"Brick and mortar won't make any difference. If the resonance states fall the wrong way, there is a substantial energy release. That's why I have insisted on test after test after test over such a long period of time."

"Big Safety tip, Felix," says LB.

"Besides, the building's metal interiors provide more shielding from those who would like to sniff around and about what we're doing."

"Shielding?" asks LB.

"Yes, the metal buildings are easier to harden against electromagnetic snooping than brick and mortar buildings."

"That makes sense. I truthfully had not considered that angle, seems like I should have, though. I used to do this stuff for a living. I suppose it is possible that at 75 I am finally getting old," says LB.

"I hope I can do the job you're doing when I get 75," says Felix.

"Yes, but with a lot fewer problems."

The lady called Suede finds herself wrapped in cotton, struggling to get free from the sheets just as she is struggling to get free from the dream. For the last several nights she has been plagued by dreams of lust that leave her feeling as if her womb is on fire. She aches deep in her belly with a want that can only satisfied one way. She squirms in her bed alone wanting nothing more than to feel dream lover's mouth on her breasts, his hands on her back, and the sensation of cupping her hands around his neck as she opens herself to his hands and their sure knowledge of how to touch her. She still feels his kisses on her knees, the insides of her thighs, and the way he pauses… his breath is still hot on her bottom.

But now I'm awake, and nothing is a real except that I have to get up and go to work.

Back in Birmingham Will is explaining his own ache to get to Atlanta, "No, you don't understand. I have to be in Atlanta at 7:30 tonight. It is now 5:00. I have to leave now in order to be there on time."

"I understand that, Will," says Felix, "But the engineers, who were supposed to be here this morning, it is true, are here now. You need to be here."

"My design specs are plain. If they can read they can get them right. I do not need to be here, in person and in the flesh. Brandon is quite capable of understanding that in order to secure the facilities you have to have a metal barrier securing all surfaces of an enclosure." A lot of information can be gathered by analyzing the electromagnetic radiation that emanates from a room, building, or vehicle. A metal enclosure that covers all significant surfaces acts as a barrier to this radiation and makes eavesdropping a lot more difficult, that and a few other things.

"If you insist, I guess there is nothing to be done. What I do not understand, however, is what you're doing in Atlanta that should be so hush-hush," says Felix.

"I am working on a project, and I am trying to help a friend," says Will.

"Okay. I can accept that. However, the quality of your work is beginning to suffer here, visibly so. I say this as a friend," says Felix. "We have all been through some very strange things, some of which were very stressful and occasionally a life-threatening, but… you cannot say that covers all sins for ever and ever amen."

"Felix, listen. I have got to go, got to. Believe me, if I didn't have to go… if there were some way I could stop wanting to go, I would do so in a heartbeat. But I am going and I will see you in morning."

LB, Felix, Brandon, and the engineers all meet that afternoon, about 4:00. Will is not in attendance and no one questions his absence.

Brandon, well prepared by Will, does an extremely acceptable job of seeing to the security issues with the engineers as Will sees them. There are a few things that Will would have done differently, but the minor inconveniences are well worth his not having to be there. He has his hands full, too, trying to rescue a forgetful queen.

On the way back the last time, Will had been struck hard in the face by several little revelations about Suede. She smelled like lavender, she was preternaturally quick when startled, and he has never seen her eat normal food in all the times he had been there. Lavender had been a single, suddenly blinding thought that in conjunction with the rain and the oncoming headlights had made him pull over to think without even the distraction of driving last week.

Will arrives at the Piper Club about an hour late, in spite of having left on time. He is in a fine fit about it, too. *It isn't as if I don't work most of my waking hours anyway. When it is time to come see her, they can kiss my ass because I am in the wind.* He is not really angry at them, he is nervous because he is considering telling Suede what it is clear she has forgotten.

Will parks the car himself, as usual. He is walking across the parking lot, waving to Rueben as he opens the big double doors leading into the foyer of the club. It takes his eyes just seconds to adjust to the dimness of the interior, but they are already searching. Will leans against one of the columns and relaxes. He hopes he looks like any other patron-just there to watch the show, have a good time, and relax.

But his eyes are hungry, searching out the crowd looking for her shape, her hair, and listening for the sound of her voice or for her name coming from the deejays booth.

"Okay, guys. Remember, looking doesn't pay the bills. The more you tip, the faster she gets naked!" The DJ sounds obscenely happy. *That, or he really is getting soused back there.*

"You okay, Doll?" asks one of the waitresses. They all know Will by sight by now just as they all knew he wanted only a diet soda, with Rose's lime or vanilla syrup. Like his former Queen, he is a teetotaler and does not consume alcohol.

"I'm OK. You look like you're doing well," says Will.

"Doing great... Need any thing?" asks the waitress.

"What I usually get, coke and lime," says Will.

"Coming right up, Baby," says the waitress.

"… Ask Suede if she'll sit with me as well?" asks Will.

"Sure."

The waitress walks away, smiling. Will is thinking to himself that he must sometimes look like it pure- D fool, but he can't stop. He is thinking maybe he dreamed of her when he was a kid. Then, she walks into his life for real, only to be taken from him when she thinks he is dead. Now, here she is for a mind popping third time. *Maybe she is here.*

"Suede says she has to take care of things in back and then she'll be right out, OK?" says the waitress.

"Great," says Will.

After about 30 minutes, Will begins to get a little bit antsy. Suede is always nice and pays attention to him, but it is clear that she does not remember him or their life together. *If it is her.* For about 10 seconds he thinks maybe he's not sure where he stands. Then a thought occurs to him, *It doesn't matter where I stand right now. She knew me before and she knew my heart. She'll know me again. Suede IS Crystal, there are a few differences, but she is Crystal. She even smells the same.*

"Evening, Will," says Suede as she slides in beside him.

As she sits down, Will is struck by a familiar rush of blood throughout his body.

"Hey, Baby Doll," says Will.

Suede sits. All something like 100 lbs. of her showing just how much shit she has to put up with in her line of work. She is glad to see him and it shows.

"Those guys are just dicks," says Suede. "They escorted him out-or at least one of them, anyway."

"What were they doing?" Will is curious.

"Oh, just acting a fool, like some have to do."

"Yeah, I think it's like a national law or something for rednecks, or maybe it's part of their religion. You know, that shalt publicly act a fool at least once a week."

"Yeah, that must be it." She had only a ghost of a smile, but it is better than nothing.

"Or maybe they have to prove they have a double digit IQ, you know, below 100 in order to keep their redneck journeyman's card active," says Will.

"Yeah, that MUST be it." She is more in her happy place in her mind now.

"Let's sit in the back, okay?" says Will.

"I will meet you back there. Let me handle one thing first," says Suede.

"Hey!" Will is trying to get the attention of one of the waitresses. "Can you bring whatever Suede is drinking to me in the back corner?"

"Sure thing, Babe," says the waitress, "Be right there."

Will walks on through the club, meandering through the path left by the daytime traffic in the maze of chairs and tables populating the club floor. He has his drink in hand and waves to a couple of the other regulars that he is beginning to recognize by sight if not by name. Sometimes Will finds himself trying analyze the motives of men who come to strip clubs as a rule rather than the occasion and those of women who dance there, but gives it up as a bad job. Everyone is different and trying to classify this group of people would be insane. Besides, Will is here to see only one woman, and that is Suede.

"Evening," says Suede as she sits and props her feet on the stage.

"Evening, Baby Doll."

"How goes your construction project?" asks Suede.

"Well, considering," says Will.

"Considering what?" asks Suede.

"Considering that even folks I know and respect sometimes want me to sit and hold their hand when it is completely unnecessary. They want me to supervise every little detail of a project. I mean if I wanted to do everything, I would not hire project managers, right? "

"I guess not," says Suede. She really didn't know if you would or not, but she figures agreeing with him on something he is so passionate about and she is so ignorant of is a good idea.

"Besides, I'm really beginning to get tired of dealing with all that I have to deal with. I'm simply trying to do my job…" Will is worked up, perhaps even more than a little aggravated. He realizes he should be talking to Suede about anything but work, but finds himself unleashing the irritation he felt with Felix earlier on that afternoon. Will finally catches himself and stops with, "Sorry, Angel. I'm done with MY bitch and moan session for the day. How have you been?"

"Fine, thanks," says Suede. Her tone is one of rye amusement. Suede sometimes comes in early and works a transition shift that patches between the day and night shifts. The differences in the rhythms of the clientele and in the groups of girls who work the different shifts sometimes make for interesting sparks. Having worked both shifts, Suede can see things from both sides, so she knows that Will is just venting. Like Will, she is there to do a job and wants as little peripheral interference as possible. Early on Suede has a fit over being asked to work the day shift, but it has turned out to be pretty much okay. She still prefers to work night shifts, though, and does so almost exclusively.

"Well, that's good. I brought you a big sleeper shirt."

"Thank you, Will. But why?" says Suede.

"Because I want to know that when you sleep sometimes it is clothes that I bought next to your skin," says Will.

Suede looks at Will, seeing the want on his face and how hard he is trying to hide it. He is an average looking guy, but there is something different about him. She is unable to put her finger on it, but it does seem to speak to her.

"Thank you, Will," says Suede. "I love to sleep in these big T-shirts."

"Looks like it will be more like a house dress than a T-shirt on you."

"Whatever, it will be comfortable." Suede is folding the shirt. She reclines back in her seat, folds her legs and props them on the stage again. "Thanks again, Will. I really appreciate this."

They talk on and off through the night. Sometimes Suede has to take a break and go dance on the main stages or sometimes a table dance for a customer that wants one specifically from her. What did they talk about? Only they know for sure, but over the weeks and days that follow they form a bond between themselves that was not built on sex or need or loneliness but purely on the fact that their minds enjoy each other.

Theoretically, Will has known in the past that his attraction to Crystal is more than just looks or sex. It is some spark dancing behind her eyes that he just can't get enough of. He has to be around her. Over the last 8 to 10 years Will has come to believe that there are certain people whose lot in life is to never be warm inside. While that may or may not be true, Crystal has kept Will warm.

Why can she not remember me? What has happened to make her completely forget everything? Why did Monica and Melissa tell me she had died? Here she is, living and breathing, thank God, so, why the amnesia? Where has she been since she disappeared? What has taken her memory? And now, she even has the ability to walk in the daylight.

"What are you thinking about so hard?" asks Suede.

"Just thinking me thinks," says Will.

"Well, I have an answer for you," says Suede.

"What answer?" says Will.

"Yes, an answer," says Suede.

"Okay," says Will.

"I do want see you outside the club," says Suede. "That is, if you still want to see me. Do you?"

"I suppose I do," says Will. "Yes, I definitely do." *What I want to do is to pick you up and carry you home.* "What is the next night you have off?" asks Will. *I know, quit this job so you have every night off.*

"Friday is my next night off. 6:00 ok with you?" asks Suede.

"Sounds good to me," says Will. "But why don't we make a day of it? I will pick you up around noon." The last word is raised in a semi-question.

"I guess that's okay. I don't work Thursday night either, so, sure. 12:00 sounds good."

The rest of the night is a blur in Will's mind. He is as excited about the prospect of seeing her on Friday as he was about seeing her the first time in Infosurge's top floor offices. The fact that he is going to see his sweetheart Friday pretty much puts Will's senses a tad over into the soft focus area. While Suede dances on the main floor, the waitress tries to check on Will to see if he needs anything. She is there a good 30 seconds before she realizes Will is not entirely home.

"Earth to Will," says the waitress while waving her hand in front of his face to get his attention. "Good grief, man. You need to breathe once in awhile." The waitress is good naturedly ribbing will. Some guys were jerks, but it is clear to her that Will cares for Suede in a way that most men are incapable of. He is definitely on her good guy list.

"I'm sorry," says Will. "I was just zoned out, I guess."

"I said to you need anything to drink?" says the waitress.

"Sounds good to me," says Will handing her a $5 bill, "and go ahead and freshen up Suede's drink, too."

"Will do," says the waitress.

Will watches Suede finish her dance, trying like hell as he has said in the past to burn her image into his brain. She comes down the stairs to the side of the stage and goes through the backdoor to the dressing room area. Will knows it will be a good 20 minutes before she gets out so he makes a restroom run.

As Will exits the restroom, he is surprised to find Suede already back at their seats. Walking up to her and sitting down, he sees that she is anxious.

"Will, while I was in back I was thinking," says Suede. "I was thinking why wait until Friday? That is, if you're up for it."

"Am I up for it?" says Will. "Sure." Then he thinks for a second about having to be back in Birmingham and at a meeting at 7:30 in the morning, but it is a short-lived thought. "What time do you think you'll be finished tonight?"

"I have one more stage left. Then I'm done today," says Suede.

"Good deal," says Will, then under his breath, "Good friggin' deal."

"Felix, LB here. Have you heard from Will yet?"

"No, LB, I have not heard from him. I do know he was headed over to Atlanta for whatever he's working on over there. Why?"

"No big deal, I guess. I just thought he was going to call and confirm our appointment for in the morning. Has he said anything to you?" asks LB.

"No, hasn't said a thing to me. Have you checked with Kyle?"

"No, I have not. Well, I guess he's working late. It's not even midnight yet so I don't know why I am paranoid all of a sudden about his getting there on time."

"Well, LB. I have to say that here lately Will has had some punctuality problems. His work is fine, as always. But I think he's distracted over something, most likely whatever he's working on in Atlanta. If it were me," and here Felix pauses. Then he continues on, "If it were me I would not worry too much about being there on time unless he calls and confirms. That's the track I'm running on with him…for about the last two weeks, I guess."

"Sounds like good advice. How are the accelerators coming?" asks LB.

"Fairly well, we don't expect to be through with the larger loops until Christmas, which is about what we expected," says Felix.

"Very good, I'll let you go."

Will made it to work, but not until noon the next day. No one was surprised.

After Suede's last dance, she tells Will to meet her outside. A dancer leaving with one of the patrons is a practice frowned upon by the management. She laughs as she is explaining this. Upon further thought, Suede decides that the better thing to do is to meet in the speed-for-cheap parking lot down the street.

"They just get all freaked. Anything that looks like prostitution can cause them problems. Just meet me there and we'll leave from there," says Suede.

"Alright, I will see you there," says Will.

Sitting in the speed-for-cheap parking lot, Will calls and checks his messages. There is a call from LB wanting to confirm their 7:30 appointment in the morning, but since it is 1:30 a.m., Will decides against calling him. I will do it in the morning, thinks Will. Besides, he so old that a phone ringing in the middle of the night usually means someone has died. Will decides against stressing LB out with a midnight phone call and waits for Suede to show up.

She isn't long in getting there. Getting out of her car, she looks quite different with no makeup, wearing jeans and a sweat top. She is just as beautiful without all that makeup.

Suede shuts the door to her F-150 and walks towards Will's ZR-1. As before losing her memory, she drives a big American truck.

The Corvette is Will's present to himself for disentangling from all the other crap that OEE is involved in. It is blue with twin white racing stripes down the center line. The tag says 'BEAR.'

As Suede approaches Will's car, he gets out and walks

around to get her door for her. She gets in and he closes her door, thinking just how good she looks sitting in his car.

Will cranks his car, listens to the large V-8 rumble into life thinking there really is no substitute for eight cylinders or more. Looking over, he sees Suede agrees.

"You hungry?" asks Will. He isn't going rush this.

"Not just yet. Besides, you might find my appetites a little different."

"You might be surprised, but ok," says Will. "So, what do we do in the Atlanta at 1:30 on a Thursday morning?"

"Let's just ride around. That okay with you?" asks Suede.

"Fine with me. Let's go down by the civic center."

"Let's go," says Suede.

Will and Suede ride around Atlanta for about an hour-and-a-half. They continue their conversation from the club and Will is pleased to see that while she may not remember their time together, she is still very easy to talk to and interesting to listen to. Like before, it is almost as if they've known each other for centuries, *which with all the weird-ass shit that I have been going through the last year may be true.*

Around 5:00 a.m., Will begins to get a little bit sandy eyed. "Doll, I am having a good time but I've been up since 6 yesterday morning. I guess I need to drop you off at your car. I'm probably going to be late to my meeting 7:30 anyway."

"Will, if you are late anyway, just stay with me. You can call in sick, can't you?" asks Suede.

Will looks at Suede, he knows he is going to call in sick. He knew it when she got to the words 'late anyway.'

"Yes, I can."

"Do it, then. I want you to be with me, OK?" asks Suede. "I want you to stay the day with me."

"Then I will," says Will.

Chapter 30

Suede is finally Mine

"Suede, I have wanted you to say that for so long," Will says as he reaches across for her hand. "God, you make me shake." Then Will is reaching for her across the car seat embracing her and kissing her with a hunger that terrifies him.

"Oh, my Bear," says Suede as she reaches for him in return, matching his hunger and running her hands over his shoulders as he wraps his arms around her, crushing her breasts to him.

This is no mere fling, not some one-stand set off by pure physical attraction. This is a hunger in the soul. Suede feels this and realizes she is in the arms of a man who will die for her and count the cost of his life as cheap.

"Why do you feel this way, Bear? You don't even know me," says Suede.

"I know your heart. I see your bravery in the face of all you have to put up with. I see the way you carry past wrongs and how you never let them stop you from pressing forward."

Now Will is pulling her over into his lap, cradling her in his arms. His hands are shaking as he slides his right hand up under her shirt to cup her breast.

"Not much are they?" asks Suede. She is not voluptuous, but rather built along athletic lines, for speed.

"Hush, my angel. You're so perfect you make every vein in my body burn," says Will.

They kiss and there is nothing else in Will's universe

but Suede's mouth, how she tastes, the smell of her hair, and her hands on the back of his neck.

"Take me home, Will. Take me home and take me." Suede's heart is beating so fast that Will feels its flutter as his lips, hungry to taste all of her, kisses her on her mouth, her cheeks, her chin, and the sides of her throat.

"Suede, my beautiful, little Suede. You know I will. But you have to tell me how to get there."

They both break out laughing, like a couple of inexperienced teenagers. It takes the edge off the passion for the moment. *I don't know that I should be driving when I am like that, thinks Will. His hands are still trembling with the touch of her skin on his fingertips.* The speed, with which he flips the ignition, guns the engine and engages the clutch make that thought silly.

"Hang a right out of the parking lot, and catch 285 North."

"My Lady, we go," says Will.

The ride back to Suede's place is quiet. It is only 20 minutes long, but it seems to contain a lifetime. In the days that follow Will remembers how she feels as she holds his hand and gives directions to her home where she will give herself to him. Her voice, her scent, everything about her is intoxicating. Will knows he is lost. The rebellion, all his successes, nothing means anything next to this siren. The radio, set to a mid-range volume, seems to be swallowed by the white noise in Will's head. He is nervous. The first time is always different, and while he remembers how the first time was with Crystal, Suede is a different person from that Crystal.

What the hell are you worrying about? Here you are,

some transformed supposed super being worried like some 16 year old virgin. It is a good thing you don't have your thoughts written across your forehead, dumb ass. Then, I guess you only get nervous if you really care.

Together they walk up the stairs to Suede's town home. She slides home her key, thinking that some things in life really are omens of things to come. As she moves to one side to let Will in, she laughs a rueful laugh.

"What's funny?" asks Will.

"I was just thinking how funny it is that something as simple as opening a lock can make you think about making love," says Suede.

This is Crystal. She goes by Suede because she can't remember. But she is Crystal and she belongs to me.

Together they go through the front door. No words are necessary as she takes him by one hand and pulls him up the stairs towards her bedroom.

"No, my love," says Will as he pulls her to him and picks her up in both arms. "You're mine and I intend to carry you both tonight and…" the sentence goes unfinished as he crushes her to his chest, kissing her.

There is no sensation of carrying her weight as he mounts the stairs with his lover cradled in his arms. Suede is kissing his throat, tasting the salt on his skin. His breath is ragged in her ears. She knows it is not from exertion but from a raging want for her.

Reaching the top of the stairs, Will asks, desperation plain in his voice, "Where?"

"Down there, Bear," says Suede, pointing to a doorway at the end of the hallway.

Will fairly flies down the hall and into his angel's bedroom. Groaning with a lust so powerful he feels as if his heart will surely burst Will lays his angel on her bed. His pants have drawn painfully tight across is groin, and he almost howls in frustration as he tries to work his belt buckle, but even his fingers feel engorged.

Suede unbuttons her blouse, whimpering with desire as a wave of lust ripples through her. This is like her dreams. She squirms on the bed and rolls over and slaps Will's hands away from his waist and undoes his belt. She pulls his pants down loving the feeling of her hands on his muscular butt, then his hands are on her shoulders pushing her back on to the bed. She leans back, feeling his erection trace a line down between her breasts and across the concavity of her stomach.

Will is on top of her kissing her. Civilization deserts him as he pulls Suede's jeans over her hips raising her legs. Her cotton panties come with her jeans and Will is struck by the scent of her want.

The urge to simply take her is overwhelming, but he doesn't want to hurt her. Suede senses his turmoil as he holds her close.

Will kisses her, kisses her cheeks, kisses her eyes, her ears, her throat all the while marveling at her softness and the completeness he feels at finally being with his angel. The simple fact of her existence, which such a creature could be makes him know there is a God. Her being here in his arms makes him understand that that same God loved him.

Will reaches down and caresses her flower. She is slick and wet with want. Suede is his and she cries out as his turgid manhood begins to enter her. Will moves slowly to fill her completely, allowing her time to accommodate him. She grips him like a wet velvet glove.

She pulls him down, hungry for his mouth on hers as he pushes forward burying himself inside her.

"Oh, Suede, my beautiful little angel…" Will says as she begins to rock. They're swept away on a wave that blurs the senses and the boundaries of reality.

She meets his thrust for thrust as his kisses burn her throat. As she feels herself skirting towards the edge she looks up into his eyes and knows he will meet her there.

As they climax together, the bear and his butterfly, their eyes lock. They both cry out as Will floods her.

"Will, I… Oh!" Suede cries out again and again as Will holds her close and continues to love her and drown in her eyes.

Exhausted, finally, Will lays beside Suede. She rolls over toward him, laying her head on his shoulder and draping one arm and one leg across his body, running her hand across his muscular, hairy chest.

"Never before…" begins Will as he reaches around her and cups a single, beautiful breast in his hand.

"Bear?" asks Suede. "What?"

"I don't think I have ever really made love before this," Will says as he rolls towards her and kisses her, perhaps to hide the wetness in his eyes.

"My Bear…" and then they are lost again.

Chapter 31

Nag and counternag

"Brandon did a fairly good job of spotting for you the other day," says LB.

"I had no doubts that he was the man for the job while I handled the situation in Atlanta," says Will. "Is he here?"

"Not yet, but he should arrive shortly," LB says.

"Good. Do you remember whether or not he was able to get all the specs on the microwave relay from Unicom?" asks Will.

"No, but I do remember that he had a checklist and he went down the list with the Unicom representative," says LB. "He was quite pleased with having worked his way through the entire list."

"It showed, huh?" says Will.

"No, he said and I quote, 'I am quite pleased with having worked my way through the entire list,'" says LB.

"Very good," says Will. Then, *if he worked his way through the entire list that I left him, I don't have a hell of a lot to do today. Cool.*

"I think Felix wanted to see you today, though," says LB. "So don't go haring off to Atlanta until you check with him, okay?"

"I will check with him," says Will. "Do you know if he had any particular aspect that he needed me to help him with?" asks Will. "I would like to go ahead and prepare before I see him."

"No, I don't. I do know that he expressed concern about

the possibility of being able to collect data from radiation leakage when running the accelerators."

"Good point. Still, I'm not sure how we can accurately determine the scope of that particular threat until we get the accelerators up and running. We'll just need to be doing a bunch of dry runs once construction on the loops is complete and then do a threat analysis at that point."

"Just cover that with him directly," says LB. "I understand less and less of the technical aspects of this project." His face is pensive, like a man who isn't quite sure what he has hold of, which is indeed the case.

This attitude is new with LB. It concerns Will that the old man seems to be losing some faith in the project's long-term chances of success. It must be showing.

"Don't sweat it, Will," says LB. "I've complete confidence in the two of you. It is just that with the new administrative overhead that has been added since cutting our staff so drastically what with all the changes involved in cutting OEE loose, I am rapidly losing the ability to put much time into grasping the technical details of what it is we're doing. I mean, just from the high fly by's that Felix has done with me point-blank indicates that we are redefining many physical laws. Don't you agree?"

"I certainly do. Now, let me ask you. I am right in my assumption that preliminary experiments based on Felix's research do corroborate his predictions for what we can do with this technology, correct?" asks Will. It only just occurs to Will that he has no way of knowing whether or not Felix actually knows what he is doing. Being a whiz with computers does not a physicist make.

"Absolutely," says LB. "In fact, many of his senior research assistants all anticipate turning physics on its ear within five years. They all seem to agree that we're on the verge not only of redefining physics, but laying the groundwork for an entirely new set of mathematics."

"Heavy-duty stuff," says Will.

"Yup," says LB.

"It is her Monica. Crystal is alive," says Will.

"How can that be possible? Both Melissa and I watched her burn up outside Norn's Lair?" says Monica.

"I have no idea," says Will. "But I don't really care. All I care about is the fact Crystal is alive."

"Will, I'm sending Melissa and Salome the guardian to you. I want them to see this Suede is Crystal up close. You're too valuable and I cannot take any chances that some of our enemies have come up with a very clever way of getting to you," says Monica.

"Monica, they can't get to me. I've engaged numerous arachnids in person…multiple arachnids simultaneously. I'm able to walk in the daylight; I'm more than a match for scores of arachnids, why are you so concerned about this? I would think you would be happy to hear she is alive," says Will. This is not going as he had planned.

"I watched her die," says Monica. *Too harsh by half.* Then, in a kind voice, she continues, "Will, this Suede can reach you in ways enemies you recognize cannot. How do you know she is not working on the side of the rebels? You've only known her… what? Three months?"

"Something like that," says Will. Actually, it was more like six weeks, but Will didn't feel like bringing that point up to his Queen. Especially when she is in a chew-his-ass mode; when he knew that if he were on the outside looking in, he would agree with Monica's comments. *Chew my ass mode?*

That really isn't fair to her. But she is wrong! It is Crystal.

"I will be careful. I do not need babysitters watching after me as if I were retarded." Will is crossing over into belligerence, but he catches himself. "Send only Melissa, Monica. I understand your concern. So, let's get right to it, resolve it and move on. Deal?"

"That sounds fair enough, Will," says Monica. "Don't you understand, though, how important you are to our efforts?"

"Yes…" begins Will.

"I don't think you do understand, Will," says Monica. "If you did you wouldn't be running after somebody you've only known for six weeks like a crazy man." She knows he'd only known her for six weeks, he is of the people and transparent to her now. Not always, but often enough that she is learning how to read him. *You can be read, but like everything else connected with you, Will, I have to do things a little differently.*

"Monica…" she is right, of course. He is acting like a crazy man and he knows it. He doesn't feel in control of himself and it scares the hell out of him, too.

"No, don't Monica me," says Monica. She is a fine fit now. "You have responsibilities. You are critical to our efforts, yet… unbelievable. Will, you cannot be sure."

"Hell, you think I don't know this? But it is Crystal. I don't know how. Nor do I know why and I really don't care. Somehow she survived walking out into the daylight at Norn's lair," says Will.

"I understand you may think that this person is Crystal," says Monica. "Will, very seldom in my millennia of living have I met a man so completely devoted to his Lady. You don't know what you are doing. Wait for Melissa before you see Suede again. She will know if this person is Crystal or if you are just projecting Crystal on to this poor stripper who probably thinks you've lost your mind."

"Monica, when will she be here?" asks Will. "You don't understand, the woman is Crystal, I am positive. If I'm sitting 6 in. away face-to-face, I know damn well whether this is Crystal or not."

"Will you wait one week?" asks Monica. "It will take Melissa that long to finish up here and then she can come and go to Atlanta with you. Atlanta is where Suede, this Suede is, correct?" says Monica.

Will didn't know whether he could wait a week or not, which fact also made him think that, possibly, Monica has a point and is right. It is clear he is not in control of himself. That as much as anything else indicates there might be another vector at work. *Besides, if she's correct I need to know it now and not later.*

"Can she make it in three days?" asks Will.

"I'll make it happen," says Monica. "Do not go and see Suede before Melissa gets there."

Three days? No problem. I mean, 72 hours is not that long. In any case, I need to concentrate on getting Brandon ready to move over to being my personal full-time assistant anyway. Sharing Kyle just isn't practical amongst the three of us. Besides, Brandon seems to have taken to me and a little personal loyalty is always a good thing.

"Yes, darling," says LB. "I know it has been a long time, but with these new projects I'm involved with it is hard to get away."

LB looks down at his desk while his forehead wrinkles

up in concentration as he listens to the other end of this conversation. Pleadingly, he looks over to Kyle and mouths the question, *where are they?*

Kyle writes a note and holds it up. It says that Felix and Will are stuck on the two-lane highway leading in from Sylacauga behind a pulp wood truck that has overturned.

"Why, no, I am not terribly busy right now," *not now that my boys are bollixed up in a traffic wreck.* "We can talk a bit," says LB as he looks at Kyle with aggravation plain on his face. He supposes it is a blessing in disguise. LB and his estranged daughter have not spoken in months and this is as good a time as any to talk.

"Well, you know my views and I cannot apologize for what I see as a clear case of not thinking clearly. Honey, you can live your life any way you see fit. Just don't ask me to approve."

LB leans back in his chair and looks at the ceiling as if there might be a Rosetta stone that would help him understand his daughter. Not seeing any help there, he spins back around and leans over his desk on both elbows.

Everybody has problems, thinks Kyle as he watches his boss deal with his daughter. *No matter who you are you still have problems.* He didn't know the nature of his boss's and his daughter's disagreement, and does not want to. Kyle is afraid that if the old man ever did start confiding in him about this it will be added to the plate he is carrying.

Which is fine, I guess. I work my eight hours and go home, so I think it doesn't matter what I do. It just seems to me that they're letting personal things get in the way of doing what they need to do for the company. All three of them are. Well, not so much Felix. But what with LB's family falling apart, and Will's doing whatever the hell it is he is in Atlanta which I will just bet is some skirt... here Kyle really starts to fume.

Kyle has come to realize that he resents Will's refusal to be on the job at 8 in the morning until 5 or 7 at night like an employee. *He is an employee, just like me. So where the hell does he get off not showing up for days at a time?*

Kyle is your archetype for the company man. His job is the first thing he thinks about in the morning when he gets up and tomorrow's list of things to do is the last thing he thinks about when he goes to bed. LB had worried about the boy when he hired him, but Kyle had put him at ease.

"Look, Mr. Browning," Kyle had said. "I don't have all these other distractions that most people have to deal with. I don't have to worry about fights during the holidays or someone not liking what I got them for their birthday, or someone thinking I like someone else's kids better. Really, think about it. I don't have to carry half the crap you have to carry simply because I have made the decision to concentrate purely on my career. I'm happy."

"Yes, Kyle. I can see the logic in what you're saying. "But what about when you get old? Don't you want kids and grandkids around you?"

"What? This way I don't have to worry about what my kids are getting into or whether not my kids can afford to send my grand kids to college. I'm telling you, this way means less trouble, period."

LB thought it was the saddest damn conversation he'd ever had with a 20 year old.

I am just about ready to speak my piece on this, thinks Kyle. The project cannot afford to be screwed up because these guys have a bunch of women with their balls set up on a mantle for safekeeping. These thoughts are the beginning of a whole lot of trouble.

It is amazing how just little things can snowball into really big problems.

"Sure." LB is silent for a long time. "Honey, you're always welcome." The warmth in LB's voice is clear. Whatever their disagreement is, it is clear he loves his daughter.

I'm glad that I don't have to deal with that kind of thing, thinks Kyle. His thinking about it for the next 45 minutes being seen as ironic wouldn't even have slowed him down. Kyle had achieved a 50 year-old mind set at the age of 25. Had he thought about it, he would have been quite proud.

Felix and Will arrived three hours late. LB is glad to see them, while Kyle makes his excuses and leaves.

Wonder what is wrong with him? Thinks Will. Then LB is sitting down to get the meeting started.

"Okay, guys," says LB. "let's make sure we're all on the same page. Will, tell us where we are on communications and security."

"We're going with the microwave relay," says Will. "We are going to link to Birmingham via microwave link, that is. We'll also have a microwave link to Atlanta, and an ISDN link to one of the local ISP providers."

"Rockford has an ISP? More than one?" Felix is astonished.

"Well, actually there is a small one and then there is Gulf Bell." Gulf Bell is the local phone company. Will continues, "Our goal there is to make sure that e-mail never goes down even if for some reason both microwave links go down. Unlikely, MAE East has been known to go through a meltdown from time to time, especially when they go through an equipment upgrade. I think they may be up for an upgrade now, so I just want to make sure."

"So that gives us…what? Four links, two by microwave and one or two by landline?" asks Felix.

"Correct," says Will.

"Good," says LB. "Redundancy seems satisfactory."

"I have to give Brandon credit for the ISDN line idea," says Will. "I knew that we needed backup coverage through the microwave links, but Brandon pointed out that ISDN to the phone company grid would enable us to overcome even a failure at MAE east by routing through the phone system."

"Brandon is turning out to be quite the young man, isn't he?" asks LB.

"Yes, he is. Since we're on the subject of Brandon I want to broach this before I forget. Kyle is working with you two and is quite overloaded in my opinion. I want Brandon promoted to work directly with me, not unlike Kyle's position with you, LB, if you're agreeable," says Will.

"I suppose that'll be fine," says LB. "but let's not spend a lot of time on that right now. We need to finish this updating session and then move on to the issue of Brandon, okay? Felix?" says LB. LB indicates that Felix should move on with the material he has brought.

Will interjects, "Alright, I just wanted to bring it up before I forgot," says Will.

"LB, for the record I agree with Will on Brandon," and here Felix has to grin a little bit because he is doing exactly what LB does not want to do. He continues on, "I think Kyle is overloaded handling all three of our schedules." LB opens his mouth but Felix continues on, "Brandon is energetic and smart and understands what Will is doing and he understands Will's designs. When Will is off doing one of his side projects, Brandon is the best man to have in the No. 2 spot in the IT department. Now" and here he does continue on into talking about the accelerator's because LB is about to pop a vein, "it is time to move on to the accelerators. We'll be done in approximately 10 days, well ahead of schedule."

Here Will pipes up. They are not just ahead of schedule, they are months early. "How did you manage that?"

"The delays weren't caused by the construction process itself, but by actually being able to take delivery of parts. The DOE cancelled one of the California projects so the manufacturer-I don't remember the name-is looking for a place to dump the coils," says Felix. "I told them to bring them on if they would do it for the same price quoted on the coils we asked for originally," says Felix. Felix is thumbing through the paperwork in front him but he does not succeed in finding the quote on the upgraded coils. "I guess it's still on my desk."

"Amazing how you got the very coils you needed months early," says Will.

"Well, they are not exactly what I ordered. They are a lot more powerful, which is great because now we can avoid the upgrades we were talking about in 20 months," says Felix.

"So, we won't need to upgrade the coils in 20 months?" asks LB.

"Correct," says Felix.

"I think you just saved us $30 million," says LB. Clearly, he is in his happy place.

"More like 42," says Felix.

"Got to hate that," says LB. Yes, he is definitely in his happy place.

"Then it is time for me to get started on coming up with some ways to collect data from leakage in the loops," says Will.

"I think so," says Felix.

"Melissa, Will is in trouble," says Monica.

"What kind of trouble?" asks Melissa. Trouble for Will has a different meaning now since he's been changed. Trouble for somebody like Will is most likely trouble for everybody.

"We thought he had dealt with Crystal's death, but we were wrong, very wrong," says Monica. "He seems to think he has found Crystal in a stripper in Atlanta."

"A stripper." It is not exactly a question.

"Yes. Apparently, he went with a bunch of men he works with, saw this woman, and lost his mind. She must look a lot like Crystal. That, combined with whatever he is holding in has him thinking she is Crystal," says Monica.

"Poor Will. I knew he had taken it very badly, but I never expected him to go mental over it."

"Indeed. I don't what he's thinking," says Monica after several minutes of silence during which she searches for something, anything that will help her get a handle on Will's state of mind. She is not successful. "Just go, and check on the man. He didn't want you to, but I insist you take Salome with you."

"Why would I need to take a guardian with me to check on Will's infatuation with a dancer?" asks Melissa. "She can't be any threat to a man or am I missing something?"

"The arachnids nor the rebels can either individually nor severally defeat Will in a fight. I am concerned that this may be the spearhead of an initiative aimed at Will specifically," says Monica. "Our being able to put off the blind spot by some several months caused more than a little bit of the uproar in their leadership. I understand there were a few executions over this."

"If they can't harm him, why are you so concerned then?" asks Melissa.

"They caught us unawares with this obscene alliance with the arachnids. No one could've seen that coming because it was just too bizarre. They already have a record of doing the unexpected. I don't want Will to fall due to over confidence… or distraction."

"So, you want me to go and be with Will and protect him from his heart."

"That is exactly it, Melissa. I want you to go protect Will from his heart," says Monica. "Also, I want you to take Salome with you as an extra level of protection," says Monica. "Maybe heart isn't exactly what you are protecting him from, but check it out. I'm curious."

"Very well, Salome is good company, and smaller than most guardians so she won't stand out in a crowd. Well, she won't stand out quite as much as some of the others would," says Melissa.

While they are having this conversation one of the guardians along the wall is paying close attention. It is Dallas, the guardian who had headed up will's security detail before the change and accompanied him for his first battle against arachnids in the desert.

"My lady," says Dallas. "I would like to volunteer to go

in Salome's place."

"Why would you want to do that?" asks Monica.

"Because I would like to see to his safety personally," says Dallas.

"Well," says Monica. "I certainly have no objections. Are you agreeable, Melissa?"

"Sure. Although, I will need to use glamour to conceal Dallas's bulk," says Melissa.

"So why are you volunteering, Dallas?" asks Monica. Guardians as a rule are taciturn and uninvolved. Asking to leave her assignment is very odd. Guardians don't exactly have what most people would consider freewill. Driven by instinct, they're loyal to their charges with a fanaticism that would scare even the most rabid Middle Eastern zealot.

"Because I would like to see the wizard again," says Dallas. "I suspect that they don't even know he is a wizard."

"The wizard?" says Monica.

"Dallas, what are you talking about?" says Melissa. "Who is a wizard?"

"The one called Felix," says Dallas. "He acts as if he is completely unaware of the fact. It may be possible to manipulate such a one by a very clever person, possibly to the extent that great harm could be carried out."

There are no wizards. At least, that is the common wisdom amongst the people. Wizards, or witches or shamans or what ever you want to call them are simply faery tales.

"Dallas, there aren't any wizards," says Melissa.

"As my lady wishes, may I accompany you?" asks Dallas.

"Yes."

"Melissa, when you get to Will keep your eyes open. Dallas's question makes me think that someone close to Will may be attempting to manipulate him and his companions. I do not think Felix is a wizard," and here Monica looks over to the hulking Dallas, "but perhaps the idea that they're being manipulated merits investigation. Will is not himself, and we cannot afford that."

Dallas keeps her peace and her own counsel.

"No, Baby Doll. I will not be making it over tonight." Will isn't going to Atlanta to see Suede. He is not happy about it, but he did promise Monica he would wait until Melissa arrives.

"Okay, Bear. When all I see you again?" asks Suede.

"Most likely by the weekend. I have a few odds and ends to clear up here," says Will. "We're running way ahead of schedule, so I want to start with some project outlines and such. Hopefully, I'll have the work schedules and timelines worked out by Wednesday afternoon."

"Sounds like too much fun to be legal," says Suede. "Want me to come keep your company?"

"Well, no, not really. You can't seem to control yourself, so you need to stay over there, or I won't get any work done at all. I mean, really, Suede, do you have to throw yourself at me? Have a little self-control, you know?"

Suede giggles at this. They both know who has no self-control, but it is a sweet knowledge. And if her bear says he can't come, he really can't come. "Oh yeah, who's gonna be all knotted up in his underwear about 2:00 in the morning?"

"Why don't you just fl…" Will catches himself. He had been about to say fly, but she wouldn't and he did not know if it was good for her to be reminded of things she can no longer do, or remember how to do, at any rate. "I started to say to catch a flight to Birmingham, but you have to work so that's out."

But he thinks about telling her to quit her job and come home, you are a princess, a vampire, but he doesn't. She is right about the underwear thing, though. About 2:00 a.m. I will really miss her.

"I will see you this weekend, butterfly, " says Will.

"Bye, Bear. I love you," says Suede. His response is cut off by the click of her hanging up.

Will is still looking at the headset when Felix steps into his office.

"Will, my man. Hungry?" says Felix. Felix is very hungry and ready to leave. Will, even in his current state, notices that Felix looks wired.

"Sure. Let's go. What's got you pumped up?" asks Will.

"Oh, just a few little surprises coming out of the last set of trials on the accelerators. Come on, and I'll buy your lunch and talk your head off about it."

Chapter 32

"So, you are done," says Felix.

"Yes, Felix, I am done with the final project outlines and the time lines," says Will. "What? You think I would just put those things slide?" He is furious. But it is time to put a stop to this now. *It is bad enough that Melissa is coming to make sure I'm not off'n my rocker about Crystal, now I have Felix crawling...you know, this is why I should never have gotten into this shit.* Then, ruefully, *Of course, if I hadn't, the world might have already ended.*

Felix is running on the assumption all day that Will is not finished with any of the project outlines or the time lines. No one is able to say exactly where he gets the idea that Will is not indeed up to speed with his planning, but whatever the source it really causes a stink. Will is more than just aggravated. He is infuriated, hurt, and embarrassed. Having taken the position that he intends to date an erotic dancer, Will had mistakenly assumes that his close friends will just laugh it off, accept it, and move on with their own business. He is wrong.

"Well, you haven't really been concentrating on the issues at hand the way you did in the past, even you'll have to admit that," says Felix.

"No, Felix, that is not the case. Point to me one issue over which it has not been resolved in a timely fashion. Just one," says Will.

"That's not the point, Will," says Felix. "You used to spend time thinking about where to take the company and what nifty neat ideas and all kinds of variations you could come up with...all that's gone," says Felix. "You just don't have the fire since you've hooked up with that stripper."

"Felix, you're my friend. Do NOT presume to interfere in my personal affairs. You're stepping over the bounds," says Will.

"Stepping over the bounds? Have you lost your mind? I'm trying to help you. Can't see that?" asks Felix.

"Well, see, it's this way, and you need to pass this on to whomever else you need to pass it on to. I'm doing everything I am required to do. I own part of this company. I am meeting the time ETAs on the various segments I promised. What I do after I leave this place is none of your damn business. I want you to understand that fact. What I do after I leave here is none of your damn business, so stay out of it," says Will.

Now Felix realizes his friend is truly incensed about the situation. Not so much of how he is being viewed by everybody, but because he feels like people are losing confidence in him even though he is doing as good a job as ever.

And so it goes, nag and counter nag, one person trying to care and the other to appreciate it.

Things had reached a screaming state of silent static while the two remaining queens, Will, and the majority of the Joint Chiefs' staff tried to map out a plan of attack against the rebels without upsetting the relative calm in which the world believed itself to be. Perception is often reality's determinate. The problem is also that many people who are sympathetic to the rebels have positions of influence. Maintaining strict secrecy concerning the people in the vampire nations is an overriding concern and has, in fact, brought all actions against the rebels to a stop. Why? It is because no one knows how to proceed without compromising a wall of anonymity that has stood for centuries with few breaches.

As the debates rage on in Colorado Springs, Norn's Lair, and Birmingham, innocent people continue to die in northern Europe. As the death toll continues to mount, outbreaks occur in the northern provinces of Russia and Alaska.

The panic and desperation amongst those in power is demonstrated by a major television network having its charter yanked by the FCC, an entire building seized and padlocked, and over 200 employees incarcerated. It is Brandon who observes that the individuals arrested form a chain of folks that runs from the chairman of the board all the way down to the fellow who empties wastebaskets. Most of the arrests are nuisances. The main targets are the reporters who, having had a conversation with someone on the Joint Chiefs' staff, could not keep their mouths shut. The deal had been that the reporters would receive a phone call once the operation was underway and it was too late, or too difficult, to stop them from following through.

Monica and Melissa are confident of having found those areas that contain the true leaders of the rebels. Monica decides to go along with the consensus between the vice president and the Joint Chiefs and move ahead with an extermination project aimed at eliminating the leaders of the Norn's enemies. There really is no choice. They will neither negotiate nor even consider concessions in return for maintaining the secrecy and stopping the violence.

I wish this could be avoided, thinks Monica, *all this bloodshed and for what? No one involved in this rebellion is in danger of hunger, disease or poverty. It is a pure selfish grab for power. I intend this to be a lesson to others who would pursue this course. It should deter some in the future who try to make this planet a hell.*

It is with these facts in hand that Monica decides to give Will her leave to go and do what he has wanted to do all along: simply cut them down individually or in groups wherever he finds them.

"Melissa, I am going to Birmingham to see Will. I am going to let the boy loose on the rebels and the arachnids. It is not as if we will compromise the people any further by sending him to rampage among them," says Monica.

"You're sending him alone?" asks Melissa.

"No, I'm sending both Salome and Dallas's battalions with him," says Monica.

"I will accompany them," says Melissa.

"Yes, of course you will. Your glamours will be critical for their success, especially since we're sending a relatively small force against them," says Monica.

"Why such a small force? We want success, do we not? Why not go and finish the fight?" asks Melissa.

"Because we will be providing support to the humans, more like the edge of the blade rather than the backbone of the knife. Will is to be our ace held back in reserve," says Monica. "It has to be this way. There are those amongst the humans who would prefer to walk through and take us all out simply: the people, children, the guardians, and rebels alike. They see us giving them intelligence and guiding them to a successful expulsion of the rebels, with no interference, and that means help, too, as proof that, as a whole, the people simply want to live in peace."

"So, Will is not to engage unless absolutely necessary? " asks Melissa.

"That is correct," says Monica. "We do not want them to see Will's full abilities unleashed."

"I can see the wisdom in that," says Melissa.

Humans attack what they fear. If confronted with a creature of Will's abilities, it is almost sure to set off a firestorm among some military leaders to find a way to take him out. Paranoia is already running rampant amongst world leaders due to many heads of state, particularly in the Third World and smaller countries who, having no idea that the people existed until recently, suddenly don't know where they stand in the world. Rumors, ideas, and midnight whisperings about who might actually be human and who might not only be fed the fire.

It looks as if there is a war coming between humans and the people in any case. Perhaps they're having taken out the rebels by themselves will make them feel safe. Melissa can see from Monica's face that her hope is shared but isn't a strong one for either queen.

"Will, you have company," says Brandon.

Will has been in the office since 3:00 a.m. He is trying to finish up, and it seems like one distraction after the other is hell-bent on sucking the time out of his day. "I really can't see anybody from Unicom today. I just don't have the time. Too," and here he hesitates, turns, looks down at his calendar and confirms he has no appointments. Will turns back to Brandon and begins to tell him why they will have to come back another day. Then his company walks in the door.

"My Lady Monica," says Will. Melissa is also with her. "Lady Melissa."

"Lord Will," says Monica.

"Will," says Melissa.

"Lord?" says Brandon. *You just never know with these guys. Wonder where this game is going.* "You need anything else?"

"No, Brandon. That is all. Thank you," says Will.

After Brandon leaves, they all move to the conference table. The table is next to a large window looking out over acreage with a creek running through it on the one side, backed by Will's collection of books that he really can't be without on the backside. It is an eclectic mixture of technology, philosophy, and scripture, a collection of a man in search of truth.

"This is entirely unexpected," says Will.

"Yes, I'm sure it is. So let me get right to the heart of why I'm here," says Monica.

"Monica," begins Melissa. "We do have time to take a few seconds to observe the rules of polite company, I think. After all, Will is on our side."

"Of course, you're right about it. Will, I'm sorry," says Monica.

"It is quite all right. Let's just all take a deep breath and tell me what's going on," says Will.

"We have been working with your joint chiefs of staff and your vice-president. I am sure you know of whom I speak," says Monica.

"I do. I guess we're finally going to go do something, am I right?" asks Will. *It is about damn time. Why is it always this way? It never fails. Hem and haw about what to do until the situation is cataclysmic and then rail because nothing you're doing is working because you started too late to be effective.*

"Well, yes. To be more precise, we're going to take the action you wanted to take some months ago but with a few twists," says Monica. Monica recognizes that Will is simply anxious to get it over with. She doesn't necessarily share his confidence that he cannot lose, so she is glad that at least the human military forces will take some of the bite out of the rebels and arachnids. She explains, "You and the battalions led by both Salome and Dallas will provide support for the land forces that are going to invade northern Europe and Scandinavia. You, specifically you, are not to engage unless the battle goes badly. You will engage only at the orders of Salome or Dallas, at which point you'll assume command.

"You will have to work with their leaders as to how you can effectively engage the enemy without being mistaken for the enemy. I'll leave it to you as to how that can be worked out. The shroud of secrecy has absolutely no chance of remaining intact if significant portions of the human forces make it out. Preferably, they would simply allow us and our forces to go into Europe and clean it out and be done with it, leaving the land deserted. They could then make any story they wanted for the history books. But they will have none of that as there is an issue of pride at work here and we all know there's nothing to be done for it but to step back and let them beat their brains out. And who knows? They might actually do enough damage to be of some use before the arachnids take them out."

"Monica, I don't know if I can just stand by and let those soldiers die," says Will.

"If you don't lots more people may die, and humans as well," says Monica. "Besides, this is their generals' idea, not mine. I don't want humans anywhere near this conflict. They will almost surely all die, and the survivors will be labeled as crazies or insane by their families when they return. But, as I say, it was not my call. It is theirs."

"Why?" asks Will.

"Because if the generals see you and what you are capable of, they will lay in their beds at night wondering when you'll be coming for them and their children; we cannot and must not frighten these people by allowing them to see you at your fullest. If the battle goes badly, as I said before, Salome and Dallas will make the decision as to whether or not to call on you. Understand?" says Monica.

Remembering how the bull had been worthless for months, will has to agree and says so, "As you wish."

"And I'll be going with you to aid with my glamours," says Melissa. "Not a lot of effect on the arachnids, but people are certainly susceptible, and I could direct human soldiers to some degree away from obvious dangers…I can help."

Will just sits and looks at the two women. It is finally on. "Well, I suppose I'm glad it's finally going to be resolved one way or another," says Will. And here Will is distracted, looking off into the distance.

"Will?" Monica looks concerned. "What is it? What's wrong?"

"I'm not sure. I seem to be having these moments of mental confusion lately. It seems like memories that I know cannot be memories as those things never happened fly through my head. It's almost like having a dream only I'm on my feet with my eyes awake."

"Will, do any of these things - do they speak to things to come?" asks Melissa.

"Hard to say. Sometimes I think so, but then I don't know if I'm stretching my imagination and history to fit my memory." Later, he will make a connection between his deteriorating mental state and Suede's amnesia.

Chapter 33

Finally, we're going to take some action against those bastards. Sometimes, you just have to rattle the bars and go for it in order to get anything done. Analysis is all well and good, but you can analyze your ass right on out of relevancy.

"Brandon, I am taking another leave of absence. Please get hold of Kyle and have him arrange an appointment for me with LB, preferably for this afternoon. Also, ask if he can clear his schedule this afternoon to meet with Felix and me. If Kyle objects, tell him that I want to update LB and Felix on my extracurricular activities and some other projects that will affect us in the long haul."

"I will do it," says Brandon.

"Yes, Will, I've known about the existence of the people for some time," says LB.

"Well, it is for damn sure that I didn't know," says Felix. "How can it be possible that such a thing is kept secret?"

"Felix, people lie to themselves about how much money they have in their checking accounts. What makes you think that they would be incapable of lying to themselves about whether there really are monsters under the bed?" asks Will.

"It was a good decision a hundred years ago, 50 years ago and a thousand years ago to keep the existence of the people secret from the masses," says LB. "Maybe 10 percent of humans exercise the necessary discipline to know what is real. The rest live in a dream world of credit cards, easy payments and I'll-handle-that-tomorrow. Besides, sitting on the armed services committee as I did, it is only natural that I knew about them."

"So, all the stuff he said about guardians and vampires and hell, I don't know what all it is true?" asks Felix. He is looking at LB as he talks, but he is watching Will out of the corner of his eye. Things he thinks are dreams are now coming back as memories. *Women too large, standing on air. This really is too much to take. Come on! Next thing he'll tell me is that there are dragons, faeries, and wizards.*

"And Dallas, the big one that likes you so much, Felix, says you are a wizard," says Will. "Whatever the hell that is."

Felix wants to scream something along the lines of, 'Don't mess with my world view, or I'll take out your kneecaps.'

"That means the dog we found that day was probably the victim of a spider?" asks Felix.

"Most likely," says Will. "So, LB," he continues. "I hope you understand now why I'm gone a good bit."

"Certainly, you should have come to me sooner. "Why didn't you?"

"Well, let's see, I had a history of having had a nervous breakdown-due to going through a divorce, it's true, still-I was newly hired to do security work for OEE, and I had an ex-wife with pen in hand ready to send my ass off in a heartbeat with just a LITTLE bit of cause-need I continue?" asks Will.

"Not hardly." laughs LB. "It is often a terrible burden to carry to know things and not be allowed to share them."

"Sure. They don't say ignorance is bliss for no reason. Knowledge can be deadly and, at a minimum, puts a requirement for action on the person who comes into the possession of such knowledge." Will isn't laughing along with LB; this is a killing serious business. "I'm leaving Brandon in charge while I ago about the business of preparations for the European campaign. I expect I'll be gone for at least four weeks or as long as six months. Whatever, I will be gone until the rebels are defeated and the arachnids are more or less extinct."

"Why do you say more or less? " asks Felix. "Just one of those things…"

"It wouldn't matter if I stayed for 10 years and killed every spider I came across. As long as people are converting humans, some arachnids will be borne. There is nothing to be done about that."

Felix doesn't know if he agrees with that or not. The thought occurs to him that if there are no people, then no people will convert humans, and no arachnids will be born. He intends to keep the thought to himself and think about it later-again by himself. Will sees the thought blaze behind Felix's eyes.

I will have to deal with that sooner or later. But today is not the day, thinks Will.

"So, you understand what we need?" asks Will. He is speaking with a two star general. Looking at the terrain of the mountains where Monica and Melissa indicate a majority of the rebel leadership call home, Will is convinced that the mountains are probably honeycombed with tunnels and warrens. Making sure that they get everybody is going to be any more than just problematic. *We should just nuke the place, but even that solution will come back on us in five years when the Europeans scream and holler about American aggression causing a radioactive hell. Never mind that the French knew that People were building this site and could have warned us or stopped it.*

"Don't worry, Will. At 7:00 AM, the sun will be nice and bright. The F-16s will begin cracking those mountains open..."

"Yes, but you don't understand. The arachnids are extremely hardy. Cut the sons of bitches up, and they reassemble themselves..."

"Will, we have read the briefings you provided. Now listen up and learn. These beasties aren't supernatural, based on your data. This has been amply demonstrated."

"Then how?" asks Will.

"Ever heard of napalm?" asks the general.

"Beautiful," says Will.

On the morning of March 14th, 2001, a combined force made up of Americans who, as usual, provided the bulk of the forces, Germans, and Russian air forces assaulted the rebel leadership in the Ural Mountains. They opened the earth with their bombs and then filled it with napalm. Seeing the ground crack open and thousands of arachnids swarming out to meet the invader made many pilots think of someone who kicked an anthill. The monsters are quickly covered with jellied gasoline and turned into so much powder and charcoal.

Neither Will nor the battalions of guardians led by Dallas and Salome are needed. Will and Salome provide what technical consulting services the human forces need. Cleanup forces led by volunteers, in battle suits of titanium alloys and armed with flame-throwers and explosive rounds make fairly quick work of the several hundred arachnids and rebels left. Several specimens are even captured and imprisoned in Plexiglas rooms. This turns out to be an almost fatal mistake before Will informs them that the arachnids really have no oxygen needs and can deform themselves and squeeze through holes as small as a quarter of an inch given time.

After three days, the common wisdom is that the threat has been ended as far as the leadership goes. As for cleaning up the rest of Europe, they now know how to fight the things on the ground and in the air. If there are any concerns about humanity's ability to stand against the people and fight, they are soundly answered by that initial battle and the ensuing weeks. Only once is Will called on with Dallas and Salome's battalions, and that is to revisit the desert territory where Will had his first taste of combat after his change.

"I'm not going to screw around on this, Will," says General Cordner. "We sent multiple forces in, always with the same result."

"That result being the loss of the forces?" asks Will.

"I suppose loss is one way of looking at it. Not only do we not know the fate of our men, but all their armor has been left at the east end of the perimeter." The general is furious. A lot of men are been lost and they still have no idea what new beast they are facing out in the desert. He is told that Will is now one of the People who has single-handedly faced multiple arachnids and even walked out of the zone in the desert.

"They needed no help. None at all," says Monica. Her face carries a mix of emotions. She is pleased that no People were lost and that the rebel leadership with the exception of a few folks is completely decimated. The fact the humans succeeded so completely and overwhelmingly against what they regard as an almost unstoppable force is what's troubling her.

"My lady," begins Salome. She is interrupted by the

entrance of Lord Tamerlane, who, without so much as a by your leave, launches into a tirade about the human threat.

"But Lord Tamerlane, you of all people should understand what we would be letting go by not having commerce with human populations. You yourself have said on many occasions that your wealth is contingent upon the success of humanity." Monica understands his concern. It is unsettling for him to realize that humanity has grown past being threatened by the People. Like a lot of liberal-thinking folks, it is all well and good to theorize about how things should be. But those you consider beneath your station suddenly becoming equals is upsetting. *This is what we said we wanted it, Roger. Don't you remember?* The thought is without rancor of any kind, though a certain amount of amusement is present. Looking at Roger Tamerlane's face, Monica decides not to tease him.

"Will, let's continue our discussion later this afternoon. It is clear that Lord Tamerlane is in a state. Otherwise, I would have to consider his behavior and barging into my court as a complete lack of respect for myself and my position." Monica's face grows redder. She can't help it. Consciously, she knows that Lord Tamerlane is one of her most loyal followers, but millennia of being a queen did make one used to being respected. That, combined with the stresses of the last several weeks, years even, make her ready to go off and she does.

"Lord Tamerlane, I'm not used to uninvited interruptions in my court, particularly not in my own throne room. Please explain why I should continue to listen rather than have Salome throw you out into the sunshine."

Realizing his peril, Lord Tamerlane immediately goes to one bowed knee.

"My lady, you know you have but to ask, and my life is yours to spend. My apologies for my familiarity, but never in a million years would I have expected human forces to so thoroughly route the rebels with which we have been able to do nothing for years. I think it's possible that your rule is in more danger now than before the rebels were destroyed."

She is entirely unprepared for this line of discussion, as it had occurred to her as well. She didn't think it would come so soon, nor in the body of one of our most trusted allies, Lord Tamerlane, however. She thinks perhaps a contact from the southern counties or possibly even a pre-emptive contact from NORAD, or NATO or maybe even the few surviving rebels, but not Roger.

"Tell me what the people are saying, Roger. Tell me all of it."

"They are saying that you have grown weak. They are saying Sven and Draco may have been right to want to conquer the human populations before they turn on us. Some are running around saying it's already too late. Because of your lack of leadership, humans are now all our equals."

"Why? Because we provided them with the knowledge to defeat Sven and his obscene alliance with not one Person lost?" asks Monica. "If we had not allowed them to carry out this battle by themselves, they would have seen Will and his capabilities. There would have surely been war." Monica looks at Lord Tamerlane and blows out a gust of air, signaling her frustration. "While we may not be happy with the current state of affairs, I am positive that had we not allowed the human forces to route the rebels, we would have to attack the human camps because they would give us no choice. The problem, Roger, is that neither of us sees ourselves in a common group. We have learned the value of Commerce from the humans, and they have benefited from our ability to live long spans as well as our willingness to remove from their population the true socio-paths that crop up from time to time."

"This will mean little if you have one of these socio-paths slip through into a position of power, especially in the US military."

"Roger, I am ending this discussion for today. Come tomorrow…and make an appointment. Good day, Roger."

"Will, May I come in?" asks Monica.

"Certainly, Monica, you do not need to ask," says Will.

"So all the ugly beasties you all were so terrified for weeks fell to modern human technology. Isn't it ironic?" says Will. "What do we do next? They're going to probably want some sort of concessions with you guys as to how they can protect themselves from such a thing happening again. So, what is to be done? They are going to want to move fast and hard. And I'll bet a dollar to a dime that you guys don't even have a contingency plan set up for this set of circumstances. Am I right?"

"We can deal with the issue of what will come next with the humans later," says Monica. "Where we now want to focus on is our trip back to Alabama to finish up with this business of whether or not this Girl IS Crystal."

"Okay, fine. I'm completely agreeable. But, Monica, it is Crystal. She looks like her. Suede sounds like her. And while there are little… a few little differences, it is Crystal," says Will. "Now answer the question."

"Why are you so certain? And which question are you talking about?" asks Monica.

"Do you have any kind of contingency plan that addresses the possibility of the people being in a bad bargaining position relative to human technology?" says Will.

"Well, not exactly. We have had to deal with the fact that the humans control the nuclear arsenal of this planet and that there are 8 billion of you and about 700 million of us, so we tend to stay in the shadows… in more than one way. So, answer the question: how do you know this is Crystal?" says Monica.

"Because she smells like Crystal, you can't fake that. I can track a man all the way across this planet just on smell. I am not deceived here, Suede is Crystal," says Will.

"Yes, so you say. So you keep saying. But you can say it a million times and it doesn't prove it's her. I'm going as well as Melissa and Salome…all of us together with you to see this woman." She turns, then stops, thinking, and asks, "What will you do if it isn't her?"

"Monica, I can't think about that," Will says, *but it is for sure that I cannot give up Suede.*

"LB, you have experience in dealing with these so-called vampires, or People or whatever the hell they are," says his lunch companion.

"What you say is true. What I need you to tell me now is why after 18 years you need to pick my brain about a project that was abandoned years ago as completely unnecessary," says LB.

"I think the abandoning was premature. We have a race of folks here that can do heaven knows what and they're basically immortal, unless burned to death. It is clear they're weak now. Now is the time to strike and remove their threat to humanity, don't you agree?" says the man.

"I've personally dealt with the Queens from time to time.

They've never hidden their motives and they never fail to carry out their promises. I trust them more than I trust you," says LB.

"I'm sorry you feel that way. What happened in the past wasn't personal, it was just business."

"Yes, just business. The difference between you and the Queens is that it's never just business with them. You would stab someone in the back and watch him bleed to death, literally, with no remorse thinking its just business. The Queens would find a way to preserve their honor and even if it costs them. They would not betray me," says LB.

"Well, you cannot conduct an intelligence initiative with scruples standing in your way. You said so yourself in the past. What? Beginning to become moral in your old age?"

"No, I suppose I'm not," says LB, sighing. He realizes that his lunch companion is correct. *Well, I did try to take the high road.* "I suppose you're right. I don't know what I was thinking," says LB. "What did you have in mind?"

"We have several arachnids in quarantine. What we need now are several people who have been changed and several people who were born as vampires. We want you to use your contacts with Will and the Queens to help us collect some specimens for research."

"Specimens for research, I can do that," says LB. *Yes, I feel much better about my decision now.*

They have desultory conversation for about the next 20 minutes. It is agreed that the threat can and should be removed by any means necessary. Excusing himself, LB walks his lunch companion through the parking lot.

As he reaches for his door handle, he feels a hand reach across from the right side over a shoulder and grab the left side of his jaw snapping his head to the right and back. Out of reflex both his hands fly to the hand that is turning his head. He tries to call out to LB, but his throat is constricted by the angle of the pressure. While he is fighting to grab control of that hand he feels the razor across his carotid artery. He is dead before he can figure out that the red jet was his arterial spray.

Your right, thinks LB as he catches the weight of the man and shoves him into the side of his car door and opens the driver's side door. *Sometimes in order to do what you have to you do stuff you don't want to. I am really going to hurt tomorrow.*

LB pops the gas cap and slams the door. Looking in, he realizes there may be a trace of consciousness left. Smiling a small, sad smile LB whispers, "Remember, it's not personal. It's just business. I may have learned about patriotism as a young man, but in my old age I have come to value honor."

Making do, LB stuffs his handkerchief into the opening of the gas cap, uses his lighter to ignite it, and walks away as fast as his arthritic legs will let him. He makes it.

Back the plant, LB says, "Felix, I want you to get with Will as soon as he returns from crazy town and see about coming up with a design for the plant that the only way they can get information is by court order enforced by federal officers," says LB.

"What in the hell is going on now?" says Felix. "I am sick of these bastards constantly screwing around with my life. All I want to do is my research. But what… I'm tired of having to fight this kind of shit. LB, it's getting to where it is not worth it."

"I agree, but as long as they follow the letter of the law,

and we take proper measures here, we can free you up to do your research and close the gates to the sons of bitches. Now that Will is loose from having to deal with the rebellion we can focus his talents on building this thing the way it needs to be built and securing it," says LB.

"You know, I don't... I don't know, LB. We've done everything imaginable it and we still keep running into those bastards. My research is 10, 15…who knows how far away success is?" says Felix.

"What do you mean?" says LB.

"I mean, LB, I spend so much time hiding from the law when I have broken none, running from the Fed's, locking my drawers and bolting my doors that I cannot get the damn work done." Felix stops. He mutters under his breath, "Do it now." He continues on, "Let me go ahead and go on the record now with you."

"Sure, Felix, you got something on your chest? Let's hear it, all of it. I'm determined that we're going to resolve all the crap now so you can do what you say you wanted," says LB.

"LB, you are my friend. You let me pursue my research even when everyone else says I am crazy. But I cannot function in an environment where I am worried that a bunch of jackbooted, dressed in black, federales are going to bust down my door at any time. LB, I just cannot live that way. Make it stop or consider me resigned."

LB is astonished. Well, maybe astonished is a strong word. The days and months of harassment have begun to mount and they are spending an inordinate amount time just trying to get the damn thing built so they can go to work. That, in conjunction with trying to protect their network from unauthorized wiretap efforts and other forms of clandestinely sanctioned initiatives against their company and their research have made it to where Felix has precious little time to do any serious work. But now that LB understands why Will is absent so much, taking full advantage of the language of his contract, LB can see how things are going to improve and rapidly.

"I see what you're saying, Felix. Now, you have to understand that only recently have I understood the actual parameters of the things arrayed against us and why. I believe, and I'm not making any promises, but I believe I can turn this thing around."

"Go on," says Felix.

"Our legal standing is clear. We are being harassed by several government agencies. We've broken no laws and violated no ethics. Even after our complying with everything they said they wanted before, they continue to harass us. That in my mind means that the former agreements are no longer binding on us for our actions."

"Alright, then what now?" asks Felix.

"With new investors we can foot the bill that it takes to completely enclose and shut in you and all your equipment and all your research to where they cannot be monitored," says LB.

"Well? Let's try," says Felix. "So what you are saying is we can now spend the time and money to do every single thing the way it needs to be done? What's our budget?"

"As far as I can tell, we have an investor who's going to let us have access to very nearly unlimited funds," says LB.

"The Queens," says Felix.

"Absolutely."

On the evening of their arrival, Will and his entourage arrive at about 10:30 p.m. It is a Saturday and Suede is working. Despite his hunger to see her he finds himself torn by a desire to stay away. Suede seemed a little distant the last time he was there and he has no urge to walk into the club with two beautiful women and Hilda the roller blade point guard in tow. Will just has a sneaking suspicion that it will not go over well.

"You guys need to get comfortable and settled," Will says when the ladies object to waiting until Monday to go see Suede. "And I need to get back and get caught up at work for a few days so you guys can just chill out and see the night sites. I should be caught up by Monday," says Will, fighting a severe case of yawning as he tries to shake the cobwebs of his brain off to focus on planning the next 36 hours or so.

"I would think you would want to resolve this as quickly as possible," says Monica.

"As far as I'm concerned, it is resolved. Suede is Crystal. Now, since the rebels are not currently a major threat, I have to be about the business of helping to make this company go," says Will.

"As you wish, Will, we'll wait until Monday night to go and see Suede."

"Crystal. You can and should call her by Crystal. At least until you're in the club, then you should call her by Suede," says Will. Will then makes his goodnights and excuses himself.

"Melissa?" Monica has a job for the second queen.

"Yes, Monica?" Melissa really doesn't even have to be told what to do next. This is really why they came and she's looking forward to it. As for herself, she hopes Will is correct and that she is indeed Crystal. Like Monica, however, Melissa did watch Crystal burn up in the daylight during Will's transformation. "I suppose I'm going out tonight and Atlanta is my first stop?"

"Yes. Check on Suede and see if you can determine whether or not she has lost her memory or Will has lost his mind."

The trip from Birmingham to Atlanta for one of the People with the power flight is inconsequential. Melissa arrives at the Piper Club well into the evening. She sees no one that looks like Crystal and finally asks one of the waitresses if Suede is working tonight.

"Sure, honey. She's working tonight but she's in the back and will be out doing her stage about 10 minutes. You can talk to her after that. Want me to tell her you're here?"

"No, that will be fine. I will just talk to her after she gets done."

Suede strides out on to the stage about 10 minutes later right on schedule. Melissa has to laugh a little as she watches Crystal take control of her audience. *Men really are visual creatures,* she thinks to herself. *Show a pair of breasts, wear a G-string, have a little attitude, and they just lose their minds. Well, some of them do.*

Melissa has seen this activity over the years and it doesn't change much, women entertaining men and getting paid for it. She had one gentleman tell her in the old Roman Empire that women had no idea the magic they wove when they danced.

That was a long time ago. Now let's see this Suede up close.

Melissa walks up to the stage with her dollar bills in

hand. This isn't new to her and she really doesn't know why Will is so enthralled about the whole thing.

Suede is in the Middle of a move that has what few customers there that early completely mesmerized. She is on her belly supporting herself on hands and knees. She has her butt stuck up an air and moves her feet in small circles as her knees move her back towards the dance pole at the end of the main stage. Every man beast among them has his eyes firmly planted on her butt and thighs as she slowly comes in for a landing on the poll cupping it close between her legs, finally straightening her legs and clutching it with her butt.

Well, I can see why that is effective. Melissa is laughing and enjoying the show. Suede leaps up to the top of the pole and winds her way down it as her hair spins out and around.

If she isn't Crystal, she is very talented. No wonder Will wants her to be Crystal if she isn't. Melissa can't seem to focus on her face. She seems to be having a good night, though, looks like maybe $30 to $50 in her g-string.

Finally Melissa's able to pinpoint what looks strange about the girl. She is looking out over the crowd as if she is looking for someone in particular. It doesn't seem to be affecting her performance, but she definitely seems to be on the look out for someone.

Melissa is so busy watching the girl and watching the crowd that she almost stumbles when Suede kneels down in front of her in order to be tipped. Suddenly, Suede and Melissa are face to face.

While Melissa is getting to know Suede in Atlanta, Will, Felix, LB, Kyle, and Brandon are all doing the Saturday night meeting thing.

"Felix, LB…everybody. Thanks for coming," says Will.

"Oh yeah, I'm just fired up about sitting in a meeting on Saturday night." This is Brandon. He is not happy about being told 20 minutes prior to the road trip to Atlanta and the Piper club that he has to sit in a meeting.

"I am just spiffy," is Brandon's response to Kyle's question concerning how he was doing. Kyle felt his pain and said so.

Yes I'd just bet you do. But it's probably a date with a spreadsheet or a calendar, Freak. The hell of this all is that he can't even lie to his boss and say that he has other plans that cannot be broken. Will knows what his habits have become. Besides, about three-quarters of the time while he is there seeing the girls he goes to see, Will sits over in the corner with Suede. *I can't even let go and get really drunk in there anymore.*

After maybe 20 minutes of catching up Will sets down an outline of the basic idea of how he is prepared to protect them from outside snooping interference.

"What we will do, gentleman, is to build this in stages. The first stage will consist of going about finishing the buildings as currently configured. While Felix goes ahead with doing some due diligence-that is repeating some experiments that have questionable results-am I right, Felix?" Felix nods his head in agreement and Will continues, "They already have that data so I can't see any harm in Felix going ahead with that portion of this plans while we change gears on the security measures." Here Will turns to a map of the plant, as it will be once finished on the wall. Reaching into his pocket he pulls out a Sharpie pen and begins to illustrate what he plans to do.

"First what we will do is to build a wall surrounding the entire property and this wall is approximately 8 ft. thick and

12 ft. high. This will give us the ability to integrate enough metal to block electronic eavesdropping and efforts without compromising the strength of the wall as it should be." Here Will proceeds to sketch a wall around the property line.

"Second, we will establish a number of pylons across the property ranging from 3 ft. thick all the way to highway Interstate exchange type pylons over the area where the accelerator's magnets are concentrated. This will take approximately a year, which will give Felix time to duplicate his experiments in their entirety and also for us to evaluate the different security measures because, frankly, the field is changing quite significantly right now. I can implement all kinds of measures and they might be completely meaningless within weeks."

"By moving on to the third stage which involves stretching a concrete and metal roof between the pylons over the property, we'll create an electronic barrier that's also a fairly strong barrier to forced entry. To some degree this will make all their new technology irrelevant."

During all battles and the furor over whether or not Crystal is indeed dead, Circe continues to see what she can see past the blind spot that set off all these events in the first place. She finds herself confused but encouraged because of what she can sometimes see.

Peace, a world at peace. How nice. But it fades, it fades, almost like the world is trying to tune into a frequency that will get them there, but can't quite get it just right. There is still danger and I must tell Monica when she arrives back from the United States. Then, because she is curious for Monica's sake and because the youngest queen is quite nice to her, Circe tries to focus and see if Crystal is there in their future.

That makes no sense…

Loki is enjoying his retirement. He is still bitter over the affair at OEE, but like most traitors, he manages, with a set of semi-facts, to make himself look like an unfortunate rather than a dastardly villain.

After the firing and his subsequent achievement of financial independence- only as he deserves, though, don't you know- he moves back to the D.C. area and is doing consulting work for several environmental law firms. It is enjoyable enough work. Loki is not popular at OEE, and he did manage to piss off nearly everybody he ran into while there, but he did sincerely care about environmental issues and works fairly regularly to advance what he considers good causes.

None of which is able to quench a burning coal of hatred he has for all things connected to LB Browning.

Sooner or later, LB. Sooner or later, this mantra is becoming more or less constant in Loki's mind. Often he whispers it under his breath and sometimes actually sings it out loud in traffic with no idea he is doing so. Loki is a man slowly but surely becoming obsessed with the idea of revenge. Had he taken a lie detector test and been asked, 'Do you intend to take revenge on LB for your downfall at OEE?' he would have quite seriously answered in the negative, believing it when he said it. But there are things in a man's mind he cannot control-or chooses to put in some dark room in his mind so he can shut the door and let it grow, ripen, and birth itself into existence, just as he wants all along while denying responsibility.

Sooner or later, LB, sooner or later, the phone rings, startling Loki. As he reaches for the handset, the blade of his hand tips the top of his glass, sending it crashing to the floor, spewing grape soda in all directions on his crème carpet.

"Damn it, LB. Sooner or later…"

As Loki brings the phone to his ear, he hears a familiar clicking in the background. *Recorder, I should have known they would call on me again.*

"Loki, I hope you are well. Your country has need of you again."

She did die, thinks Circe. Crystal did indeed die, but she is not dead. How can that be? Circe sees both into the past and into the future. Sometimes she isn't sure in which direction she is seeing, but she sees herself talking to Crystal in a conversation she has never had talking about her death.

"There wasn't really a lot of time to be in pain, little sister," says Crystal. "But I would not live without Will."

"You care for him a lot, don't you?"

"Enough to pursue him into the next life," says Crystal.

"But isn't suicide against your personal code?"

"You know, it is. The funny thing is, while I was running towards the door 'suicide' as a concept never entered my mind. I just knew that he had crossed over and I was going after him. I never thought to myself, 'He is dead and I am going to kill myself.' It was more of a 'I know where he went and now I will follow' kind of thinking. I didn't want to die; I just had to follow Will."

"Maybe that is why you lived, then."

"Why?"

"Because you never intended suicide; you intended to follow Will. You followed him back to the Southeastern United States."

"True enough."

"Do you remember anything else about the time between when you were incinerated and you regained your memory?"

There was something, something about spending time in several minds. I may have spent time in other's heads, I think. But I shouldn't talk about it, not yet. Crystal is under a burden of silence-a strong urge to not talk about this aspect of her time before…

Circe wakes. *It IS Crystal, but not entirely…*

It is Crystal, My Lover

Will is convinced of Suede's identity and is tired of hearing that there is no way to be sure that she is Crystal or not. Suede is living a somewhat strange life that she has managed to successfully hide from Will despite his best efforts to monitor the situation.

He isn't looking to 'catch' her per say, but to confirm to Monica and Melissa that she is Crystal. Besides, if she is or she isn't is really very immaterial. *If she is, I have my baby back and I can go on with where I wanted my life to go. If Suede isn't then Crystal is really dead and the universe is a cold hell that at least God doesn't want me to be alone in. Suede can keep me sane because I do love her, Crystal or not.* Will is past the only one love in life stage, as most people are. It had been one bloody, gut-wrenching trip, though.

"Brandon, can you get the prep files for the meeting this afternoon and meet me in the exec lunchroom in an hour? I want to do a walk over on the coils again."

"Why, is everything cool? I did a walk over yesterday and so did Felix." Brandon takes his job of keeping Will efficient very seriously. Will sometimes repeats himself or does things repeatedly when he is caught in a loop in his brain and Brandon knows this. When he sees his boss in 'skip mode' as he calls it now, he knows Will is looking for trouble.

"I know, I know, but something is eating at me under the surface where I can't seem to get to it. I keep seeing the coils in my mind. Last night I kept seeing them in my head and thinking 'That's not right' and I don't know why. You are sure Felix has signed off on the installation already?"

"Positive. I was there myself when he finished the last inspection."

Well, that is good, then. I suppose I am probably just having worries for no reason-or maybe I am worried about something I don't want to confront directly... Will has become extremely introspective since his change. His thinking is that people may indeed be colony organisms rather than individuals and the thing we define as 'individuality' is just the collective sum of the parts that make up a human being. He explains this to a perplexed Melissa one day.

"Colony organisms, humans?" Melissa loves Will to death, but sometimes he really charges off the map. Today is a good example as he is telling her why they may be really more than one person inside.

"Yes, it isn't really that far fetched when you understand that the mitochondria in the cells are more like symbiotic bacteria than part of the cell itself. We are a collective organism physically, why should we be surprised to find out that we are the same mentally?"

"Well, because...hell, I don't know. It just seems bothersome to think that I may not really be me sometimes."

"Look at the way some people go into a rage and…think back. Have you ever had someone tell you that I was just so mad that it was like I wasn't there, I was just sitting back watching it happen?" Will asks.

"Yes…" she does and it makes sense what Will is saying.

"Just for arguments sake let's suppose that what is happening here is that one of you just throws a switch and exerts total control while the collective consciousness sits back and takes a time out. That would explain the whole thing, right?"

"Yes, it would, but just because all the facts fit the explanation doesn't mean you are right."

"I know, but you have to start somewhere."

"Start somewhere to do what?"

"To explain why certain males turn arachnid after the change and why whatever agent is doing it is targeting males of European descent almost exclusively."

"Why, it is for the same reason that 80% or more of serial killers come from the same stock. The nature/nurture argument is over…"

"When I changed, something invaded me, some THING. I saw things and heard things and understood things about whom and what humans are that I can't get back in my mind and I don't know why. Sometimes when I wake up, I can almost see it, hear it again, taste with my eyes and hear with my tongue…" An image keeps coming to his mind, of humans lined up in a line, stretching from infinity to infinity, holding hands as a series of doughnut like shapes rolled past them and around them…

"Sounds like you have been licking some microdot to

me," says Melissa.

"I know. It almost is like that. Whatever tried to roll me over to spider out land opened a part of my mind that I can't seem to get back to and it is driving me bananas because I am certain it is important."

"Why? We beat them. Hell, WE didn't beat them. A bunch of humans with their techno toys beat them without any significant help from us."

"Yes, I know, but we didn't kill whatever tried to turn me. I don't know if it can be killed because I am not certain it has ever been alive."

"Okay, we can maybe not kill it but anything can be destroyed, Will. Anything."

Will isn't so sure, but lets it go for now.

"Anyway, Brandon, something has my wind up over the coils and I want another inspection. Care to come?"

"No, I wouldn't have time to get the files to the exec room if I do that. Let me get you guys set up, and I will try to catch up."

"Of course, you are right," says Will. Brandon is a good kid, thinks Will.

While Will is heading over to the accelerators, Felix decides to do the same, thinking he may have left his planner over there as he can't seem to lay his hands on it.

Why I cannot remember to just stuff it in my pocket, I don't know. Felix bought a pocket size planner specifically because he keeps forgetting to pick it up and carry it with him, *doesn't look like being smaller is helping any.*

Over in the administrative building, LB thinks to himself, *You know, I think I would like to see those coils again, really neat stuff. If Felix is right, we'll change the world...*

The three meet at the primary coil assembly at about 11:00 AM.

"Will!" LB hadn't expected to see Will until Monday what with the drive to meet Monday's deadline for a full scale test run pushing everyone on their perspective to do lists.

"LB, I thought you were covered up until Monday with paperwork. Had to get out of there a bit, huh?"

"Well, yes I..." says LB.

Felix interrupts, distractedly, "Bugger all, will you look at that? It was in my pocket the whole time. What a waste."

"What?" LB asks.

"I thought I had left my planner over here and came to look for it. It was in my pocket the whole time. Guess I am losing my mind."

"That, or the gray hairs are beginning to grow into your brain," says LB.

"Well, you are certainly qualified to make that judgment call, in spite of most of your gray hairs having fallen out," quips Felix.

Will is just watching this exchange when he understands that the three of them wound up at the point of the complex that has been on his mind more or less constantly for the last 36 hours or so.

"Felix, why are you here?"

"Huh? Because I thought I had lost my planner and this was the last place I remembered having it in my hand, but the stupid thing was in my pocket the whole time anyway, why?"

"LB, why are you here?" Will has an intense look on his face and LB knows the boy is going somewhere.

"I don't know, I just got up from my desk about two hours ago with this hobby horse about getting over here to look at the coils again."

"But you were just here yesterday, right?" asks Will.

"Right," says LB.

"Guys, there is something wrong with the coils and I don't know what it is, but we have got to postpone the test on Monday."

"How can…?" begins Felix.

"Shit…" says LB.

"For some reason I have been seeing the coils in my mind for the last day and a half or so and you guys show up here with me at the same instant I am determined to find out what the hell is going on, so…yeah. I have to insist that we have a security problem that is as yet undetermined."

Will is adamant about the situation being a security issue and he pulls rank and cancels the test. LB and Felix are both just about apoplectic about it. Nothing is found for three days after the tests should have been completed. Will is just about ready to concede that he may have been wrong when they go ahead with the powering up procedure for the magnets. Just for safety's sake and for no other reason than a whim, a low power run is carried out first.

BLAM!

Everyone in the instrument room covers their eyes and one technician, his ass trying to leave the room without any notice to the rest of his person, falls over backwards in his chair and has to be helped up.

"Everyone okay?" yells Felix.

Coughing and low level cursing accompany a mostly positive response. A few bruises is the worst of the damage to people, but not the control room viewing windows.

The windows are 8 inch Plexiglas, like that used in high security installations and it is considered armor. It now has somewhere between 15 and 20 foot long, one inch thick bolts driven almost all the way through it in various orientations. Right in front of where the tech who had fallen had been sitting, at eye level, one bolt had been driven to where almost ten inches protruded on this side.

Looking down at the assembly, it is clear that damage has been done, though how much is unclear.

"Damn it!" Felix is charging down the stairs now, taking two and three at a time. Will is right behind him.

The two walk up to the coils, which now sit some three feet off center, walking over to the mounts Will kneels down and begins to pick up pieces of metal.

"What is it?" Felix is incensed.

"Here is what was keeping me up at night," says Will. He is holding the nuts that shattered under the strain of keeping the coils on the mounts. "It looks like we need to look at the mount specs again."

"Bullshit. The specs are correct and should have been more than sufficient."

"Yeah, then we have a defective set of mount nuts," says Will.

Felix just scratches the crown of his forehead and curses

as he turns to the task of seeing how long the repairs will take. After a few phone calls and a conversation with LB that ends with his shrugging his shoulders and leaving for the admin building, Felix turns to Will.

"How did you know?" asks Felix.

"I kept returning here in my dreams. I could never pinpoint any problem per se, but I just couldn't get the coils out of my mind."

"Well, see if you can get the tuner working a little bit better."

"You're welcome." Will is only half kidding. He had been beating his brains out trying to figure out what the hell was going on and even called a halt by pulling security director rank on everyone, but no one had listened. *Though to be fair, even I had given up after three days.*

"You know what I mean…though you are right you did raise blue hell and sit down in the middle of the road…"

"Like some stubborn, hard headed mule was the term, I believe…"

"Yeah, Will, you were right and I was wrong. I apologize."

Enough, thinks Will. "Whatever, Felix, buddy. How do we keep this from happening again? I mean, how do we know something else isn't cracked?"

"We'll just have to go over the shipping lists and find out what all came from the same supplier as these nuts and determine if other risks exist." Felix is very unhappy. This could delay them for months.

"Want to do dinner?" asks Felix.

"Nah, I have a date," says Will.

"With Suede?"

"Oh, yeah," Will's face lights up.

"Look, Will, can you move it? We really need to get on this. Can't you move it to Friday?"

Will can and he knows he should. "Okay, I'll do that. I just hope you understand what I am giving up."

"Wellllll…I GUESS I can wear a skirt and t-back if that will make it easier for you…"

Snorting and choking on his soda, Will says, "You know, while I appreciate the offer, I think I will pass. I just can't see you having the same effect." Here his eyes glaze over as he thinks about his little butterfly…his built for speed, in your face and you still can't take your eyes away cause the attitude just makes it better butterfly.

Lucky guy, I wonder if he knows how he looks when he starts talking about her.

Suede is dreaming again. She is looking out on a circle of folks who seem to be bowing to her. She wants to respond, to move, to offer comfort to these who are so obviously in great distress.

"Wait! No!" There is a young woman who is a prisoner of the others. They intend to shame her. Suede can feel the heat rising in her face and chest as anger takes her. It is useless, though. She cannot move. She tries to look away but her neck seems to be bound.

The young woman is pleading.

"This isn't what you promised, Eric. You lied to me, you told me you…"

"Yeah, yeah, what the fuck ever, you are stupid, cunt." Eric laughs now and his friends join in, though some are looking nervous now as the one or two others who are women begin to realize that they are in a very bad place with men who are not what they had seemed.

It seems like a good time, talking about the old religions that Christianity replaced. Most of the group thinks it is an excuse to get dressed up, get drunk, and get laid. If you want to dress it up in religion and call it a fertility rite…well, then, that is just spiffy.

The young woman, who is now covered in a fear sweat because she has looked at Eric's eyes, REALLY LOOKED and knows that Eric is not alone inside his head. She knows she is to be shamed, soiled, and slaughtered. She is crying softly because Eric slaps her when she cries out loud.

Suede looks down as the woman looks up directly into her face and mutters a "Please, God, help me, I don't want to die and…"

The young woman is about to apologize for being here in a pagan ceremony to be with the man she thinks she might be in love with the way he wants, but Eric cuts her off with a sharp slap to the mouth.

Suede ceases to have much rationality and begins pushing against her bonds. She tries to turn and look at how she is caught, but can't seem to move, still. With a force of will she finally tears loose her left arm and reaches across to free her right arm. It isn't her arm she sees cross her line of sight, though, it is an oak branch about 6 inches in diameter. A thought crosses her mind *I will NOT have my rituals used to destroy those I am sworn to protect.* There is a tearing sound like roots pulling from the ground…

The phone rings and Suede sits up with her chest aching for the woman-child's fear. As she grabs the handset, she mutters into the mouth piece, "Hold on."

Holding the phone to her chest, she goes ahead and gets out the sobs of pain she has for the girl. *Get it together, girl, it was just a dream. It wasn't real.*

But it feels real, real enough to physically hurt. She hears her name in the phone against her chest and knows that it is Will.

Bringing the phone to her ear, she listens as Will asks her if she is awake yet or what.

Suede in seconds thinks about her dream, the fear, her paralysis and the fact that Will would burn down half the planet and trash the rest before he will let something like that happen to the nastiest crack whore you could imagine even if he didn't know her.

"It is nothing, Will, I just had a bad dream…" then she is crying and Will listens as she tells him of her nightmare.

They talk a few minutes and Will indicates that he will be there, the dinner plans with Felix entirely forgotten in his need to comfort Suede.

Crap. Oh, well. I will meet Felix and cut it short and tell her I will be late.

"LB, will you at least tell me what it is you are working on? This can't be good. I don't think you understand how many folks are antsy about what you are doing over here."

"What do YOU think we are doing?" LB is comfortable that he knows where the company is. He is wrong.

"Look, the intelligence community in the states, MI5 in England, and a crew of other folks have point blank come to NSA and accused you of wholesale industrial espionage. They even have meetings arranged where they will present formal charges against you, Felix Dorcai, and Will, your CIO."

"You can't be serious! We haven't done anything. Hell, the whole point of what we are doing is that we don't NEED anyone else's technology. How can they hope to make it stick?" LB isn't worried just mystified at the lengths the folks are going with very little information.

"You don't get it, they don't care if it sticks or not. They want the technology and looks to me as if they aren't worried about breaking the law or infringing on patents or trade secrets…or possibly even more drastic measures."

Now LB is worried because he is beginning to understand that his friend, or what passes for a friend amongst men who respect each other and may be called on to kill each other next week, is trying to tell him that it is reaching a level where his enemies don't care about the law or legalities because in order to get what they want they will just as soon kill a judge as him.

His companion continues, "LB, get a security detail and keep it with you 24X7. And wear a vest."

"I can see you understand, finally, that you are in danger of being killed- you are truly hardheaded, you know, and need to do something."

"Okay. I am going to take steps. Now, on the legal side, why are you helping me?"

"I don't really know." A lie, but it is harder to get LB to focus than in the past. *Age, I guess. How old is he?* "As for what they are going to do, they are bent on making sure you aren't able to patent it or USE it. Teams of folks sit around wondering what you might be building. When they have an idea that looks like it may fit all your shipping labels and invoices, the patent paper work machine kicks in and they submit it so they can get a provisional patent."

"That is truly the weirdest thing I have heard in a few days," says LB. "What is funny is they may actually come up with some good ideas. Which they naturally will not develop because they are too busy pursuing us."

"Yes."

"How long has this been going on?"

"Several months."

"I can't remember if non-related folks can have access to provisional patents or not," says LB.

"I don't know, why?"

"Well, if they have their best and brightest sitting around wondering what Felix is coming up with, perhaps they really HAVE come up with some good ideas. Maybe we can use them."

"Siggy, LB here." Good as his word, LB is swinging into action on the security issue and calling Siggy, his physical security chief. He knows there is a need for security, *but not an armed escort all the time. That wears on your nerves.*

"Sir."

"We have a problem. There are threats against myself and Felix."

"Okay, I will get an escort out there for the two of you."

"Not good enough."

"Sir?"

"Just come to my office after you have placed guards with Felix, too."

"I am on my way. What about Will?"

"What about him?"

"Don't we need to put a crew with him as well?"

"No. Will has his own measures in place. You don't have to worry about him."

It is an amazing thing to watch as humanity reasserts, without any help or urging by the Norn's, its own code of silence concerning the People.

Some areas of northern Europe are devastated by the arachnids and the rebels. Monica steps in and says that it is to end and end now. The humans want to go first and are successful in crushing the rebels altogether. The analogy of a bug getting hit by an 18-wheeler aptly describes the rebel's fate when they confronted humanity's technology. Those of the divine right to rule crowd, the ones who are low enough on the totem pole not to warrant execution- are now sitting home, stunned not only at their defeat but a defeat received from the hands of ordinary humans.

Now, governments are cleaning house using some test that supposedly can detect exposure to People, either by long association or being fed on.

Bullshit. It is a good time to clean house.

The trouble is, a new era of McCarthy-ism is being born. The governments are not only seeking out rebel sympathizers, they are going ahead in the more repressive countries and branding dissidents and other political enemies of the state as rebel sympathizers. Executions are swift and in several countries, on the spot.

Only it isn't People or rebels and arachnids now. Now, the war is being blamed on distribution of a powerful halleucinogenic that now contaminates maybe 10% of the water supply in Scandanavia and a few Bavarian countries.

Those who are found to be responsible are being dealt with harshly, even in the Western democracies, the test for exposure to 'People' or 'arachnids' is not seen as contradictory to the contaminant theory.

The People, loyalists and rebels alike, hunker down and keep their mouths shut as so called rebel encampments in the European countries are burned out and the Sahara Desert becomes an explosives testing area. The only organization to object is the Sierra Club.

The Sierra Club's objections are unanimously withdrawn. Why? The directors are given a tour by the new Sahara Reclamation Authority. Of the Sierra group, all returned but one. The idiot tried techniques he had used to observe mammalian large predators. No one sees it happen, it is so quick.

The disappearance evokes a reaction in the reclamation people. Shoving their guests into the two Hummers they drove here to what they think is a safe area they head back towards the reclamation post. The folks in the second vehicle are looking back towards the spot where the fellow disappeared. A dust devil seems to be winding up and begins a run down the centerline of the dirt tracks left by the hummers in the sand.

"Interesting."

"What?" asks the driver.

"No biggie, just a dust devil," says the woman.

The driver's reaction is to goose the hummer to a higher speed as he radios to the point truck.

"Pick it up! We got one on the tail!"

Both hummers are now accelerating, the second one to put as much distance as possible between itself and what is almost certainly an arachnid and the first one in an effort to keep from getting run over.

"Carl, we have one on our tail, can we get some air cover?" *I knew this was a bad idea.*

"We see you and are on our way, ETA 90 seconds."

We should be able to keep ahead for that long, anyway.

Carl, in his Apache attack chopper tops the hill to see the two hummers running at breakneck speed over the dunes away from the heart of the desert, what look to be several huge crabs are on an intercept course with the lead vehicle.

"This is Carl, I am confirming sighting of…" here he hesitates as he counts, "…6 hostiles."

"Take them out, Carl."

It is over quickly. The Apache is in no danger in the air and its weapons can reach deep into the sand before the spider can burrow deep for protection.

"Thanks, man," says the lead driver.

"No problem, just call me the pest control man," says Carl as he banks the Apache away in search of possible other targets.

"Sorry I am late, Babe. Work tied me up. We had an accident that we had to sit and bitch about for two hours before we felt like we could move forward." Will is with Suede in the back of the club. He is responding to Suede's question.

"Where were you?"

When a woman asks you where you were, that is a good thing, I think. It means you are on her mind when you aren't in her sight. Yes, that can only be a good thing.

"Oh, okay." She isn't worried about where he was so much; she was just concerned because he has never been late before…which is not true. *It is Saturday night and I was wondering where he was, deal with it, Suede. You wanted to know where he was when you wanted him here and he wasn't.*

"I was just worried about you in traffic and, I don't know…the dream has me STILL upset. It was just a nightmare."

"Well, here lately my dreams have been pretty much on point in warning me about stuff." Will proceeds to tell her how he and his two partners had wound up at the coils at one time and the subsequent explosion.

"You were forewarned and it saved your life and most likely several others. You could have died."

"I did once…"

Will didn't catch himself in time. When he says 'I did once' Suede sits back in her chair and gets very still. She turns her head slowly to look at Will and it seems all the music in the club fades back into the white noise that sometimes fills your head after a severe thunderclap, only it isn't her hearing that is overwhelmed, it is her memory.

She is back in her dream now and the club scene seems to have narrowed in focus as Suede is back in the grove where the young woman had pleaded with Divinity to help her.

"Please, God, help me, I don't want to die and…"

Suede feels her arm rip free of its bindings again and again she sees a thick oak branch pass in front of her face. As she steps forward she is thinking her mind, My Bear is dead. He is dead…I will not live unless he is…

But there is the young girl looking on in horror as Crystal tries to step forward, but her feet seem to be caught in the mud or tangled in something. Looking down she sees only the base of an oak tree.

I have to get free! She hears a ripping pulling noise like fabric being ripped apart and finally her feet are free. Suede begins to move forward. This man will pay, because Bridgette is here.

The young woman knows now that Eric is going to kill her, all his talk about how it will just be a blast; like the Society for Creative Anachronism, and how much he cares for her are lies.

"Suede, baby, are you alright?" Will knows something is happening, but not what. Suede appears to be okay, but she closes her eyes and doesn't speak for minutes. She just looks to be thinking really hard, but there are tears beginning to run from the corners of her eyes.

Eric looks up as he hears the ripping noises begin. *Finally! I knew my loyalty would be rewarded. Finally! It is all real, just as I knew it was! Finally, I am going to receive and be an actual Druid.* He feels vindicated and honored.

As both Eric and his girlfriend, who in his mind now loses first name importance, watch, the old oak tree they had picked out for their ceremonies pulls itself out of the ground.

At first it is unsteady, rocking back and forth. As it steadies itself, never completely ceasing its forward motion, its form begins to shift and roil. It is becoming humanoid in shape and its movements more assured.

I am watching one of the old gods become incarnate. I did this, thinks Eric. *This is better even than the mages of old.* Eric is quite satisfied with himself.

The girl, Kelly, is in shock too great to try to escape. Even her tears have dried up now as she watches her death approach. Looking up at Eric's face, she sees no fear, only a raging surety of destiny fulfilled.

As the tree approaches them, a whirlwind of sparks, like multicolored fireflies begins to wrap around it and through its limbs. Lightening begins to stretch from a clear sky as the limbs and leaves become skin and hair. The tree is now a young blonde woman. Eric has only seconds to be confused.

"You will harm no one else and you will never again dishonor a woman or my rites."

"Who are you?" says Eric as the blonde woman reaches out with one hand shifting into an armored, killing thing.

"Why, fool, I am Bridgette, the Celtic goddess you thought you summoned." With that she squeezes and Eric's neck pulps. Only belatedly does the woman begin to feed on the last few surges of blood from Eric's neck.

"Please…" begins Kelly and the thing the woman has become focuses her attention on her.

Falling back into childhood behavior, with no where to run, Kelly shuts her eyes tight and tries like hell to wake up in her bed at home.

"Please, please, please…"

A hand touches Kelly on the shoulder and she flinches, but her eyes open involuntarily. The thing is gone, replaced by the young blonde woman who faints.

"You were dead." This statement is Will's first evidence that Suede is indeed Crystal. "Bear, how are you here? They told me you had…"

Suede stops, looks around at her surroundings and starts

to laugh out loud and hold her stomach.

"I knew it was you…"

"But you had your doubts."

"Yes."

"What made you doubt?"

"Your butterfly wings are new."

"My…yes. They are. Well, I always heard that sunlight was hell on the skin." Memories are flooding back into her mind now, of the last several months. Feeding on the scum of Atlanta, watching Will watch her and wondering why he was so adamant in being here as she worked the crowd.

"You were so cute."

"Cute."

"Yes, trying to be cool and it just isn't you."

Cute, the kiss of death, well, as long as she doesn't tell me I'm a nice guy, I'll be okay.

"Will, my Bear, you are such a sweetheart."

Pretty freaking close but I will just act like…

"And you are alive, and oh, you are still mine!" Suede/Crystal is hugging Will close now.

Being a nice guy is okay if your girl loves you anyway.

"Hey! Break it up, damn it! Suede, you know better than to do that shit." The bouncer knows Will is here to only see Suede and frankly wonders that it took this long to have to say anything, so he is not too aggravated with them.

"You know what, Sweetie?" Suede is looking at the bouncer and a few of the other girls.

"What's that Suede?"

"I am done. I quit."

The club manager, Troy, overhears her and says, "Dammit, you can't leave me in a lurch here. We only have 9 girls as it is tonight."

"Will?" Crystal has an evil look on her face.

"Oh, shit. Don't hurt them baby. These girls will need to be getting paid tomorrow, you know."

"Well, I will hold back a little bit, but I need to finish out the night anyway. Wouldn't be polite to do otherwise, you know."

"Okay, go for it."

Suede spent the night doing her things but this time she was doing as one of the Norn's, with glamours. The traffic for the club was down significantly for weeks afterwards.

"Wow." They are riding together back to Birmingham.

"What?" She is smiling innocently, which only makes her look so completely guilty of something. What did she do?

"Okay, give. What did you do?"

Giggling, Crystal explains.

"I am not as good as Melissa at the glamour thing, but I am no slouch. I am only suck in comparison, get me?"

"You can play the pros, but you're not Joe Montana?"

"Exactly! I did glamour, but every man of them saw what he saw in his wife when he first met her. I was their sweetheart if they ever did love her. Hopefully, they will see her for what she was and what she is when they get home tonight."

"Are we a couple of hopeless romantics or what?"

"Oh, baby girl…" Will is pulling his Corvette over to the side of the interstate. Reaching for his angel, he is leaving the earthbound and carrying his butterfly with him. They are lost in the clouds for hours.

She is mine and she is Crystal. Then, *But I am glad she is Suede, too, because this Crystal is more able to love me, I think. I wouldn't have her hurt for the world, but somehow she is more with me.*

Solomon

"So, Will, how have you been?"

"How have I been?" Will is addressing his cat—the one he placed in a shelter on leaving the states.

I forgot about him.

"Yeah, you did, just wanted to thank you for that." Solomon reaches out and does a slow rake down Will's chest and it burns like fire.

"Shit that hurts!" It does and Will is surprised to find that his skin doesn't armor up in response to the pain.

"You didn't change because you are in my realm now, I am de' boss here. I didn't want you to. I wanted to rake the hell out of you for leaving me in that place. They couldn't find a home for me so they put me down."

"Really?" Looking down, Will sees that the claw marks are healed up completely already. "Where is here?"

"Well, for me, this is the next life, Heaven, Nirvana, the Greek fire, yadda, yadda, yadda. What? You didn't think cats have soul? IN spite of the green eyes, I do have soul, m'man." As if to prove it, BB King starts playing the background and switches over to Aretha Franklin singing the

House that Jack Built.

Jack? Jack was another cat that Will owned but had died in a fire.

"Jack? Good dude, I mean, for a tabby, that is. He made out okay. He is two universes over."

Weirder and weirder.

"No, you mean curiouser and curiouser. Got to keep those literary references straight, you know."

"Okay, Solomon, I am sorry about leaving you there."

"Yeah, I know you were stressed. Cats and dogs have it simpler, do the nasty and go on. No emotional ties and no right or wrong. That is you guys special challenge."

"What?"

"Boy, bring you through three or four dimensions and you just revert to a one word vocabulary. Humans, right and wrong, The CHOICE to create, to make, to be other than you are, it is your special gift. A tree is the best tree it can be, no choices, no DECIDING, no regrets, it just IS."

"Okay, so why is this important?"

Solomon just looks at Will as if he just reached up through his own butthole and pulled his head out of his ass. "Hah?"

"I said," and now you have two very different beings looking at each other as if the other had been slapped out of his mind, "why is this so important? I mean, I know it is important, but are you going somewhere specific?"

"Yes, and see if you can remember things here that you can't remember on earth. It is important because you need to understand that humans are the crux of the forces that oppose destruction. As your buddy, Rush, used to say, you ARE equal time."

"Equal time," Will is confused.

"Entropy, remember how all the eggheads kept telling you that entropy is always increasing?"

"Yes. I never did…"

"Believe them. Yes, I know. And you were right. Either every action has an equal and opposite reaction or entropy is always increasing in the universe. You were right, you can't have both and that is one of the reasons science in your neighborhood is so fractured. You have a bunch of priests, who call themselves scientists, running around screwing up the lives of anyone who goes against accepted practice."

"Okay, so why is this so important?"

"Because…"

"Will," Crystal's voice.

"…and if you don't takes steps now…"

"Will, wake up." Crystal is calling.

"…humanity's development will…"

"Will, wake UP!"

There is a sudden flaring pain in Will's side as he rolls out of the bed.

"Shit, that hurts!" It does, too.

Crystal is looking at Will with wide eyes as he rubs his side down the ribs and finds himself sitting on the floor of their bedroom.

"What did you do?" He had gotten used to not getting hurt. Twice now he had had the crap raked out of him.

"You were…fading out like you were going somewhere else." The last word was slightly raised as if it were a question rather than a statement. "You were talking to someone. Who is Solomon?"

"One of my dead cats, I was dreaming that he was trying to tell me something about what I saw during my change. He was trying to help me remember what I had seen in the thing's mind." Will hesitates and goes on, "Maybe that's not accurate. Maybe as it was trying to flip me to spider out, it opened my mind to be able to see in directions I can only define mathematically…" Will is going off again in the search of whatever it was he had seen. He forgets Crystal is upset.

"Will, please focus."

"Oh, hell, I don't know. What do you I mean I was fading?"

"It was as if you were ceasing to be here and it wasn't just a glamour, either. I tried to reach you and my hand just sank into where you were as if you weren't really there…just some kind of projection."

"Well, I WAS there and that must have been what hurt so bad…your hand and my ribs sort of occupying the same place…"

"Are you alright now?" Crystal is running her hand up and down his ribs.

"Fine. Only I still can't remember what it is Solomon was trying to tell me."

"Well, if it was important and more than just a nightmare it will come again. Most dreams that are important come to you three times."

"Yeah, I would hope so. I need to make sure I have a

notebook by the bed in case so I can write just as I wake up."

"Monica, it is indeed her." Melissa is talking to her queen. Her tone is one of relieved happiness.

"Oh." Monica puts her head in her hands and softly begins to cry. "My daughter, you live."

Monica never had children as one of the People, though it wasn't for lack of trying. In People just as in humans, some people are just not capable of having children. The sadness is the same and the remedies are similar. Adapt or adopt.

Melissa walks over and puts her hands around Monica and says, "We need to go and see her, you know."

"Of course, of course," says Monica.

Monica and Melissa seek out Circe to see if she would like to visit the states. She has never been to America. Circe declines with thanks. After speaking with Salome, who is jubilant to find out Crystal lives, and giving her some last minute instructions for duties to be carried out in their absence, the two queens depart for Alabama.

Watching the two queens, Circe turns to Salome and says, "You know, Will is still standing at the center of a storm."

"I know. I think he may always stand at the center of one. It may simply be what he does."

"Crystal is what keeps him going, though. She is his anchor."

"At least he has one," Salome says.

"And now he has a future. We all do."

"You see that or you think that?" asks Salome.

"I can finally see it. We are safe, for now. It fades

sometimes, but Will is there as things fade and he brings it back into focus.”

“Then all is well.”

“Well, his three companions are not here yet, but they are own their way.”

“Who are his three companions?”

“Plague, Famine, and War.”

“Excuse me? Circe?”

“Don’t you know who Will is from looking at him? I saw a rider on a pale horse and his name was death. Will is the first of the four horsemen of the apocalypse. He fits so perfectly into the different prophecies I am shocked you all didn’t see it sooner.”

“Who are the other three? I don’t mean which horsemen, I mean do we know where they are or who they are?”

“No, I don’t have a clue. Lucky for us, I am pretty sure they will reveal themselves when they get here or they figure out who they are.”

Troublemaker

“Loki, your country has need of you again.”

Bullshit. You just can’t figure out how to get to the info you need on the Project.

“Un huh, now what?” Loki isn’t impressed and he would rather be pursuing environmental issues anyway. From what he was able to understand about the Project, there are no inconsistencies between what they are trying to do and what he, personally, is trying to do. Loki just hates LB. *...kind of like dear old Mum must’ve had an irrational hatred* *for me, naimg me after the Norse god of mischief...*

"We need you to come in and do a debriefing on your experiences at OEE."

"I have already done that, twice."

Loki has had reason and time to reflect on his former employer. *It is true that he is a genuine hard ass. I don't think I knew what I was doing when I signed on with 'helping' the NSA. So far, it has been more like having done business with the mafia and they just keep coming back for more. I am being run like a bitch who is trying to stay out of jail, only now I am trying to stay alive.*

"Yes, we understand that but we have some new relaxation techniques that we feel will be beneficial in helping you focus…and remember."

"When would you want to do this?"

"Oh, no sooner than the 5th of next month, is that agreeable?"

"Sure." Click.

Loki called the office of his attorney. *Fucker hates my guts, but he is my lawyer.* Loki didn't really hold it against him. He had lied to his attorney and it had made him unable to mount an effective defense.

Sooner or later, LB, sooner or later.

"Mr. Browning, I am Loki's attorney, I am sure you remember me. Do you?"

"Yes," says LB. He does.

"Well, I am calling to remind you of your promise to protect my former client."

"Your former client?"

"Don't be a smartass, Mr. Browning. I didn't like him then and I don't like him now. Fulfilling my professional responsibilities to a client does not mean I have to like him. Of course, I am speaking my personal feelings which have absolutely no reflection on his character or person."

"Right, you have a point?"

"The man is in danger, and you agreed to protect him or at least do all possible to protect him."

"That is true, I did. What is the situation?"

"The NSA is putting pressure on him to undergo repeated debriefings. Does that mean anything to you? I only ask because it is my understanding that you used to have significant influence in that arena."

"That is true. I am somewhat familiar with the field."

A smile that was more of a smirk, the lawyer looks LB dead in the face and says, "Look, I really couldn't give a shit if the SOB is dead tomorrow. I am fulfilling my professional duty to the man. You DO what you promised and get him out of my life."

"You have had threats to your family?" LB is looking at the man with pity. Many people do not really know what kind of world they live in. Generally, if you keep your nose clean, pay your bills, show up for work, pay your taxes and go along for the most part, you are okay. Life is only hard for those who want nothing and those who want everything.

This guy is between the NSA and what they want. Bad place to be, "How many times?"

"I don't know how many times." *Am I breaking any rules here?* He doesn't really care now. "Many times, I have taken to answering the door with a shotgun."

Won't do you any good, "Won't do you any good. In fact, they will now simply execute you from a distance when they decide to get rid of you. Which is good, I guess. There is a better chance of them missing you than your overcoming a field agent in a fight."

"I used to be a marine."

"Then you have a marginal chance. Most of these…screw it. I am not going to argue with you over how tough you are. Marines are Marines, after all. Do you want protection as well?"

"For my family, yes."

"Consider it done."

"Thanks. By the way, I am pretty sure I have violated something or other, here."

"Don't worry about it. I know we paid through the nose, but it was a cheap price to get rid of Loki. The man is a train wreck waiting to happen."

"I believe I see his train on the horizon…"

"Yes," says LB. "I almost feel like letting him get run over."

"You will provide him protection then?"

"Yes, but yours will happen first. Kyle?" LB is leaning over and yelling out the door.

"Yes, Sir."

"I need you to get a few of the ART guys and send them with this gentleman. He is a target by some supposed white hats."

'Supposed white hats' is the term that Felix and Will agree on for government agents who are supposed to uphold the law. The problem with something like the NSA is that their interpretation of the 'law' and their 'duty' is quite fuzzy, especially when the moment's needs interfere.

"Sir."

LB wonders if Kyle knows that he understands that when he says 'Sir' rather than 'Yes, Sir' he does not agree with what he is doing. *Well, as long as he doesn't bring it up, we don't need to discuss it.* This attitude, while tolerant, will come back to haunt LB in the future. *He is way too rigid to be as young as he is,* thinks LB. *Not only do I not know what he does to relax, I don't know if he does ANYTHING to relax.*

"Kyle, when is the last time you had a day off?"

"Sir?"

"When was the last time you had a day off?"

"I am thinking."

This tells me what I need to know, thinks LB. "Well…?"

But Kyle cuts him off with, "I haven't had a day off since before we split with OEE!" Rather than looking put upon, Kyle is beaming.

He is proud of not having taken a day off. Oh, geez. "Well, come see me Thursday afternoon, just before you knock off. For now, I want you to see this fellow out the door and to the ART guys. Then I want you to tell the ART folks to see to Loki as well."

"Should I delay or forget to call them until next week?"

"Regretfully, no."

"Okay."

Queens Reunited

"Crystal."

"My Queen, I remember you." The two queens look at each other as Will and Melissa look on from the side.

"We thought you were dead."

"I think I was. For a long time, I don't think all of me was in my body." Then Crystal adds, "I really don't think that explains it correctly, but it will have to do as it is as close as I can get in this frame." Her eyes are just a little glazed.

Will thinks *that is where I am when I see what the thing showed me. If I can get back there, I will remember.*

"What matters, my little sister, is that you are alive, and you are back with us."

Will mutters, "It was meant to be."

Melissa turns and looks at him as Monica and Crystal continue to speak. Her face tells the question.

"What I mean is that the way I found her was so fortuitous that the only way it could have happened was that there was some divine intervention."

"You think?" Melissa is amused that Will would spend so much time on the obvious.

"Well, it was."

"Oh, I know. I completely agree. It is just amazing that even after all the thousands of years of miracles and close saves and…everything else miraculous, people still are shocked when they see the hand of the divine in their lives."

"Yeah, I guess."

Monica turns to Will. "Good Sir, I stand corrected. Suede is indeed Crystal."

"I know. I told you. I was up close and personal, and I

knew it was her. There is only one angel for me."

Crystal is looking the three over as they talk. Having assembled in Norn's Lair, it is ironic that the atmosphere is one found in a funeral home, only without sadness and regret. It may be only comparable to when the Tibetan monks find the Dali Llama child again. Claiming to know him personally, they treat the child as one who has returned rather than a new addition to the household. Crystal has returned.

"Well, it is true that I am Crystal, but not entirely true."

Hah? Will turns to Crystal.

"I am Crystal, but this body is new. Also, it is aging."

Looking at the youngest queen, Monica notices for the first time that, indeed, Crystal now has crow's feet around her eyes.

"Butterfly wings is what we have decided to call them," says Crystal, reading Monica's face.

"Butterfly wings?"

"Yes, the girls who worked with me in the club and I decided that rather than use that awful term wrinkles, we would use butterfly wings."

"What the hell ever," says Will. "I just know you are my Crystal and your back and I don't care about anything BUT that." He is aggravated and uncharacteristically short.

"I know, Bear, I know, and it's okay. I AM Crystal, but somehow I am someone else who wanted to leave as badly as I wanted to stay."

Monica and Melissa have lived thousands of years and have seen a lot of strange things. Will, however, is new to all this, in spite of being super pest control guy. *What now?*

What now. It seems I have been asking that a lot in the last several months.

Crystal explains how she had been summoned to a grove of oak trees outside Atlanta.

"When I thought you were going to be killed for going arachnid, Will, I refused to live. I knew that, for some reason, I had been spared back in Pictland and that I had to be here for some purpose."

"Okay," Will is having trouble concentrating. *Why?*

"Will?" Melissa is watching Will's back. It is twitching as if there is a change coming on.

"Yes, what is it?" His eyes have gone a bright, almost fluorescent orange.

Great, something new, thinks Melissa. He *doesn't look as if he is going to be in control, either.*

Will continues to plate up, turning into a towering white centaur with the body of a scorpion and its stinger. As he continues the transformation, the insectile changes race up his torso.

Inside Will's mind, he is no longer with his Queens. Will is now standing on a barren landscape with almost no light. There is only rock and pebble and grit under his feet. He can see what looks to be a trail of rubble where the moon should be. It is crisscrossed by another stream of rubble in the sky. He doesn't recognize the sky, mostly because it is almost empty of stars.

At first, Will thinks there must be some cloud cover blocking the sky, but then he sees a meteor streak into a fireball and disappears. It isn't that I can't see the stars; there are no stars here to see! Will suddenly realizes that he is no longer on earth. A noise distracts him, and he turns to see what the scrabbling noise is.

"Will!" Crystal, Monica and Melissa all try to approach him, but they are held at bay by a white circle of light. It doesn't hurt them. They are calmed by touching the light.

Melissa suddenly knows that Will is truly her friend. He would die for her as surely as he would for Crystal.

Monica knows that Will is truly loyal to her and has empathy for her she didn't know could exist. *He knows that the decisions I sometimes have to make cause my heart to bleed.* Her eyes begin to water as she knows this man's heart.

Crystal sees into his heart for her and knows that she is indeed the blood that runs in his veins and that she is the center of his existence. She knows what it is for him to smell her hair after she was gone for so long and how her scent is the sweetest thing…her laugh, her hands on his skin…of how he thought his heart would burst in his chest when he made love to her for the first time while she was still only Suede. She knows how he swore to God that he would work like three crazy devils if he would only make it so she could be part of his life forever. She knows what it was like for him to sit and watch her dance for others before she committed back to him, never knowing if he really had a chance or not but not able to walk away. She sees in his mind how he pulls over to the side of the road one night because he is so frustrated at finally having found a woman who makes him want something more than to get by and to want it badly enough to do whatever it takes with no slacking off. Crystal realizes that he now believes many men look for their REASON, what will drive them to greatness, what will let them reach down into their guts when they have done all they can and keep going, and she realizes that SHE, Crystal, is the spark that has made Will able to fight off Legion, SHE is why Will has never lost a battle to the arachnids, and she is why he continues to fight to be a good man, an honorable man…a man even by Kipling's standard.

She tries to reach through the circle of white light, and two bands of light cup her wrists and gently push her back to her sisters. Crystal gasps as she realizes that Will is not doing the circle of light but is composed of tiny little beings, all blazing white, like snow, with delicate little butterfly wings. A single creature flies up to about 6 inches in front of her face and holds a single finger to her lips.

Hush, now. Your knight is busy. The creature, male or female, Crystal really can't tell, flies back into the circle around Will. All the creatures then turn to watch Will. As the three queens watch, all the white butterflies lift their eyes towards heaven and hold onto one another, forming a ring around Will.

Are they giving him their strength? Or praying for him? Melissa looks to Monica, who looks as mystified as she feels. *Monica has never seen this, either. Wow.* Melissa is dumbfounded because Monica is so old. It's not so old as to start showing age. But that isn't it, either. There are people younger than her that age horribly but never die.

Her thoughts are interrupted as the butterfly folks begin a chant. Three times, they chant and are silent.

Will finds himself standing on a plain surrounded by cliffs in 360 degrees□. *I am in a crater,* he thinks. Looking up along the cliff tops, Will sees that he is not alone and that the noise he heard must have been them lining up along the face's edge. This horde of people, what appears to be thousands, are doing the mob two-step. He can barely hear the crowd noise because they are so far away. *Make that tens of thousands,* he thinks.

Suddenly, the crowd begins running down the cliff face,

and Will hears what sounds like clicking in the distance. *Not people, arachnids. Well, I will get the fight I said I wanted.*

The horde stops maybe 200 yards away from Will and, several steps forward begins walking towards him. These are not arachnids but seem to be normal human beings.

As they draw closer to Will, he can see that they are men, well-dressed in what appear to be priestly robes.

"Hello, Brother. It has been long and long."

"Do I know you?"

"You do not remember, but that is okay. It was not our choice."

"Again, do I know you?" Will is antsy. Along the perimeter, he can see thousands of arachnids moving back and forth like caged lions. Occasionally, one swipes at another. It is always a fatal blow, and the victim's neighbors immediately fall on him, and he quickly disappears down several arachnid gullets.

Laughing, one of the men turns back to Will as the conversation continues. "They are vicious once you remove the consciousness."

"So I see," says Will. "What do you want?" He doesn't understand why he is not changing in the face of this threat.

"You are not changing, Will, because you are already in your most dangerous form."

"Really, I can't see how bare hands can prevail against claws and teeth and speed."

Laughing again, the first man, apparently the guy in charge, says, "That is why you will either bow down before us or you will die here and your body will die there."

"Well, let's talk about this." Will doesn't have a clue what to do. He isn't changing and he doesn't know what the rules are here. He can be hurt. For a bit, he had thought he was invulnerable, like some centaur superman. *Getting ass slammed as he called it in the desert and Crystal's reaching for him as he was talking to Solomon now have him not so sure of himself.*

"What's to talk about? You will join us, or you will die."

Will could feel his irritation beginning to rise, "Once again, I am asking who you are."

"Very well, we are Legion, for we are many. We were your brothers once but were betrayed. Billions of your brothers and sisters were lost because…"

Will. A thought flies across Will's mind.

What? Who is that? Instinctively, Will closes his eyes.

Legion says, "It is okay, Will. There is no shame in surrendering to a superior force."

Will, he spoke true when he said you are in your most dangerous form now. You are dangerous to them, says the voice in his mind. *Your power is greatest now.*

What do I do?

Use your imagination. All things are possible with God. Have the faith of a grain of mustard seed. Don't hope, just do. Don't think or believe or suppose, be certain you can win and you will.

Have a positive mental attitude? Geezus pleezus.

That is as good a way to put what I am telling you as anything.

Who are you, now?

Doesn't matter. This fight must be won and you can win it. Simply know that you can and that the battle is already won.

Okay.

"Well, I have considered your offer."

"Yes?"

"Well, I would tell you to go fuck yourself, but you can't. You can never do anything because of your betrayal of the light that loved you. You are done, finished. I know not what your final fate is to be, but today you will suffer another defeat."

The man looks at Will, and his face begins to redden. Finally, his face is a true beat red as it begins to swell with blood.

"You look like a tick about to bust, loser."

The man cries out in bloody anger, and as he does, he begins to change.

Well, here we go. He is going to spider out. Boy, I hope I begin to suit up, soon.

The man doesn't change into an arachnid, however. His companions all stand closer to him as they all begin to change.

They, too, begin to metamorph and as they do, their forms begin to run together. As Will watches, the group who call themselves Legion wrap themselves into a single, towering monster with three heads and dozens of legs.

"You will bow down, or you will die," the thing rumbles.

So this is the dragon? Thinks Will, *one of them anyway.*

Well, if I am in my most dangerous form, let's get to it. With that thought, Will walks up to the dragon and does his best to kick the shit out of him. He kicks one leg squarely in what he hopes is a sensitive shin area and makes plans to climb right up the front of Legion's throat and throttle him to death. *It doesn't go real well.*

Reaching down, Will is grabbed by the head and slung into the crowd of arachnids. Will has time to look down into the waiting crowd of spiders and think this is going to hurt.

As he strikes the ground, crushing one spider under him, Will reaches down and yanks the front two legs off. Both are tipped with wicked 18 inch blades of chitin. Using them as two swords, Will begins to hack and cut.

The battle rages across the field, until the arachnid body count begins to mount. Again, Will is aided to some extent by the spider's willingness to fall on wounded comrades for a quick bite before returning to the fray with their target.

Will is beginning to tire and to accumulate injuries. Blood is beginning to pool in one shoe to the point it squishes as he moves. *I don't see how I can win.*

With this thought, the horde begins to press its advantage.

"The light around Will is weakening," says Melissa.

"I see it," says Monica.

Crystal is saying nothing. She looks down at the tiny beings that make up the circle of light and sees that some of the tiny faces are concentrating fiercely, gripping each other with an intensity that is palpable. Crystal says nothing, only telling herself that *he is okay, he is okay, he is okay.*

"Just kill him, pets. Just kill him. Then we can move on to those meddlesome witches."

Will has fallen to the ground under the weight of thousands of arachnids as they fight each other to get to him. He hears Legion say kill him so they can move on to the queens.

"Crystal, my butterfly," The arachnids now have Will restrained and one walks forward to disembowel him. A large foot stamps the would be executioner into so much yellow pulp.

"I will do the honors."

"I never bowed and I never will," says Will.

"I know and I am impressed. But see now I will kill you. Once you are dead, the heart will go out of the Queens and I can move forward."

"They will never give up. You will lose, eventually." This last is spoken in a bubbly voice. Will's lungs are filling up with blood and he is beginning to lose focus. *I lose and I die, am dying. I thought it would hurt more or that I would be frightened.*

Legion places a single claw tip in the center of Will's throat where the collar bones meet.

"Ready to get unzipped?" asks Legion.

"Piss on you," gurgles Will.

"No, not on me, but I think I will do that to your butterfly after I pull her damn wings off. Don't worry, I will do you the favor of not letting you live long enough to watch me pull her apart."

Crystal. No.

Looking on, the three queens see Will start to bleed from the mouth.

"Oh, my Bear."

Will sinks to his knees. The three Queens try to move forward, but are still restrained by the light, though it looks to be weaker now.

You are in your most dangerous form now.

Not my butterfly.

Legion's claw pierces the skin in Will's neck.

This battle is already won. I am a son of light and cannot die.

Strength begins to flood back into Will's body. Legion's claw stops its downward rake as it catches on the bones of Will's ribcage. This causes Will to scream as Legion places another hand on Will's forehead to steady the man's body so he can rip him open.

Back in the room with the three queens, the ring of light begins to become even more blindingly white.

Will screams and as he does, a break in the ring of light opens in front of Crystal. She walks forward and lays her hand on his chest as it begins to be plated in chitin and says, "Bear? Fight it. You are stronger than they. You were born."

Will hears his butterfly's voice in his head as he had heard the other voices. *Bear? Fight it. You are stronger than they. You were born.*

My butterfly. Will feels power flood him as Legion grunts in surprise. Reaching up, Will takes the dragon by the arm and twists it away as he feels his lungs begin to clear. An itching momentarily takes his attention away. He looks down to see what is causing him to itch so badly.

The arachnids see Will's distraction as an opportunity to reassert their hold. They have no effect as Will continues to stand. He now sees that the itching is wherever he has been cut or torn. The wounds are healing over. It looks like accelerated film footage as the tears close themselves without even leaving a scar.

I wish it would stop itching so badly.

The itching stopped.

Too bad I won't have any scars left.

The scars reappear on his body.

Cool. Now it is time to whup some arachnid ass.

As Will turns to look at his enemies, many of which are still tearing at him, now to absolutely no effect, he imagines that what he needs is a killing light to simply burn them down, burn them all down to ash. With that thought, Will feels his eyes become full of a warm heat. He closes his eyes because at first he thinks something has blown into them.

Open your eyes, Will, and burn them down.

Will looks on his enemies and as he does a white light emanates from his eyes and his hands. He begins to turn and everywhere the beams fall, arachnids are consumed and left as ash.

Will becomes a spinning dervish as he fills the crater with the ash of burned arachnids. Finally, there is only Legion left. Will wades into them, trying to burn them into ash as well.

"You cannot kill us, but you have won for now." Legion's form does join the other piles of ash on the crater floor. The surroundings begin to lose their depth and become indistinct, less there.

As she says the word born, a light, a white light, begins to burn through the pupils of his orange eyes. It spreads to the corneas and starts to spread over his face and down. It races down his skin until it reaches the chitin, where it hesitates.

Back and forth the battle of chitin versus white light rages over Will's skin. Finally, his face settles into a white marble of determination and calmness. The white light then races over his skin and banishes the insect like traits.

Will collapses to the floor. Crystal kneels down with him as he rolls into a fetal position and begins shuddering.

"Will? Look at me, Baby. Bear?" Crystal is trying to get Will to look at her and give her some sign of recognition. He looks to be going into shock. Then, *that can't be right. He no longer has a heartbeat.*

Monica and Melissa crowd around the fallen man. As usual, his clothes are shredded around him after the change.

"Will, look at us." Monica is talking to Will as she looks around at Salome and says, "Go get a healer." A healer is what passes for a doctor amongst the people. They are not in great demand since a Person hardly gets sick or hurt so badly they can't recover. In general, if a vampire is hurt badly enough to require assistance to get over, they die anyway.

The three Queens pick Will up and carry him into his room and lay him on the bed. Monica and Melissa stand to the right of the bed as Crystal crawls up into the bed with Will and kneels beside him and wipes his forehead. He is sweating copiously now.

"Crystal. I know what the thing is now."

"The thing."

"The presence that tried to draw me over into being an arachnid."

"What is it?"

Will chuckles a little, here. "It is famous and I am not surprised."

"Okay," says Crystal. "Why are you not surprised?"

"Because its name is Legion, for they are many. I beat them, but they will be back, attacking someone else, but not yet. We have a little period of peace now."

Know Thy Enemy

"Legion. The Christian devil?"

"A group of devils."

"They are real then?"

Like much of the world, the idea of devils and forces of good and evil has been somewhat put on the back burner.

Like someone said, the greatest lie the devil ever told was that he didn't really exist. *Well, now I know, for sure.*

"What do they want?" Monica is worried. Will never exaggerates. With the exception of talking about Crystal, he is a low key kind of guy.

"I don't know if we should use 'they,' 'it,' or 'him.' I do know that to a great extent that Legion sees itself as one unit. It may actually be one or one with multiple personalities..."

"Demons with personality disorders, next on Jerry Springer..." Crystal has picked up some of Will's strange humor.

"Uh-huh. Yep. Anyway," Will continues on, "I think its goal is the simple destruction of everything that lives. I kept getting a picture in my mind of a perfectly cold diamond as its goal." Will is not going to tell them everything. For some reason, he feels like he is under a burden of silence on the battle that went on. Besides, I don't know if I was really there or if it was just some allegory of what was going on in my mind. Then, *I will deal with that later with Crystal.*

"A cold diamond?"

"Yes, if everything…and I am doing some extrapolation here…were dead and the universe had come to a complete halt, I think this thing would be happy."

"Perfect entropy, Entropy would be at a maximum. No life, no heat, no change; the universe is just one big, silent graveyard of a universe where all things had reached the lowest possible state."

"No hope, no life, no expectations…"

"Which is a just fate for traitors!" a scream came from the left side of the bed as a hole appears to take form in the air, just about six feet off the ground and a head pushes its way through. Its form couldn't maintain any cohesiveness, as it shifts from one hideous visage to another, sometimes unbearably beautiful, sometimes just unbearable. Multiple heads and multiple voices occasionally sit on the single neck that protrudes seemingly from nothing.

"Will, you will be ours. You will fail. Just as we told you when you were a child, when you were a teenager, when you…" here the thing seems to collapse in on itself as if it can't keep focus, but it reasserts itself long enough to say, "Will, you will bow down to us before you die. You will or you will lose everything and everyone you love. You will beg for our help…"

"Leave. I am my father's son and you have no power over me."

"We were betrayed! We would have lost no one! We should have been given the power…"

"In Christ's name I rebuke you and tell you to leave my home."

With a bang the thing is gone.

Monica, Melissa, and Crystal all have ashy looks on their faces. Will wonders why they are so freaked.

"What is wrong with all of you?"

The three queens are visibly upset and flashing towards battle state maybe 30% before backing off. Three heads twitching in random directions until finally Monica says, "Guardians, show yourselves."

Six hulks shimmer into view.

"My lady?"

"Nothing, I just feel better with you ladies taking up space around us right now."

Melissa asks, "Was that real?"

"You heard the bang when it left, so, yes, it was real."

"The bang?"

"There was a bang because when the thing vanished, air collapsed into the empty space it left. It was truly, physically here. Where it came from or where it went is a different matter, no, I do not know."

He is lying, thinks Monica. *Why?*

Now it is Melissa's turn to have a stomp fit like Crystal's reaction to thinking a spider was in Will's apartment.

"Damn it!" She is rubbing her arms as if she is freezing. It is colder here, in fact, a result of their uninvited guest, no doubt.

"Wait. You guys are way too freaked out over this. Why? I have told you from day one that some thing invaded my mind."

"Demons? You have to ask why we are so freaked?"

"Well, you guys are vampires and I am a shape shifter. Why would the concept of demons freak you out so much? I expect the werewolf and creature from the black lagoon to show up any day."

"Not funny."

"Okay. So, what do we do now?"

"What else is out there waiting on us? We haven't had any confrontations like this before," says Monica.

"What about the stories of the dragon wars and…"

"Crystal, those are just old wives tales. Tales to frighten children with," says Monica.

Will holds his peace. He has just fought a dragon.

"Are they?" asks Melissa.

Will, the three queens, and the six guardians all just look at each other and around the room.

"I only ask because we thought Will was just a tale, we thought demons were just ideas brought by priests trying to control their people. What else is really out there?"

"Well, we now have a verified case of resurrection, too," says Will. "Crystal."

"I couldn't live with you dead."

"I am alive so, tell me how this can be? Monica and Melissa did see you die. You burned up in view of guardians."

"I ran out the door into the light and…let's see. Yes. I did. I ran through the doors at Norn's Lair, and my thoughts were basically, 'I will not live without my Bear. You took him, and I am coming to get him or be with him on the other side.'"

"So, you just decided."

"Yes. I had no doubts and I meant to see you even if it meant I came on over to the other side. I think I remember telling myself that I WAS going to have you and if it meant dying, I would do it. It wasn't so much I wanted to die, though. I just meant that whatever doors I had to walk through to get to you, I was going through those doors."

Will is touched. He knows Crystal loves him, but he didn't know how unconditional it is.

The Wizard

"Well, will you look at that," says Felix. "We made those changes to the entry angle for the particle accelerators and just as we had hoped…well, the efficiencies are actually even better than predicted."

"So, something is wrong with our calculations?" This is Brandon. He is intensely interested in the technical side of the Project.

"Brandon, there is something wrong with our whole system of mathematics. We just don't know what."

"So, how are we able to do this?"

"Well, about half the time, I go to sleep and just before I fall into a really deep sleep, I find my head full of pictures, or fuzzy calculations. I wake up throughout the night, making notes and doodling. This is how I figured out why superstrings are so massive."

"Why are they so massive?"

"Another time," says Felix. "Right now I think I can safely say that I can keep from blowing us up when we run a load through the accelerator."

"A load?"

"Sure. A macro-mass, something other than protons or particle beams, and something that is big enough to do some good. I think we'll go for a kilogram mass on Friday.

Later that night, Brandon is watching nothing in particular, just doing the channel surf bit, when a thought occurs to him.

He runs to his kitchen table and sits down with a calculator. Twenty minutes later he is calling Felix at home.

"Felix, this is Brandon."

"Yes? Is everything okay at the site?"

"What? Oh, sure. I guess. I mean, I haven't heard anything."

"Okay, so, what's up?"

"Well, I was thinking back to what you said today. You know, about not blowing us up?"

"Yes."

"…And about moving a macro-mass of a kilogram?"

"Yes."

"Well, see, I just did a napkin calculation of how much energy it will take to accelerate a kilogram to relativistic speeds."

"Un-huh."

"I also calculated how much energy would be released

by a kilogram mass hitting the wall or any of the receivers in the lab."

Felix is silent.

"Felix, you there…"

"Silence, Brandon. Don't say anything else."

"What's wrong…?"

"Meet me at the lab, wow."

Shit, now what did I step into?

On the way over, Brandon is kicking himself for not just sticking to his business and letting them do whatever the hell it is they are doing.

Brandon is waved on through security and stops just inside the gates. Several of the Attitude Response Team guys approach his car.

"Please unlock your doors so the three of us can accompany you to the lab, Sir."

"Okay." *Man, I really screwed this up. This is a sweet job, too.*

As they approach the lab, the doors swing open and out steps a few more ART guys. Brandon leaves his car and the ART guys who rode with him take up positions around his car and the door to the lab.

As Brandon steps through into the lab, which now looks at once familiar and alien, Felix walks up to him.

"Sit down, Brandon."

"Okay."

"I want you to understand that I am not angry and that your job is in no danger."

Man, oh, man. Thank you, Lord. "Okay, thanks for making that clear."

"We do have a situation, though. You spoke to me concerning sensitive issues on a public phone."

"I…uh…just thought. Well, you said if I ever had any questions to call you."

"That is true, but here is the thing. Do NOT discuss these things over a public phone network. Hopefully, we weren't being monitored. They can't watch us all, all the time, I don't think."

"Okay. I apologize."

"There is nothing to apologize for. You didn't know and you thought you were not violating your non-disclosure agreement by speaking to me. In the future, though, you need to know that even when talking to me, Will, or even LB, that there may be other interested listeners, okay?"

"Got it."

"So, what we do in here only gets discussed here."

"10-4."

"In any case, based on what I assume to be your knowledge of mass-to-energy conversions, you are right. It would be much energy."

"Isn't it, like, dangerous?"

"Only if your math was correct, Brandon; it is dangerous only if your math was correct, which it is not."

"So, show me the math."

"Follow me."

Brandon follows Felix into his office and observes as Felix opens up his cloak closet. Felix turns to Brandon and says, "You coming?"

Cool. "Yes, I am."

The back of Felix's closet was a door, too. It opened into a well lit room that was some 24 x 24 feet. Several tower PCs were in the middle on a table, arranged so that all the hubs and everything were easily accessible. What walls were not lined with book shelves full of 50 lbs. tomes of science were covered in whiteboard from about 2 feet from the floor to the ceiling. These whiteboards were covered in small neat, symbols, many of which Brandon, a math hobbyist, had never seen.

"What are these?"

"Oh, that is a new calculus I am developing. It should give me the tools I need to accurately explain the conversions that run through the 6th and 9th dimensions, which is where the conversions from electromagnetic energy to gravitational get hairy."

"Uh-huh. I can see how that would be." He could. It was line after line of iterations of the same calculations. Brandon notices something and asks about it.

"I see here that on the odd-numbered conversions, the math seems to collapse many of the expressions. Is that significant?" Brandon stops and asks for clarification, "Did you say 'from electromagnetic to gravitational conversions'?"

"Yes, I did."

"What does that mean?" Brandon thinks he knows and his expression pretty clearly tells that he knows. Felix is proud of him.

"It means inertia control, which means we can accelerate the hell out of macro mass."

"I thought that was impossible."

"Yeah, well, so did I. When I got pissed off out riding one and decided to throw out the word 'impossible' I started making progress."

"Uh-huh. So I see." Brandon is amazed and lost in the calculations.

"It only looks complex, Brandon. If you look closely," and Felix's face takes on a peculiar intensity now, "you will see the underlying simplicity of where I am trying to go."

Brandon looks again, seeing how Felix breaks down the apparent contradictions of two objects moving at 180 degrees to each other both ceasing to move with respect to time as they approach the speed of light. It is a localized affect caused by…

"So, you just decided to live, and you did?" That seems to be the gist of what Crystal is saying, but many people have been strong-willed about things, and Will says so.

"Yes, but no one opposed me, Will. I think I am supposed to be here, too. There is a Divine power in the universe, and I think it just decided to support my determination."

"You know, I know you must be right if for no other reason than you are standing right here in my sight. I just…"

Crystal touches Will's lips and says, "Will, it is late. Can we retire? I am exhausted."

"You're tired?" Monica asks.

"Yes, it is one of the new things about this body. It does get tired. I am as strong, as fast, and I still change as I did, but I do get tired now."

"You bet," says Will. "Goodnight, all." Will takes

Crystal by the hand and leads her down the hallway. He places his arm around her and she leans her head against his shoulder as her right arm circles his waist. It is the embrace of a couple that has a warm, gentle love for each other.

Monica and Melissa watch the two disappear down the hallway. Monica reaches her hand out to Melissa and pulls her into a hug. "She lives, she truly lives," Monica is hoarse as she whispers this into Melissa's ear.

"Yes, and Will still has at least one more destiny to fulfill."

Will, lying in bed with Crystal, the Bear and his Butterfly, thinks *Whatever comes, I can face it calmly now. I can meet my fate as long as I have my heart with me.*

November 1999 to April 12, 2001

Edited, November 9, 2023 to March 2, 2024

Timothy Lynn Singleton